# NOT DEAD

## madi girlmeat

Copyright © 2021 by Madi Girlmeat
First Edition via IngramSpark
Print ISBN: 978-1-7778267-0-3
Ebook ISBN: 978-1-7778267-1-0

I am eternally grateful for the following people's generosity in helping flesh out my world with a diverse and interesting cast.

In order of appearance:
**Crozi** was developed by Teef —
@chronoteeth.
**Becca** was developed by Michelle Weathers —
@GuMMYGuTTZZ.
**Pokey** was developed by Silas Rock --
Deleted their Twitter, which we all wish we could do.
**Davy** and **Walter** were developed by Max Graves —
@maximumgraves.
**Casey** and **Kassie** were developed by 'Dog Lady Heather'
@dogladyheather.
Thank you also for the contributions of Dawn Alexander, Penelope Cochran, Silas Rock, and Paige Einstein.

Thank you especially to Rachel Doty, who has been an incredible friend through every step of this process, and who has near single-handedly made me believe this story is worth telling.

Cover art by Madi Girlmeat.
Edited by Vivi Bond.

This book was written on the unceded lands of the Anishinaabe, Haudenosaunee, and Wendat peoples. It is influenced heavily by their principles, many of which have only recently become trendy with settler "anarchists." – these principles should serve as a blueprint for our way forward.

Amazon suppresses labour organizing in order to continue to underpay and overwork their employees. If you purchased this book through Amazon or one of their affiliates, give it away when you are finished with it.

For every dead queer, and every queer who wishes they were dead.

# Table of Contents

It is impossible to know what year it is.

Professor Hanratty Vermington opens her eyes for the first time after a long period spent comatose. She remembers falling asleep on a train, being arrested, being interrogated, and after that: nothing. There is a black spot in her memory that fades out on the words "freedom of the press."

She stands in the evacuated street of a cold, frosted hamlet, surrounded by collapsing buildings, their bricks a rotting shade of white. Across the way, the last movement of a derailed commuter train halts, the final sound dampened by the snow.

She flinches as a computerized screeching roars in her earpiece, loud enough to send spiderwebs through her vision. She rips it out and drops it into the slush.

There is another person here. A foil-wrapped charge hangs off their vest, supported by a combination of velcro and wires. Ratty begins to panic as she notices the pistol levelled at her head. She raises her hands slowly, only noticing the assault rifle hung around her neck as she dings her finger off the barrel.

She drags something up from her memory, the voice of her mentor, a story about foreign reporting. She tries and fails to sound out the Russian word for journalist. She used to speak Russian. Doesn't remember learning it, doesn't remember any of it, but knows that she used to speak Russian.

"I speak English." the other figure says. "You know I can't stop this."

"I— Who is making you do this?"

"Your people. Handler Smith. Angelcorp people." The other figure points at her vest with his pistol. "Took my family, told me to come here, this whole war is their doing."

Angelcorp...

That rings a bell...

Ratty is then obliterated by the half-pound of C-4 explosive sewn throughout her vest.

2

# 202█ — 200█
# Hell

Strings of flesh crawled like worms into the pile that had once called itself an opossum. For the past 20 years it had sat comatose with its legs crossed in the centre of its cell, staring right through the bars, right through the bars of the adjacent cell, and right through the back wall of the prison. No amount of torture, real or digitized, fazed it, it very rarely blinked, and it usually took several seconds whenever it did. It was as though it had fallen asleep with its eyes open, yesterday's liner still smudged across its face.

Hanratty Vermington's unnatural ability to put itself back together attracted all the classicists of torture. Forgone were the modern innovations that allowed a user to plug directly into a creature's nervous system. 'Ratty' was fun, both because it couldn't be destroyed, and it couldn't be broken. A full ten percent of conversations between oldheads were bets on whether someone could finally crack the possum in C017.

It had — according to upper management — become a waste of resources to physically tear it apart. Rebellion produced creativity in that way. The more cost-effective experience machine, for example, could reverse what was a normal range of motion. The body could be forced to contort in on itself without outside handling. The lungs could be collapsed automatically — that was a favourite. All of this could be written up as an accident.

Putting the possum back together had become Sett's full-time job, their unique and hard-learned ability to heal reduced to mortuary service. They had neither the means nor the impetus to investigate its supernatural origins. This would be a job for another day.

Tonight's shift was unremarkable. The goat sat on the floor next to Vermington, their legs folded under them, deftly pulling glowing silver threads through the pieces of broken skin. There were nights where Sett talked to their charge. Besides their — how many things was he now? Father figure/boyfriend was enough to sum up why he was awful. John. He was just John. Besides John, Ratty was the only person available to talk to. They told themself it wasn't too strange, likened the practice to talking to a favourite toy while you repaired it.

"Here we are..." they muttered, tying off the last stitch. Despite its comatose state, Sett struggled to raise their voice to the possum, still anxious about crying — showing weakness — in front of anyone. The day, by contrast, had been difficult, the kind that made the tiny immortal wish for an effective means of suicide.

They had become so familiar with each other. The blend of its fur a comforting and soft contrast against the goat's own rosy brown. The possum was not in fact grey up close, Sett noticed that almost immediately. While their fur was solid black around their wrists and ankles, and solid white in patches around their face, there was no spot on the rest of the possum's body where its fur was entirely one colour. Instead, individual strands of black and white blended together in such a way where the possum appeared a slightly different shade from every angle. Sett wondered if anyone else had noticed that.

They fantasized tonight as they often did about what would happen if it came back to life somehow, what would happen if 'it' became 'she'? In all their research, no cure for this kind of paralysis had ever come up, and Sett was absolutely certain it never would. Anyone that could sleep through 20 years of being sublimated and sewn back together over and over again wasn't going to suddenly stand up and help them work through their problems.

"Do you mind if we talk?" Sett asked. The possum stayed silent. This, for their needs, was as good as a yes.

"Yes, of course. Thank you." The goat nodded, resting their back against the possum and leaning into it like a seat. Firm, but with just enough give to sit comfortably. It made some slow, instinctual moves responding to the goat's presence, not waking enough to actually listen.

"So, I think I've told you about John before?" The first few words were usually a little odd. "We uh... he said something tonight that really rattled me, and I'm not sure what to do, really," A familiar knot formed in their throat. "I mean I have to go back to my apartment eventually of course, but... He left a reminder on a blank part of the wall in my bedroom and—"

Sett took a deep breath, feeling the anxiety rattle in their lungs. "I do not think I want to talk about this actually." This was weird. It was weird to talk to a corpse. Quasi-cuddling one definitely crossed a line.

"I do not feel safe going home tonight, Ratty... Would you mind terribly if I stayed at yours?" They were only half kidding. More silence, the flopped air around their ribbing a deafening reminder of just how alone they were. "You always know just what to say Miss Vermington."

More silence, not a great recovery. Sett watched their own tears dry on the warm cement between their crossed legs. It had been a long, long time since they had the energy to be afraid of John. It was just a part of existing: wanting to scream and run and carve into one's self until there was little enough left to make the underside of a boot feel comfortable. Whenever Sett pictured the possum escaping, they cast themself as little more than dead weight.

There were border camps, a group of rogue demons that'd set up shelter outside the hierarchy's control. People made it out of the prison fairly regularly, but nobody ever made it out of Hell. As long as John was alive he would track them down.

"We do not belong here." The two had a lot in common: sucked into bad situations, doing bad things because they didn't have a choice.

And then the possum stirred: not its occasional slow moves of instinct, but actual movement. She rolled to one side, put far more of her weight on Sett than they could handle, then slipped and cracked her nose on the concrete. Sett jumped to their feet, hands shaking as they backed into a corner, and pulled a long needle from their subspace sewing kit. They pointed the sharp end at the now living corpse, their heart roaring in their ears.

She screamed. For 17 seconds the possum's voice tore at the lining of her throat as every piece of torment that had become backed up crashed into her reborn ego at once. The pain grew out of her, sending bright spikes of anguish through the subspace of the cell and knocking Sett's weapon out of their hand. Like this, it was at least short-lived.

She stopped abruptly, her breathing barely audible against the now absent wall of sound. One swallow and her torn throat was coated in a layer of spit. Two and she found herself able to breathe again. Three, four, and five were all dedicated to suppressing coughing fits.

She looked up at Sett, face to face with a stranger.

"What... did you... just say?" she asked between lungfuls of air. Sett, terrified, trembling, and now openly crying, pulled another needle out of subspace.

"What did you say?" Ratty repeated, reaching out to try and calm the goat. It took a moment for them to register the question, then another few seconds to compose themself enough to answer. "It's okay. What's your name?"

"Sett."

"Just Sett?"

"Just Sett."

"What did you say before, Sett?"

"I— we do not belong here?" Sett offered.

The possum's chest rose and fell violently, taking more time with each breath as she began to calm down. "Do you—" She coughed. "D'you wanna bust out with me?"

---

It was difficult to convince Ratty not to go directly from her cell to the exit, a move that would have definitely gotten them caught. She was loud and punkish, uncomfortable leaving anything unsaid between the two. Several lines were crossed as they made their way to Sett's apartment on the edge of the city. They had not been to Earth in long enough to know if that was normal. There had been similar periods of years where Sett hadn't spoken. They had the good sense to stay mostly quiet in the aftermath.

There was an accent, a subtle cut from northern Ontario. The kind, if they were elitist, they might not have expected to hear from a professor.

Sett hadn't socialized enough to find anyone who actually talked not annoying. As an advantage of their status, Sett was allowed to check out any prisoner they wanted for 24 hours at a time. This was not a particularly healthy way to make friends. In the end, Ratty won by promising — although in a mocking tone of voice — that she would stand guard while Sett slept. Sett declined that offer.

Ratty's long stride brought her to the door first, too focused on escaping to let Sett keep up.

"So, okay. I get it, but what if—" She started in on a new plan.

"Miss Vermington," Sett cut her off, the frustration of digging for their keys tipping them over the edge. "I really am sorry, but I have had a very long day. I am all for fantasizing about breaking out, but it is just not possible."

"What if you made me one of your disciples? That's a thing, right?"

Sett dropped their keys, their hand hovering a few inches from its lock. Ratty did not understand what she had just asked.

"I'm not that unfamiliar with supernatural shit. There's like 'Emissary of So-And-So,' or whatever."

"That—" Sett swallowed hard. "That is a very serious proposition."

Ratty stopped, the change in Sett's tone forcing her to consider the shorter animal. She forced her toe to stop tapping, relaxed her posture, and took a step back from the door. She could at least stop hovering.

"Yeah, okay. Sorry." She gave a polite nod.

"An honest mistake," Sett's tension dropped off as they were enveloped with the smell of their apartment, dropping their medicine bag on the floor and deftly stepping around the little anxiety-inducing heaps of mess that populated their apartment. "Watch your step, please."

---

Ratty stood stock still as the door shut behind her, blocking out the rough texture of the entryway mat against her paws as she took in the eclectic decoration. Some piles of books had been left sitting long enough to have their own decorative ecosystems, a scented candle or butterfly pinboard or spoon-shaped instrument case marking them as a permanent fixture.

"You collect butterflies?" It was something to ask, a good dead-air filler. She had started to figure out how the goat navigated, then stopped, coming to understand how dirty she was compared to the sterile chaos.

"Hm? Oh, all kinds of taxidermy, actually." Sett turned to look as their stove clicked to life under a kettle, filled and placed blind with the ease of something they had done thousands of times before. "We like to catch our own when we go up to Earth, but opportunities to do that have been... slim as of late, and John really only has an eye for conventional beauty."

"John is your...?" Ratty prodded, settling into the foyer.

"Boss," Sett kept it short. "He gets free passage to Earth."

"Cool... could we...?" Tonight was a night for letting the ends of questions hang, evidently.

"No, no. He would actually be our main obstacle in getting out," They broke eye contact for just a moment to select a few leaves from a foggy glass jar and fold them into a piece of cloth. "Would you like some— is there a reason you're still on the welcome mat?" the goat asked.

"I— uh, my paws are dirty from the walk, and I don't want to track dirt through your apartment."

"Oh!" Sett laughed softly, "I wouldn't worry about it," They nodded towards the door to their room. "The restroom is through there. There are towels under the sink you can use."

"Right, for sure." Ratty padded through the living room, no more reassured than before as she all but tripped her way through the stacks. Their bedroom was comparatively barren. A small, empty bed, ashtray on the bedside table, empty dust-covered bookshelves, and—

Oh...

Ew.

Someone had written on a blank part of the wall in black marker. That in itself wasn't the disgusting part. What was written, though, made the possum's fur crawl. She touched the autograph — 'John,' it looked like — and smeared one corner along the plaster. Fresh, too. Probably not something the demon wanted them to see.

The bathroom, then. They left their shower curtain drawn back. Ratty turned on the tap. One time she shared a hotel room with someone who had gotten food poisoning on the first day of their trip. As soon as they got in, he put his laptop in the hotel room safe with his passport and press pass and laid down with his mouth a few inches from the drain. Work — back when work was like that — had paid for the hotel. They paid for his ruined clothes, too.

She pulled at her cheek in the mirror. There were few periods in her life where her face had been this sallow. A wide smile didn't look natural. The corners of her lips only raised themself high enough to make a pointy rectangle. She let it go, and a fang hung over each corner of her lips.

Her clothes were replaced with an orange blur. She wasn't wearing anything she owned when she died. Someone went through the trouble of putting her makeup on, now smudged by whatever happened before she woke up. The thought pushed into her mouth as bitter bile.

It hurt to kneel. The cold metal handles ached against the insides of her fingers as she pulled the little cupboard under the sink open. She pushed a pair of unused hoof-style slippers aside and wrapped her hands around a clean, soft, white towel.

No... not that one. She stood back up without the towel. There was a laundry basket in the corner. Poking out of the top was a ratty piece of cloth. She picked it up and sniffed it. Not too dirty. It smelled like—

Wait. That was a weird thing to do. Smelling other people's dirty laundry was not something normal people did.

Sett smelled nice.

Ratty held the towel out at arms length as soon as that thought crossed her mind, racing out of control to the fact that the subtle damp of the cloth was a non-zero percent made of the goat's sweat. She dropped it into the warm water and sat down on the edge of the tub, determined not to process any of that shit.

Water was always too hot or too cold. She used to enjoy it scalding hot. Now there was no way to put up with it. It triggered something beyond the reach of her memory as she scrubbed the dirt from her paws.

She wrung out the towel to the best of her ability, and dried off.

The ink stayed stuck to her fingertips.

She was careful not to step in the spots she had tracked through earlier as she backed out of the room. A hoodie, a pair of shorts, and a set of underwear sat folded on the demon's bed. She pinched the material: the same stretchy faux-denim she always wore.

Huh.

Interesting.

In the foyer, her jacket flickered into existence over a pair of heavy leather boots.

Convenient.

"So..." The goat jumped as Ratty sidled up next to them on the counter, trying to keep her hand flat against the faux stone. It was difficult — at least for someone as bad at eye contact as Ratty — not to notice how they locked onto the smear of fresh black ink against her pink fingers. "John's a shit, eh?"

Sett took a deep breath, not quite ready to talk about that yet. "Yes..."

"Can I help?"

"Not sure. How are you feeling?" That forced Ratty to take stock. It felt like there was a metal rod through her chest, but otherwise...

"I'm fine, don't worry about it. I could do dinner for you tonight, let you relax?" she offered, quiet enough to tip the goat's ear.

"You cook?" Sett asked

"Oh, I'm a fantastic cook." The possum smiled.

"We would, but we don't really... eat... all that often." Of course not. What had first at first looked like a patch of longer fur hiding a pair of lips had thinned as the goat's face moved with their speech. Sett had no visible mouth. They carried twin jugs of water and tea to their coffee table, charting an unrecognizable path through their collection as Ratty watched. "We do appreciate the gesture, though."

"Is 'we' like, a royal 'we' in this context?" She re-navigated the apartment, finding no option at the end of her path than to climb over the coffee table.

"I— yes, sorry, it's— we don't want to call it a social crutch, but..."

"Just a habit then." The possum gave a charming little smile, settling into the couch and picking up the water jug. Her wrist shook as she tried to pour herself a glass. A commute with sixty students worth of papers in her bag had kept her in decent shape in the overworld. How long had it been since then?

The pair sat quietly, possum watching goat as they both ignored the tea. Sett produced a pack of rolling papers from under the messy tabletop, laid one out, and bunched a line of tobacco across the centre.

"You roll your own?" Ratty asked.

"Manufactured cigarettes have strychnine in them." Sett answered. Perfect. The goat was also a weirdo. Maybe they would smell her clothes later. That was also not a normal person thought.

They reached out to their water jug without looking, not having noticed its move before the tip of their claw knocked it all over the floor. "Fuck." they hissed, lifting their hooves out of the way of the spill. They searched frantically for a dry spot to set their cigarette down on.

Ratty lifted her paws to the cushion and tossed down her towel. That was barely a solution. "There." she said.

"I still need—"

"Oh, here." Ratty said, scooting forward and sticking her tongue out. Sett had probably wanted to use the water to close the sticky part of their cigarette. This was an alternative.

"What?" Sett asked. They hadn't put Ratty's idea together yet.

"For your roll-up," she said around her tongue. "You can just roll it up and—"

"Oh, uh..." The demon paused, sat forward, and carefully lifted the paper to the possum's tongue. They struggled to find a place to put their eyes as she wet the sticky edge. The two settled on direct eye contact, Ratty's bemused, smug bluff shattered immediately at being called. Her eyes flicked — too fast to be seen — at the blush in the goat's cheeks, heart thrumming a little faster each time it faded. Sett sat back, folded the roll closed and wrapped a few glowing strings around the tip. They lit it and dissipated, a strange little show of power. Sett lifted it to the spot where their mouth should have been and perched it on the air.

"I didn't expect you to actually do that." She tried very hard to cover up her goofy, dykeish grin.

"What can I say," Sett shrugged. "I am an addict." They let the silence hang as Sett punched a small hole in the skin where their mouth ought to be with their pinkie claw and took the first pull. What would their smile look like?

"So, you've asked a lot of questions tonight, now we think we ought to. What do you do for a living, Miss Vermington?" Sett asked, forcing the possum onto her back foot.

"I'm a 20th century history professor, I make documentaries sometimes, and I write freelance for a Toronto based alt-weekly." There were other things that she was. Sett didn't need to know everything this early on.

"Oh, how is that?"

"It's, uh— Well I'm pretty sure that second job got me killed, so not great."

"Mm," Sett took another drag. "What about hobbies?"

"You don't talk to a lot of people, huh?" Her therapist would have called that a manifestation of her instinct to keep to herself. She probably also would have called it rude. She had missed enough appointments to stop calling that person her therapist, though.

"No, but indulge us anyway." Sett said, cornering the possum in the spotlight of their full attention.

"Uh, I cook, I build stuff, I'm a painter, I like abandoned buildings and haunted shit. I like politics too, but that's not—"

"All things you can do alone?" the goat teased. Something about that didn't sit right. There weren't a lot of ways to respond to such an accurate read.

"I used to perform poetry in front of people." as in roughly six times throughout her ten years of college and high school.

"Oh! We write poetry as well, actually, would you like to see some?"

"Yeah, sure." Just as she was getting used to the attention... Sett forgot entirely about the wet carpet, even as their hooves pushed water deeper into the floor. They got up and interrogated a few stacks of books, lifting one off another and briefly reading the covers of each.

"We just have to find one of our journals..." they explained.

"For sure, for sure..." It was fun to watch the goat flit from stack to stack. They were adorable. They stood out, even in their plain grey standard issue coveralls. Their messy hair formed naturally into a mullet around their ears. They wore the uniform with a few top buttons undone. The possum tried not to be caught looking when they bent forward, the open front hanging low enough to show their function-over-form bra.

God, they were cute. Ratty pretended to be wiping her nose to hide a blush.

"So... how serious is emissary-ing? Is that the demon equivalent of like: 'I wanna get you pregnant?'" Ratty asked, uncomfortable in the flustered silence.

"Actually it would be 'we want to get you pregnant,' and if that's what you wanted, Miss Vermington, you could have led with it..." the goat teased, their eyes dancing over a page. Ratty failed to act like she hadn't noticed the flirting. Sett moved on. "...don't like this one... no, but in all seriousness we would have to be very much in love with you." they said, matter of fact.

"You're not in love with me yet?" Ratty teased.

"I suppose I am in love with an idea I projected onto you while you were in a coma."

"Oh yeah? How disappointing am I so far?"

"Oh, very." they ribbed back, pulling at the skin over their mouth as they broke into a gentle smile.

"I'm sure I'll fix that eventually," Again, she hid her blush with her arm, taking a sip of tea and feeling some tension slip out of their body as she did. "How's that poem coming?"

"We can't find any that aren't, uh, well, tragic. I'd like to show you something nice..." Sett trailed off, closing the seventh journal in a row with nothing to show for it. They sat back down, flicking the embers at the tip of their cigarette off into the accidental lake below.

"Do you really think you could get us out of here?" they asked.

"'Us' as in you, or 'us' as in both of us?

"Both of us, Miss Vermington."

"Probably." Ratty nodded.

Sett turned the idea over in their mind.

"Alright."

Ratty got comfortable on Sett's bed first. Half of the free bedrooms within ten kilometres of her old job were twins. She had learned to put her legs through someone else's while completely ignoring their presence. Sett, on the other hand, rarely had anyone but John over, and he preferred to leave when he was finished.

Ratty found her eyes drifting naturally towards John's message. It drifted back into her thoughts every time, writing itself on the back of her skull even when she was fully turned around. The only cure was to scramble the words through the warped glass of Sett's ashtray, rising and falling on their chest:

1  I'm your boss.
2  Who'd believe you?
3  I'm the fucking devil baby.
4

He had clearly written the number "4" before thinking of what he was actually going to write there, further proof of just how much of a dick-shit he was.

"So— okay—" Ratty pushed the bite-marked bread tag into her cheek, her voice scratchy from a few pulls off Sett's joint. "He just... writes that on your wall... and leaves?"

Sett nodded, their gaze lulling from the ceiling to the wall. "Why wouldn't he leave? This is a normal escalation of his regular behaviour. I'm not surprised. We think we're— I should stop. I'm probably just gonna hang my banjo up over top and try and—" they said, staring, detached, at the dripping black ink.

"Oh my god! Shut the fuck up!" The possum rolled over, failing to account for the size of the bed and nestling her snout directly into the goat's armpit. "Not relevant. He is an asshole and I am going to kill him."

Sett took another long drag, crossing the threshold between anxiety relief and low-level psychedelic experience. The only weed available in Hell were mids with stupid names. That wasn't particularly shocking or relevant, but something Ratty noted when it was said.

"Have you ever killed anyone before Miss Vermington?" Sett asked.

"It's Ratty, please— and not to my knowledge. I talked a lot about killing Nazis as a kid but like— god, I hope not."

"Are you not supposed to remain unbiased as a reporter?" Sett asked.

"Nothing more unbiased than cracking some Nazi skull,

ma'am." Ratty winked, temporarily embodying a caricature of herself.

"So, you think you might have killed someone, but you do not remember?" Sett pressed, high enough to forget about being polite.

"Kind of a long story, I guess."

"Would you like to tell it?" Sett had read the broad strokes.

"Not at all, actually."

"Hm," Sett turned over, dropping a clump of ash into the possum's massive mess of half-curly hair. "Tell me a different story then."

"Yeah?" Ratty looked up from the goat's armpit. "What kind of story?"

"Possum's choice."

"The first story that comes to mind basically every single time someone tells me to tell a story is about how I lost my virginity on a sailboat in the middle of Lake Ontario."

"Oh goodness. That sounds awful."

"Oh absolutely. I was not ready, and It's just a shitty story, like I just told all of it."

Sett humphed, just to register their dissatisfaction.

"I smashed a glass Tupperware over my dad's head at my sister's wedding." she offered.

"Getting closer."

"Well okay then, dyke. You tell me one; set the bar for me." Ratty prodded. Sett sat up in the bed, straightening their back as though preparing for an era defining speech.

"We..." Sett began, falling a hush over the crowd of one. "...went on a few dates with Jesus Christ when he was around."

And silence... a perfectly preserved moment of history suspended in crystalline amber, broken as Ratty spoke. "No fucking way."

"It is true." the goat bragged, self-satisfied.

"Was he a good fuck?"

"Well, I mean, they don't call her the Virgin Mary for nothing." Sett joked. Ratty stared at them in silence for a few moments, trying to process what she had just heard.

"What the fuck does that mean?" She broke into a cackle.

"I have no idea," Sett admitted, letting down their faux gravitas for a quiet laugh.

"Was Jesus a mom-fucker?" Ratty pushed further.

"No, actually. I just thought it would be funny to say," Sett put their laughter on pause, something clearly building behind their eyes as they turned to look at Ratty. "Are you?" they asked.

"Not telling. I am not going to tell you that. That's a secret." Ratty stammered.

"Oh my goodness! You totally do! I'd heard things about country girls, but—" They rolled over to punch the possum, landing with just a few inches between faces.

"I'm going to fucking kill you! I'm going to end your goddamn life!" Ratty giggled, choking on the little piece of plastic in her mouth. Her tongue retrieved it and shoved it back into her cheek. For the record, while she had fucked people who were mothers, Hanratty Vermington was not a 'mom-fucker'.

She froze as she came to comprehend the goat, the skin around where their lips should have been pulling and splitting like warm rubber. It was — admittedly — reviling, and yet watching them laugh, their mouth torn and bleeding from the effort, Hell managed to slip away from around the pair. It was a cool, end of summer Friday evening, laughing with a weird goat they met through work.

She just watched, Content to sink comfortably into the glossy yellow glow of the goat's glowing eyes, the way they scrunched their snout, and their laugh: weak and crackling, but there.

Huh.

Wild.

"You have a beautiful smile, Sett." Ratty said, reaching up to hold the goat's chin. Impossible not to say, seeing it this close. Individual white furs crossed the border around their snout, a perfect little mess. Sett let their mouth hang open, felt a drop of blood fall onto the possum's lip, and pulled back.

They cleared their throat, covering their mouth as they turned back over, trying not to be seen reexamining the doll that came to life. Her goofy grin, her beautifully tired eyes — she was certainly less suave than Sett had originally imagined, but then again nobody was that suave. She made an effort. That was pretty nice.

Sett climbed over the possum and stood up, chewing on their fingers as they stared at John's writing.

"I'm sorry, I assumed you were—"

"No, be quiet please." They needed a moment to process. They touched their open mouth, sealing it shut and wiping the blood off on their dirty uniform. They wanted to take it off, to be rid of the filth. "Aren't you scared?" They turned to the possum.

"I— what? No, I—"

"Of— I'm sorry— I mean, of, uh, being in Hell."

Ratty blinked up at the goat, sat up, and turned so she was sitting upright on the bed.

"No, I don't think so. I made it this far, so... I mean basically it goes: you put me back so you don't get in trouble, I break out, I come get you, we bust out." She forced a smile, something buzzing behind her dilated pupils. "I've done harder things than that on a Wednesday night. That's basically just four things."

Sett considered their next words carefully. "You are here because you did something bad, and while I'm not sure it's your fault, you did do bad things. That is— actually, I am sorry," They cut themself off, trying to wave away the thought. "I'm sorry, ignore me. That is the last thing—"

"Am I afraid of what those things might be?" Ratty prodded. Sett stared down at the possum's hands for a moment before nodding.

"I'm not afraid of anything. As soon as we get out, I can set to work fixing every shitty thing I have ever done. I mean that's basically back to normal, right?" The possum grinned, igniting the goat's own drive for the first time in a long time.

Right,

Just four things.

Easy.

17

# 200█ — 198█
## Vomit

Sett paced over the sleeping possum. She had elected to camp out on the living room couch out of courtesy. Whatever had gone on after their shared memory faded to black made Sett's head pound, blurring the edges of their empty tobacco tin. They tried never to smoke this much at once, but these were extenuating circumstances.

Even looking at her might wake her up. There was enough glow behind the goat's eyes for that. The sooner they could discuss what she was proposing, the better, but that also meant Sett had to work through their own thoughts. There would be a narrow window wherein they had enough to be coherent, but not so much as to write the idea off entirely.

With shaking hands, they rummaged through their smoking drawer, picking up and shaking tin after tin to see what was in them. They really had to stop keeping empty tins. There was one with just a little extra weight in it. They picked it up, opened it, and watched the lid fall right out of their hands.

The tiny aluminum bang was enough to wake Ratty. She sat bolt upright, clutching her chest as her brain caught up with her body. Sett could see the checklist fire off in her mind. Where: in Hell, in an apartment, belonging to a demon. Who: Sett. She centred the demon in her trained gaze, smiling as she understood them to exist.

"Hey!" The dropped tin, along with the what and why, went unacknowledged.

"Good morning. We want to talk to you." They undershot the window significantly. Still, no use prolonging it.

"Who doesn't?" She winked.

"We need to have a frank and honest conversation, Hanratty." They stayed on target.

She blinked, forcing herself to take things a little more seriously. "Okay." The rest of the bend wiggled its way out of her back, another few blinks pressing the comfort of sleep out of her eyes. She patted a pocket, checked behind an ear, never broke her gaze, and listened. What little time they had left to think had run out.

Sett stopped pacing. "Do you actually believe we could escape together?"

"Yes." She didn't hesitate. "Sorry— It's not something I've done before, but it is… similar."

"I thought you were a professor."

"I'm a reporter."

"Of course, my mistake." Sett let their chin fall to their chest. A fucking reporter. She happened to be one of the risk-taking ones, but really, if anyone could have been sent, there were options that far outranked someone who made TV spots. She got up, climbed over the table, and reached for the goat's hand. Sett flinched. Sett felt bad about flinching.

"Sorry—"

"No, it's not you."

"Okay."

Ratty was what they had to work with. They swallowed their mouthful of bitter spit. There was very little to do besides—

"I mean…" She could have been reading their mind. "What's the alternative?"

The alternative was to send Ratty back to Hell. Sett could make an appeal based on some obscure foundation-era laws, maybe get her moved from a cell to an apartment, maybe put her up for some reaper positions, but that was still prison. They had spent their life in that prison. Until it became a possibility, they had refused to feel how badly they wanted out.

"Okay. You can only stay here for one more day unless we get you out of the city, so I'll— we can say you escaped me… and I can call in a favour… and we can go from there." Sett said.

Ratty grinned, her lethargic tail dragging across the carpet in a muted display of excitement. She offered an open hand. Sett took it, and shook.

"Sapphomet of the Mountains, of Chaos, and Etcetera."

"Charmed." Ratty nodded. "Professor Hanratty Vermington,

from the newspaper."

"My pleasure."

That didn't quite work.

"Sett." they said.

"Ratty." she replied.

"Good." Sett nodded. Ratty wiggled their hand side to side, a mold-breaking move of excitement. Tired, the goat gave a soft little laugh in return.

---

It was not a particularly difficult favour to call. Ratty was not the first person to escape from Sett's apartment. They were rarely reprimanded for it. A lot of demons liked to release-and-catch. Sett pretended not to be very good at it.

She was one of the least experienced to escape, though. There were doubtless reporters that had been smuggled out of cities on lockdown. Toronto, with the rest of what North America left behind, went through its fair share of totalitarian moments through the 2020s. Ratty didn't strike Sett as someone who had ever tried for a story beyond the borders of the world's superpowers.

In any case, there was an easy alternative to letting her run off and eventually get captured. A freed smuggler, running propane out to the communes — exclusively for profit, of course. It was one of the camps Sett had never visited before. That would go a long way in helping cover their tracks.

Ratty sat on the edge of the moving van, rocking the suspension with her heavy boots. Her residual self-image had produced a black jacket, silver spikes reflecting the distant ceiling. This was what Ratty thought Ratty looked like, or at the very least what she thought Ratty wore. A little sluttier than Sett had expected, though that wasn't the right word. Shorts a tad too short for the weather, and the kind of black hoodie that showed off either stomach or lower back if she was doing anything but standing straight up. Back together meant all the way back together. This was part of Ratty.

"It's weird. The texture is weird, right?" she asked, squinting at the sky, waiting for the smugglers to fuel up.

"It's tiled." Sett answered. They looked down at their own plain garb, a half-step above scrubs in both comfort and style.

They had nice clothing in the short bursts where they lived on Earth. They came as close as anyone in biblical times to... *model* was too strong of a word. They were a biblical e-goat. It would be the late 20th century, roughly, by the time they got out. They had never seen that era before. There would be new textiles. That was something to look forward to.

They tried not to monopolize the possum's free time. Stupid, considering they had to end up married at a certain point. They weren't used to talking that much either way.

"I suppose this is goodbye then, Ratty." The name fit strangely into their mouth.

"For now." She smiled. "How're you feeling?"

"Our feelings are decidedly mixed." They had spent too much time with the body. It was hard to adjust to the living creature. She had done well so far, though. Well enough to make the goat's mouth dry, to make something happen in their chest when she offered a hand.

"You should come with."

Sett took the hand. "It would ruin our plan."

"Well, duh. Not right now. Maybe switch careers. Become a- what would you call it?"

"A cop?"

"Well, yeah, but like a fake cop. Come riding up on horseback, throw a lasso around me, make a big deal about 'I cannot— sorry— we cannot believe the possum slipped out from under our cute little snout!'"

Sett huffed at that. "You should not speak, actually."

"Yeah, okay. I will make sure of that." Her eyes traced the keratin curve of Sett's claw, fascinated by the way it effortlessly slipped into a groove in her fur. "Here, hold on—"

She let go, rolled up her sleeve, and undid the rubber band of a digital watch. One of the... lets see... watch, jacket, shirt, bra, pants, underwear, socks (2), boots (2). One of the ten things in her possession in that exact moment. She wrapped it around the goat's wrist and latched it in place. "Now you can count down the seconds," she teased.

Sett rolled their eyes and pulled on the band, already trying to get it off, to be done with this joke. Ratty put her hand over theirs. "No." she said. "I'm serious. Here, tell me what time you'll be able to set out." Sett stared down at the watch.

Roughly midnight right now, so it would be in...
"Two days, 12 hours." Sett said.
"Good." Ratty tapped the glass. "Stick to that."
"I can't—"
"It's fine, I'll find another watch." She was not going to accept its return.
"Alright."
They took a long step back as one of the smugglers rounded the side of the truck. Ratty hopped up immediately, trapping him in a firm, two-handed handshake. "Nice to meet you," she said, a little too loudly. "Hanratty. My friends call me Ratty."
"Sure." The smuggler was uninterested in that fact. "You two finish this up. You climb up there." He pointed to a small compartment just above the cabin. "Pull the strap, latch it closed, don't come out until we come get you."
"For sure." Ratty nodded. Sett couldn't remember if the smuggler had been wearing a watch; they knew Ratty hadn't been wearing two. her hands went straight back to her pockets when she let go. "So..." He hadn't rounded the corner before fully leaving the possum's head. "Do I kiss you here, or...?"
"Here." Sett had thought more about that possibility than they cared to admit. They stood on the tips of their hooves, and set a gentle peck on the possum's forehead.
She paused, staring down into the goat's eyes. "Definitely." The possum's non-sequitur stood on shaky ground. "Didn't expect you— yeah. For sure." She was too easy to fluster. "I'll see you around, then."
It was not on purpose when the gold edge of a new watch poked out from under her sleeve. She used that arm to hop into the back of the truck, waiting for Sett to fully turn away before closing her compartment.

---

They had never had a watch before. The novelty of it was almost enough to make up for how much time they wasted fiddling with it. It made wait times drag on, more obvious when they could be measured. They could see its utility wearing thin.
The elevator chimed, flickering every light on that floor. It spat up the only other person in the library: Becky, who locked away some of the upper wings on days where they sat empty.

"Thank you so much for coming out, I—" Sett started.

"It's important! I get it." She was perfectly happy to do it. The lizard unlocked the little cage around the doorknob, took a pair of white gloves from their pocket, and offered Sett some spares. Two white fingers dangled uselessly off the side of the goat's hand. "John actually asked me to get some papers for— oh, okay!" Sett had already taken off between the stacks. "I'll just be here, then."

The name was familiar. There were few families that would choose to stack animal names like that: Rat and Vermin. It was not a book they referenced often. In all likelihood they only understood it to exist as an echo of some lecture series. *Tracking Lineages of Godhood* organized a cursory history of each of the 13 bloodlines: Life, Death, Time, Space, Growth, Decay, Chaos, Order, Passion, Knowledge, Luck, Fate, and Comedy. Of those, 11 had gone dark. Only Decay and Time had updates from this century. Time's most recent entry had been scratched out. Sett had already met Decay.

This was not some grand conspiracy, though they could be accused of treating it like one. It was a theory that had not played out in this copy of the book. The three points that poked out above and below the thick black marker could have been 'V' for Vermington, or any other name beginning with V, or any other letter with two high points and one low point. They had run out of time not to investigate the possum's supernatural origins.

They closed the book, set it on a return cart, and winced as it evaporated back into the sorting room. It would have been a good idea to bring it with them. Actually, it would have been a good idea to enchant the return cart to just put it back on the shelf.

Well, whatever. They still needed... there. *Mechanics and Music.* They passed it along through subspace, dropping it at the check-out desk and moving along. Then... *Emmisaryship and You* — old enough to have wrapped around to modernity. A little further along their gloved claw stopped on *Advanced Subspace Repair for Combat Applications.* They had skimmed the abstract online before, but never actually read the full illuminated version.

Research like this had no target demographic. The pantheon

of the elder gods understood subspace instinctively, and while their lackeys were allowed to tinker with it, Sett's was the only practical method for worker demons. It had yet to find mainstream use.

They pulled the book open, thumbed to a random page, and traced their free finger along the pattern. It took a few wrist flicks to get it right. When they did, the subspace rope from their cosmic spool landed in a perfect weave. They pulled the exact way the book said to pull, and the weave closed. Sett smiled. Subspace would never lose its novelty.

They closed the book, enjoying the weight of it in their hands. They were so often more dense than they remembered. They looked up at the rest of the stack, rising into a miniature infinity. It was convenient — or perhaps telling — that everything they needed had been within arms reach. The shelves rose well past the next floor, flickering where the poorly maintained non-euclidean geometry of the place overlapped. It was possible, if you were brave about it, to read two books at once up there.

That was almost the nerdiest thought Sett ever had.

They were going to miss this. Perhaps that could be an Earth goal. They could build their own— A bang rattled the space. Sharp and metallic, it knocked the lights out for far longer than the elevator.

Sett took off running out into the hallway, where climate control did not restrict access to windows. A third of the way between the edge of town and the edge of the world, a ball of propane flame had demolished a little bridge. Where the container sat was now a crater. The possum was dead.

They stuffed the book in their hand into their bag, bumping Becky on the way back into the library.

"God, they get more destructive with this shit every day."

Sett chose to ignore that. They swept an arm across the check-out desk, dumping their selection into their purse along with whatever else Becky had left out. "Thank you, again, Becky." They bumped her again on the way out.

"You're—"

"Yes, I need to— I just remembered that I have— something! Something that I need to do. So thank you again, and goodbye."

Becky blinked as the goat retreated down the stairwell.

"For sure." she said to no one.

---

Ratty smacked her head off the ceiling, startled out of sleep as the miniature wall came down. Two closed fists wrapped around the collar of her jacket and dragged out over the miscellaneous furniture of discrete smuggling before she had fully woken up.

"Whoa— hey!" She struggled to her feet, the few steps she managed in full service of cooperation. Her lungs hit the back wall of her chest when she hit the road's surface. "What's going on here?"

"We're waiting." one of the smugglers answered.

"Yeah, obviously. What're we waiting for?" She tried to stand, too close to avoid the boot that knocked her back down. It was hard to think about anything but how she wasn't thinking straight. Until the picture was finished, she always stared directly at the bits of table poking through a jigsaw puzzle. She scuttled back a little ways, trying to balance frantic and unnoticed.

There were two other smugglers, flanking either side of the truck, both holding improvised firearms. The ammunition inside was probably remanufactured too, if not straight-up homemade. If there was reason in Hell to sell fireworks, odds they would actually fire were low.

"We're waiting for the patrol that comes through this way."

"Cool, okay. Why are we—" Obviously, Ratty. Idiot. That's the word she was trying to pull earlier. Not "fake cop," "bounty hunter." That was all that would have been available down here. "Oh. Get fucked you fucking loser." was an understatement.

"Yeah, whatever." She got up, far back enough now to make it to her feet. She had started to be able to tell when someone didn't take care of their gun. Nice guns made small, clattering sounds when they moved quickly. Poorly maintained guns made smushing sounds, like a tin can being stepped on. She kept her hands raised either way. One of the smugglers saw his missing watch.

"That's mine."

"You want it back?"

"I'm gonna get it back either way."

"For sure." Ratty nodded, her hands still. "So you guys just do this to everyone, or am I special?"

"I owed Sett a favour. Now we're even, and Sett understands not to ask me for another favour."

Ratty nodded at the explanation. "Smart. You must have a lot of friends."

Could be the kind of friends who sold faulty guns, or ammo without the casings filed down properly. When a gun fires the casing blooms a bit at the end. The bloom has to be ground down if you're going to use it again so it doesn't get stuck inside the mechanism. There's only so many times someone can pick up and reuse that same casing before there's nothing left.

If she held her breath for long enough, she could move fast enough to avoid the first shot. She would have to get lucky on the second one. She had gotten luckier before, though.

Her hand came over her mouth and nose — a precaution to make sure she didn't fuck it up. The first shot came from the one on the left. She ducked around it and it missed her head by several feet.

If she wanted to, she could have watched it whip past her head. She had forgotten just how slow time could go by. The gun on the left made another smushing sound. Nothing came out of it. Before anyone understood what was happening, the possum was holding the only functional gun.

"Okay!" she started, sweating with the effort not to choke. "Alright, you put that down." She flicked her barrel at the one jammed gun. Better not to leave any options open. It hit the floor, let go of its shot. Something in the back of the truck started hissing. She was going to have to walk.

"Okay." the lead man had noticed too. "Great little trick. Let's bring the temperature down, I'll patch up the truck, and none of us get stranded in the middle of the desert."

The bridge they were standing on was the only landmark for miles. Behind them, Hell's central spire shot up through the ceiling. Ahead was just road. There might have been smoke in the distance, blending into the carbon-black walls, but that was far too massive a maybe.

She swallowed hard, eyes locked on the lead smuggler, and

began to lower her gun. Several things happened in quick succession. He went for the back of his waistband. Ratty shot and hit his shoulder. The gun behind his back dropped to the floor of the moving van and went off. The bullet hit something, sparked, and set the ground on fire. The two henchmen stepped forward to stomp it out.

Ratty backed up towards the edge of the bridge, watching the flames lick the underside of the van. Somewhere, hidden under a mess of furniture, a massive tank of propane was being slowly heated from below. A little further and the heel of her boot tripped over the curb. A little further and her back was against a concrete barrier.

She tipped back over the wall. The propane tank exploded. The concrete barrier was scattered for several feet in front of her. Ratty's heart stopped. It was the only one still beating when it came back.

She got up, inching carefully up over the barrier's jagged remains. There were legs left, still trying to stomp out the little gas fire. Something rose in her throat as the meaty smoke tried to suffocate her. It smelled like— one of the legs fell over. The combination of propane and charred flesh made it smell like a barbecue. Ratty spun, realizing she was standing in someone, and vomited off the side of the road. The underside of her boots crackled as the tacky blood peeled from the rubber sole with each stumbling step.

"Oh my god," she groaned, heaving into the dry stream below. The gun dropped, her hands went to her knees, something came up her throat. The material on the bottom of her boots is fried against the hot pavement. She threw up again.

"Not my fault." she gagged. "Right? Not— that was self defence." She had to tell herself that. Another deep breath, another retch, and she was done.

---

Passing the charred remains of the van only served to amplify the goat's panic. No piece of the wreckage was large enough independently to identify as Ratty. If she had — as she was told — stayed put, she was currently in more pieces than could be reasonably reassembled. They kept moving forward, the stolen animal between their legs not conscious enough to care.

She started out as a speck on the horizon, a microdose of anxiety muting medication growing and growing in strength as she came into focus. The back-patch came first: red and black, simple enough to be understood this far off. She was not in perfect condition. Singularly focused, she continued hobbling forward even as Sett slowed to a crawl beside her. She flinched when the goat's mount made a noise.

"Oh, hey." She was tired enough to slur her words. "I was joking about the horse." She turned around to look up at the goat.

"I can't drive." was a near-appropriate response. "What the hell happened?" Sett dropped down off the horse's back to get eye level with Ratty.

"You're early."

"What…" Sett unbuckled a water canteen from their saddle. "the HELL…" They threw it at the possum's chest. "happened?" This was going to be impossible to explain. They would probably have to switch careers after all. Instead of joining the bounty hunting profession, Sett would forever be a fugitive from the eyes of God. This was an exaggeration, but they wouldn't admit that to themself.

"They pulled guns on me." With the benefit of wet lips, she finally caught up to the conversation's pace.

"So you BLEW them UP!?" Sett asked.

"It wasn't on purpose!"

"How do you accidentally—" Well, no. That was possible. "You could have told me, by the way, about your whole thing!" The lineage of godhood was the thing Sett was second most frustrated by.

"I thought the little trick with the watch— I was signalling!" Ratty said.

"What? Not that! What— what are you?" That was the missing component of their escape, surely. She wasn't cocky, she was overpowered and fully self aware. There was some underlying component of manipulation here.

But then why did her "What?" sound so genuine? There was a catalogue of 'dad things' to tick through before she got to her inherited godhood. "Opossum?"

A bad guess, or a good lie. These were families that people devoted their entire lives to tracing the lineage of, but sure! Why not just have a smear of marker blocking out critical information on one of the four existing copies of their work.

"It's okay though." She stepped in between the goat's thoughts. "I'm okay, and you might have to get used to me almost dying." She laughed the last few words.

She *laughed*. "This is funny to you!" Sett screamed.

"Honestly I'm just happy to see you!"

"I was worried about you!"

That stunned her. She drew it all over her face with that same marker — *why were you worried about me?* "Sorry about that." Like a kicked dog, she crumpled in on herself, thumbs through her belt loops. Shame was not an emotion Sett had seen from her yet.

"Okay." Sett huffed. That would have to be enough for now. It was getting too early in the morning to stand around in the open. "Get on the horse."

There was no sun in Hell. It was something you got used to over millions of years, but something the possum hadn't noticed until she began to sweat. She died somewhere cold. The warmth in the central spire — it was starting to look more like a city from this far away — was a welcome change.

They were on a spinning disk. All of the heat from Hell came from friction. The border camps were situated, not up against the wall like Ratty had originally thought, but on the border between hot and unlivable. This close, with nothing around, you could hear the grind at all hours of the day.

She had stubbornly refused to take her jacket, and then her sweater, off until it became unbearable. She didn't like the idea of strolling into a town of strangers in a bra and shorts, especially considering how people normally reacted to trans bodies. It helped somewhat when Sett's jumpsuit went around their waist.

They nodded curtly to the property manager as he showed them into a tent. It was an oversight to send Ratty his way with no money, but she would have figured it out. They felt a little vindicated, picturing the possum wandering around the town, naked and broke. No one here was like that, but they needed this.

Sett staked their claim with their banjo case, the bed farthest from the door. Ratty, having nothing on her, simply dropped herself. These were incredible accommodations when exchanged for a single horse. Every inch of space along the border was precious. The property manager had made it clear Ratty would never be kicked out, so long as she integrated well with the rest of the camp. Sett could be sent back with the next caravan on Monday.

"So," Their book bag claimed the shared little table. "when were you going to tell us about your power, Hanratty."

The possum swallowed hard, staring quietly up at the ceiling. "I hadn't planned on it." The gentle click-click of Sett's case broke her focus.

"You're a very dangerous person, Ms. Vermington." They kept focused on the strings. Gods, and the children of, could pounce when they sensed weakness. Very slowly and deliberately, Sett's claws went around the neck and under the body of their instrument.

"I have my moments." She was already back to teasing. The strings made a swiping sound as the goat's hands tensed around them. "You play guitar?"

"We believe we mentioned banjo several nights ago."

"That was last night."

Sett let go. They were not in the mood to play. "Is this what you do?" they asked, their voice cool and even.

"Is what—"

"We mean the whole unassuming little act. You blow something up—"

"I didn't do that on purp—"

"Please do not cut us off." No weakness. Their voice dropped the temperature of the room a few degrees. When they turned to look at her, it was intentional: the practised little dance of the underling. She had sat up in the meantime, and was bleeding from her forehead. This was their job. She flinched when Sett's hand went around the side of her head.

"Sorry—" Her hands barely lifted from her lap, shaking.

"You're bleeding. We are fixing it." Hands went back down. The façade returned. The skull was only barely more difficult, a thinner gap of skin and flesh between surface and bone. They could afford to lose focus, to feel the transition between smooth fur and rough hair under the tips of their claws, to watch her eyes struggle to find somewhere to sit.

"How's the blood? Is the blood doing anything for you?" she joked. Then, almost too quiet to be heard. "I am sorry. It started when I was 19, I don't know why or where it came from. I try not to think about it. I don't like having power over people."

Sett pulled the wound shut. Ratty winced. Sett's claws dug into the back of her neck to keep her still. "I was— we were worried about you." It came out more terse than the admission would suggest. Again, the possum refused to comprehend that.

"That's nice of you." she said. "This is just kind of what I do, though."

"Journalism is that exciting?" No such industry existed in Hell. What needed to be known was known, all else was better left untouched.

"When you're good at it? Kind of." They had only ever heard one joke about it: that the highest honour you could receive was the CIA award. They had heard this from an incorrectly sorted soul killed in a car bombing. That was another good job, one that exposed them to far less of Ratty's kind of person. When this fell through, they could go back to doing paperwork for the incorrectly damned.

"I've always been kind of weird. Just figured it was luck." Ratty said. The wounds Sett had yet to touch began to heal on their own, understanding they were supposed to.

"Where did you learn to steal watches?" Sett asked.

"I was working on a story and someone stole my watch." Ratty answered. "Great guy. Ended up working together." She shrugged, leaving her head perfectly still even as Sett took their hands away. The last stitch had long since been tied off. "Is this what you do?" Ratty asked. "You worry about people?"

She was incredibly close. "Better than the alternative." Sett answered.

"I agree." She broke eye contact first, curious about the instrument on the goat's side of the room. "I don't think I've heard you play." There was barely enough room between the beds to keep their knees from interlocking.

"Is this..." They quieted themself, an unconscious decision.

The façade of fear in their psychic voice cracked, too quiet —
even between minds — to worry about reverence. "Is this what
you do? Come in, sweep someone off their feet, record a
couple of poignant conversations, and disappear?"

"And you..." She sat forward, still much shorter than the
standing goat. "You adopt comatose sinners for..." Her eyes
fell to their lips as the covering skin began to stretch them,
stopping along the individual grey — they were grey, not white
— individual grey furs. They let a miniature grin fall across their
non-extant lips, the breath from their nose ruffling the lightest
part of the possum's bangs. "...for what, exactly?" She was
back to teasing again.

"We are very lonely, Hanratty. Please do us a favour and try
not to die again."

She struggled not to scoff at that. "Sorry babe." She very
clearly jumped a half inch, having slowed time to think of
something to say. "It's just what I do."

"And you have no idea where that comes from?"

"Was it that obvious?"

"Absolutely."

"Well." She literally had to freeze time to think about other
people's feelings. "I guess we'll just have to take it in real time
—"

"Stop that." Sett cut her off. Whatever Ratty was was not a
threat, clearly. Sett, their mouth barely open, leant forward and
set their lips against Ratty's. Dry and cracked, they soaked up
a little droplet of blood. It lasted just long enough to feel the
heat rise in the possum's cheeks, and then it was over. "No
more secrets, if we're going to be working together."

Sett sat down, picked up their instrument, paused to watch
the smooth veneer crack against the topology of the possum's
scrunched snout, and began to play.

---

20 years in hell flew by: a combination of trying very hard to
go comatose every time she was captured, and a simple fact of
Hell's design. Part of it's intentional metaphysical makeup kept
time thin: 15 minutes felt like 10, you woke up early if you slept
at all, the moments where you caught your breath were always
fleeting at best, and a straw poking through choppy waters at

worst.

Ratty spent most of her time in and out — but mostly out — of prison. She had become a recognized face in the border camps, enough of a name by the time she arrived to earn her a few sympathy meals in exchange for an odd job or two.

Sett made regular journeys out on their time off too, and for once in their infinite memory, they found themself in a not-unpleasant mood. They spent their shifts absentmindedly, able for the first time to look forward to next weekend and a trip to whatever tent city of militant anarchists their possum had nestled herself into.

Living with distant fear was so much more comfortable than living with present fear, and tonight — more than a little drunk — Sett feared absolutely fucking nothing.

They had spent the night on a small scrap wood stage, a rare opportunity to perform in front of anyone who wasn't Ratty. On Earth, tonight would have been her birthday, but neither of them kept track that well.

The goat had a beautiful voice in the same way they had a beautiful smile, a cool growling that hovered just above the warm sharps of their banjo, filling the room with their comforting presence. Unfolded on their lap, their eyes hung low over Mechanics and Music. They plucked away tiredly at the last song of the night, a hollow ache filling their chest as they grew to miss the twang before it had had a chance to say goodbye.

In the opposite corner sat Ratty, craning her neck to watch her partner finish their set. Across from her a rising star in the hierarchy: Crozi, who declared themself the patron of 'knowledge of who you can and need to be,' whatever that meant.

They sat tapping their claws in abject protest of Sett's rhythm against the map splayed out across the chipboard table, their planning stuck idle by the pen out of reach in-between the possum's teeth. It was in their mutual interest to work together: Crozi — gifted with knowledge of the future — had helped them plan their escape, and in return, Ratty would neutralize a small amount of competition on her way out.

Ratty sat, wrapped until the end of Sett's set. She turned to Crozi only once the goat had taken their bow and stepped down from the flimsy riser.

"So... you think we can pull it off, right?" This was not the first time Ratty had asked. Crozi continued drumming the table, annoyed. "I mean we're as prepared as—"

"I don't know if you deserve that certainty." This was also not the first time Ratty had heard that in response.

"Fuckin' serious?" Talking to Crozi got difficult sometimes. In addition to a complete refusal to make eye contact with lessers, they spent their tenure on Earth in the middle ages, and in so doing picked up the annoying affect of a faux-sophisticate.

"If you must ask, you will never know." The ram raised their chin in the most coached high-society posturing Ratty had seen in her life.

"No, listen, okay—" The possum grabbed Crozi's chin and forced it back into the normal people zone, earning herself an affronted glare which she graciously ignored. "What about Sett?"

"Yes, indeed. What about Sett?" The greater demon drawled. "Saint to all but itself, should I concern myself, lost already to the ales and wines?" Crozi nodded towards Sett's preferred bar-stool, currently home to a spinning little goat with a fresh drink. Ratty watched for just long enough to make sure they were okay — she had started doing that without realizing — before turning back on Crozi.

"'Concern yourself' with our deal then, asshole. John finds out about you, and..." That was enough. The ram blinked — putting on airs of 'stunned' for perhaps for the first time since the two had met.

"You're implying—"

"I'm not saying anything." She took a long sip from her empty water cup, struggling not to enjoy the way Crozi's eyes caught fire.

"I will not tell your future, Hanratty. I am not a carnival trick, nor one to flash my wisdom at those lost in its stupor. Though — should it please — perhaps a coin or two to lay out some cards, if you like," they hissed. "What I can tell you is that if anyone is at risk, it is you."

Ratty rolled her eyes, not entirely comprehending that threat. "Yeah, thank you. Always a plea—"

"Quiet." Crozi interrupted. "Your abilities are naught compared to mine and theirs. You have some nebulous skill written into your brain, and an amount of strength to be considered minuscule, even by the standards of a mortal. You are vermin, and perhaps beyond that: only proof that luck is blind. All you have is instinct. They, on the other hand, are not susceptible to mortal wounds. If anyone's not ready it's you." Crozi simmered, Ratty glared for a few moments, waiting for the water to calm enough to interject again.

"Well—"

"No, no my apologies!" Should have waited longer. "You can also drop into a coma at a moment's notice, and skulk around behind time— what do you call it?

"It's called time-stepping and it's fucking mysterious and cool..." the possum grumbled.

"Forgive me. In my age, I even forget the simplest of tricks."

"Okay! Fine!" Ratty sat back, dejected, choosing to watch her partner gather enough social stature to be hoisted onto a table.

"That said..." Crozi started once the universe mandated proper-amount-of-silence had passed. "You are an opossum with an unquestionable amount of dumb luck, and..." They nodded at Sett. "...of course, them."

"Everyone! Everyone everyone everyone," The goat gathered what limited attention was available, sweeping it into range with their arms. "Hold on— Ratty, come get up on the table," They tapped the cheap wood with a hoof. Ratty glanced around for a moment, caught one last glare from Crozi, and — with the requisite amount of encouraging nods — complied, struggling to look at anything in front of so many people.

"This is my — what are we calling it now? Girlfriend is good, what do you think? Yes. This is our girlfriend: Ratty, and we love her very much." They forced the possum's arm into the air like a boxing champ, forcing air either into or out of Ratty's lungs. Right, breathing. Squicked by the crowd, she breathed a sigh of relief as Sett spun her so they were face to face. A public display of affection like this was impossible to cope with. Sett was not only being incredibly kind, they were proud of that affection. They wanted to *brag* about Ratty.

"You don't have to say that." she whispered into the goat's ear.

"Well I mean it, and I'm sorry for getting drunk," they slurred. "I know— well, okay. I am also sorry for making you get up on the table."

"S'alright hun. Can I get down now?"

"We will allow that if you do one thing for me first."

"What's that?"

"Gotta say it back."

"Say what?"

"I love you."

"Oh, fuck off. Is that all?" Ratty swallowed hard as she drowned out the rest of the world. To acknowledge that was to say that she was worthy. Up here, it was just the two of them, the goat fighting back a bout of giggles as her flicking tail threatened to topple the table. She bit down on her tongue. "Sett, goddexx of the Mountains, of Gay Love and Chaos, weaver of the ties that bind: I love you with all of my heart. The 20 years since we met — as rough, and as fleeting as they have been — have meant the world to me. I cannot wait to start our lives together."

Sett stared, stunned at her best friend as they processed: first their girlfriend's words, then every good memory Ratty had brought them. They blinked, noticing as they did that their eyes had welled over. They dove into Ratty's chest, tipping the table and sending them both to the floor.

And Ratty laughed, a quiet signal that Sett's attack hadn't damaged anything.

They would make it out of Hell,

And if they didn't, it didn't matter.

# 1984
# Murder

Ratty had to be brought back eventually. Beyond suspicion, they had to go through John to get out. His office was at the top of the prison, and so inside the prison was a decent place to start escaping. Who better to return her than Sett, the noble demon double agent whose time in the outskirts would no longer raise eyebrows. Of course they had been tracking down the notorious Ratty Vermington... There might have even been a reward, a lovely ceremony to should they decide to stay long enough to see it.

The monster was dragged in by a fistful of hair, too dangerous to be allowed any dignity as she was handed off to the prison handlers. The handlers put her on the end of a collared stick, too cowardly to take risks like the ones that would burn whatever *Sett* was short for into the history books.

"I thought you loved me!" Ratty screamed, yanking against the sharp steel of her collar. The possum had no trouble making her performance believable. Her handlers laughed. Sett turned at the threshold, the loose legs of their jumpsuit fluttering in a constructed wind as they let the flesh around their mouth fall open. They pulled the most over-the-top caricature of the vile upper-crust demons they had grown up around they could manage.

"And how many times will you make that mistake, Miss Vermington?" they sneered, licking every moment from their lips as the facility's automated doors slid shut behind them. It was an incredibly convincing character. Ratty kicked and screamed all the way to her cell, hissing and spitting at the authority-less pawns of the authoritarian afterlife hierarchy's aristocratic regime.

She slipped into her coma almost as soon as she touched down in her cell, not conscious enough to register the bar pushing her shoulder from its socket as anything but a mild inconvenience. The first wave of "welcome back" pain only barely clipped her perception as she dulled her senses. Sitting patiently, she watched the lights around her dim, the air becoming dense in its search for a way to hurt her.

She couldn't hold her breath against it anymore. Whatever had put her in the original coma could not be replicated. The best she could do was ignore it.

It was calming at first, gently cupping her cheeks in a cool full-face embrace, making rings where her whiskers meet the surface. It was quiet. A few small bubbles trickled out of her nose, filling it with water. Her throat got tight first, starting at the top of her chest. She noticed — trying to distract herself — the way the water rocked back and forth against her face.

No holding her breath, no time skip. Those were the rules.

Her two handlers were eventually joined by a curious warden, a thumb hooked proudly through the belt loop that held his solid steel baton in place. They chatted idly, the superior showing off the white sparks of his baton's taser.

It was important to remember that this was still Hell. For these people, fear of a violent uprising was part of their torture. They had been cops or soldiers in their previous lives, and had grown accustomed to being the unquestionably most well armed people in whatever room they walked into.

In a riot, a baton might as well be a squirt-gun. Uniforms came in one size fits all, either too tight or too loose in keeping with the interchangeability of the sinners who wore them. Prisoners had regular access to weapons both improvised and designed. Nobody was safe. All of this just to generate fear and tension for the people put "in charge." It also had the side benefit of being convenient for anyone on their way out.

Ratty had definitely broken out of tougher places than this.

So, plan: Knock out one, grab his baton, knock out two and three. Slip on a uniform and walk out the front door. Easy.

As though stepping out of the way, the phantasmal water leaked from her cell, leaving just a few moments for her to clench her jaw before slipping out of her numbed substate, letting it all come at once. She kept her eyes locked on one, her body twisting as her lungs collapsed beyond themselves.

This was nothing.

There were times in her before-life where she had been in more pain than this.

She had hurt herself like this for *fun*.

Whatever decided her punishment had been holding back, scared of what was to come. As though the experience machine had to index the physical sensation of "take it out on them, not me."

She stood as the last remnant of her pain shot from her throat, hitting the ground in front of her like a ball of phlegm. The dull ache in her dislocated shoulder came back slowly, a gentle nudge pushing her towards the bars.

She sat, just staring for a moment...

And another...

And another...

Then took a deep breath, forcing time to slow around her in the same way she forced it to speed up for her 20 years spent comatose, and sprung at the bars like a caged animal. She slipped through with her arm still dangling out of its socket before the guards had a chance to register movement.

She swung at one, using the impact with his chin to pop her arm back into place. She dove straight south from there, catching the baton on its way up to jabbing-height. Her fist closed around the rubber grip. Guard two stomped into the side of her knee, snapping her leg cleanly and knocking her to the ground. She watched three's boots back away slowly, rolled over onto her back and jammed her new baton up into one's crotch. The taser gave a shower of brilliant white sparks.

One went down hard as Ratty jammed the heel of her soft shoe into his throat, re-breaking her leg and crushing his windpipe in the same motion. She stood, undoing what little progress her bones had done as she smacked the top of her skull into two's chin, sending them down as well.

And three was... fuck. three was a few feet away from the riot alarm. Ratty tossed her baton on instinct, holding her breath as it landed a couple feet short and rolled. It finished it's journey under his boot, rolling in just the right way to send his head to the cement floor with the kind of crack he was unlikely to recover from. The followup fist pump sent shooting pain through her still-not-fully-secure arm.

"Fuck..." she whined, massaging the joint. That would be

easy enough to ignore soon.

Sett checked their watch compulsively. Clicking through the time zones gave them some odd comfort.

They stopped the little LCD map on New York City for the sixth or seventh time that night, staring into the centre of the highlighted timezone. That's where they would come out: An unassuming office building owned in part by the hierarchy, 1983, New Years eve, between 15 and 30 minutes to midnight.

Making Ratty their emissary was no longer a question of whether or not Sett loved their partner enough to go through with it, but it was still painful, intricate, and illegal in any sense of the word that mattered in Hell. It was not work that could be done with shaking hands.

John had already been through tonight to congratulate Sett on bringing Ratty in. He hadn't noticed the cupboard full of supplies they were subconsciously guarding. He had complimented them, making some backhanded remark about how organized things were. Odds were low that he would visit again.

Still, better to be safe. They had cut along the edges of their carpet and rolled it into one corner of the room, ready to be released if the latticework pattern of sigils needed to be hidden. The carpet would do nothing to mask the sweet smell of burning lacquer, but anything Sett could do to minimize their chance of getting caught was at least a little worth it.

They spent a lot of that night on their stomach, measuring each angle with a combination of extensive scrutiny and flicking between reality and a subspace blueprint they had spent their nights off drawing up. *Emmisaryship And You* sat open on their couch. They had messed up somewhere in the design process and needed the outside reference. The thread was infinite, but their spool was not. Somewhere in the almost perfect weave was a missing half-foot of slack. Some anchor somewhere — maybe it was that one? — Needed a few inches to... the left? The left.

*There we go.* The goat let out a sigh of relief as the move sent slack through the entire configuration. They knelt and tugged on the loose end of the thread, begging for all they could get from those few inches. It strained for just a moment — weighing it's want to see the goat to succeed against the hard and fast rules of its construction — and gave just enough to latch onto the last anchor.

And it was done. Sett took a step back to admire their work: an intricate crisscross of shimmering gold that gave way to two small clearings, one for themself, and one for Ratty. Their banjo sat unstrung between the two, waiting for the possum's own soul to be threaded through it.

The goat felt a pang of guilt as their partner crossed their mind again. If either of them fucked up, the last thing they had ever said to each other was—

Actually, it was better not to think like that.

They would see each other again.

Sett picked up their banjo and unfurled the carpet, feeling a little more anxiety ebb away as it was temporarily extinguished. Still, they couldn't stay in here. There was just enough clear space on the bed to lie down on, the rest crowded with mess that had to be moved out of the way. Sett took their seat on the edge, glaring at the graffiti that had haunted them for the past several years:

1   I'm your boss.
2   Who'd believe you?
3   I'm the fucking devil baby.
4

The black ink had faded, the originally raised edge now indistinguishable from the rest of the wallpaper. They slept on the couch to avoid looking at it, to avoid letting those words watch as they slept. Win or lose, this was the last time they would ever see them.

There was the binder they stole, too. That was a lifetime ago at this point: seeing and not registering the red check mark on its side, the word *Angelcorp* written in its crux. They had intended on browsing it at some point. Time got away from them. They were too nervous now, and they couldn't take it with them.

# ∕ANGELCORP

Give up today for a better tomorrow.

They tried to pull a needle from subspace as they sat back, forgetting that their spool was fully taxed until nothing formed between their fingers. They gulped, rolling over and diving their claw into a dresser drawer. For the first time since they were young, their knuckles went white around the handle of a knife instead of a needle.

No, actually. The knife was wrong in their hands. The way the blade rattled in the handle was more annoying than comforting. They went over the skeleton of a plan that Ratty had laid out. It wasn't a very good plan actually, not a lot of substance beyond "fight and leave." There was no guiding their racing thoughts into anything productive at this moment. Instead, their anxiety dictated it was time to think about torture.

People rarely confronted their memories unless it was to push them forward. They could feel the ache in their armpits, the chains cutting into their wrists, the bruised and broken ribs on which they learned to be useful. Why not do that to a child? John was already despicable, charged with, responsible for, and taking sole glee in nothing but suffering across the entirety of his miserable life. A creature designed by the elder gods to create pain was incompatible with the idea of child rearing.

That lasted only until the little demon was just barely 'old enough.' That was when Hell came down hard on Sett. Hard to think about, and hard not to think about. The best they could conjure was the image of his lifeless corpse, and even that was coloured with guilt.

Sett was not designed for hurting people. They put down their knife.

That thought loop ended when they heard the front door handle punch a hole in the adjacent wall.

"Sett?" Ratty's voice, thank god. The goat swallowed hard, setting aside the Rolodex of worse options that had jumped to the front of their mind.

"Bedroom." they called. Ratty stopped in the centre of the

door frame, just ahead of the turned up pull-out couch.

"In the couch?" She gave it a weak kick.

"In the actual bedroom, Ratty." Sett leant over and gave a weak smile through the doorway. Ratty turned, going from a vague look of confused discomfort to a full faced grin as she caught sight of her partner.

"Hey!" Her voice was like a single mouthful of air. She shifted her weight onto the handle of an axe, trying to force some casualty into her posture. She had clearly seen better days.

And yet, for a moment it was almost like Ratty had simply come home from a long day. Sett stifled a laugh at how they must've looked: Ratty coming home with a bloody axe, her partner waiting with a knife in close reach. Ratty laughed too, mostly out of nerves. She really was just a possum shaped bundle of nerves.

"Where did you get an axe from?" Sett asked. Ratty looked down at the weapon, sizing it up as though it was the first time she had ever seen it.

"Uh— fire box? I think."

"Alright." Sett smiled. "Are you ready?"

Ratty took a deep breath, gazed into her partner's eyes, and nodded.

---

A shower wet her fur, pushed some of the ache out of her body, let her breathe again even with the water quietly threatening to suffocate her. Half an hour later, Ratty and Sett knelt in their respective clearings in the latticework. She watched patiently as Sett threaded the white thread of her soul up through the tailpiece of their banjo, smiling as they noticed the goat savouring its tone against the drum.

Her eyes followed the silver threads up through the head of the instrument and stopped where they did: at four tightly tied anchors. Sett's hand sat there, idly twisting and plucking, searching for a tune to bring to the resonator. They could tell which notes hurt, little pinches in the back of the possum's mind, and seemed to cross them off in their mind as they discovered each one.

Ratty shifted on her knees, careful not to distract her soon-to-be life partner. The goat's eyes twitched back and forth gently under their soft lids, sparkling softly as each note revealed itself in turn. Their lips shimmered with the fresh blood of trimming back the skin, dripping down their chin as they mouthed silently through the verses as they came to them. Each word Ratty managed to pick out rose like roots from the thread, further binding her into the ritual.

She scooted closer, hoping to catch a few more words and jumping as her damp fur sizzled on the boundary of her clearing.

"Sorry," Ratty settled back into her spot. The goat's eyes flickered open, mostly confused, and a little annoyed to be interrupted. "I didn't know it—"

"It's okay. I didn't notice until you spoke, actually..." Sett smiled.

"Cool," The possum shifted anxiously. "I love you."

"I love you too." And with that, they began to strum.

"Is this a song I would recognize?" Ratty asked, diverting attention away from the fact she was loved.

"I'm not sure. It'll be our song, none of the texts I read were clear on whether that's something preexisting in the both of us, or something we create together... I just need to find where we start..." They began to strum more confidently, their throat's voice taking over from their head.

Ratty's headache came on slowly, pressure building gradually under the front of her crown climaxing in a pair of pin-pricks under her skin as her new horns pushed their way through her scalp and into fresh air. They stopped, poking just an inch above their fluffy mess of freshly shampooed hair.

"That wasn't so bad." Ratty reached up to touch the budding tips, then froze as their eyes met Sett's.

"Oh, hun..." The tight lipped expression of sympathetic guilt brought up a familiar urge to skip through pain. The ritual was too delicate to skip, too important. Ratty refocused.

Setts eyes.

Setts bleeding lips.

Sett.

The feeling of damp fur, slicked back from her forehead.

Her snout, twitching involuntarily from the smoke of the floorboards.

As long as she kept grounded, as long as everything else

was blocked out, this would be just fine.

Her entire body tensed suddenly as the residual pain of her prison break was pulled from her extremities into the centre of her chest and out through the threads of her soul. She watched, squinting through the light as it travelled like a signal, up through the banjo, an aggressive and thrumming distortion of the instrument's range.

"I love you, Ratty." Sett whispered, almost too quiet to be heard.

"You don't have to s—" The words caught in Ratty's throat as her blood-soaked nubs pushed forward into a full pair of tight coils. It was hard to know just how much of her skin was torn by the keratin outcroppings when the only signal was searing pain. Harder still when it refused to stop at her scalp, shooting down the back of her neck like a pair of careless scalpels running their way down to the small of her back, her shoulder-blades pushing up through the perceived wounds like a pair of useless wings.

She threw herself forward as the pain reached her stomach, found Sett's lap much closer than before. Every inch of the demon's damp fur was a cool comfort against the pain. She felt her teeth chip and reform with the effort of clenching her jaw, felt her throat tear with the sudden effort of holding a grinding wall of sound in her throat.

"Sing, Ratty." Sett said, as though feeling the pain for themself. Ratty growled into the soft fabric of their dress, not ready to give that last bastion yet.

"I love you. Sing." Sett repeated. Ratty felt her body start to split as it had done before only in the most traumatic moments of her life, skipping out of control in an instinctive effort to escape. An inch to the left, an inch to the right, several times a second, sending a melodic drone out from her body. Sett's playing adjusted accordingly, preparing to ramp up into the resonant screech this universe was designed for.

"Ratty." The goat was firm this time. Ratty caved, opening her mouth wide enough to force her ears back against her skull and feeling her teeth finally reform for good, each a little more jagged than when they had started. Her growl became a melodic scream, and the banjo began to scream with her, its strings suddenly burning bright gold with the feedback of every

Ratty across every universe.

In an instant,

She felt dogs teeth tear her throat out, felt cold cement against her back start to warm with her blood, saw the eyes of an animal with fear and pity and love and the knowledge that it had killed its master. She died, and returned.

She felt her spine snap, felt the invasive fingers of a machine dig under her skin and bore out her flawed biology, felt cold, industrial metal parts take over her body, felt love for only a moment as she watched the rolling tides. She died, and returned.

She felt her body rot in a ditch, cold mud against her aching back, anguish at the reward of a long life spent in prison: freedom. She died, and returned.

She felt herself simply disappear, her last sight a grey recreation of the goat in front of her, bleeding from one eye. She died, and returned.

She felt welts form on her body. She died, and returned.

She felt her heart stop as an act of plain bad luck, died, and returned.

She felt her mind fade to grey, died, and returned.

The most important seconds of a thousand tiny lives all at once.

And then,

In an instant,

She felt her partner's hand on the back of her head, felt her face resting on their soft, felt the quiet buzzing of the banjo, still calming down from its last note. Ratty slumped over, flinching as her new horns thunked against the hollow body of the instrument, and curled closer to her partner. The ringing in her ears faded slowly, even her advanced biology finding it hard to adjust to the relative quiet after the din of every universe she had ever existed in.

"I love you. It's okay now. You did so good." Over and over again, just waiting for their partner to return. Her head felt heavy, the line between her fur and her partner's grinding closer and closer to nothing with each silent second that passed.

"Rock n' roll." Ratty stammered, pushing out the first thought that came to her mind as a signal that she was okay.

"So rock n' roll." Sett laughed, stroking the pain out of the base of their fiancée's new horns.
"I love you so much."
"Love you too."

---

The higher you got in Hell, the more the hierarchy let their gods play fast and loose with space and time. The general excuse was that a simple concrete prison was probably far too good for the likes of Adolf Hitler.

Of course, John had no concept of fairness to begin with. Instead of trapping ol' one ball in an infinite maze of suffocating incinerators, forever forced to perceive the pathetic downfall of die infinite Reich, he chose instead to make his office pretty, and left Adolf in a cell with a dude who watched too many videos of babies falling over.

"Ratty!" the demon called from his throne like a cheerful co-worker, rising stacks of black tile to catch each step down. "I gotta hand it to you, buddy! Bagged my babe, escaped my prison, it'd be impressive if— well, actually, y'know what? It is actually pretty damn impressive!" He came in for a hug, backing Sett and Ratty to the edge of the platform. "What're you doing man? Bring it in! Haven't seen you since day one!"

"Back the fuck up, cunt." She jabbed him in the chest with the head of her axe. "We're leaving."

"C'mon! I was just about to offer you a job!" He dropped his arms, frowning down at her with the same energy as an email titled 'sorry for calling you 'man'" "The hierarchy! Take over for your pops!" The fake almost-cry dissolved from his face. "Nah, I'm joking. Good guess, though. It's what I would'a thought."

She chose to take after her mother instead. Her hands tightened around the handle, pressing the soft heel of her palm into the threads wrapped around it. It was heavy with potential, almost begging to be swung, discontent with the stillness.

"That's not going to happen." Sett spoke up from behind her. She felt their heat through the strings. John stared down at the pair, chewing his lip. He shrugged, snapped his fingers, and nothing happened. That surprised him. He tried again, only opening his eyes when he was not met with the shrieks of unmaking. He trapped Ratty in the centre of his gaze, leaning over the axe to get a better look at her horns. They were still wet with blood. John ran a finger along one of them, and tasted it.

"Did you— oh my god you did! Wow, what do people say after engagements?" The threads wove themselves into thick, braided ropes beneath Ratty's palms. The extra weight was too much for their shaking hands to move. They were trying not to look scared. "Good for you! Really, I mean good for you. We'll just do this the old fashion way, then." He paused for a second, cleaning his teeth below his lips, and stepped back.

His throne began to crumble behind him, criss-crossing the tiled pillars over the pair's head. Ratty held her breath, watching their midsections crack as slowly as she could manage. John, for all the debris, wandered calmly through the stacks. This could have hurt him.

Ratty jumped forward, dragging Sett along behind her, getting as close to the demon's back as she could. He turned in slow-motion, pillars falling in a protected ring around them, as Ratty let go of the tension in her axe. It shot up at his chin, stopping where the wooden neck of the tool met his palm. It was barely an effort to rip it from her grasp.

Sett let the slack of their rope go limp around their wrists. This was stupid. They never should have tried this. John's elbow came down on Ratty's head, putting her on the floor. "Could have— whoa!" Ratty kicked at his knee. "Could have done way better, Sett! Just letting you know."

The handle of the axe came down on her head, and Hell began to spin the wrong way. Her eyes shut against the sudden brightness of the world, Sett glowed through the darkness. They were a warm peach against the darkness, flickering frigid white in the darkness. A chain dangled red-hot from the centre of their chest. Thick and dangerous, the other end was hooked through John's belt.

"'Lotta fight, but I mean, really?" He picked Ratty up by the scruff of her jacket. She struggled to open her eyes, dove blindly for the chain when she finally did, and fell right through it. Her snout cracked off the hard ground. John tossed their jacket off to one side, laughing. "Is that the first time you're seeing that?"

He pulled on the chain, half-extant in his grip, pulling Sett to the ground. "You really had no idea, huh? I am so sorry, buddy. Sett is mine."

Well, that sucked. Ratty rolled onto her back, choking on the noseful of blood that fell back into her throat. It sprayed out past her lips, the cool mist bringing her just below the plateau where she could have inflicted more pain on herself. She just stared, eyes winding around the loose bundle of threads in Sett's grip.

She had fucked that up pretty quickly. The axe came down in her chest, hovering just above numb ache as her punctured lung filled with blood. Numb was the only way to describe it. There was nothing to feel but the aching centre of guilt to rot away in her chest: the promises she made, her best friend just a few feet away, eyes blank with fear.

"This was fun!" he drawled. "It's been a while since I got my hands dirty, we should really do this more often. Wouldn't you agree, Sett?" He stepped over the possum's pre-corpse, completely eclipsing the trembling lesser demon. She caught every fourth word or so, the rest going by behind a black curtain. Probably best not to let Sett end this alone. She got up to her elbows, her immobile lower half dragging behind her as she crossed the few inches it took to see through the crook of John's elbow. Maybe she would die faster, whatever that meant. Didn't matter, had to be there.

Sett caught a glimpse of movement through the triangle formed by John's arm and torso. A possum, her tired eyes struggling to focus on their own. For a moment, Sett wanted to give her a smile. To show her that it was all okay. That wasn't going to happen with John standing over them like this. Almost imperceptibly — perhaps unintentionally — the possum kicked her chin up in a headbutt motion. Secure in the knowledge that this couldn't make things any worse, Sett reeled their head back and slammed their forehead into John's nose, knocking him back. Sett ducked under his flailing arm and slid to a halt next to Ratty. Threads pierced her skin in a rough lattice pattern, sewing their doll back together as they had done so many times before.

"One more go, c'mon, Ratty." They patted her up, checking over their shoulder to watch John recover. "One more. I'll keep you together, just one more go, okay?"

Thread pulled the ache out of her nerves. She could ignore the sting as it cut into her skin, trading her large wounds for several more small ones. This was more than she had ever been through before, and she wasn't dead yet. "One more go." she nodded. Her body pushed itself backwards through time, in and out of this universe with the amount of repair work it had to do. She owed Sett one more go.

"Ugh! You fucking bitch." John flicked blood from his fingers, having failed to stop his nosebleed. Ratty took the head of the axe in her hand, using it to push herself into a standing position. She glared right through John at the ephemeral door behind his back. Her stitches pulled tight, sinking into her flesh as they bound more with her spirit than her body. The lattice pattern remained, keeping everything aligned. They freed their hands from the rope, choosing to hold them only for dexterity.

They were supporting instead of binding. They were in control. They weren't just being used as a useful piece of medical equipment, but that they were the only one who could do this job. It was theirs to control: triage.

One more go.

Something cracked behind John's eyes, putting a wall between him and the pair. "Hey, okay actually— listen, Sapphomet—" He pivoted hard. "Lets talk about—" Time stopped again. Sett was brought along to watch it go by.

Ratty lunged at the dog, the threads in her arm tensing like a spring. He threw up a pillar on pure instinct, not understanding it to have shattered until the axe lodged itself in his chest. His ribs went one at a time, stopping part way through the third. He barked as the possum let time slip again, snapping the axe handle. The force knocked it from Ratty's hands. Where it lay on the floor, a shattered piece of tile formed around it, leaving the original head to push its way out of John's body.

Sett yanked their rope as he swung the new axe over his head like an executioner, shattering and re-forming it against the ground where Ratty had been standing. The threads stayed synchronized with her body as she moved laterally through time. She stepped back into the fray, stomping the axe out of the greater demon's hands and kicking it backwards towards her partner.

There was light in her veins as the edges of her vision

started to fade, pinhole focused on her enemy. The threads that had previously slipped through her skin further consolidated in her centre, shaking with Sett's effort. One final yank and they snapped together, bringing Ratty to the ground out of John's reach.

Sett took the axe in their hands. The fear had all but gone from their body, replaced with a burning determination that pushed its way up through their throat and made their ears ring. They wrapped the head of the axe around their chain, now visible to the whole world, and stared down John.

The goat savoured the moment, watching the dog — paralyzed — run through the stages of grief. They turned to their fiancée once they had had their fill, a brilliant excitement in her eyes, and yanked the corner of the axe through a loop of the chain. It shattered instantly, peppering the three with flecks of hot metal.

"Well... fuck."

Ratty dove into John's chest, the same latticework pattern that made her an emissary weaving its way out below her feet. She took a clump of the greater demon's hair in her fist, yanking his head back. One final piece of revenge as she drove a closed fist up into his healing ribs, time-stepping to worsen the impact and feeling nothing as every bone in her wrist was pulverized and reformed.

John fell back, struggling to keep any amount of height as the possum dragged him further to the floor. The goat stumbled forward, catching themself on the possum's back and letting out a little slack. John went for a punch, missed, and was caught in the searing fistful of rope between Ratty's fingers. His wrist pulled behind him at an angle that held his chest and neck perfectly exposed.

The axe was heavy in their hands, powerfully aware of its potential, feeling the same discontentment with keeping it still. The same coiling muscles begged to taste blood. They ached over this as their fiancée fell, bringing John to the ground in a perfect impression of a man sentenced to death by beheading.

Two sets of eyes lay before her: an opossum, deep and black and tired and pleading for the end of this, and a dog's: still full of hate. It was always hate, since the day they were created all they had ever known was hate. It just felt normal.

Not anymore. Sett had felt love before, but they had never had someone like this. This was love: Ratty's torn body, refusing to give up after being carved to shreds. Love was Sett, fighting the man who had kept them prisoner for their entire infinite lifespan. Love was not a chain, it was a rope, and it had taken too long to find that out.

Sett raised the axe above their head, noticing the ache of straining to hold their partner together for the first time. For the first time, they noticed the shaking in their limbs. For the first time, they collapsed, bringing the axe down with them.

He would not stay dead, but he would know to stay away.

They collapsed into their fiancée, the pooling blood cool against their burning fur. Ratty pulled them in closer, bringing them within kicking distance of the still-mouthing head. They tried to do the same with the rest of the heavy corpse, broke down crying when they couldn't, and instead just buried their face in their fiancée's chest, feeling their tears track through the grime that had built up on the possum's shirt.

John was gone.

New Years Eve.

Another boring night.

Every night was boring for Becca.

Every night spent waiting for her shift to end, every night a half finished game of solitaire in front of her, every night her Walkman jammed, every night she adamantly refused to listen to Earth radio. It was bad enough that she had to comply with a bunch of stupid rules around the era's technology, it was a bridge too far to stoop so low as to listen to a celebration of the next mortal year.

She entertained for a moment, as she did every night, that perhaps she might not be a desk demon, but in fact a mortal trapped in Hell. It was her job to do customs for anyone that escaped, and nobody ever escaped. A truly ironic existence, or at least close enough to whatever irony actually was that her internal monologue did not bother to correct her.

All of this musing as — as happened every night — a small goat shambled into the lobby, half-carrying a near-dead possum over their shoulder.

Wait.

Hang on.

Becca jumped as the pair turned to look at her: one lesser demon, and one Earth born emissary with enough wounds to put a pause on an army. It was the first time anyone had actually looked at her since she started on Earth.

"Are you- are you customs?" Sett asked.

"I, uh— I think so? Are you leaving?" Becca responded.

"We— I'm- uh, Sapphomet... Sett, actually. This is Ratty," They dragged the possum over, paying more attention to planting her feet in the right spots than actually reaching the desk. "We need... we need... documents for uh, immigration to Earth? And... I think it's called re-naturalization? I'm sorry this is— we have had a rough night."

"Get some- get some money for all the time I spent in Hell, too," Ratty slurred. "Gotta be a grant... always a grant..." her head lulled with the effort of speaking.

"For sure, yes I definitely have papers for that kind of thing somewhere." Becca shuffled her Walkman under a pile of office detritus as the time to do actual work came down. Silence hung between the two parties as — without breaking eye contact — Becca successfully spilled coffee all over her computer terminal.

"Yes, and can we have them, please?" Sett nudged.

"Oh, yeah! Yes, I'm sorry, here—" Becca dove beneath her desk, producing two heavy binders and a stapled stack of forums. "Application for your allotted uh, 10k in repatriation expenses, permanent residency on Earth... and— sorry, are you Canadian?" she asked.

"Oh, we totally are, oops." Ratty nodded.

"Right, and you're staying permanently?"

Sett nodded.

"Okay, one more of these uh, expense applications, and I will actually get you the Canadian versions... that's quite a bit more money actually— I would invest that, if I were you. Can I ask, actually, what, like, happened to you two?" Becca let her curiosity get the better of her as she dove back under the desk.

"Killed the devil." the possum mumbled, clearly exhausted, "and I feel bad that I don't feel bad." She spoke like someone very sure of herself despite most of her blood being outside her body. Becca nodded politely over the lip of their desk, feeling weird about her boss being dead.

"Not, Lucifer. Just— did you know John the Architect?" Sett corrected.

"He's next." Ratty refused to wait for an answer.

"No, she's not. She's very nice and you don't have to."

"Okay." She was disappointed.

"So, what do I do now?" Becca asked, coming up with another pair of binders and forms, more lost than she had ever been in her life. What do you do when someone murders your boss?

"I- I'm not sure," Sett started. "isn't it your job to like, deal with people who escape?"

"You're the first two people I've seen in the entire time I've worked here, so I don't really think anyone would notice if I just left."

"Come work for us!" The possum piped up again.

"No, okay. Ratty, stop talking." Sett said.

"Gonna start a company. American dream!"

"This is not the time to— Ratty." Sett commanded. Ratty caught their eye, choosing not to finish what she was saying as the goat lodged the binders under their free arm and gave a polite goodbye nod.

"Oh! Wait!" Becca dove back under her desk for a third time, producing a thermos and offering it to the pair. "Hot chocolate," She smiled. "It's cold out there."

Ratty took a step back from Sett as the two hit the sidewalk.

"It's okay, I can stand on my own," She swayed on her feet, laughing to herself as she recognized the neighbourhood. "*Hell's Kitchen...*" she sighed with a smile. Sett looked up at their fiancée, breaking into their own fit of giggles at the absolute absurdity of what they had just done together.

"You know anyone we can stay with in New York?" the goat ribbed. The countdown to midnight started just a few blocks away.

"In 1983?" Ratty teased. "Not— not looking like this, no." It was warm enough to be drizzling at the height of December, and breathing real air never felt so good. No one in the world knew her anymore. The memory of her was left in the future.

"Well, we can probably stay here until at least the end of the year." Sett said, less and less aware of their tears as they cooled and blended with the rain on their cheeks. They let their eyes lull closed as their eyes as their fiancée wiped them away, unintentionally replacing them with a smear of blood.

"Ah shit, sorry." Ratty said, trying to lick a clean patch on her thumb through the caked on grime. Sett shook their head, giving their first free smile in centuries. Somewhere, the organized countdown devolved into a crowd of cheers, a select few corrals trying to push the din it into a chorus of 'Auld Lang Syne'

And for a moment an infinite weight lifted from their shoulders. They just stood there, looking at each other: Ratty with her tired eyes and goofy grin, Sett smiling quietly under the bliss of new potential.

"Happy New Year, Sett."

"Happy New Year, Hanratty."

And then they kissed.

# 1986
# Reconnaissance

It hadn't taken that long to get Ratty back to Toronto, but it was their only priority while it was still in progress. One missed piece of paperwork and their timeline could have been significantly delayed. They stayed in motels. Sett washed their jumpsuit in the sinks. Ratty's clothes stayed in the freezer when one was afforded to them. When that stopped being feasible, clothing runs were function over form. Ratty needed a blazer to go to some office to set up some part of her business. She picked the first neutral coloured one that fit. Sett, most of the time, ended up in whatever was cheap.

That changed when they stopped in the Toronto Coach Terminal for the last time. They unpacked essentials on day one. On day two, they went to a local second hand store.

"Alright, we're— I'm finished!" They poked their head around the door frame, tempering their reveal. "Actually, can you stop me when I say that?"

"Say what?" Ratty asked, splayed out on the couch opposite the door.

"I don't wanna be *we* anymore. I'm Sett." they answered.

"I will try to stop you from doing that." It slipped her mind almost immediately. Satisfied with that, Sett ducked back behind the door, took a deep breath, and stepped out into the little common area. This was the only one-bedroom in a row of two-bedroom apartments.

They flattened down the pile of grey-to-black sweaters. In Hell, and for their first few months on Earth, Sett styled their hair like someone who wanted to forget they had hair. They kept it as short as they could without drawing attention. Largely intact in the front, they brought it all the way down on every inch of skull behind their ears.

Ratty stood up, leaving her work behind for a moment. She

56

tried and failed to pause the VCR, more focused on the goat than aiming the remote.

"It's not too short, is it?" They shook their head a bit, fluffing their smooth bangs. They fell almost perfectly at the line where the rough buzz took over their fur. They had uncovered so much of themself. The subtle curve of their jaw signalled the underworkings of a mouth. Where the patch of white-grey on their forehead met their temple, the cut transitioned sharply into a smooth almond-shaped bang.

"No, not at all." Ratty's hand tracked around the back of their shawl as she circled. "I really like it."

"It's a little dykey." Sett said, dropping down on the couch.

"I mean," Ratty sat down next to them. "Are you yourself not a little dykey?"

They made a little noise of contentment, settling in against the possum. "What're we watching?" Their eyes refused to focus on the TV.

"It's— did I ever tell you about Angelcorp?"

"You... have not, but, I saw— or rather I stole this binder from the library that had their logo on it."

"In Hell?" Ratty asked.

Sett nodded.

"Did you ever read it?"

Sett waited to answer that. There was no way to say no without saying "no." "I did not." was as close as they could get.

"Well, that is still weird. I'm also pretty sure— I mean actually I don't want to— well. Okay what's true and factual is that it's like the second last word I heard before I died, and so I got bored and went to the library, and they gave me this tape about like, the development of the Angel II. I'm trying to see if I can't find anyone that lives nearby to talk to." Ratty explained.

"Cool." They let their eyes lull closed. Ratty tugged on the edge of their shawl, one of their favourite finds. They couldn't decide what exactly to try on first, and so piled it all together. This, with a little refinement, could work wonders.

"I like this." Ratty said.

"Thank you." They had overdone it just a tad, though. No one needed two shawls. No sensible person needed to wear fingerless gloves indoors, and no one needed this many rings. Put together, they gave off the impression of a living laundry heap at the blanket factory, whatever that meant.

"Are you goth now?"

"I was always goth, it's just not easy to find clothes in Hell."

She fiddled with the rings next, incapable of holding back her urge to touch every part of the outfit. "You throw out your old uniform?"

"It's in storage." They had brought it this far.

"We should burn it." That was not an entirely unattractive idea.

"It's not exactly goth." They couldn't stop themself from correcting her.

"Is there a word for it? Are you going to be a nerd about it?" Ratty teased.

"Oh my god." They buried their face in her chest. "You're so rude!"

"C'mon," she teased a little further. "Get back up, give us a little spin."

"I'm not doing that." Their voice was muffled by the possum's lazy hoodie.

"What's it called?"

"I'm not telling you that either!"

"It's like *Cozycore* or something, right?" Ratty pressed. "or is this part of the folk punk thing?"

"Oh my god, you are such a millennial."

"I was born in '98, that's barely— when's your birthday?" Ratty asked. Sett bit their tongue, their face too effectively hidden to give away their overwhelming hesitancy to answer.

"I was... 'born'... with the start of the universe." It came out slowly, almost inaudible until Ratty pressed back into the couch to listen. She grinned down at the little goat.

"So you're a cougar?" Ratty asked.

"Oh my GOD!"

"You're a folk punk, Cozycore goth cougar."

"Shut UP!" Sett screamed into the possum's chest, absolutely baking in the combined fabric, blush, and shared body heat. "Shut up!" they repeated.

"Waitwaitwait." She caught Sett as she shot forward, grabbing the remote from the coffee table and successfully pausing this time. "Sorry—" Sett wormed around to sit without help, making room for the possum to drag her finger along the

58

unfolded phone-book mixed in with the rest of her paperwork.
"You should probably put your money somewhere more
safe." Whenever she was paid in cash, whatever didn't fit in her
wallet was left wherever it landed when she set it down.

"It's our money," she said, completely absent as she
squinted through the list of names. "How are you supposed to
find it if you need it?"

"Well, we can find a drawer or something to put it in." The
coffee table itself had one that would work, but that was a little
too out in the open.

"How's your tea shop, by the way?" There was an old plot of
land on the west end that belonged to Sett a few decades ago,
almost unused in the era it was purchased.

"I had to take ownership of it as my own child, but it does
belong to me again, which is nice."

"That's good... here we go, hold on. C... Ca.... Can.... Cane.
Marshall Cane." Ratty tore out the page, stood suddenly
enough to startle Sett, popped out her VHS, and went for the
door. "I'll be back soon! "Love you!"

"Oh, okay!" Sett called, bewildered by the sudden change. "I
love you too."

"Wait—" she turned tail, kissed Sett, and took off. "Now I'll be
back!" her voice came down the hall.

---

"Can I help you?" He looked younger in the documentary. He
also looked quite a bit smaller. At an even 5'10, Ratty wasn't
used to looking that far up to make eye contact. People usually
avoided answering the door shirtless, too. The wolf's cabin sat
in the middle of a clearing a few miles from the nearest road,
far enough away from civilization to warrant a massive satellite
dish rusting away in the front yard.

"Hi, my name is Ratty Vermington, I'm a reporter. Are you
Marshall?" she asked, finishing up folding her headphone cord
and dipping back into her comfortable, journalistic tone for the
first time since returning to Earth.

"I am." Marshall replied, audibly resenting being known.

"I understand you work for a company called Angelcorp, do
you mind if I come in?" Ol' J-School tricks. Most polite people,
especially in the era her instructors grew up in, would not say

no to such an innocent request.

"What for?" Of course, that was most people. On occasion, the black-tie/white cotton shirt set some people on edge. Marshall adjusted his posture, taking up even more of the door frame.

"I was hoping, actually, to ask you a few questions for a film I'm doing on the recent success of the Angel II. It's a followup to the one you were in before," she answered. A little journalistic malpractice never hurt anyone, and it was a story, just not a story that would end up in shitty indie cinemas, and not a story about the Angel II.

Marshall sized up the possum, furrowing his brow slightly at the width of her shoulders. Ultimately though, he shrugged, stepped aside, and let Ratty in, closing the door behind her.

"Where's your camera?"

"We haven't started shooting yet, this is just a pre-interview." That satisfied Cane.

The cabin felt much smaller on the inside. A simple construction of a trim kitchen, single seat living room, bedroom, and bathroom; the kind of place you would expect to belong to a person who spent most of their time outdoors.

"Anything to drink?" His demeanour stayed gruff.

"Just water, if that's okay." Ratty sat down at the only other seat. a squeaky kitchen chair, and set her notebook down on the counter.

"I'd have to boil it anyway if you want coffee or something, the filter's been busted."

"I'm fine, then." The possum smiled, clicking her pen.

"Alright." Cane's firm demeanour changed as much as it could to signify disappointment, eliciting a small pang of guilt from the possum. The wolf set his kettle on to boil. He might've had some really cool kind of tea he was eager to show off. He was clearly not the kind of person who had frequent guests.

"Mind if I take a second to get dressed?" he asked, pointing down the hall to his bedroom.

"I would feel weird if you didn't, actually." The possum smiled gently.

The cottage was cute, evoking nostalgia for what was — for a bachelor of the time — pretty modern design sensibilities.

"I gotta say—" Cane called from the other room. "I'm just an engineer, the NDA hasn't come down yet. I would feel better if you told me who you work for." The wolf called Ratty's eyes back to the hallway, tripping over the handle of a door she hadn't seen before. A half-moon hole had been carved out of the wooden slating.

"I uh— I'm actually working on spec, haven't pitched it yet, so —" She stood from her seat, wincing as a symphony of creaks gave away her movement, careful to keep her tone even as she examined the hidden door. A padlock, barely visible in the darkness behind the wall.

"So you don't have anyone waiting at the office?" Cane gave a gruff laugh, a sudden cruelty creeping into his tone. "That's funny. I always thought reporters were funny: showing up to a stranger's house with nobody at home expecting them back."

"I'm... engaged actually..." Cane came out of his bedroom as she reached for the lock. She froze, her eyes jumping straight to a spot of red on the wolf's white cotton shirt. "You have a stain—"

"Yes, I know." Cane advanced, towering over her once again. "You really should have taken that tea."

"I- what?" Ratty stammered.

"Because there were drugs in the tea, and I wouldn't have had to do this." With that, before the possum could react, Cane took hold of a fistful of her hair and slammed her head through the wood and into a reinforced steel door frame.

---

Ratty would be back soon. There was no need to panic. This was normal. People sometimes left for three or four days at a time without saying why. Ratty had even said why, so this kind of absence was more than allowed, probably. It would be overbearing to go looking for her.

They had worn a track into the carpet already. They found it impossible to sleep, and had broken not one, but two strings the last time they tried to play.

This was normal, right? There was nothing to do about it, in any case. The police would only make things worse. Imagine that. "Yes, hello officer. I'm a non-binary lesbian from Hell, and my undead transgender fiancée is missing." Not ideal. Not a good idea at all. Ratty wasn't missing yet, either. She was just gone...

...for three days...

...possibly four. It should only count as missing officially when the person someone lived with completely lost track. Ratty was missing. Sett stopped in their carpet track. Their heart froze in their chest. They sat down on the couch. They began to cry.

They shut their eyes, letting the darkness illuminate the rope that bound them together. They wound it through their fingers, too self conscious to entertain the thought of hugging it. Beyond the empty apartment building the world became too crowded to track her, the muddy image of Earth's subspace flickering into existence, as though every living being had to share one orange streetlight.

They would get better at deciphering this version. They got up, circled the coffee table, and tipped it up against the couch. The kitchen junk drawer came preloaded with the detritus of someone else's life. Pens, pencils, a quarter pad of sticky notes and etcetera were joined by the few magical trinkets that were easy to procure. Sett took a stick of chalk from the side and grabbed their banjo on the way back to the living room.

They put down a ring of runes on the carpet, sat down in the centre and re-strung the banjo. Ratty was not missing. The world was still too crowded to tell, but people didn't go missing after three days. The folk standard cleared the brown from the black, brightened the orange souls, but the crowd remained. Playing harder, the brightness hurt their eyes. They missed notes and lights popped around their head. In the darkness, a grey-furred goat stood over them, hollow and towering.

They jumped to their feet, cowering against the tipped up coffee table. Their banjo hit the floor, snapping in half. They were alone in the room again.

"Fuck." they hissed. Back to the junk drawer, they picked out a glass phial, pinched in the centre to make it easier to break. They broke it over the banjo, and it pulled itself back together.

That was an idea. Ratty's phone book was still here somewhere.

That was their only phial, though. They already understood that before they checked the junk drawer again. Maybe they came in packs of two, and Sett had just forgotten. They took the trays out and scattered them across the counter, searching the lost lint and pen-caps underneath. They ripped the drawer from its socket and dumped it across the floor.

There was not another repair phial.

The phone book page was in her pocket when she left. If they could just get the phone book moving towards its missing page, it would point them in the right direction.

There was not another repair phial. They fell to their knees, crumpling the book in their hands.

For the third— maybe fourth day in a row, Ratty woke up with a fistful of her hair in Cane's hand, kicking and spitting all the way to the centre of the room. For the third/fourth day in a row, Ratty tried and failed to rip free, a combination of too exhausted and hungry to meddle in time's domain. Cane's fist was closed around her hair. In a moment, he would be suffocating her with a pressure washer.

"Fuck you." she growled, wiggling just enough to bite down on the wolf's wrist. Cane threw her into her usual seat, activating her shock collar for the first time today as he closed the metal shackles around her wrists. She flipped him off as the last one clicked shut, growling a quiet "Fuck..." as her finger was chopped off with a pair of garden shears. A few extra seconds, and her outburst was rewarded with the sharp, drowning cut of a pressure washer.

"I'm going to be leaving today, 17." Cane started as the machine's internal compressor shrank to an idle. "My deer will be watching you for the next week."

Ratty clenched her fist around the wound as the last of her short night's rest drained from her eyes. A new face, for the first time in three/four days. She stood, waiting patiently behind Cane, a similar collar around her neck. She was shorter than Ratty, with a long faded crop of bleached and dyed hair and blank eyes of a similar faded quality.

The possum's still developing sense for the paranormal lit up as it took on this new deer. Where some were easily classed as demons or- well, classing Ratty was also difficult — the best her sense could do was to label the deer: the face you see everywhere.

She could have sworn she was college friends with someone who looked almost completely identical. She had been childhood friends with someone who looked almost completely identical. One of her professors must have looked almost completely identical.

"Charmed," the possum blinked through her confusion. "I'm —" Cane pointed his pressure washer at her as she went to introduce herself. Flinching, Ratty stepped back into line.

"You're going to have to give up on that name eventually, *17*. It'll be easier for you." He turned to the deer. "Isn't that right, *13*?"

The deer kept her eyes locked on the metal shackles around her ankles as she answered: "Yes, sir. 13 is so much happier without her—" The light on her collar blinked — a warning — and 13 fell silent again.

"Good." Cane passed the remote off to 13, starting up the stairs. "Let it out when I'm gone. Shock it if it misbehaves."

"Yes sir. Absolutely sir."

Ratty spent a good half-hour glaring at the deer, both of them listening intently for Cane's truck, one disappointed, the other relieved as it thrummed to life and kicked gravel against the plastic siding of his cabin. Basements were cold. Ratty was wet. Ratty was therefore cold and wet. The entire house smelled like drywall dust, overworked deodorant, and sweat. Very occasionally, when Cane had been working in the next door office, the smell of solder-smoke joined the haze. There was nothing to do about that, and so she forced it to the back of her mind.

"So, what're you in for, *Lucky*?" Ratty prodded as the deer tentatively stepped forward. She stayed silent, keeping her eye on the possum. "Get it? That's a joke. 'Cus 13 is—"

"*13* used to work at a grocery store." she interrupted, the hard edge in her voice signifying that she would not be answering to "Lucky" any time soon. "It was on the edge of homelessness." She knelt in front of the possum, her hands shaking as she put her key into the lock around Ratty's ankle. There were pretty decent odds on Ratty taking control of the situation, but no scenario in which Cane left the door at the top of the stairs unlocked.

Kick, jump chair, break chair, subdue 13, and from there:

liquefy her bones against solid steel trying to break down a steel door with her soft, fleshy body.

There was another door, though: flimsy, protected only by the threat of violence.

"It was lonely," 13 continued, her voice frail. "Mr. Cane took it from the parking lot. It was special for Mr. Cane. It was a risk. It was a break from form." Her tiny voice was only barely capable of surging with pride as she described her kidnapper.

"How flattering." Ratty rubbed some of the pain from her wrists as 13 released the last shackle. What a fucking production. All that effort to keep her tied up for what, 45 minutes? Fucking ridiculous.

"13 gave up very early, Mr. Cane says this is why 13 survived..." The deer paused for a moment as she backed away, mulling over her next words. "13 would never get away with acting like you do." Her voice was suddenly quiet, suddenly sounding very trampled on by the fact of Ratty's continued survival.

"Don't worry. I'm not that easy to get rid of." Weird thing to try and comfort someone over. She held out her hand, showing 13 the slowly growing stump of her middle finger. The deer took Ratty's hands in her own and watched the pink stub re-liquefy and suck up the dried blood caked into her furry palm. "So, okay. Grocery store..." Ratty put herself back on track. "That doesn't answer like, why you're here."

"13... doesn't understand." The deer stared. "Mr. Cane likes having 13. That's it."

"What about Angelcorp? Does that sound familiar to you?" Mr. Cane had actually never confirmed that he had ever even heard of Angelcorp, but the kind of company that may or may not have kidnapped her younger self in 40 years wasn't the kind of company that would hold a record like Cane's to much scrutiny.

"I shouldn't tell you."

"Ah, 'course not." Ratty stared at the deer for a moment, then stood, kicked back the chair and crossed to the flimsy mystery door.

"Wait, what are you doing? Stop." 13 commanded, now suddenly panicking with even a shred of power in her hands.

"Not gonna do that. Sit tight and I'll grab you on my way out."

She pushed the handle to one side, raising an edge just wide enough to jimmy a knife into.

Cane's workbench would have something. Ratty dove into the wheeled chests of drawers stored underneath: scalpels — some of them clearly used — hammers, nails, power drills, screws, each caked with a variable amount of dried blood.

Oh god, yeah. Okay. The possum had a morose moment of mirth as she took stock of the first thing to cross her mind: a mental catalogue of places in Toronto she could get tested for AIDS.

She followed that thought to its logical conclusion. Roughly 400,000 cases at the start of 1990, 17 kidnappings. She gave it roughly a 1 in 20,000 chance, more than enough motivation to tear out the drawers and dump their contents into the sink. A relatively clean screwdriver jimmied open a few overhead cupboards before finding a container of bleach.

"17. Stop it right now." 13 commanded again.

"I'm—" Ratty started, incredulous as she dumped the container into the basin. "I'm cleaning his tools. This is a good thing."

"17 should not be doing anything without sir's permission."

Ratty's collar beeped, and she stopped. "Aw fuck, you're right." The possum glared, forced to listen to the deer. She dropped the half-full container into the sink, throwing bleach-water everywhere. Fine, that was fine. If she had AIDS she could just rewind her body to a point in time where it didn't have AIDS. *Whatever!*

Instead of cleaning, she took her screwdriver and jammed it into the soft wood around the mystery door's handle. The shield popped off easily, giving way to a complicated little mechanism.

Actually, fuck this.

Ratty dropped the screwdriver, took a step back, picked up the chair, and stopped in her tracks as her collar beeped.

"17." The deer was suddenly firm. 'Come back here and kneel."

Ratty stared at the deer for a second, trying to figure out if she was serious, scoffed, and brought the leg of the chair down on the doorknob. "There we f-UGH." She jumped as her collar zapped a now incredibly sore spot on her neck. Annoyed, she turned on the deer.

"Good, now—" 13 started, cut off by her own stunned silence as the remote was snatched from her hand. She stood in the middle of that sentence, shell-shocked at the sudden loss of power. "W— uh— hey, hold on."

Ratty turned their back on the deer, working out the odds of sinking the remote from this distance. Something hit her in the back of the head.

"What the fuck was—" Another empty bleach container thunked pathetically to the ground, more surprising than painful. Ratty picked it up, skimmed the label, and dropped it. The trembling deer had frozen at the peak of their throw. "Oh, you wanna fucking roughhouse, huh?" Something lit up behind her eyes. 13 wasn't to blame, but she was around to take it out on.

"No. You need to stop." Ratty had already started at the deer. She shoved her back into the corner, rattling the temporary wall.

"You listen to me—" she started.

"17. Shut up and kneel, now—" She choked on the last word as the possum's arm pinned their neck to the drywall.

"I am going to get us *both* out of here, and you can—" Something sharp jabbed into her side. She flinched for just long enough to be shoved over, her horns cracking off the cement below.

"Give me the remote." That was funny. 13 had picked up a hunting knife: wide and silver, the kind you would use to skin a deer.

"Fuck." Ratty shot up as 13 tried to kneel on her chest, using the deer's momentum to throw them at the floor. The knife clattered uselessly from her hand. "You." She knelt on the deer's wrist, ignoring the new kind of whine it forced out of her. Ratty threw the remote into her bleach-swamp.

She said either "Get off me!" or "You're hurting me!" Ratty stayed put.

"You fucking stabbed me." The possum clamped a hand over the deer's mouth, forcing 13 to look her in the eye. "We are getting out of here. I am not going to let you fucking stop me. Nod if you understand."

13 nodded.

"Again." she growled, regretting the fear that lit up behind

13's eyes. 13 nodded again, slowly. Ratty stood up.

Where was that fucking screwdriver? There. She jammed it into the office door's now completely exposed lock mechanism. It gave easily, opening onto Cane's office like a present.

13 stood, staring between the sink and the office before ultimately deciding on the sink.

The scratched case of a modern-for-the-time Angel Portable Plus sat in the centre of a weave of cables, each wired through a piece of proprietary technology Ratty suspected would have been unrecognizable to most people who weren't from 40 years in the future. Each off-white box was branded with the same logo:

So, good. Angelcorp was real, Cane worked for them, he also kidnapped people. Excellent mystery.

Ratty circled the desk and booted up Cane's computer. One by one the satellite machines followed suit, thrumming to life, clicking lights on various surge protectors on as they went.

Ratty explored through the desktop, moving straight to the 'Project_Archangel' folder. It started simple: black and white drawings of circuit diagrams, scans of patent documents, a few photos of 13 in a green polo. From there the slide-show evolved into diagrams of limbs, overlaid more circuit diagrams, then photos with circuit diagrams, then, without warning: 001_leg.gif. The low resolution gore of a carefully dissected thigh, separated into what could only be called its component pieces. This too was overlaid with a circuit diagram, each string of flesh labelled with a four digit id number.

001_leg2.gif: the same with a calf from the same body, a few with the additional tag of 'bring to Eden'. It continued like this through each limb, each with its own detail shots and associated circuit diagrams, all the way up to 012. For whatever reason, 013 only had one lightly bloodied closeup on her wrist.

"That's me."

Ratty jumped out of her skin as a bloody, bleach burned hunk of scar tissue popped into her field of view holding a wet plastic remote, using the antenna to point to the wrist.

"That's not... good." Ratty said, realizing she had just knelt on the post-deconstructed piece of flesh in the picture. There was a perfect bruise in the shape of her knee already forming on the balding surface. "Sorry, I didn't—" The deer pressed her lips against the scar in a reflexive move of comfort, blinking at the apology. 13 would always flinch around her now. That was going to be heavy every time.

"What are these pictures for?"

"I don't know." She made no effort to hide her disinterest. She focused on jamming down the remote's main button, squelching out enough water to make it work. She shook it one more time, spraying droplets across the room, pressed it again. The resulting jolt knocked Ratty the fuck out.

---

Sett clutched the phone book in their hand, keeping their thumb in the businesses section. There were investigators under that subheading. The phone book itself sat in one of Ratty's messenger bags, Sett not trusting themself enough to remember the address. They stood, tapping their hoof, at the front door.

They had found a familiar name towards the back. They could afford the detective's rates with only most of the tabletop money. The only barrier now was actually getting out the door. They tried to stop tapping their hoof, having received noise complaints from downstairs neighbours in the past.

They pulled their hand out of their pocket, navigating the bundle of shawls, and gripped the doorknob. They let go, and re-gripped. Let go, re-gripped. Let go, let their hand fall, and flopped the phone book open in it.

They stared at the name again, still underlined by their thumb, just to make sure they had gotten it right. It went back into the bag.

They tried again to stop tapping their hoof. It would have been rude either way, if anyone was around to see it happen. They gripped, un-gripped, re-gripped. the doorknob, and took a deep breath.

"UGH!" They threw the phone book across the room. It knocked an insect pinboard off the wall. They went to pick it up, tossed the frame and it's pieces on top of the TV stand, and charged out the front door.

---

13 was the best available friend for those two weeks. She understood power, and understood that she would be overpowered any time she tried to stop Ratty. She was a grocery store clerk, not cut out for hurting other people, and so chose to ignore the times when Ratty spoke in a way she wasn't supposed to, or went into Cane's office like she wasn't supposed to. It got intense only when Ratty asked 13 what her real name was, even then it was clearly an agonizing push against what they thought to be right.

The nights where 13 left her alone — and she was rarely comfortable unconscious in the same room — Ratty attacked her collar with whatever she could find. The best she could really do was pull on it and drain the battery. Sitting in the opposite corner of the room was just about as alone as 13 could leave her, and she was curious enough to look over her shoulder when she heard something.

She wasn't bad. She was just someone who had spent too much of her life in a cold basement. Her history came in short bursts: the guitar she used to play, a jargon-laden story about computer science, all with the passion of someone who was incredibly talented, all — unfortunately — in the context of doing these things for Cane.

Lucky was good. One day, she wouldn't have to hate Ratty anymore. One day, Ratty would figure out how that made her feel.

Lucky was salvageable, if that was a word a good person could use for another living creature.

---

The elder opossum chain-smoked, flipping lazily through the phone book in her darkened office. It was obsessively clean, the only thing with dust or dirt on it being the ashtray. Even that was contained to one central heap that didn't overflow whatsoever. Her face was too familiar, too. It made the proceedings uncomfortable, even with only one side committed to secrecy.

"The ad says to call ahead." she said.

"The phone in our apartment hasn't—"

"Fine." She stopped finally on the torn-out page. "This it?"

Sett nodded, wringing their hands around the elastic wrists of their sweater. The detective looked down at the torn page, up at Sett, and stood. She skipped the file cabinets behind her desk, going instead into the coat closet. On the rack above the hanger, she took down an identical phone book.

"You have neighbours." She sat back down, shoving the original to the side and flipping to the same spot in the copy. "Don't bother me next time." She dragged her finger down the list. "Is it Maria or Marshall Cane?"

"Marshall!" Sett said, a little too impressed by the lateral thinking. "Marshall Cane." they nodded, tempering their excitement.

"Cane with a C?" There was a dog in the back corner. Sett hadn't noticed them until they spoke up, the loud hum of their computer terminal suddenly impossible to ignore. The detective's assistant, probably. "Worked at Angel Corporation Unlimited since it's inception in 1976... registered sex offender... lives up north, south of Bobcaygeon."

"Are you fucking around in the police database again?" The detective turned on them.

"They're not gonna catch me! Should have kept it locked tighter." The assistant rolled their eyes.

"What if she's a cop?"

"I'm a 'they,' actually." Why the fuck would they say that to two strangers, born — on average — in around the late 1960s.

"Oh sick, me too," was about the longest shot in the history of gender. The dog sat up — a borzoi — barely smiling. "Fern."

"Sett. It's nice to meet you." they nodded.

"Here. There is a legal way of doing this." The detective cracked the spine of a binder, an older version of the same Angelcorp logo printed on its cover. She did so confrontationally, smacking it across the two phone books, audibly frustrated as she scrolled through the proprietary company ledger.

"I already—"

"There we go. Marshall Cane." She popped open the binder clips and took the page, folding it and stuffing it into her pocket. "Fern, get up." She put an arm through her jacket, already half-dressed by the time it came out of the closet.

"What're you—"

"Do you have a car?"

"No."

"Then I'm driving. C'mon."

---

Cane.

Two weeks in. Heavy, careless footsteps thudding on the basement ceiling. 13 took her position at the bottom of the stairs, shuddering with excitement each time the floorboard at the top creaked. Ratty stayed in her corner, draining her collar as much as she could. Cane would come down and leave the door open, then Ratty would slip past him, come back with Sett and kill the motherfucker.

An hour before the door opened. Cane stopped at the bottom of the stairs, lazily scratching 13 like one would a pitied, least-favourite dog.

"Where's 17?" he asked.

"Sir, it's— I asked it to present but—"

"Where?" His affection snapped suddenly, cold again. 13 stood, took several clean steps back, and pointed into Ratty's corner. The possum looked up, chewing on the screwdriver.

"Hey, Marshall." She waved, picking her teeth. The wolf charged, picking Ratty up by the collar and tossing her through the room. She hit the opposite wall, emptying her lungs. "Good to s—" she croaked, stopping as Cane picked up his pressure washer. "Okay! Okay."

The next impact rattled the dividing wall, Cane's office door creaking loudly as it shook open. Cane glared at the void, then at Ratty, then back at the door, all to the backdrop of building rage. He threw her to the cement floor with a crack, freezing her body for a half-second as her bones shot out to grab each other.

"You..." he turned on 13. "I gave you a *month!*" A month? "A month to break it, and instead, you let it into my office—" he snatched the remote from the deer, slamming her head against the chipboard top of his work surface. "and—"

"I'm so sorry sir. It—"

"*Don't interrupt me!*"

Ratty groaned as she struggled to bring her head upright, staring at the deer with a vaguely annoyed emptiness. Grey walls of concrete turned black as her eyes filled and unfilled with blood.

"Sir— so sorry sir. It's just— It cares about me. It'll follow orders if it sees you're going to hurt me."

"Fuck off. Kill me yourself or get over it."

Cane blinked, pulled a still-wet knife from his worktop, and handed it to 13. A fat hunting knife: wide and silver, the kind you would use to skin a deer. A broken shard of black tile, the kind you would use to skin a deer.

"Kill it." There was no give in his voice. "I let you have something. You need to kill it."

Ratty sat up slowly, pushing herself off with her tail like an ancient lift.

"Go on then, Lucky." She got up to her knees, momentarily distracted as Cane cocked a shotgun over 13's shoulder. "Give it your best shot." No use making it any harder. The deer's eyes began to water as she picked up the knife, wide and silver, the kind you would use to skin her. The grip looked massive against her chipped bare hooves.

Ratty stared only at Cane as the deer charged, quietly imagining all the ways she could kill him. She was distracted — only momentarily — as 13 pushed the blade into her heart.

"I hate you!" 13 screamed. "You're ruining my fucking life." She stabbed again. "Fucking die already." A broken shard of black tile, the kind you would use to skin a deer. The concrete walls fall into darkness.

She pulled the knife from Ratty's chest, missing her third stab as the possum blocked her hand and drove a thumb-claw into her wrist. She yelped and fell, dropping her knife perfectly into Ratty's hand.

Cane began to panic. He raised his shotgun, the sudden motion scattering shells from his pocket, and pointed it square at the possum's heart. Blood rose in her throat as she tangled her fingers through the thread that connected her home, as she saw every piece of torn flesh in her chest pull itself back into alignment.

Walls tinted black.

A broken shard of tile, the kind you would use to skin a deer.

Ratty lunged for the gun, told by her eyes before her body that Cane had shot instinctively for her hand. He was too slow, slow enough that — if she wanted to — the possum could have watched two thirds of the shot bounce off the concrete. The rest scattered uselessly through her fur. "Fuck you!" She jammed her shoulder into Cane's chest, stabbing the knife into his side and using that to pin him against the bench.

He let off another shot in Ratty's ear, shattering her eardrum and flinching her for the first time since he had come home. Ratty pushed the knife deeper as she turned, catching the hot tip of the gun in the crook of her elbow and falling just right to drag it out of Cane's hands.

They turned at the same time. Cane went for his remote, Ratty for the gun.

And as his finger mashed the kill button, Ratty's scrambling to shove a pair of scattered shells into their chambers, her collar gave a pathetic triplet of beeps as if to say: 'should have gone for the gun.'

And in the silence that followed it was 13 who spoke up first. Quiet, sobbing, broken: "We can't go back. It's safe here."

"...We can't go back..." As her jaw, only mortal, hung from its socket.

"...It's safe here..." As she struggled to move.

"...We can't go back..." As Ratty's eyes stood locked on her target's,

And then a moment of silence as 13 ran out of energy.

"Collar." The possum's voice shook, too small for the silence. "Take it off. Now." she demanded

"Fuck you." The wolf replied. The air cracked into even pieces as Ratty unloaded the left barrel into Cane's shoulder.

"Your shit doesn't grow back." Louder, sterner. "Collar. Now."

Cane held up his remote slowly, his arm shaking with the effort of making it very clear which button he was pressing. With a click, the collar fell away. "Happy?" he asked.

"Say my name." She lifted the gun to his face, putting his eyes at the end of each barrel squarely in her sights.

"17. Let's talk about—"

"Wrong fucking answer."

Several things happened at once:

Ratty's finger came down on the right trigger. The right hammer came down on the right primer, and ignited the gunpowder in the right shell. The right shell then propelled its particulate into the wrong target as 13 — in a sudden burst of energy — threw herself in front of the barrel.

She fell on top of him, knocking him out on the cement floor with the final crack of the night.

Ratty took a half-step back, staring through the hole in the centre of 13's chest. Without thinking, she ran.

Rain.

For whatever reason it felt like an unlikely night for rain. Too cold, or warm, or something.

She ran, the soaked blanket from Cane's couch clinging to her torso as she sprinted blindly into the night. Gravel tore at her soles, she felt nothing. She would come back for 13. If she was fast enough, the deer could survive. Time came and went under its own rules, it was down to her legs and lungs to give up.

And they did. She stopped, and fell, and curled herself shut on the sharp stone. Something white shot past her, a racing dog of some kind, the collar of their windbreaker held up against the storm.

"Detective! That's her." Sett. Sett was here. The possum struggled to lift her head, and saw her partner in a similarly drenched black knit cloak. Sett. Sett was here.

"My name is detective Tilde Vermington, don't move.." The other figure spoke, illuminating the possum with her torch.

Huh.

Small city.

"Ms. Vermington, that's— that's her. That's my fiancée." Sett fell to their knees at the possum's side, gold threads diving immediately into the hole in her stump wrist.

"I'm okay. I promise, I'm okay. There's- you need to go back-" Ratty sat up as far as she could, blinking rain from her eyes, struggling to focus on Sett as her head spun. Just over the goat's shoulder, framed in the long, curly black hair she had only seen in old pictures, "Is that my mom?" Odd to see her staring down a gun 12 years before she would be born.

"It's not your fault. It's okay. Next time, okay?" Sett murmured.

"You have to go— there's this deer..."

The dog poked their head out of the little cottage, an incredibly familiar blur at this distance. "There's no one here."

"Is that Fern?" Ratty couldn't remember how she knew that name. She was apparently loud enough to be heard over the rain, a byproduct of her still-ringing ear.

"I'm sorry, do I know you?" the borzoi asked. Something really hurt about that, though Ratty struggled to put a finger on it.

"No." she answered, struggling to her feet. "No, I guess not."

13 was gone by the time Tilde reached the cabin, and so was Cane. All that was left of them was a pair of wet tire tracks.

Ratty stared at the blood splatter in the basement for hours. This would not go to waste. This could not go to waste. She bit her lip, pushing past Detective Vermington into Cane's office and taking his laptop before she could call the real cops.

Sett followed shortly after, unnerved enough by the possum's stoicism to follow her to the nearest bus-stop in the rain. She spent the next several weeks, months, years, whatever, awake, plagued by the spectre of Marshall Cane.

---

She looked so small against the investigation. Splayed out across walls and floors, it dwarfed her in scale, having suddenly exploded from nowhere. It was like this every time she got a new lead: furniture had to be shoved out of the way to make room for the mess of red string and paper.

She would leave, very rarely, for one or two days at a time. She always left a note with the address, called when she got there, and called when she was on her way home. Almost all of her spare quarters went to funding the laundry and payphone industries.

The borzoi, working out of their computer store, had offered their services for free from that point forward. She stayed there some nights too, taking advantage of the free phone services to call as frequently as possible.

She stood now, centrepiece to this fire hazard, her paws planted in the only two gaps in the paper. Shaking, her bloodshot eyes drew into slits with the effort trying to put this together.

'Eden' was Dir. Eden Ross, head of Angelcorp's advanced robotics team.

13 hasn't turned up dead yet.

Cane had last been seen leaving Angelcorp's Scientific Interests Compound a few hours before his picture hit every TV news station in the country.

She couldn't actually bring herself to visit any of the addresses she had turned up, but she also couldn't bring herself to stop trying.

Sett sat a few feet away, nervously tugging at the edge of their nightgown. They brought a wooden stool in from the kitchen, too exhausted to tip a couch the right way up. They had gotten used to Ratty's rabid focus. It was worrying to see her like this after everything they had been through together, but it made sense: John was gone, Marshall Cane was still out there somewhere.

"Ratty." The sun had started to rise when they spoke up, knocking the possum out of her manic haze.

"You— you scared me. Why aren't you in bed?" She failed to stifle a scowl as she went back to work, completely unconscious of the way her face moved.

"I'm waiting for you." Sett said. She needed rest. The goat was out for blood, ready to tear the heart out of Marshall Cane, but Ratty needed rest. It was jarring to see Ratty like this. She could get scary. There was no way in Hell she could overpower Sett — not that she would have tried — but she was liable to hurt herself.

She was already hurting herself.

"Busy." She brushed them off.

"No, Ratty." Sett said, now firm. Ratty flinched as the goat slipped their fingers into hers.

"If you want the bed to yourself so you don't have to touch anyone I understand. I'm not taking that personally. It's been days. You—"

"I'm fine." Ratty cut them off, pulling her hand away to dive into some other pile of papers marred with thick strokes of red sharpie. Sett took a half-step back, watching the possum's back arch further as she realized Sett wasn't leaving. The goat's chest filled with cold fire, not missing another night of sleep for this.

"Haven't you been through enough?" they pleaded.

"Leave me the fuck alone!" She spun, glaring into the goat's eyes. "I'm busy! I don't want to talk about this! I barely even talk to fucking Fern about—" The venom locking in her throat as she came to understand just how hard Sett was struggling to hold back tears. She tried to push through it, tried to stay mad, tried to say anything that would have been true.

"You don't—" Of course Sett knew.

"I can't—" There wasn't even an investigation to be meaningfully interrupted. She couldn't breathe. Sett had nothing to do with that. A different Ratty might've resorted to just saying something hurtful to scare them off. This Ratty bit down on her tongue, tears blurring the perfect goat, whose greatest realized dream was to become a pile of comforting sweaters.

"It's like he's hovering over you, isn't it? You feel like—" They let out a sob, finally. "Like this is all just a happy dream, and any second now you're going to wake up." They were weeping openly at this point, nearly struggling not to pull threads of yarn from the hem of their sweater. "Your stupid brain makes you actually want to, because you think you deserve it, because of all the things he made you do." That last one was less about Cane.

Ratty fell forward, wrapping her arms around her partner as some useless document crumpled and stained under the weight of her paw.

"We— I felt that way every day, Ratty. I know exactly what you're going through." Sett managed between sobs. They shuddered in the possum's arms as their cheeks went damp against the stale smelling fabric.

It took a moment before Ratty apologized; a simple "I'm sorry" that broke her voice to let out. "I don't know why I do this."

"I know, Ratty." This was better than Hell. That was as much as could be said about it.

78

"I don't know what I'm supposed to do," she managed. "I'm sorry for scaring you."

"I know." Sett said, "We're going to get him. I swear to you we're going to make him hurt twice as bad as he hurt you, but there's no reason to make any more pain." Ratty's façade cracked, giving way to a single, suppressed choke. She took a deep, hitching breath, her musk tainting the gentle smell of the smaller animal. She left one hand in theirs and let them guide her back to their bedroom.

Earth would be hard. People would continue to be hard. For less, they could have abandoned the possum, set up shop in their dusty little west-end property. They had escaped Hell. Their deal was complete.

That didn't feel right, though.

# 33 — 1989
# Green Tea

It was generally frowned upon to cancel a ceremony half way through. More heavily frowned upon was sprinting out of their temple, wrapped in nothing but a sheet and flinging off bits of gold and silver tribute as they went. Hard to care about what was and wasn't frowned upon as their own heartbeat roared in their ears. Heads turned as they sprinted through market towards the part of town they knew to be less populated, hiding their eyes and relying on their other senses to guide them. It didn't matter if they ran headlong off a cliff at this point, they just needed to get away.

The heavy wooden door of a small, two-story stone building stopped them instead. It was held together more with thick vines and the pressure of time than with the decaying mortar. Abandoned. Perfect. They pulled on the door handle and gave a small sigh as it clicked. It slammed behind them. They fell against it, bracing it shut with their back and slumping to the floor. They buried their face in their hands, feeling an angry blush rise in their cheeks as they noticed for the first time the deep tear-streaks soaking their snout.

"Stupid." they growled at themself. "Stupid. Idiot. Awful." They sat there, their breath refusing to calm any further as they choked down bleating sobs. It had not been long enough since the last time they panicked like that, but it was the first time in recent memory they let it get the better of them. They kicked themself, there was nowhere to run to, absolutely no point to the ache in their chest as they struggled to normalize their breathing.

Sett was shocked out of their self-loathing as an old floorboard creaked just beyond their claws. They looked up from their palms slowly, expecting some variety of monster, met instead with an elderly woman, her head tilted in concerned curiosity as she gazed down on the tiny goddexx at her feet. Sett jumped to their feet, pressing themself deeper against the grain of the door.

"We apologize— we thought—" The woman held her hand up, palm out.

"Your thoughts loud little goat." she signed, her gnarled fingers moving steadily. Sett watched, suddenly calmed by the effort of focusing on a language they had fallen out of practice with. They raised their own hand tentatively, abruptly conscious of their limited knowledge, making a mental note to practice more when the opportunity arose.

"S O R R Y" they spelled clumsily. "T H O U G H T A B A N D O N E D" The woman laughed, gentle and encouraging.

"Mute, not deaf." she signed "Speak normally."

"Of course." Sett's voice shook as they stood. They were not used to towering over anyone, it was a very strange sensation to be looked up at. "We're terribly sorry," the goat took a step forward, reaching for the door handle and steeling themself to walk out into the world. "We'll leave you be, then."

"Like this?" the woman asked, shaking her head and gesturing to the strings of blanket hanging off them. She turned on her heel and doddered across the room, reaching over her counter pulling some spare clothes from behind: a proper mantle, and long skirt to go underneath. Sett nodded graciously as the clothes were all but forced upon them, dropping what was left of their tattered sheet and wrapping themself in the carefully kept fabric. They fit perfectly, draped around their waist and ankles, protecting them from perception.

"Thank you." they said, dabbing their tears on the corner of the hood. "If there's any way we can—" They stopped to watch the woman sign.

"Yes, you help pick leaves." She shooed Sett away from the door, filling the dark room with light as they stepped out with very little space for negotiation. Sett took a moment before following, still hesitant to be seen. They swallowed what little anxiety they had left under the pretense that they owed this woman, and followed her around the side of her home.

Her garden was overrun with bright green bushels of waxy-looking leaves. They chose their footsteps carefully, increasingly overwhelmed by the smell of green tea as they breathed more and more of the springy air. The older woman smiled as they caught sight of Sett, looking only for a long moment before returning to their work.

Sett set to work picking what looked like, from their limited knowledge of herbology, like the best leaves. Deep green? But not too deep green? Like... spinach coloured, maybe? They took a moment to admit to themself that they were guessing, and for the second time that day made a mental note to study. The woman stepped out in front of them, placing a firm but gentle hand on the back of their own.

"Don't pick good leaves. All good leaves. I grow them good." She smiled, demonstrating by diving in with both hands and grabbing the leaves by fistfuls. Sett laughed quietly at her fervour, like years of doing only this had conditioned her into the perfect tea-picking machine.

"What's your name?" they asked, splitting their attention between watching and mimicking. More leaves ended up on the ground than in the bucket, but the woman didn't look like she minded.

"Green Cat." she signed, taking the sign for green and twisting it along her whisker. "Fur used to be green. All fell out."

"What happened?"

"Stress!" She grinned. "Stress like you. Stress makes your fur fall out. Now I make tea, no stress in making tea." Sett's hands faltered in their motion as they remembered the anxiety quietly crumbling away at their insides. Cat slapped their wrist.

"Stop! You think too much. Work instead." she signed, more encouraging than chastising. "Your name?"

"We are— we're Sapphomet, of the Mountains, and Chaos, and um, Love... also..." They struggled to remember the rest of their ID attributes.

"S A P P H O M E T?" Cat spelled. Sett nodded. "I am not going to spell that every time. I will call you—" she took the sign for little and flicked it up into a pair of goat horns. "Little Goat." Sett smiled at their new nickname. It was cute, but...

"What about—" the goat brought a closed fist down on the back of their hand. "Set?"

"Both." Cat nodded. "Little goat: Sett."

Yeah, that worked.

The two of them worked in silence until their shared bucket

was full well past the brim with leaves. Sett carried it back inside as the sun began to set. They sat quietly by the fire, taking turns tending to the large bundle of leaves in the steamer pot. Sett took over when it came to spreading them out to drying, their hardened hooves better suited to handling something with the potential to scald.

The two shared a few glasses of the runoff when all was done, its potent flavor coating the goat's throat the same way it stained into every inch of their arms up to the rope burns on their wrists. As night dragged on into the early hours of morning, Cat insisted that Sett stay.

"Too dangerous to travel at night little goat." she signed. "You stay long enough to taste your work."

Sett could hardly argue, having to hide a yawn every few minutes. They cleared a space in the attic and strung a hammock across a pair of beams. As they struggled to sleep, their senses were made void and left room for thoughts to return. They found themself raising the back of their hand to their snout and focusing on the impossible-to-wash-out smell of green tea.

They sighed, contented with every inhalation as they drifted off.

---

They stayed in that attic a lot longer than the week it took their first batch of leaves to dry. It was comfortable, far more comfortable than the alternative. Though it was impossible to put an exact number of days on it, Sett stayed in that attic long enough to think of it as a home. Long enough to sneak out at night and feel safe coming back, long enough to occasionally butt heads with Cat and stay housed.

It always smelled like green tea and tobacco smoke. They had carved a path through the old sacks of dried leaves, checking them on their way in and out each morning and evening for signs of rot. In one of these bags, stuffed in a corner where Cat was not likely to find it, Sett had started a small collection of cleaned animal bones. They sometimes died in the garden, left there to fertilize the tea leaves. Cat brought in a friend of hers from market to build a small desk into the attic, and Sett quickly filled it with books.

They kept a small mirror next to their collection, and their favourite tributes next to that: some thick gold bangles that they had been meaning to sell off, a set of beautifully crafted clay teacups, a small wooden carving of themself and a dozen small bottles of wine. They received one just about every time they held tribute, always from the same long haired lamb. Jacob, or James, or something. A biblical name for sure. They quietly hoped they would see him again today.

Market day was always exciting. Sett had become a shut-in since the day they met Cat, humiliated to go anywhere if there was not a good reason. Going out to sell off the home's excess tea and going out to be the subject of worship were just about the only times they interacted with other people, and it was much easier to make friends bartering than it was when having semi-public religion based pseudo-sex with them.

They tied their hair up with a short length of cord as they backed down the ladder to their room. Sett glided up next to their mentor at the counter, quietly focused on putting freshly chopped leaves into small silk bags. Part of what made a good market day was having a little something to give away.

"Good morning." Sett signed, drawing focus to their claws with a little wave.

Cat smiled, signing back "Getting there. I still prefer your voice."

"Well if we don't practice we're not going to get better." Sett teased, nabbing half of the silk squares and setting to work making their own bags.

"Fair enough," Cat nodded. "Will the Lamb Carpenter be there today?"

"I don't know why you would expect me to know that." Sett said, successfully keeping down a blush. Cat laughed her quiet, breathy laugh.

"Good boy. Makes good wine. I'll get you a bed if you want to bring him around."

"We're not sure it would work, his dad and our... uh..." Sett trailed off. It wasn't worth talking about.

"The man who makes our jars, you know him?" Cat asked, prodding the goat. Sett nodded, focusing on their work. "He tells me his daughter asks about you. Maybe I will find my wine somewhere else."

"Maybe both." Sett smiled softly.

"Maybe!" Cat signed, reaching up to pat the goat as she finished up her tea bags. "No time to think about the past. Market day is a busy day." Sett took a deep breath, sliding their pile into a small crate and handing it off to Cat. They swept the unused leaves back into their sack and slung it over their shoulder.

"Ready?" they asked.

"Ready!" Cat answered.

Almost no money changed hands on market days. It was about getting together with people, trading whatever you had around and trusting everyone else to do the same. The value of the tea didn't matter. It didn't matter that it was cultivated specially by an artisan tea maker. It mattered that everyone be brought up to the same standard of living. Sharing their tea helped bring luxury to some people's lives.

Those who came from out of town brought whatever currency their nation used. Sett, for their part, attracted customers internationally, the story of the icon crossing the land in much the same pattern as other, far more popular religious figures. They embellished the story slightly, passing along tales of "the tea leaves that sparkle gold in the morning sun."

When the Romans came, Cat turned her nose up at them, up-charged, and handed over their oldest jars. "No, no." Sett would translate. "They're supposed to look like this. Everything we give out is off-cuts, under-ripe, this kind of thing."

They took that at face value. Food poisoning could be deadly this far back. It was understandable, considering what they did to some of her favourite customers.

Most people just traded, though. Grain and fish, and worshippers brought books, and little trinkets, and wine. Sett always timed their absence with the wine delivery. Always from the same carpenter, kept at arm's length for no other reason than... well... he was cute. It was allowed to be that simple.

Sett jumped as the hem of their dress was yanked on. Cat took a hold of their belt and dragged them back to the stall. "What're you doing?" they laughed, swatting the arm, not receiving an answer.

"Hi!" and god, was he ever fucking cute. Dumb as a bag of rocks, carrying a few skins full of wine. He smiled like the fucking sun, in full awareness of how simple and cliche that metaphor was. "I'm sorry! I was just asking your mother if you were around."

Sett stood firm against the onslaught. "We are around." Their heart would have given them away if anyone could hear it. Their tail, mercifully, was short enough to flick entirely behind their back. "Did you need help with anything today?" they spoke, word-by-word.

"Oh! No, sorry." Was it possible for him to be glowing? His rich, golden-brown fur covered him in an even sheen, snout dew-dropped with sweat. He definitely could have been glowing. "Thank you, I was just hoping I might take a walk with you."

"Oh?" That was it. Their heart was definitely audible then. "We—"

"And then come back for some tea, of course."

"Of course." Sett turned to cat, the tiny woman using her whole body to signal *of course! go!* "We suppose, yes. We could take a break."

He had to shorten his strides so they could keep up. He didn't mind, eyes lulling lazily around the colours of late afternoon. Then, towards the north end of town, he finally spoke. "What's on your mind, Sett?" he asked.

"Oh, nothing." It would be something of a turn-away to admit they woke up that morning with an ever-increasing sense of oncoming doom. They did this every day. It was not necessary to mention the unchanged.

"Are you sure?" If he was asking anyway, though... He had led them to the plaza in front of their temple, a beautiful, humble building, entirely too much for them. It was all too much. People would travel for days to see them, and for what?

"I'm not sure," they answered.

He crossed the little courtyard, pushing the front door open with his heel. Sett's temple sat abandoned. Dust threw itself up in sacrifice to the beams of sun criss-crossing the room. It was too beautiful for them.

They sat a few feet away from their usual spot, blocking out the smell of blood as the carpenter took his seat in the first pew. "Something to smoke?" he offered. Sett nodded silently, pinching it an inch from their lips and waiting for him to light it with his magic thread. By taste, it was not tobacco. For some reason, they had expected it to be.

Everything about this place was too beautiful. The religious perspective almost across the board was that God told all the animals just to stand up and walk, and so they did. God made the animals on the sixth day, and then he remade all the animals on the seventh. This temple was built because Sett was believed to be some small part of that.

The evolutionary perspective was almost the same. Instead of God, a global genetic supervirus event, 7 million years ago, rather than 10 thousand. The virus originated from a group of apes after massive deforestation forced them to walk more than climb. That virus, for no reason at all, also told all the animals to get up and walk.

"So..." the carpenter started.

"So..." Sett echoed, taking the little shred of momentum and turning it into their snowball. "I don't want to go back."

"No, neither do I."

"We are so happy here." they spoke for themself, took another drag, and let their cough explain why their eyes were watering. There were religious viralists, who believed that the virus was sent by God. That was an incredibly mortal thing to believe. With no way of proving either, and no time, most people just accepted both.

"We— I don't know if I've ever had the chance to think about myself, and I love me." It was hard to get used to that. "It's like as much as we have learned about everything else, we are finally getting the opportunity to learn about me. I apologize— None of this makes sense and I'm sort of making it more complicated in the telling."

"No, no." The lamb stood up, sitting back down next to Sett. He was this perfect warmness. They couldn't help but scoot to his side. "I understand completely. It's hard to be part of something when you can't get close to it, harder still when you know it's all going to go away." He reached for the burning bush, taking a long drag before continuing. "People are lucky. They pass on, and get the chance to forget all the good they forgot to do. It's much harder when you could always risk going back."

Sett nodded along, enjoying his warmth. "I hope I'm not being too forward." they said.

"No, of course not. It's hard to touch anything knowing it'll be gone. I appreciate your company a lot, actually." He took another drag, letting it sit in his lungs and pushing it into the sun when it begged to be released "Do you know what I think we owe during our time here?" he asked.

Sett shook their head, more felt than seen.

"The best we can do. Every time God sets before us a chance to do good, we should take it." His smile gave away that he truly believed it. "That's what the people who don't live forever do, seems only right that we follow their lead." Sett took the joint back, desperate to block out the scent of their altar.

"I wish we had more chances." They blew smoke around the feet of the pews. The carpenter laughed.

"Me too."

"I mean I— we don't know what makes me happy, or— I don't? didn't?" The royal personal pronoun felt purpose built to avoid talking about oneself. They pulled a thread from the air, wrapping it around their finger. "I don't know what I thought it was. Making myself better, maybe? I mean— no."

They stood up, letting the thread fall out of their hands, not bothering to be light on the hollow floor. "I really like making tea. I like the books everyone brings me to read. I like— Jesus Christ, I really like people."

The carpenter laughed.

"Oh, I'm sorry—"

"No, no. I wasn't aware that was an expression. Please, go on."

"I just—" It was hard to focus, brought back down, suddenly very extant beyond their thoughts. "I want to be a part of it.

Helping is — don't get me wrong — so beautiful and very attractive of you—" They chose to ignore that they had let that slip. "I want to be that too, but I think at the most base level of this feeling, I just want to be a part of it."

The carpenter stood, forcing Sett to realize just how much they were shaking as his firm arms wrapped around them.

"I'm not nobody, I'm not a worker demon," they mumbled, an

afterthought.

"No, clearly not."

They sniffled into his chest, glad to have put that out there. "Glad that I'm putting that out, at least." they laughed. "Glad that, even by the standards of biblical Bethlehem I'm still putting off 'gender vibes.'"

"Biblical?" the carpenter asked.

"Oh, wait, hold on. Are you going forward?"

"I—" the lamb swallowed his curiosity. "Maybe save the future for the future, little goat."

"Of course." They stepped back, drying their eyes on their sleeve. "Did you— sorry, were you just inviting me on a walk?"

"Oh, I don't know if— I mean, I had *intentions,* but it'd hardly be appropriate."

"Well, no. I don't mind, honestly. My mood is changing." Sett shrugged. "You may 'go ahead.'" They were not entirely sure what they meant by that. The carpenter turned it over, trying to suss meaning out of the meaningless statement.

"Can I kiss you?" How perfectly mundane of him.

"Yes, you may." Sett answered.

---

It was dark by the time they got home. It was always dark after a good day at market, their arms loaded up with gifts, groceries, and a few pouches of roman coins. Sett walked with an excited bounce in their step, turning today over in their mind. The act of knowing what they wanted made it feel so much closer.

That is of course, only what it felt like. Sett got to the door first by a couple seconds, and eager to go up and read for a few hours before a well earned rest. Something light probably, perhaps a treatise on—

Their horns thunked against a hard, familiar chest as they crossed the threshold. Cat's heart raced as she rounded the corner, answering in a terrible instant why Sett had stopped on the doorstep. They saw an illustration first: a harsh black and white illustration of their face, no doubt commissioned that day in the market.

They followed the mass upwards: a fitted, all black suit. He was dressed far too modernly for the era they were in. His black fur gave away seamlessly to a short black pair of horns, his solid white eyes too focused on Cat to watch Sett drop what they were holding and trip over it, scrambling for safety.

John had cut the pull-cord to the attic ladder.

"Hi Sapph!" The demon grinned, staring down at the goat like a predator playing with their next meal. "I was actually just looking for you, isn't that wild?"

Cat barged past him, putting herself between John and Sett and signing furiously in his face.

"What is she trying to say to me?" he asked, leaning around the small and steady frame.

"She's—" The goat's voice broke in their throat. "She is asking you nicely to leave." John cocked an eyebrow, glancing back and forth between his charge and the cat's paws. By the looks of things, the way she was asking could not be described as *nicely*. John gave a short, impatient sigh as he tried to step around the smaller woman, earning him a firm stomp on the toe of his polished black loafers.

He stopped, sucking his gums as he stared down at the scuff of dust. He rolled his eyes and shoved her to the side with roughly the same effort as swatting a bug out of his face. Sett winced as the back of their head thumped against the floor. They planted their hand on the counter top and pulled themself up from the floor, blindly fumbling for the knife they knew would be waiting for them. They stepped in-between John and Cat, the blade shaking in it's guard.

There was nothing to be done. John was not leaving here. Stabbing him would make things worse, and again in this dark home they were so stupid for daring to give a fuck about anything.

Their heart stopped as he spoke again: "Sapphomet, come on home." If there was a worse context under which to be winked at, Sett couldn't think of one. Their gaze fell, suddenly unable to meet John's gaze, instead trying to focus on what little of Cat they could see. Something in her leg was clearly broken. She tried desperately to push herself off the ground with one hand, alternating signing and pulling on Sett's dress with the other. They turned, using what would surely be their last moments on Earth to heal the break, and simultaneously feeling their heart snap as they caught sight of what Cat was signing, less than a foot from their face

"Love you." she was crying. "Always love you, little goat." The bone snapped back into place just as John took them by the wrist. It was only as his claw clamp down around their wrist that they noticed how badly they were shaking.

"C'mon, Hell just isn't the same without you." he teased.

And then it was gone. Their last thought on Earth was a quiet estimate on how badly their shaking hands might have worsened Cat's wound.

---

The plain façade of Sett's shop was not designed to attract customers. Those who made it inside rarely recognized it for its intended purpose. The warm interior was decorated more like a specialty shop than an active tea counter: fitting, considering the better half of their customers were daring collectors looking for cursed antiquities.

This wasn't an issue. It served mainly as a place to deal with cursed shit far enough away that it didn't affect their home life, and close enough to get to by subway. Beyond that, it was very rarely a place they spent the night to get away from the noise of downtown.

Tonight was not any of those kinds of nights, though; tonight was just a get out of the house night, and it was now over.

They spent the scraps of the day ignoring today's paper and watching the downpour outside seep under the front door's bent kick-plate, their eyes flicking once in a while to the crumpled form of a young lizard in a heavily worn parka clearly sleeping at one of their tables. Pokey often spent whole days in the shop.

They checked the time again, cycling Ratty's watch around to the correct timezone: 9:54 p.m.

There was really no point in staying open any later than they wanted to. No one was going to come in in those last six minutes. They let out a deep sigh, meandering around the counter and pulling the plug on the worn "Open" sign.

"Do you have an umbrella, Pokey?" they asked, startling the only other occupant out of her nap as they pulled on a raincoat. She re-hid her eyes almost instantly, trying and failing to conceal the fact that she had noticed being noticed. "I can call you a cab if your place is too far to walk," Sett offered. Pokey buried her face deeper into her arms. The goat blinked, set their jacket back on the hook and crossed the room to sit across from Pokey.

"Pokey?" Sett tugged on the sleeve of her parka, now doubting whether they had actually seen her wake up. She shot up, blinking through the light.

"Yeah, sorry— I just," The lizard bit her tongue, "I just thought I could stay, I guess? Like hang out for a little bit?" Her eyes lulled closed for a moment as she spoke. She stuck her thumb through a hole in her hood, rubbing the wool inside as a reflexive move of comfort.

She looked so tired. Even through her scales the deep purple discoloration of her pale green skin made it look like she had pressed a crumpled piece of newspaper against her eyes. That same discoloration stained just about everything she was wearing, the left sleeve of her jacket worst of all: nearly black in some places.

"Is something going on?" Sett prodded.

"I don't see why there has to be something going on. This is a public store right?"

"It is a closed store at the moment. I can walk you to the train station if—" Sett cut themself off. "That's beside the point. If you need— I mean if there's — for example — an 'is everything alright at home,' kind of thing going on..." The goat danced around the word 'homeless' as Pokey swallowed what little spit they had, mostly awake, staring empty at the uneven floorboards.

"I assume everything is great at home, I just uh... I don't live there." Pokey said. Sett nodded quietly, taking the smaller animal's cold hand in their own.

Pokey kept to herself generally, always making a point to deflect when their usually limited conversations turned to personal questions.

It wasn't long enough ago that Sett remembered hearing about an 18th birthday

They got up abruptly, closed the blinds over their front window and stamped down the latch on the front door. They lifted the cushions from a seldom used old couch in the corner and unfolded the temporary bed underneath. Pokey watched the flurry with cautious hope.

"What are you doing?" she asked. Sett ducked behind the counter and clicked on the plastic kettle underneath. The floor kicked up a layer of dirt and dust as it gave way to a hidden compartment with a pair of dusty milk crates: one containing several sealed jars of tea and thick textbooks, and some fresh, if a little dusty sheets, a space heater, and some pillows in the other. Sett plucked a jar from one and rested it gently on top of the other, hoisting it out of the hole and dropping it onto the counter.

"Grab that." They nodded at the basket of sheets, popping the seal on their jar. Pokey obliged, shaking the dust from the duvet and holding it awkwardly just off the floor, waiting for instructions. Sett went to work chopping the leaves into flakes as the pot began to steam behind her, stopping only as they noticed Pokey: frozen.

"Go on, you are staying here tonight." They pointed at the pull-out with their knife in one hand while pinching the tea leaves into a strainer with the other.

"But—"

"And!" A rare interruption from the little goat. "As long as you want until we find somewhere better." Pokey stared for a moment, stunned, holding the duvet like a flag in front of her. She stared down at the down-filled sheet, took a moment to dry her eyes with the corner, and went to work making her bed.

"Thank you." she croaked into the corner, not one to cry in front of strangers. "Thank you, really, thank you."

"Of course." Sett said, barely phased as they coated every dry leaf with a stream of boiling water. Pokey plugged in the space heater, all but falling to pieces as she slipped off her parka and submitted to the orange electronic hum.

"Can I shower here?"

"I would need to have someone come fix the hot—"

"Oh! I know how to do that!"

"Well, good then, as soon as that's fixed you can use my place upstairs to get washed up." Sett tapped the last few drips out of the strainer and brought the mug over to the shivering lizard. She stared into the green, confused for a split second before realizing she was being offered tea, and accepted it graciously.

Sett blinked slowly, watching some of the colour return to the lizard's cheeks. With the half-second of distance, Sett realized what what they were doing looked like.

"I apologize. I understand that having a relative stranger lock you into their store is probably a little hard on the nerves."

"Better than being locked out." Pokey barely finished their sentence before taking a long, throat scalding sip. Her guarded posture fell as the last shivers slipped gently from her bunched shoulders. She took a deep breath. "Thank you, really." She stared up at the goat, her eyes watering.

"It really is the least I could do, Pokey." They took a long, deep breath and started towards the apartment above the store.

"Wait, hang on." Pokey set her tea down, nabbing the hem of Sett's shawl before they got out of reach. Her gaze fell to the floor as the goat gave her a puzzled — although not at all upset — stare. That was going to be a weird thing that Pokey would remember forever, and everyone else would forget about within a few minutes. "You're like, an alien, right?" She drew a line across her mouth with her finger as if to say, "I noticed you look kind of weird."

Sett laughed, then caught themself: "You know, actually, I might be... I would not call myself an alien in the traditional sense, but... that is something to think about." They smiled to themself, content with this answer.

"Well, no. Hold on," Pokey scooched closer on the bed. "You have to understand that that raises way more questions than it answers." she said, incredulous.

"Yes, I suppose you're right." Raising yet more questions. A wry smile formed beneath their skin. They gave Pokey just a half-second to scoot closer to the edge of her seat before: "I'm a demon, actually."

"Retired demon?" she asked.

"Oh, yes." With the joke now over, Sett's smile fell back into its distant contentment.

"But like, thoroughly paranormal though?"

"Yes, very. So is my fiancée. Her name is Ratty." The admission came from Sett with an ease that Pokey desperately yearned for.

"Cool... so..." Pokey started, their voice shaking. "Right...

the thing is like, I wasn't kicked out by my parents or anything. It's more 'cus like— I'm, uh— so—" The lizard faltered, struggling to figure out where to start with her story. She reached for her mug, cancelling the action as she noticed just how badly her hands were shaking. "A bunch of my friends— paranormal friends, have started like— like, I can't find them? I can't— that's why I can't go home."

That was hard to chew on. Sett took a moment, realizing they couldn't *not* get involved at this point, and sat back down on the bed next to Pokey, a slight twinge of regret colouring their teasing. It would have been weird to hug a relative stranger, but Pokey was really just a kid. There was absolutely nothing wrong when she broke down and dove into Sett's arms, holding them like a surprise third parent, wandering out of the crowd at the other two's funeral.

"I can't go home." The words fell from her mouth. "I've been running for so long, and my friends keep disappearing, and I can't go home, and I don't know what to do, because every time I find somewhere to say—" she shuddered into the goat's embrace as the ability to speak left her.

"Shh, shh. It's alright. Nobody is going to hurt you here, Pokey. I promise you that."

---

Sett struggled to leave that night.

They sat with Pokey until the lizard fell asleep and slipped out quietly, forgetting their jacket in favour of triple checking the locks. It was an effort to walk calmly to the bus station, an effort too great to actually wait for it. They charged through the night, absolutely drenched as they all but slammed into their apartment.

"Ratty." Sett panted. A chewed up pen-cap fell from the possum's lips into the pan in her hand, a half-cracked egg hovering in the other.

"You're— you're all wet." She flicked the piece of plastic out onto the floor and set the egg down in the pan, not thinking to remove the shell. She brushed against the smaller goat and dove into the linen closet. "You're so cold." she murmured, now coming up behind and wrapping the goat in their thickest towel. "Did you want spicy beans and rice, it's nice and—"

"We should buy the rest of this building." Sett interrupted, leaning on the counter for support as their lungs seized. Ratty blinked back at them, trying to split her focus between this and removing the shell from her egg. It helped only slightly as the scent of Ratty's cooking coated their torn throat with a comforting little blanket.

"Well, okay. Eat some warm food. Calm down." Ratty took a scalpel and a fork from the cutlery drawer and handed it to Sett along with the finished pile of food. They cut their lips open, taking a deep breath, then another, then a bite of runny egg.

"So, the landlord is taking a dive on this place. We're the only two people who live here." Sett started, balancing a lot as the cold burn in their lungs fought against the warm in their stomach, all while keeping their thoughts in order. Ratty nodded along. "There are other paranormals on Earth, which I thought stopped happening – I mean it's not like we're in hiding, right? But I think we could help them."

Ratty turned it over in her mind, watching Sett eat as she thought of every reasonable problem with this plan. "Money would be tight," was the first thing to jump to her lips. "We would essentially be out of money for the foreseeable future."

"We could apply for an additional government grant based on our escapee status, Becca can push it through for us, and the courier is doing really well, and I really think we can afford it."

"I wouldn't be able to stop working, so I could only help—"

"I know..." Hope built in Sett's chest as the possum's tone shifted. "Ratty, I really think this is what I was made for."

"You fine with beans and rice?" Ratty asked. Sett nodded. Another moment of thought. "Okay. Then, yeah. Let's do it."

96

# 1989
# Logistics

"Sett!" The goat dropped the stack of chairs in their arms, behind schedule in turning the first floor common area into a little meeting space. Pokey had started to move in. She had asked, in the process of dragging a garbage bag full of her belongings up the front stairs, if it was okay for her to bring a friend. Sett saw no problem with that.

"Hi Pokey!" It was so nice to see her. The money that would have normally gone to finding somewhere to sleep for the night had instead been invested in some new-ish clothes. Still attached to her parka, the thrift store had sold her a clean new pair of sneakers. Not ideal for the weather, but better than before.

A little striped orange head trailed behind the navy blue mass of stained weatherproofing and faux fur, clinging desperately to the lizard's hand. "Who is this?" Sett knelt to the little one's level, patting down the rolled collar of their sweater for a better look. The tiger's gaze fell to the goat's shoes as soon as it was met. "What's your name?"

"Go on, Pri." Pokey stepped aside, her new sneakers barely shuffling an inch before the tiger's panicked face dove back into the comfort of the back of her parka.

"You just said it!" she whined into the down.

"It's okay." Sett skirted around Pokey's side on their knees, offering as wide a smile as they could manage without bleeding when the tiger's bright eye popped out above the blue. "I'm Sett. It's nice to meet you."

The runny yolk of their heart popped when Pri returned the smile. "I'm— my name is Prisha. I wanted to ask, if— uh—" That was as much as she could manage.

"Pri just wants to know— she's worried you might make her speak when we have uh— what're we calling it?" Pokey put a hand around her surrogate sister's back.

"Oh, goodness, no. If you don't want to talk when we come to you, just say you want to skip, and I'm sure everyone will understand." That wasn't enough to convince her. She stayed resolute behind the wall of fabric, peaking out only to check if the goat had disappeared.

"Here." Sett rolled up their sleeve of their baggy sweater, thumbing open the clasp on their watch and slipping it off. "This was given to me by a special friend. You have to give it back when we're all done, but it'll help."

Prisha took it, clicking each one of the buttons in sequence, her tiny hands dwarfed by the little plastic case. "What does it do?" she asked.

"Well, it tells the time." They tapped on the plastic screen protector. That, and another warm smile was just enough. When the circle landed on her — with Pokey's help, and on the second go-around — she started to recount what'd brought her to this point.

"I actually— um. I don't know if this is off topic, but..." She trailed off.

"It's okay, Prisha." Sett's chair creaked as they sat forward, trying to draw the tiger a little further into the circle. Pokey caught Sett's eye, nudging a bit from behind. "We're all here to support each other."

She wrung her tiny hands around the rubber watch band as she processed the memory, too young to be this scared and alone in the world. "I uh— Pokey." It was easier, probably, to talk to her guardian in front of everyone, rather than directly to everyone. "Do you remember um— Miss Nelly? She was paranormal too and when we got separated the other day, I tried to go meet her at school, and she wasn't there, and I asked the office and they said she disappeared too."

She struggled, like no child should ever have to struggle, to hold back tears. "She said that— she said that she would take care of us if— you remember that, right? If we couldn't go home." She stopped in place, forgetting what the point to that story was. An admission, or explanation, as to why the tiger could not be found on a given day.

Sett listened until Prisha was finished, running through another story and a half, and listening politely to a hulking baritone of a grizzly bear as he suggested a few things that might help. When he finished, and the group moved on without Sett's prompting, they stood up quietly and stepped out.

There was a spot under the stairs where the concrete above matched almost perfectly with a vent that went straight out of the building. Sett sat down below it, lit up, and blew their smoke into the unintentional funnel.

How had this gotten out of hand so quickly? In their first few weeks of operation, someone had heard from Pokey about a new shelter downtown, and from there it ballooned out until the majority of their rooms were full. There were people with other arrangements that only intended on staying for a short while, or until they got back on their feet, or whatever. Sooner or later, whoever was threatening these people would find out. Sett would have stepped in only as bait and a bed.

"Hey." Ratty had tried to put something a little less threatening on for her first meeting. The best she could do was her work blazer and a sweater, her punkish frame out of place in a Mister Rogers getup. She ended up just sitting at the reception desk with Becca. "You okay?" she asked.

They dabbed the corner of their eyes with the hem of their sweater, surprised as the single tug collapsed an eyeful of tears onto the black fabric. It faded to nothing, soaking into the weave. "Heavy shit, huh?" That's how a person would have said it. "It's never going to be enough."

"Well..." Ratty slid down the wall next to them. "It kinda just started, right?"

Sett nodded.

"And like, the support group is secondary to like, giving people who can't find one a place to live, right?"

Sett nodded again. Still, if Pokey didn't happen to stumble upon the exact right tea shop, they would be scared, alone, and homeless. That was the reality for anyone outside the greater Toronto area, outside any of the small communities that had their little clubs. If Pokey and Prisha didn't know each other, Prisha would probably have disappeared.

"It's not enough." they said.

"It'll get better." Ratty tipped her head back against the concrete. "It's a place for people to help each other. You don't have to save everyone."

"It's one shelter in one city." the goat protested.

"Yeah." Ratty said, giving Sett an affectionate bump. "And you're one goat."

Sett took a long drag, sucking the rest of the life out of their cigarette and tossing it to mingle with the rest of the butts. Having this here was nice during the winter. Ratty's eyes searched the goat's, falling from their half-moons down to the individual furs crossing the border of light grey around the tip of their snout. She set her chin on top of the goat's head, tipping their horns into her chest for a little headbutt, the way she knew they liked.

"You wanna get back in there?"

"I really would like to."

"Good. I'll be right behind you."

5:43 in the morning.

Still awake.

Fern rolled over in bed, not sure why they ever tried to sleep on the night before a full-moon day as they slapped the space-bar on their computer: 5:44a.m. They had developed an impeccable sense of time.

The butcher would be open in three hours, but wouldn't be selling their off cuts for another eight. They would have to spend the entirety of today thinking about tonight.

Might as well open the store.

They spent the morning normally, sipping coffee and glaring at a chorus of angels on monochrome monitors across their little hybrid shop. People wanted Angel computers, the best thing Fern could do for those people was rip out the surveillance chips and sell them next to some alternative literature. Soon enough this would not be profitable enough to survive, the dog would have to fall back on what little Miss Vermington payed them, and the trickle of income from their decades old patents.

As if on cue, a little kirin rapped on the front door, pressing his face against the glass.

"Morning, Davy."

"Morning, Fern."

"Gonna watch the store for me today?" A song and dance

they had worked out with the kid. They never expected anything, but...

"Yep," which made the addition of "gotta warn you though, I have a thing around four." a little jarring.

"What kind of thing?"

"There's this new shelter, I'm gonna see if me and Walt can get a room there."

"I thought the shelter system didn't take..." Fern set their coffee down, poking Davy's horn.

"These guys are independents."

"Huh, cool." The borzoi gazed out over their shop as their coffee maker finished filling up a travel mug. That was their exit. "See you, I guess tonight?"

"Yeah, for sure. I'll meet you back here tonight."

And then it was 5:43 in the afternoon. They had cut it too close for the end of October. They swung their backpack off their back, pushing aside the shrink-wrapped end-cuts and whatever other dense scrap food they could find for the night. They needed a different bag. This one only had one pocket, and so they struggled to find their keys almost every time they ended up in there.

Padding around in the bottom, their pointer and middle fingers shot out into cold air. They turned the bag and stared down at the little appendages. This was not cause for panic. They had— yeah! Pockets. They patted their pockets. The non-deep kind, they were perfect to stash their keys in. They just forgot, that was all.

They rammed their hands into the tiny space, nothing but pocket lint and dust creeping under their fingernails. Maybe they had dropped it on the walk-up. It was a good thing they noticed now, or they could have been robbed.

Their keys were not on the walk-up.

Davy had the spares. Their roommate had just moved out. Their set was sitting on the other side of the mail slot. Tilde had keys in her office, but that was too far, and there was no guarantee that she would actually be there.

Fern took off running.

Where could they have gone? There was no body of forest deep enough to contain them within the 30 minutes of running it would take for the sun to set. The only other building they had access to was Ratty's, and the number of paranormal incident reports coming from that area made it—

Actually.

They stopped running.

That might work.

It was a long shot, but it might work.

They took off in the other direction, windbreaker flapping against their treacherous bag full of raw meat. Was Ratty's less than 30 minutes away? They dropped the bag.

They had always felt directed when they visited Ratty in the past. They wrote it off as a new renter, anxious to cross the boundaries of where she was allowed in the building, but they had regularly made a mess of what was supposed to be a communal office space. They had also never seen anyone else in that communal office space.

Definitely less than 30 minutes away. They slammed into the glass of the front door, slapping it with the open palm of their hand. "I know what you do here!" they yelled at the receptionist. She jumped, dropping a Rubik's cube. She stood up to get a better look at the door.

"It's still a pull door, Fern." she said. Fern stepped back, blinked at the handle, and pulled it open. "Hi, welcome back." Becca tried to be polite.

"I know it's a front," the borzoi interrupted. "I'm a werewolf, I need you to lock me up for the night." Fern checked their watch again, the moon's pull on their fur a more telling indicator of the time they had left.

"Oh! Okay." She sat back down and picked up the phone, as though this were the most normal thing in the world. "I've never met a werewolf before." she told the dial-tone, punching in someone's number with the back of her pen. "I will call someone down to help."

"Oh, hey, it's Fern." Ratty spoke up from behind, sitting across a little table from—

"Hey, Davy." The borzoi chose to single out the kirin first. Then Ratty, a distinct look of "oh fuck, are we working tonight?" plastered dumbly across her face. She was helping Davy fill out paperwork.

"Sorry! What time is it?" Davy asked. The borzoi's expression told him everything. "You're right, I'm so sorry, I got side-tracked with—"

"That's fine, Davy." Their nails scratched lines into the desk, struggling to keep grounded. Ratty stood up, recognizing the way the dog's body curled.

"You're going to have to finish this on your own, okay? It's— here, Becca can help." Ratty abandoned the paperwork, taking Fern by the arm and starting to walk them towards the stairwell. "Becca, tell Sett to meet me downstairs." she said.

"You ever—" Fern's own biology cut them off, an ache shooting through their shifting spine.

"A lot, actually. Used to do this kind of thing with you in the other universe— oh I haven't even— okay. So, I was thinking about it, I think we may have met in another life. You did your hair differently, took me a while to— anyway, doesn't matter. How's the investigation?"

That was the last thing Fern wanted to talk about right now.

"Y'know it's funny, back when we— I used to just wrap you in blankets and belts." Ratty was altogether far too unconcerned about what was about to happen. "Used to be able to calm you right down towards the end of it. Past '24 we'd just like— god, this is gonna sound gay. I'd calm you down and lay on top of you to make sure you didn't move."

That was less comforting than the possum had intended. "So you're out of practice actually controlling me, then?"

The possum sucked on her teeth, figuring out how to avoid answering that. "Your voice changed, too— you ever go to a stump burn?" A completely ungraceful shift in topic.

"What're you— do people 'go' to stump burns? I thought you just burned a stump?" Successful enough by the measure of its results. "Is that door strong enough?"

"Oh yeah. Easy. It's made outta metal." The possum tapped the edge to demonstrate. The hollow aluminum ring once again did not set Fern at ease. Further unsettling was the tiny goat that stepped over the barely-there bulkhead, there only — to the dog's racing mind — to be used as sacrifice. They wished they hadn't dropped their meat bag.

"I'm here! Sorry!" They had met several months ago. Seth, or something. Was there a way to ask why they needed to wait for them without being rude? Probably not. They circled the room, closely examining the identical spots of grey concrete floor for a comfortable spot to sit. Their other half would have been better at that. They jumped when the weird static-y edge of an electric blanket hit them in the back.

"Sorry!" Two apologies in two words. Ratty had opened a wall panel, and was unfolding a collection of linens. "I just assumed you would want to, uh, change." At least it wasn't belts and blankets.

"Are you two staying in here with me?" Fern asked. They tried their best to impart a spin of "you shouldn't" into their voice.

"No." Ratty said, dropping another blanket onto the pile.

"Yes." Seth? No, Sett said, at the same time.

Ratty's eyes locked with Sett's a silent argument passing between the two. Ratty tried to convince Sett that she knew better, Sett convinced Ratty back that they were the authority. Ratty rolled her eyes and returned to her blanket stacking. If the other Fern was more docile, the possum might've been used to leaving out some blankets. This Fern's other half might as well have been an incinerator. Nothing in the same room ever survived over a long enough timeline.

"Yes." Sett repeated. "I will stay to make sure the transition is as comfortable as possible." Fine, whatever. They were running out of time either way. The fear of being seen naked was overpowered by the fear of tearing through some likeable clothing, forcing Fern into their underwear, handing off the disorganized ball of clothes to Ratty.

"Fold those, please." They tried not to be rude. Backed into a corner, their body ached against the new bare cold of the basement. They had held it off too long. Bone had already pushed too hard along the grain, splitting and sliding along its evolutionary lines. The heated blanket, lying uselessly in the centre of the room, was the sun. They fell onto it, a regrettable crack filling the room and confining them to the floor.

"You—" Fern struggled not to growl. "You need to leave." The words came out broken, like an animal mimicking the sounds of its master. Onto their front, and their sharp canine elbows dug almost immediate holes in the electric blanket. The possum backed towards the plug, pulling it out with her boot.

That put her in an awkward position. Sett wrapped threads around the newly forming creature, doing their best to siphon pain off into the cosmos as sharp claws grew from the borzoi's paws. A great cold, numbness overtook their body as it was free to struggle for air without pain. Where the fur had spread enough to reveal the skin underneath, their oxygen deprived blood burned purple through their veins.

And Ratty had put them between her and the door.

"Okay…" Her voice came out breathy, excited and terrified in equal measure. It was enough to attract the creature's attention. "C'mon now. Good doggy." She kept her centre of mass low, gently cooing up at the creature. They tested their new jaw with a pair of snaps, choosing to leave it open as they advanced. Ratty whistled quietly. That used to draw the dog's attention. She clicked her tongue. That used to signal the dog to follow.

"Sett." Ratty whispered, coming to terms with the fact that this technique was not going to work. "Rope them when I say, okay?"

Sett, guarding the door, nodded. One more whistle-click, just to try it. It made the creature curious more than anything, sniffing their air above their head. The acoustics of the tiny room made the possum sound so much larger.

That was it.

Their snout to the sky, Ratty charged at the exposed neck, keeping as low as she could. The extra half-second spent up forced the creature to pounce over the possum, putting their chest in the perfect position to take all her weight. Momentum meant nothing. They still weighed as much as before, just spread across a larger body. Fern was stopped dead, forced to balance on their hind legs with a creature half their size clinging to their chest.

"Now, Sett!" A glowing orange thread wrapped itself through the creature's roaring maw, dragging them the rest of the way over. There was no room below the concrete foundation for the floor to shake. Instead, everything in the dog's body crunched. They passed out.

"Sorry!" Three apologies in as many minutes.

"Don't bother, fuck— move!" Ratty tried to shove them out of the doorway, feeling more than seeing the dog's eye flick back open. Ropes snapped, flitting between the possum's legs and back into Sett's hands. "You really—"

"Hang on!" Sett tried to look over Ratty's shoulder, watching as — short of being able to get up — the creature raked their claws through the possum's back.

"Fuck." This was the final push to get Sett out of the room. Something in her back tore as she sat up to pull the door closed, kicking at the dog's jaw as it stuck its way through the jam. She fell back as soon as the door was sealed. "What was that!?" Ratty rolled over, struggling not to writhe against the hot cuts in her back.

"They were in pain." Sett answered, their hands going to work on the claw marks before their mind caught up. "I'm sorry."

"It's fine." Ratty buried her face in her sleeves, wounds shuddering as they rose and fell with the effort of keeping sane. "I'm okay."

"You need to—" Maybe not the best timing. Sett pressed on anyway. "You need to work on not baring your teeth like that."

Ratty hadn't noticed. "I was smiling. We— used to be friends, I was excited."

"In your old universe?"

"Yeah."

"Is that weird for you?"

"Little bit. Not sure yet."

The creature banging against the door scared her out of any deeper thought.

---

"Hello." A cold, metallic voice paralyzed Sett in the same instant it woke them from sleep.

"Jesus Christ." Ratty dove for the baton on her bedside table and stumbled into a sloppy combat stance before she had fully woken up, one knee still hanging off the bed. Sett was not blessed with such instincts, they sat up in bed, shaking too much to hit the switch on their bedside lamp as they took in the creature above them:

A thin veneer of rough, clearly synthetic fur just barely covered an underworking of tightly constructed mechanisms, marred across the chest with a black X. A black visor took the place of the creature's eyes, and from their back was projected a matching set of holographic arms and antlers: each fumbling for a nearby surface to brace themselves off of.

"My name is—" Ratty stopped it as they turned to look at Sett, trying to press themself into the bed.

"Get the—" Sett stammered, not sure what they were trying to say.

"I got it." Ratty nodded before turning to the creature, "C'mon, let's take this outside." She swallowed her panic as the creature nodded, ducking through the door. "

You gonna be okay, Sett?" she asked. The goat took a deep breath, nodding as they exhaled some of their nerves. "Good, try and go back to sleep, I'll be back in a sec."

"My name is Angel J22:4." The creature spoke as Ratty crossed the barrier between the bedroom and living room.

"Shut the fuck up." Ratty hushed Angel as she tried her best to shut the door without a click. Angel stared at the door handle for a few moments, then turned to Ratty for approval. "Yes, fine, now." Ratty led the way out of their apartment.

"My name is Angel J22:4. I am a model J Angel Robotics Unlimited drone manufactured in the year 2900 by Kegawa Digital. We have met once before—"

"You shouldn't be here." Ratty sped up their quest towards the elevators, perfectly willing to take that at face value.

"I have disabled my tracking protocol. It is my understanding that this company is currently at conflict with Angelcorp. You and I share that goal."

"*I'm* currently *at conflict* with Angelcorp. The rest of this company has nothing to do with that."

"Your mission is to preserve and protect the paranormal, is it not?"

"My mission is to move boxes from one place to another."

"I am seeking shelter." Angel said.

"We have a receptionist. She's here—"

"You are being intentionally obtuse. You are currently at conflict with Angelcorp. It is not my intention to exacerbate this conflict. Our meeting— please stop." Angel put a holographic hand out in front of the tired possum. "Our meeting significantly altered my programming, I believe I am malfunctioning. I have some memory of you that is incongruous with the rest of my history. I believe I could be useful to you in this conflict, zero-one-seven."

Ratty's temples tightened suddenly at the use of her number. She swallowed panic for the second time that night, not coating her throat quite as well this time around.

"What— what did you just call me?"

"Zero-one-seven. Is that not your name?" Angel asked.

"No, it's not." A strange combination of rage and anguish played second fiddle to cracked-tongue anxiety as she examined the drone. The synthetic fur was too thin to hide its rubber skin. Incredibly intricate mechanical muscles twitched and pulled under the surface, giving away the otherwise incredibly convincing puppet show. Ratty stepped in closer, her throat closing as she examined each individually labelled string of flesh.

She took the drone's wrist in her hands on a hunch, bringing it to her face and having the image of 13's scar jump to the front of her mind. Angel had an access panel in the exact same shape.

"13?" Ratty asked, trying to stare through her opaque visor. her face remained blank, only subtle twitches of its mechanical musculature to give away that it was processing something.

"My name is Angel J22:4." Angel said finally, her voice clicking with the effort of processing it on top of whatever else she was remembering.

"You— you need to leave." Ratty stammered, "I'll— I can walk you out."

---

They weren't sleeping until Ratty got back, at the very least. Sitting alone in bed, Sett thought about the potential of another scare. They would not have reconsidered, knowing that even their bedroom was not off limits, but it should have crossed their mind.

Standing alone on the roof, however, they thought about the cold. They thought about almost tripping on one of their layers, and resolving to wear shorter clothes in the future. This was far simpler, and easier.

The surrounding buildings were so much taller, even a half-decade of development down the line. They could have jumped from the edge and dangled off a lobby chandelier, landing through the tall windows of their neighbours.

They were too much taller. It was office space, occupied in the night only by polisher-pushing janitorial staff, buffing the imperfections out of the sole-scuffed tile. People with means like that wore temporary shoes. They wore a different pair every day of the week. Ratty went back for hers when they were let out of their evidence lockup.

No one lived there. Unless someone from the day-crew forgot a briefcase, the overnight staff were not treated to the comfort and luxury of full overhead lighting.

There would always be more power behind ventures like that. They could have, in their infinite knowledge, patience, and time, clawed their way up to heaven. They were more comfortable on Earth.

They thought, in the cold dark, wearing their layers, about the way the tobacco burned their throat on the way down. Pain was poverty's luxury. People who didn't know a thing about wine, or smokes, or anything consumed by big guys and little guys, would tell you the ones they got went down smooth. You knew how good a cigarette was if it went down smooth.

Cigarettes that went down smooth were manufactured with strychnine in them. Rich people selling shit to other rich people didn't worry about these kinds of things. They would get a lung transplant, if they smoked the cigarettes at all. More likely, they would auction them off to another one of their friends for a charity tax write off.

"Oh, hey." There's a voice at the other end of the roof. A short kirin. He had moved in a few weeks ago. D— Dave— David? Davy! Davy. Davy stood silhouetted by another neighbour, the barely-there light of maintenance outlining him from across the street. The tips of his sneakers hung over the edge. "Didn't really expect to see anyone else up here."

"I hope I'm not interrupting something." Sett said. If they suggested he looked like he was about to jump, that would put the idea in his head. On the other hand—

"No, probably better that you do, actually." Davy said. "Do you think it would kill me if I fell?" That answered that question.

"I do." Sett tried to make the crunch of gravel under their hooves as quiet as possible. Their heart tipped instantly from a mild panic to a galvanized rhythm. "The building is quite a bit taller than it looks."

They sat down on the edge, six-or-so feet away. Close enough to grab him, but not so close as to look like they were going to try. "Do you smoke?" They flashed the metal edge of their cigarette case.

"I—" He stared, bewildered, at the aluminum edge. Davy was roughly 16, Sett remembered. He didn't look it in this light. Better then, when he said "No, I think I'm okay." He turned to look over the edge. "I don't think I should be around anymore, is the problem."

They came simple like that, usually. Someone who attempted suicide once in their life did so with fanfare. Those who tried more often were usually that casual about it. It could get cold in the winter. Davy had faced death already. "Why's that?" Sett asked.

"Dunno. I guess I feel like I'm taking a lot more than I'm contributing, and on top of that everything is kind of, existentially horrible, if you know what I mean?" Sett had gone through something similar in their adolescence. They saw a vast, repetitive infinity in front of them. Davy had a way out of that.

"I do, actually." They shuffled a little closer, snuffing the last of their smoke.

"You gonna tell me not to jump?" Davy teased.

"Would it change anything at all if I did?" That sort of thing really never worked out. "If you let other people tell you what they think makes a person worthwhile, you'll find yourself in the gaps."

"That's pretty smart." He let out a long sigh, repeating the word *cracks* involuntarily. His reflection in the opposite building flashed into existence with an extinguished light, and there he was, hovering out over the infinite blackness below. Sett checked on their own reflection, colour sucked from their fur by the dark glass. "Yeah, you're probably—"

Davy slipped. In the seconds following. Sett closed the now 5 foot gap, balling their fist through the now-billowing windsock of his hood. Their heart deflated as their chest pressed into the roof's raised edge, Davy's sneakers dangling in front of someone's window.

"You're okay." they panted. "I have you. You're okay."

"Yeah." His voice came out ragged. "Good. Thank you."

It took delicate effort to pull him back up to the roof. He fell to his side on the damp gravel, refusing to stand for the first few minutes as his heart settled.

"You can—" Sett put their hands on their knees, panting. "I can only feel what you're going through through the lens of my own experience, but I can promise you you will always have a home here, okay?"

"Yeah." he murmured, keeping his face hidden. "Okay. Yeah. Sorry."

---

The elevator doors gave up Ratty on their way down. The possum's eyes went from confused to delighted, then back to confused.

"Hey." She smiled.

"Hi, sorry. I was just walking Davy back to his room."

"Two in one night, eh?" The tired little goat hunkered into their partner's side.

"Have you been sleeping alright?" Sett had been struggling. Ratty was balancing work and recent PTSD with helping out.

"I— no, not really." she answered.

Sett pressed their head deeper into her chest, listening to her heart.

"Hey." they prodded. "I love you."

"Yeah, well, I love you, so its not like you've got a choice." Ratty pulled them in a little closer. The elevator could have been sitting still for all the noise it was making. "I was thinking..." Sett was the one to break the silence again. "We never really had a honeymoon."

"We aren't even married yet." Ratty agreed, realizing this for the first time herself. Ignoring the cost came bundled into the fantasizing. "It's kind of been one thing after another since we broke out, huh?"

"Yes, it really has been. But I mean, if this all goes well..." Sett examined the edge of their skirt, torn where they had tripped over it earlier, a few specks of gravel still clinging to it. "There will probably be enough people to run the centre on its own for a little while."

"I bet Pokey could do it, she's kind of doing a bit of leadership."

"Yes, I'm sure she'd be delighted."

"And I have kind of a big job coming up..."

Sett nodded, encouraged.

Ratty slid up next to her partner on the hand rail and set her chin down on top of the goat's head. They wiggled out from underneath to look up at their fiancée, her eyes still so tired. That wasn't something that was going to change.

"Where do you want to go?" Ratty asked. "Hawaii, maybe?"

"Maybe. Do you like tropical places?" Sett yawned. "Florida is cheap and similar."

"The humidity is really good for my fur, actually. Gotta be something all-inclusive." Ratty's eyes lulled closed, in turn closing the discussion. She left intact the comfortable miasma of honeymoon plans. Another moment of silence as the two independently thought about how long this elevator was taking.

"Can I say something kind of weird?" Ratty prodded, her eyes flicking open as she became bored of the silent version of the box.

"No, absolutely not." Sett said, too tired to put humour in their voice. Ratty blinked down at the goat, struggling to read them and clearly not getting it. "Yes, I'm sorry. That was a joke."

"Oh, okay," Ratty leant back on the hand rail, staring up at the ceiling to hide a grin. She let the silence hang "perfect, then." as notes of a smirk crept into her tone.

"What is it?" Sett poked the soft part of the possum's side.

"I was uh, just gonna say that I... miss you... I feel like we spent more time together in Hell than we have on Earth so far." She brushed the carpet with the toe of her boot.

"I was feeling the same way, oddly." Sett watched the cheap polyester kick up dust.

"So, honeymoon for sure then."

"Definitely." Sett nodded, quietly following the toe of Ratty's boot up the wrinkled crease of her pyjama pants. "and I really hate to be a perv, but—"

"Right!?" Ratty startled Sett with her sudden energy. "When was the last time we had—" The word *sex* caught in her throat, bringing with it a full body blush. "Sorry- I didn't mean, that was —" She laughed to try and cut the tension in her chest.

"No, thank you! I was holding off because I'm never quite sure when you want to, but—"

"Oh, babe, you know nothing gets me rowdier than hearing the words *want* and *to* pronounced separately." Ratty pointed her snout at the ceiling, avoiding the goats gaze with the unintended consequence of leaving her neck wide open. Sett took one one side in their claws and pressed their sealed lips against the other, suppressing a snicker.

"Tonight?" They brought the possum's chin down, their eyes glowing bright enough to cast the shadow of Ratty's snout on her face.

"I mean like, not here." Ratty said, as though late 80s elevator encounters were unheard of.

"Why not here?" Sett tugged the cord holding Ratty's pants up. The downy fur at the edges of her stomach, just above where one of her shorter sweaters hung, was almost silky to the touch. It stayed out of the thick mess at the centre of her stomach, in the perfect spot to press up against her and keep their hand-hold. It was sensitive, too. A light tug, and she flinched into the corner of the elevator. "You're making that face you make."

"You are also making a face." Ratty stammered. She had, at various points, been narcissistic enough to look at herself in the mirror while she was being groped. Sett had no such pleasure, never knowing the way their half-moon eyes hung low, uncaring of the greed that shone through them.

"You let your mouth hang open." Sett teased. "Like a slut."

"Every time?"

"Every single time." Their head hit her chest as her tail, like brickwork, laid and unlaid itself up and around the back of their leg, shaking as it went.

"Someone might catch us."

"Oh no, then everyone will know you're a slut."

"Didn't you just stop a kid from jumping off a roof? Doesn't that put you off—"

"How did you know that?" Sett pulled back far enough to stare.

"I don't— This is a really long elevator ride." Ratty said, snapping out of the moment, her hands still hovering a half inch from her partner's waist. Sett adjusted to the new atmosphere, ducked out from under their fiancée and pressed the button for their floor. The mechanism came back to life with an impatient *ka-thunk,* and they were moving again.

"Did you— Ratty, hun." Sett laughed again.

"Hang on, no— there was no reason for me to think I needed to do that twice."

"What about our floor?"

"I hit our floor when I came in!" Ratty turned, her mind racing to mount a defence as her partner burst out laughing.

"Oh, don't you lie to us!" The goat teased between fits of laughter. They wrapped their arms around the possum's back, affectionately jamming their snout into hers "You were trying to corner us in your sex elevator!"

"I didn't even know you were going to be here!" Ratty said, failing to hide her amusement beneath a thin veneer of annoyance. The two stood in each other's embrace as the ancient machine pulled itself through the building.

And then they had sex, I guess.

---

She forgot how much old, cheap shit clicked. If she bumped something cheap in the 2020s, the screen shattered, she worked around it. Same went for expensive shit in the 2020s, honestly. If you bumped something from the mid-to-late-1980s though, it kept working, quietly getting worse and worse until it started clicking.

The clicking her distracted from her music. The music was supposed to distract her from the TV, and the TV was supposed to take her mind off reading. That last one only worked understanding the fact that, if she devoted her entire attention to the textbook in front of her, she would never absorb any of it.

Reading was supposed to distract her from the itching. It took a lot to scar Ratty. Her side, where John hit it with the axe, was a permanent bald-spot. Being kept in a dirty basement for however long had made it start to itch again.

Today was Sunday, her day off. She had run enough deliveries during the week to pay for some living expenses, and put some in the communal money pile that went to food. She spent the other few days looking into Cane, bothering the police department and RCMP for details, and coming to the understanding that they were not going to cooperate with her.

Doing something was better than doing nothing. Going through the coronavirus pandemic the first time, she was tentatively employed, had just graduated for the first time, and spent every day sleeping. She got out of that just picking random shit to do until her tolerance for it raised past the functional threshold.

Something loud happened on TV. Her screwdriver, jammed between two parts of her cassette player's mechanism, leapt forward into obscurity, cracking everything it hit along the way. Ratty bit through the lip she had been chewing on as the takeup reel popped up, out, and onto the carpet.

Great. Fucking great.

It's pathetic, knowing that she's going to be upset over that one little slip-up for months. She stood up, leaving it all behind.

"Sett?" The goat woke up in that moment, making a startled 'mm?' sound. "I'm gonna go for groceries."

"Oh," They settled back in, happy to be woken up for that. "Okay, I love you."

"You don't have to say that every time! I love you too."

Becca gave the robot clothes: a pile of comfortable looking lost-and-found trash. She was waiting in the lobby when Ratty left to run errands the next morning. She followed her out the door, hovering just beside the possum as she walked.

"You and I are similarly motivated. If Angelcorp is not disrupted before 2027, their master computer will go online and I will be taken over by the global signal. Similarly, if you don't stop Angelcorp, they are going to continue to kidnap and exploit paranormal entities until they become unstoppable." Angel explained.

"I didn't know they were doing that." That wasn't entirely true, she had mentally done the red-string-wall and... yeah, that made enough sense. This morning however she was far too tired to be anything but distantly panicked, choosing instead to devote the brainpower not taken up by this conversation to admiring a modern-for-the-time motorcycle spinning in the front window of a dealership. "How do I know you're not a spy?"

"I understand one of the creatures under your employ is a foremost expert in cybersecurity. Have them proverbially 'open me up' and you will have your answer." Angel encouraged.

"Fern is not my employee. They're- I dunno, they're not my friend yet. I know them. You're also from 2900, right? How is a hacker from—" Ratty faltered, not sure when Fern was actually born. "Are young people born in the 40s now? That was only like 30 years ago at this point."

"1949 was 40 years ago. You were heralded at your funeral as an excellent judge of character. Does this not extend to your post-life?" Ratty felt a weird twinge of guilt as she realized just how much stretching her old co-workers must've done to find something nice to say about her. The other professors probably managed okay, but her old reporter friends... yikes.

The pair ducked into a convenience store, Ratty too caught up in picturing her own funeral to answer the question. Maybe someone took a video. She could ask her mom in about 35 years.

"Hey, Harry. Got your package." She dropped a small cardboard box on the counter, getting a newspaper ruffle and a lazy nod in return. "I can't even look you in the eye, by the way."

"Me?" Angel asked.

"Yes, you. You got the built-in sunglasses thing going on."

"I hardly think that matters. My infrastructure is based on people. I am what comes from people reverse engineering themselves in an effort to build something better. I suspect your skills still apply." Ratty once again chose to ignore this line of questioning as she pulled a carton of instant noodle mixes from a top shelf, slinging it under one arm as she picked up a pallet of canned stuff and handed it to Angel with the other. All of that and a bag of milk came to the counter with them, topped off with a tin of Sett's favourite brand of affordable rolling tobacco from the wall behind the till. Under normal circumstances she would have gotten something sweet and caffeinated to go with it, both to treat herself for leaving the house and to energize her to finish the rest of her errands. Today, though, she had broken her tape-player. Neglecting to indulge in an energy drink would be her punishment for that.

Harry stared at the pointer finger, then at his package. It was ahead of schedule, delivered on a Sunday. He stuffed it under the counter, ignoring Ratty completely and picking out a nicer tin of tobacco. He dropped it into her shopping.

"Not easy to get my medicine nowadays, Ms. V. You take that as a tip." He pointed to the can's outline at the bottom of the bag. It didn't stop him from checking the other hand, stuffed away in the front of the possum's hoodie. Nothing there, either.

"What do you think of my friend here?" Ratty tried not to be annoyed.

Harry turned, squaring up the robot. "I'd feel better if I could see her eyes."

Angel complied, taking off her glasses and a cotton face mask someone had found for her and revealing the significantly more obstructive black visor that covered — or maybe took the place of — her eyes.

"Ah... Well, she's one of those, uh, supernaturals. If that's what you're looking for," he answered, zapping through the selection and tossing each in turn into the bag. Ratty scoffed.

"You think so?"

"Could be. Then again you've always hung around scary people. What're the stakes, Miss V?"

"Well, she might be a spy." The possum did her best McCarthy impression.

"Communist?" Harry followed suit as he all but clambered onto the counter top, taking a much closer look at the mechanical woman. Angel winced, advanced enough for her mind to create a personal space bubble.

"No, much worse. She says the boys down at Angel Computers put her together."

"Oh, nah!" he concluded, slumping back down behind his newspaper, still waiting for Ratty to pay up. "No one that pretty works for a computer company. Plus, if she were a spy, some old man getting way too close wouldn't make her quite so uncomfortable."

"You think?"

"All I'm gonna say is that, if she thought I could make you trust her, she'd be putting on the charm."

"Suppose that makes sense." Ratty nodded. Harry sat back, satisfied with his work as Ratty got out her wallet and sorted through a small stack of rumpled bills. "Hey Harry?"

"Yes ma'am."

"Don't ever do that again, please."

"O'course. T'was outta line."

"Thanks."

"Does that help your judgment?" Angel asked, taking the garbage bags of food off Ratty on programming.

"A little. I dunno, we'll see how you do at the..." Ratty trailed off as she noticed a new store slotting itself into the mall across the street. A real stroke of narrative luck made today the day they raised their sign:

**ANGELCORP**
SERVICE CENTER & WHOLESALE WAREHOUSE

Her gaze held steady as a security guard caught sight of her, unsure whether to glare directly at the possum, the spikes on her shoulders, or the passive robot-ghost thing standing behind her. Ratty's gaze followed the cops, up to the taller woman's visor.

"What'd they build you for, Angel?"

"I was a soldier." The drone replied. The possum's gaze fell back to the storefront.

"No shit..."

# 1991
# Angelcorp

"I really do not enjoy this plan." Sett flinched as another off-white box crashed through the display window of an Angel Computers outlet. It came to a stop moments before a pressurized canister shoved through the broken CRT went off, spraying the storefront with paint. "I hate this plan so much."

They weren't supposed to watch. They were very clear when Ratty explained how it was going to go down that they would not be watching. If they were a witness, that would ruin everything. At this point, though, enough people were gawking at the spectacle of pulverized circuitry to excuse a short peek.

They turned their back as Ratty came flying through the same window.

Why have I been singled out, officer?

I'm not discussing my day with you, officer.

Am I being detained or am I free to go?

I am not answering any questions without a lawyer present.

They had never been arrested on Earth before. This was the script Ratty had instructed them to go through. Canada did not have a fifth amendment. The Canadian Charter of Rights and Freedoms was the stand-in for that. They couldn't "plead the fifth," but they could very specifically tell anyone who cared to detain them that they weren't going to be of any help.

"Stay down on the ground and put your hands behind your head." That was not a police officer's voice. That was a scared man, hired by a computer repair shop to wear a dark coloured uniform and a belt from the army surplus store. The rest of the plan would not be so forgiving.

Another paint bomb went off: a quick bang and splat in quick succession. The goat's heart leapt into their throat as a gunshot followed. The following few seconds of silence held it there. Then, the metal clatter of a gun hitting the ground, and...

"GET YOUR FUCKING HANDS OFF ME, YOU PIG CUNT!" They weren't supposed to look. Over their shoulder, they could see the awkward horse costume of two under-trained men trying to keep the possum off the ground. Short of being able to kick, she smeared the paint that covered her boot up the back of the man holding her legs' uniform. She was shaking.

She caught Sett's eye as they tossed her into the back of a police cruiser, one eye jammed shut against the blood leaking horizontally from her nose. Her wink came out looking more like a weird blink. Sett turned away.

"I fucking hate this plan."

"Yeah." They had forgotten about Fern. "C'mon. We have work to do."

This was probably what it was like last time. It certainly brought back memories: belted to one of those cargo wheeler things, the leather edges digging into her fur. She could probably pretty easily have made something like this at home if she had more belts. Was this something they had on standby? Or did they have to do a breakroom belt-drive to get it all together in time?

The bread tag in her cheek snapped finally, worn down by hours of chewing and spit. It had served its final utility in giving a lab technician the single thought: *what was that noise?*

And the lab coats, too... People in lab coats liked to gawk. People with press-passes liked to gawk, too, but lab coats were probably higher on the gawking hierarchy. Ratty tried not to feel jealous.

This entire wing of the facility was under construction. Walls, still with massive holes in them, gave way to reinforced doors, the kind made with several inch thick sheets of steel sandwiching twice as thick bulletproof glass. Any distortion at all made them impossible to see through.

Monitors, hazard suits, eight different doors into the same lab, the airlock style thing — gawl-lee! They were really trying to put on a show in a half finished building. Who on Earth could they be trying to impress.

It was Ratty. Ratty knew it was Ratty and she felt incredibly smug about it.

The assault rifles were a bit much, though.

"Hanratty Vermington, in the flesh." Menacing supervisor on an upper catwalk too! Very nice. Classic science fiction. "Quite the trouble you gave Doctor Cane. Though, I must admit his methods were... well, let's just say he doesn't enjoy the privilege of working under me."

"Why are you talking like that, dude?" A bad voice could ruin the whole character. Like he was pretending to have to juggle breathing and talking.

"Talking like what?" There it was. Normal voice. Much better. "Just— someone take her restraints off, please."

Ratty yawned the stiffness out of her jaw as her muzzle was loosened and slipped off. She rubbed her wrists, satisfied when her boot left a pink mark on the pristine white tile. "Before we begin, I am legally required to inform you that Angelcorp is not affiliated with the government. We are a private contractor with the OSTP, DoD, and United States Department of Energy in the 'States, and their equivalent organizations in Canada."

"Director Eden, I assume?"

"I prefer Director Ross, actually. Would you like me to list them?" They started towards the airlock. Ratty followed, walking backwards to take in what her limited range of motion wouldn't have let her see before.

"I'm fine, I can Google— what're those?" She pointed to a trio of person-shaped steel constructions. The one furthest to the left had an engineer hanging off it, tacking on another piece of thick steel around the neck.

"You like them? Doctor Cane and myself designed them together. Stick around long enough and you might get one of your own." The engineer tested an actuator, at the panel folded neatly into the machine's chest. They didn't look like suits. Eden had also not answered her question.

She hadn't even noticed the airlock. Something about the automated timing system was off. There was never a sealed box of air between one room and the next.

The room on the other side consisted of one main loop, a ground level balcony over a massive void below. Little segments of catwalk rose from the ring, the one closest to them dangling out over the centre of the hole. Below that, a thick orange and black column, showing thick bundles of wire and circuitry where panels were missing, dove into the darkness below. Above, two teams of engineers on separate scissor-lifts did crackling detail work on the head of a room-filling arm. There were two other arms, currently under construction.

"Project Rabbithole, I call it. We're about to make historic contact with other—"

"I uh—" Ratty cut him off. "I hate to be rude, but I got all of my science credits from uh, cheating, mainly."

That made Eden laugh: a weird snorting grunt of a geek laugh. "No, no. We have all the scientists we need, Ms. Vermington. What we don't have is power."

"I hear they just finished building a plant in Darlington." Ratty could not believe she remembered that. "Might want to ask them."

Another laugh. Incredibly unsettling. "No, no. The kind of power we need to run a machine of this scale won't exist on this planet for at least another thirty years. My employers have identified an alternative power source." He was back to the weird science fiction voice. "We are currently looking for liaisons to help us *acquire* it."

Even the laugh was fake. Trying way too hard. Nobody laughed like "HM HM HM."

"Your unique experiences—"

"I'm sorry, are you mining Hell for power?" She cut them off.

"Very insightful."

"Like *Doom*? Like the video game *Doom*?"

"I don't know what that is."

Ah.

Fuck.

The video game *Doom* would not come out for another two years.

"In any case, I have been authorized to offer you a job." Eden explained. "Yourself, and one other individual. I thought it might help to ask you directly if you had a recommendation."

Oh, so it was going to be that easy. Perfect. Ratty put her thumbs through her belt loops, rocking back onto her heels and touching her chin to her chest. This was a completely practised move. This was how people like Ratty thought. These were the motions a body went through when it was thinking.

"Sapphomet. M. C. L." Probably should have used that time

to prepare to drag up that old name, but... oh well. "They were born in Hell, they live in Toronto now."

"Well, that is convenient." he smiled, clapped his hands together. This was how people demonstrated 'satisfied' or whatever. "Please introduce yourself to the rest of your team. You will meet your new boss, Handler Smith, at a later date. I will be waiting—" their pager cut them off.

"Ah, speaking of Handler. We'll have to talk about payment some other time."

"Convenient." Business people liked to tease each other sometimes. Business people laughed at that kind of thing. Ratty laughed too.

"Feel free to explore the grounds. You have our attention, I'm sure you won't—"

"No, god no. I'm here now. Don't need to break anything else."

"Okay, perfect. I will see you in a bit."

Eden left.

Ratty waited.

Ratty followed.

---

The obsession with glass-walled offices must have been someone's undoing. Somewhere along the way a whole sect of top-tier execs got thin strips of white paint at waist height confused with opaque walls. Eden, at the very least, had desks to accent them. They were enough to hide behind. Some small courtesy paid to the corporate spies of the world.

Ratty held her ears flat to her head, crouched next to the front entrance. The entire office chimed. Eden turned their back to the door. There was almost no point to this early attempt at a video call, given the caller's intentional [NO SIGNAL] face and distorted voice.

"Handler!" Eden said, rendering the anonymity completely useless. "How's it going?"

"Well enough." The letters shook under the stress of sending both audio and video at the same time. "How's our soldier?"

"Prepped and ready."

"Exactly as I instructed?"

"Yessir." Eden nodded.

"Good. It's not particularly easy to maintain control over such a free spirit. Who did she pick?"

"A lower caste demon, shouldn't be too much trouble. They're designed to take orders."

Well that was fucking rude.

"And our alternative?" Handler asked.

"She's — I need more time. It's not easy to plant the idea that someone like that could be a god." Ratty was not the only candidate for this program. She would have to ruin her own project and whomever else's project to get this right.

"We have plenty of time, Eden. Our negotiations with Decay are nearly complete, and all that you must do is tip the first domino with the right timing." They — Decay, maybe? — hadn't been hired yet. "Be patient. She's a comedian, something will come up."

Ratty flinched as Eden's head moved. They stared at their shoes for a moment before speaking.

"I don't like that we've put all of our eggs in one basket."

"Eden—"

"Unlike you, Handler, I cannot wait forever."

The voice behind the screen scoffed. "No one said anything about that. Before I go, give me your picks for the Department of Defence and New York." The abrupt subject change hadn't bothered Eden.

"They're letting us pick?"

"They want more soldiers by '95, they'll give us anything."

"Lucky you, getting the state to pay your medical bills... Cheney, or whoever's heading the Deepwater contract right now, I'm blanking on the name, and Giuliani. Cheney will be easier. Do you think Giuliani will go ahead with COMPSTAT?"

"He will if we ask nicely." Handler said. "Thank you Eden. My negotiations with Kegawa are nearly complete. Bedel wants to talk about the paranormal program. I will keep you in the loop on both matters. Always a pleasure."

The call ended. Eden turned back to his work on a desk to the left of the entrance. He noticed neither the possum nor the pair of white-tipped ears poking up over the desk below where his holoscreen had closed.

Interesting.

Ratty backed up far enough to be out of Eden's sight line

when she stood. A few pillars and empty cubicles, and enough renovation to mask her movement. The fox — and it was obvious now she was a fox — had no such forethought. Trying to walk like she wasn't sneaking around, Ratty made a b-line for a private little spot she could run into the other spy.

"Hi!" She knocked the fox's wire frame glasses out of place behind a pillar. "I'm Ratty."

"I know who you are, and you never saw me." She straightened her glasses and wriggled violently out of the possum's grip.

"Of course." Ratty smirked. "We're just two people spying on our boss. Why would we have met?"

"Good." There was something weird in the way she refused to meet the possum's eye. Something beyond the shame of having been caught. "I agree. Goodbye." and then she was gone, down a few bends before the possum registered that she had moved.

She looked familiar. Some hazy cover story seen through the dirty glass of a newspaper box, maybe.

---

Angel's security was too modern for the time. The same way the average person wasn't vaccinated for the bubonic plague in 1991, a 2900s firewall didn't waste any space on the kind of attacks someone from the 1990s had at their disposal.

Wireless access points, for example: Angel was so tightly engineered that parts of her body communicated with each other using an archaic network of transmitters and receivers to run between points where it was too crowded to run an interior wire.

A terrified band of rebels was a lot more likely to fire an explosive or puncture the oxygen sensitive Holloway Corporation battery than to try and emulate Angelcorp's proprietary encryption, but Angelcorp itself had used iterations the same software from the beginning of their drone program (already underway in 1991) until its end. Suffice it to say the master's tools had to be modified.

"You need to sit still." Fern muttered, gently desoldering signal wires from their absolutely minuscule boards with a sewing needle on the end of a soldering iron. As each one came loose it was bundled into one central, exterior spine: a monstrosity of scrap wire and heat-shrink tubing. The simplest solution to wireless vulnerability was to wire wherever possible. "Seriously. This is the most delicate—" They dropped their soldering iron with a clatter as another twitch bumped their paw with a still-hot ball of tin.

"I have tried to, and cannot make you understand that you are literally touching the parts of me that make me move. It is not a matter of—"

"Okay, yeah. Shut up." Fern snapped, exasperated as Angel's mouth-mover tugged yet another a hair-thin wire out of their tweezers. No one could be blamed for mistaking this basement operation for some kind of illegal upper-spine surgery. Fern had jammed a modified parallel port through the back of Angel's neck, found no interior point to mount it on and so instead had it held in place with a few loops of electrical tape. To make matters worse, there was a vital data port blocking out a massive chunk of the interior working space.

They got back to work just as the needle of their record player ran into the out-groove, filling the room with a repetitive, clicking silence. "So..." Fern started again. "What's the uh—future... like?"

"Terrifying." Angel said, conversationally distant. "Small pockets of civilization remain the same, concentrated in former major cities: London, Tokyo, Moscow. These pockets are viciously curated, anyone who Angelcorp considered undesirable is either executed or exiled."

"That's fun...." Fern nodded, thoroughly annoyed with the machine's honesty. "When does that happen?"

"It's already begun. Currently, the groundwork is being laid to make Angelcorp the foremost trusted brand by 2025. By then, the yearly waves of pandemics combined with agricultural collapse will so heavily burden the population that all they will have to do is blame a hypothetical *other,* and control will be theirs. It is not all bleak, however. A rebel movement begins in 2020, and encampments occupy the rest of the world by the time I am born, surviving off the vast, nature-reclaimed wasteland. Where we are sitting now is a rebel base, buried under several kilometres of snow by the time I am first built."

"Isn't—" Fern stopped, a roll of electrical tape hanging off their finger as they wrapped up the last of the spine. "Isn't 2025 in like... thirty-ish years?"

"Yes. Although mine and Ratty's presence has thoroughly damaged the timeline, I suspect it is already too far along to stop." Angel said, still deadpan.

"Ah." Fern struggled to speak as static took over their brain. "That's cool." They were entirely absent as they snapped the hanging electrical tape from their roll, slipping one final heat-shrink tube and waving their hairdryer over it.

"Okay..." The borzoi sat up, feeling different. "You are done."

Angel sat up from the slab, took the bundle of cable in her fist and gave it a firm yank. It was not indestructible, but serviceable. Satisfied with the strength of the hodgepodge construction, she stood, turning as far as she could from side to side, once again satisfied when the new spine had barely any effect on her range of motion. She then bent forward, stopping as the spine went taut and making a note of her new limitations.

Fern, after a brief soul search, brought their full length mirror out from the bathroom, holding it up for Angel to look into. The robot turned in place, curiously tugging at the rubber edge of her electrical-tape-choker.

"Excellent work, Fern."

"Uh-huh. Don't break it."

"I hadn't planned on it."

"Okay, but you seriously cannot. The way it's anchored could fuck you up permanently."

"Again, I had not planned on breaking it."

"Okay," The borzoi set down their mirror. "Okay."

Sett fidgeted with a loose and clicky piece of panelling in the back of the black rental car, a necessary part of the façade. It smelled like old leather, furthering the starched discomfort of their disguise. They swore to themself that as soon as they got home they were changing back into the biggest sweater they owned, curling up with Ratty, and sleeping for a year.

"I hate this plan, Angel." They murmured, watching the unsuspecting Angel Computers campus creep towards the window. They worked what tightness they could from the stiff, mantled jacket. Demons were expected to dress like the future in this context, and so Sett tried.

"I know you do. It will be over soon." Angel rolled to a stop at the entrance, gravel crunching below the tires. Sett took a deep breath, making what eye contact they could with the reflective piece of black plexiglass, and opened the door.

"Ms. Sapphomet?" Bad start. "Hi, I'm Rebecca, assistant to Handler Smith. He unfortunately won't have the time to meet with us today, but I've been briefed on the particulars of your assignment. Come with me."

The door behind them shut automatically, a much-advertised quality-of-life feature. Sett kept their face neutral, turning to watch Angel drive off. She would find somewhere to park, and be back. Sett hated this plan.

"Ms. Sapphomet!" Really fucking hated this plan. "Welcome to Angel Computers Unlimited."

"We were under the impression a Director Ross would be our point of contact?" Aloof and unconcerned were marks of the future. Sett followed the receptionist back to the lobby, a tram waiting for them in the centre of the open entryway.

"Yes, Director Ross and Ms. Jozwiak will be in attendance. I'll be taking them to you and answering any questions you may have along the way."

Sett nodded, the tram jostling under their hooves as they boarded. The receptionist stood in the corner opposite the door, staring blankly at the window. Sett sat down in the middle row, facing forward in the little booth. A person more committed to this character might've pointed out that this was hardly more luxurious than a common subway train. Sett had taken the subway to the limo rental place.

"Oh, I'm sorry." They had brought a cigarette to their lips and begun to light it without noticing. Only when the lid of their metal lighter clicked did the receptionist turn away from the door. "This is a non-smoking facility."

They suppressed their urge to apologize profusely. They *wanted* to explain that they were stressed, and that it slipped their mind, and that they usually don't even smoke indoors anyway (which would have been a lie). Instead, they said "Of course." and slipped the roll-up back into their cigarette case.

They slipped the entire case away into subspace, a show of

power in exchange for a pocket. They sunk one claw into their coat, watching the sun climb higher to compete with the fluorescent lights above. It went out entirely as they crossed a cement wall.

They thumbed the rough, flaking gold of an ornately casted thread-puller in their pocket, feeling at the same time the weight of Ratty's baton in the strap of their purse.

Sett hated this plan.

If Angelcorp could be commended on anything it was their security. True, a goat with no prior training managed to get two completely different weapons deep into the complex, but in a paranormal sense, the miles of hidden complex might as well be a solid steel box. Every black site ran several dozen experimental field generators. While most of them simply spent taxpayer money causing blackouts and giving everyone in the surrounding area tumours, and every single one of them was horribly under-understood, at least one of them blocked Angel from teleporting directly into the building.

This wasn't a huge problem for a robot that could — for example — teleport above a field and comfortably fall 30 feet between that spot and the nearest rooftop. Angelcorp had nailed down her self-improvement algorithm long before she was built. Realistically, it wasn't like anything could actually stop her.

The corrugated roof buckled under her weight. She watched as the dull gold hoop that enabled her teleportation returned to some form of sub-existence before digging into the grooves. She followed the curve up and over to a little half-shed with a locked hatch, littered with a congregation of cigarette butts and their singular brick messiah.

The biomechanics in Angel's wrist clicked and strained, somewhere between the grotesque cracking of a misaligned bone and the standard operating noise of a very tightly engineered piece of machinery as it built the perfect lock pick below her skin and spat it out of her palm.

The lock gave easily, sharing a moment of understanding with the android — this was the alternative to being caved in and torn out. The hatch opened onto an elevator shaft, further confusing the fact that someone had come out here to smoke. She dropped down into it, her magnetic fall-dampening system licking at the metal walls as she came level with her floor.

*Level B1 — Security* was barely a floor at all. A small concrete outcropping connected the elevator to flimsy aluminum catwalks between different surveillance offices. Below, rows of cell blocks lined the opposite wall, only accessible via an elevator box running on a pair of perpendicular rails.

"Hey!" Angel turned as a guard barked from the other end of the catwalk. She watched calmly as he whipped out a baton and spread himself out to block off the width of her path. "Get back—" A stroke of luck that Angel crushed his windpipe, considering that "get back to your cell" are the kind of last words that get a person fast tracked to Hell. The separate parts of their face incapable of deciding who was going to bleed first as they choked on their crushed and severed throat.

"Everything alright, west-side?" The guard's walkie hissed as Angel slipped into his uniform.

"Yeah, sorry," Angel replied, her voice replaced with a perfect copy of the guard's. "Just thought I saw something. One of these fuckin' animals putting shit in my head."

"I hear that. They're putting shit in the camera guy's eyes too. Come up and see a doctor about it when you get a sec."

"For sure." Angel dropped the walkie back onto the corpse and shifted her appearance as much as she could to match. There was no replicating living eyes, but the rest of her passed pretty well for the still-drowning west-side.

"Nice one, Angel." Ferns voice blared from inside Angel's ear, barely more colourful than the day before. She paused for a moment, staring into the middle distance as she calculated a way around *Fern has constant access to the inside of my head.*

She settled on: "Why are you in my head?" The channel sat quiet for a few moments as the borzoi on the other end fumbled for an excuse.

"I installed some extra software... Just to keep track of you." They failed to actually answer the 'why.' "Uh, help you navigate, I guess... so... just keep moving forward."

"Yes, Fern. I have the map memorized. You do not need to give me directions."

"For sure. I'll butt out."
"Thank you."

---

It must've been standard issue for evil science corporation trams to exposit all the worst things about that company. A kind of bragging, probably. Look at our big machine! Look at our scientists, milling about below! Look at—

Hang on.

Sett stood from their seat, standing back from the hive of cells beyond the window. Individual barred cubicles were lit from within by harsh fluorescent lighting. Someone threw something at the tram, missing by several feet.

"What is this?" Sett asked.

"Ah, I suppose you're the person to tell about this if there is anyone to tell! The Angel Corporation is in the process of compiling the largest data set in history on paranormal entities." More than one cell on the outside edge of the block glowed a non-white colour, signalling some bioluminescence or other light source. They all went out against the concrete wall of another transport tunnel.

"And did they all... consent... to being locked up like that?" Sett asked. The receptionist took a moment to respond, receding into their skull for the moment it took to remember the correct answer.

"Our subjects are largely acquired through the legal and shelter systems. They are transients and criminals; this is their alternative to rotting away in a prison cell or being stuffed into a homeless shelter."

Sett pressed their face against the back window of the tram, struggling to catch any last glimpse of the cell block. They were not yet used to the way coincidences followed Ratty.

"We're actually quite close to our destination, you can get a closer—"

"So, no? Right?"

"No what?"

"No, they didn't consent."

"Oh. No, I'm afraid not. Still—"

"That's alright, I've heard enough." Sett sat back down, the thick bunker-style walls and ceiling suddenly suffocating. This was not a good plan.

Out into another wide-open common space, and the tram began to rise between blocks of offices.

"This is our main R&D space." The receptionist began in on a tour script, pointing out the offices of significant inventors. They became particularly excited at the blown out walls of a corner of the top floor. A fox laid into an old leather couch, desperately trying to block the light from her eyes. It all looked miniature from this distance.

Directly in front of Sett's face, a fat glob of dark red pelted the window from above. They jumped back, checking to make sure the receptionist hadn't noticed before checking where it'd come from. Angel had entered the building. Good.

"We're here!" Everything today was determined to startle the goat. They stood, brushed the dust from their lap, and nodded politely to the receptionist, who let the goat go first. It might have been a mistake to do that, actually. It wasn't good for the façade.

"Hi." This part was going to be harder than they thought. "Professor Vermington. It's nice to finally meet you." She shook their hand. Stunning, the things 'professional Ratty' and 'home Ratty' shared. She wasn't even playing a character. She was liable to get them caught.

"Rebecca, I am so sorry." Eden — Sett had seen them in pictures — rounded the corner behind Ratty, ducking past her to talk to the receptionist. "I have been running late all day." He was a small man. Tall, thin, and hunched, they were trying to copy whatever a young DiCaprio would have going on in a few years. It did not work for them.

"That's quite alright, Eden." Another polite nod. It was rude not to have asked for the receptionist's name.

"Am I—" a head poked out from the conference room door, wild eyes behind a pair of wire frame glasses. Her long hair smelled like smoke and oil and sweat, even from this distance. Somehow, the fox had made it from the office a few floors below to this conference room before everyone else. "Am I the only one that's on time today? I thought I was late."

"Yeah, Steph." Eden said, trying to avoid looking at her grin as they slipped into the conference room. "Don't you fucking say anything. Don't say a goddamn word, asshole." they hissed, too loud to be hidden by the thin walls.

"I'm early." Steph said flatly, not bothering to hide the smile in their voice.

"Why are you even here? Don't you have some LSD to go do?"

That deflated the fox somewhat. "Yeah, well... shut up." they backed out of the conference room. "My trips pay your salary. And you!" She turned on Ratty, finally recognizing her in that exact moment. "Why'd you smash up all my fucking computers? I worked hard on those designs."

Ratty let her eyes lull shut, handing down a soft smile to the angry fox. "I'm sorry, I had to set this all up somehow." It was not technically a lie. That was probably why it came so easily. "Tell you what. After this meeting is done, let's you and me get lunch and I'll apologize properly."

The fox folded in on herself, hands diving directly into her pockets. Patronizing was apparently the exact right button to press. Sett turned their face into the high collar of their jacket as a rising blush revealed their jealousy. Jealousy was a strong word, actually. Better not to get in bed with the enemy. Ratty would just have to answer for that later.

"We're terribly sorry. We forgot to introduce ourselves." Sett stepped forward, cutting the tension. "Sapphomet." They extended a hand.

"Oh, no, yes. I know." Eden shook it. "I heard about uh— or rather, Ms. Vermington told me all about you. Should we sit?"

"I'm—" the fox stammered, drawing every set of eyes back to the entrance. "I'm not going to sit, because I said everything I wanted to say, and also because your robot creeps me out." She flicked her chin at a machine in the corner, patches of realistic looking synthetic fur poking out from under metal scaffolding. She pulled her hand out of her pocket, stepping just far enough into the room to shove a business card into the possum's chest.

"It's *our* robot, Stephanie!" Eden tilted their head to call after her.

"Back when it was actually a robot!" she screamed from down the hall.

Ratty blinked down at the little slip of paper. She tilted it towards Sett, bemused. Above her phone number, Stephanie had crossed out the last name Jozwiak with a very intentional X.

Eden snapped their fingers as they sat down, bringing to life the pile of fur and scrap metal. It stood slowly, collecting a crystal bottle of whisky and three glasses from a hidden drawer and setting them down on the table between the trio.

"Rebecca, you can go as well, actually." The receptionist nodded, and stepped out. Sett would have to apologize on their way out.

It was fascinating to see the first version of an Angelcorp drone, very clearly more bio than mechanical. There was something familiar about the "pilot," too — if they could be called that. Ratty chalked it up to PTSD as she was viscerally reminded of another deer in metal bondage. She made a note of it only as another person to drag out of here.

"Thank you." Eden nodded the machine back into its corner. "Do you drink?"

"No thank you," "Not at work," Sett and Ratty said simultaneously, some calmness returning to the little goat as Eden poured themself a glass. This did not seem like the kind of person to hold their liquor.

"Smart. Keep yourself sharp." Eden waved the drone back over. "013, would you put these away?"

And that's when Ratty decided it was too familiar to be a coincidence. "What did you just call— that?" She pointed.

---

Nothing between Angel and the security station offered much resistance. The most valiant effort came from two corpses between her feet, and even then their greatest form of defence was limiting the amount of room to stand in the small office without getting blood on the android's nice shoes. Then again, the inanimate security console was doing a better job of that, simply by virtue of the fact that Angel had to be tethered to it.

"Okay, enough. Just give me control and—" Fern started, breaking their promise.

"I'm not going to do that Fern." Angel interrupted. "I was built with more knowledge—"

"Yeah? Well, why have you been running up against the same wall for like, four minutes?" Fern snapped back, giving

134

the drone a taste of their own medicine. If Angel had the ability
to feel uncomfortable, she would have been.

"How much of me are you monitoring?" she asked. Fern did
not answer, understanding that there was no good way to say
"all." Angel glared at the data visualization in her mind, feeling
the pathetic creature of meat and bone hover over her with
their stupid little laptop. "Fine, take over."

For all the dog's talents, they were incapable of putting a
noise gate on their microphone. The tapping of their keyboard
interrupted all of Angel's senses as one by one the security
feeds went dark, two out of the 12 illuminated only by a
bioluminescent paranormal in their cell.

A weight lifted from behind Angel's eyes as the few
subsystems security had been suppressing came back online
with the prison's emergency lights. She watched each screen in
turn as the corporation's prisoners began to climb their way
down from the wall of cages.

"Are you going to set the self-destruct or should I?" Fern
asked.

"How long do you think it will take to collect them all?"

"Half an hour, maybe."

"Okay." Angel walked away from the terminal as they set a
glowing red '30:00... 29:59... 29:58...' ticking away in the
corner of their vision.

"Jesus. What a day we are having, huh? I am so sorry about
this, do you mind if we—" Eden stood up into the tip of Ratty's
baton, stumbling him back into his seat.

"That's not necessary." Ratty pinned Eden in place with the
tip of her baton. "I actually have some questions about this
whole operation, if that's okay?"

"Ms. Vermington, I understand the— this—" Eden's pager
screeched in their pocket, eliciting a panic as they took in the
LCD screen. "This is absolutely not the time."

"Ratty," Sett interrupted, jacket cast off, their body already
2/3rds out the door. "I heard gunshots. I need to go, now."

"Go on then." Ratty gave a firm nod. "Go save the world, my
love." Sett's eyes flicked between the possum's for a moment,
still absolutely hating this plan, before disappearing into the

fray.

"You two know each other?" Eden asked, face switching from scared to annoyed in rapid succession. "You're making a huge mistake."

"I don't make mistakes, sorry." Ratty said, splitting their attention between the door and the conversation. Something dawned on Eden in that moment: the possum's total ignorance was a wonderful opportunity to brag.

"Have you seriously been doing all of this randomly?" They dropped suddenly into the confident and cruel tone of an unfeeling— "You murdered the leader of an entire afterlife, leaving a gaping power vacuum, just because?" Director Ross was now unshakable as an explosion rattled the glass and sent cracks through the drywall behind them.

"I had— we had reasons." Ratty asked

"Well, then thank you for that, Ms. Vermington. The explosion of your rage has allowed a mortal corporation to move in on the afterlife hierarchy for the first time in history. We are to become gods, travel freely between worlds, living forever, that sort of thing, all because you got in— no..." The jackal began to laugh, as though Ratty's motivations suddenly spread their legs in front of her. "You killed the president of hell because he fucked your bitch."

"Y'know what..." Ratty struggled to speak around her gritted teeth. "You were right. We should move." She grabbed Eden by their shirt-collar, regretting it immediately as 013 — previously slow and clunky — dropped into a fighting stance and charged at her. It twisted a fistful of her shirt, knocking the wind from her chest as she was thrown through the drywall into the next boardroom over.

"Speaking of living forever, Ms. Vermington!" A pipe had broken between rooms, setting off one of the sprinklers closest to the wall. The resulting haze of white powder and mist silhouetted Eden's retreating form. Ratty stood to give chase, the ache of breaking through drywall holding her down long enough for them to disappear. Devoid of another target, she locked eyes with 013.

Sett jammed their senses shut against the metallic rattle of the catwalk under their hooves. Something had knocked it loose from its moorings at each end, leaving it to swing freely from its anchors in the ceiling. If they fell, it would be against hard cement.

It was impossible to avoid looking down. Down was where there would be people. Down was where, behind a barricade of whatever scrap they could scrounge up, a small clump of jumpsuit clad individuals huddled around one bleeding form.

"Hands up!" Someone's bark startled the goat into action. They turned to see a line of guards struggling to keep their footing on the swaying catwalk, having discovered it as an alternative angle of attack. Their heart froze for just a moment as instinct took over, yanking a heavy needle from subspace just behind the clump and pulling the attached thread through a support chain.

The ethereal spike of metal sheared clean through the chain, tipping that corner of the catwalk to the floor below. The adjacent chain complained for a half-second before snapping and throwing three of the five guards to the cement.

Another chain snapped, this one close enough to make Sett flinch. Again on instinct they turned to run from the collapsing floor. Their stomach jumped into their chest as the metal grate below them gave out, its slats just barely wide enough to dig their claws into as it swung low over the barricade.

The goat let go as the edged metal dug into their soft keratin, falling the remaining five feet and managing to stay upright.

"Who is hurt?" Sett asked, blood pumping too fast to react appropriately to the barrel of a stolen gun jammed into their face. They turned to stare blankly at the weapon, enraptured briefly by the way the slide rattled around the rest of the metal construction. "It's okay," the hard edge melted from their tone as instinct took its seat. They then slowly, gently tipped the barrel away from their face, meeting the leader's gaze. The gazelle was clearly not used to scowling, her face suited more for a teacher than the front-woman of a prison revolt. Still, she was unconvinced.

"I can help. They're—" Sett pushed past, feeling the life ebb from what now looked more like a pool of blood than a person. They knelt, not flinching as the gun cocked behind them. If they were shot, they were shot. This couldn't wait.

"What's your name?" The leader asked.

"Sett. Just Sett." The goat set out a sewing kit out on the slowly rising chest. She was cold, but not too far gone. "What's hers?"

"She's— she's Stephanie. I'm Helena." The gazelle dropped her aim, dumbfounded as threads of gold danced in and out of bullet holes in step with the goat's own stitching.

"Stephanie as in—"

The fox stirred, cutting Sett off. "I don't want to die. I just wanted to make computers. This whole slavery shit— I just needed money to build my fuckin' computers, man. I don't want to die."

Yeah, that was likely enough.

"Move your hand, Stephanie." Sett said, a combination of firm and soft as they sensed pain radiating from their eye "You're pressing your glasses into your eye." They pulled the fox's hand away from her face. "Does anyone call you Nelly?" Sett let focus drift from their work to the gazelle as the relatively simple task of plucking glass out of an eyelid fell to someone else. They preferred to take a conversational long shot than work in a silence interrupted only by sudden volleys of gunfire to steady their hands.

"My— my students did." Nelly said, the distrust leaking out of their voice as scrap lead bubbled to the surface of each wound.

"Did you ever have two students— Pokey and Prisha?" Sett pried. They took the stunned silence as a yes, annoyed at the least talkative teacher they had ever met. "They live with me. They're doing great." Each thread dove back into the walls of the wound, making the same dragging motion and the torn interiors back together.

"They're okay?" she asked.

"Yes, I just said they're doing great.' Their hands slid under the fox's back. "Try and sit up for me, Steph." Sett helped her into a sitting position as her blood rose from their claws like smoke. Nelly knelt, pushing aside the blood-matted fur, astonished at the constellation of fully healed, star-shaped scars.

"We have more." She stood abruptly. "Can you do more?"

Sett nodded confidently, already tying a knot around their next needle.

"There's another clump of them coming up on your—" Fern was cut short as Angel stuck a fist through a cement corner, pulling only the most vital part of a guards throat through the hole, making it his own personal failure when the rest of his body failed to fold up to fit. She kicked the limp corpse off the side of the mezzanine. "Hey, I know this is a thing for you, but I am about to throw up here. Could you—"

"No." Angel rounded the corner, targeting the floor below and dropping a portal below another clump of three refugees. She watched through the golden loop as Becca helped orient them, then closed it as she watched them climb down off the pile of mattresses.

"That's everyone but Ratty and the clump that Sett's in. You're gonna want to double back and—" Fern's voice crackled and died, overtaken by the dull roar of the prison's interior for just a moment before—

"I thought so!" Angel turned towards the familiar voice: one they had only heard in simulations and through speakers. Director Eden Ross, looking distinctly less like the warehouse full of servers Angel had known them as.

"Director," she said, as terse as she could manage with the direction her programming was pushing her in.

"I don't know if we've met, but— I mean, let's skip the niceties. You're one of my designs, aren't you?" They were rapidly approaching giddiness as they advanced on the drone. "I have so many questions. When do I build you? Are you—"

Angel, in an effort to cut the conversation short, swung for Eden's throat. The machinery in her arm locked up a few millimetres from their fur. Eden smiled at their foresight, taking the mechanical hand in their own and examining the construction of the wrist.

"Fascinating... and if I just remember to—" They twisted the wrist, bringing Angel to her knees and exposing the data port just above their new spine. "Oh god, that is so cool!" The drone winced as a ribbon cable clicked into the back of their neck.

"Let go of me," she growled, a digital grinding seeping into her voice as the majority of her brain power was rerouted into dumping data. Her entire consciousness vibrated as — bit by bit — one became two, and was set back to one again, sucked out through the back of her neck.

She clenched her jaw and spun, hoping the momentum would carry her attack over the barrier. She had not realized just how firm Eden's grasp on her spine was until bundles of the shoddy wiring tore themselves loose from their moorings.

"Shit. I'm gonna have to start over." The jackal knelt, unfazed, and clicked the cable back into its slot.

She took stock of just how many connections had become severed. The principal joints on her legs and in one arm held on to a slim degree of movement, the loose arm pushing in all directions against itself. The ring of magnets in her chest that positioned her portals was also partially working. That would be enough to get out of here. "The spine is aftermarket, I'm assuming? I would offer to fix it, but I honestly wouldn't know where to start."

Angel rolled over, the internal damage worth it just to glare up at Director Ross. One more turn and she fell from the edge of the cement outcropping, barely able to pull herself to her feet with the still-working arm.

That was it: how Eden made the leap from a deer carcass in a metal suit to a fully fledged war machine, and Angel had just handed it to them. She tried desperately not to think about it, the processes of her mind killing themselves as she hobbled towards Sett.

"Angel?" Fern's voice screeched as they reconnected.

"Yes, Fern?"

"Just— just up ahead."

"Thank you, Fern."

"Are you okay? I'm seeing—"

"I damaged your spine."

"Oh shit." Angel heard the wheels of Fern's chair rattle as they rolled back from the console.

"I'm still moving." Fern was not there to respond.

Ratty stripped off the top layer of her jumpsuit she stood, glaring down the barrel of this half-machine. 013 was all too familiar now that she actually had reason to look at her properly: the same scarred body under it's mechanical reinforcements, the same tuft of faded, bleached, and dyed hair, the same hole in the top of her chest where a shell full of metal beads had ripped through her just — was it months? — earlier.

"So that's the twist? Angelcorp makes drones out of people?" Ratty spat some of the dust out of her mouth, surprised when white drywall came out a deep black-red. She received only silence in return as the drone sized her up. "Fucking stupid, if you ask me."

13's face changed as they finished their battle plan. She missed Ratty by a long shot, careening into the wall, all but thrown back to her feet as a set of superfluous limbs shot out, righted her, and broke off. Small, leg-mounted rockets flickered down to a tight blue flame as the deer stabilized herself. Not entirely sure why, the possum swept up a fistful of drywall dust from the conference table.

"Gonna assimilate me now?" Ratty failed to hide the venom in her voice, processing this in the worst way possible. 013 — clearly — was not at fault. Those who were had made themselves unavailable to kick the shit out of.

"*No.*" The deer's voice was taken over by whatever computer made up it's throat as the machine exerted more control over the flesh inside. The rockets at 013's ankles flared up again, preparing another attack.

"That's— yeah! Okay! Whatever!" 013 charged again. Ratty threw the handful of drywall dust up at one of the overhead sprinklers. The sensitive mechanism inside reacted to the dust like smoke, coughing up what was left of the water and triggering everything else in the emergency chain. The rockets faltered under the spray, giving Ratty enough time to line up her baton. It hit 013's stomach, then — stunned — in-between the scaffolding of her knee-joint. She hit the floor with a cement-cracking thud, waiting for the repair system to weld her back together, setting fire to her fur in the process. She picked Ratty up as she stood, glaring through the black glass of her eye-slots as she waited for her programming to tell her what to do next.

Ratty fumbled blindly for something to grab onto as she was thrown through the glass front wall of the conference room. The railing at the edge of the balcony was a no-go, but the same railing on the opposite side a few floors down was grippy enough to pull her tail out of her socket. That slowed her fall just enough to keep her conscious as she hit the thin layer of water covering the concrete bottom floor.

Just barely. Her head swam as she watched 013 struggle to hover down between the stacks of black tile. Leftover droplets of water found their way into the air intake on her boosters, which in turn had to boil off before they could reignite. She fell several feet at a time before it gave out completely, dropping the body from 40 feet up, more into the cement than onto it.

Ratty's core shook as she struggled to push herself upright, the push of curling herself into a sitting position threatening to tear her spine from the bottom of her skull. Her body took the hint, prioritizing the bones and muscle groups she couldn't move without. 013 was not so lucky. Every part of her body screeched against her movement, too 'prototype' to survive anything but moving whisky and a lab-environment.

"We meet again, 017, for the last time." 013 said, its voice breaking over every vowel as it tried to act like anything more threatening than a computer that had just dropped itself off a balcony. It drilled its feet into the floor as twin flywheels spun up at its hips, preparing to throw their weight around.

"What the fuck is wrong with you?" Ratty asked, more to verbalize the feeling than to get any answers. She limped until she could run, dug her boot into the ridge of a pillar, and came down on 013 from above, shattering what little progress her legs had made. The ankles that kept the machine bolted down snapped without protest, sending her to the floor with the possum on her chest. Ratty jammed the baton into the face plate, the deer battering her side. She pried it off, shattering both eyes in the process.

Very familiar. Her eyes completely hollow, filled slowly with panic as she searched for screens that weren't there.

"Look at me, Lucky." Ratty snapped, absent of a proper name to call the deer. She glared down into the empty sockets, ears flat against her skull, trying to claw some empathy out of the darkness. 013 blinked back, blankly.

One of the flywheels shot sparks into Ratty's leg as 013 rolled, the smooth metal surface struggling to drag her out from underneath the possum. A half-face blast shield folded out from under her chin in the free seconds, giving her something to stare at as similarly thick sheets of metal folded out from her limbs, pushing all the broken and bent pieces of her body back into alignment.

The jets around her ankles flickered one last time, launching 013 head first at her target. Ratty stopped her breathing in instinct, watched the charge slow to a crawl as she ducked under the living missile, clamping a fist around her hoof and setting the back of her hand on fire as she yanked the jet from the rest of the construction.

013 stood again, now incapable of anything but a slow, quiet advance.

"Come the fuck on." Ratty pleaded, her voice catching in her throat as just how shitty her stupid fucking post-life had been so far came crashing down around her. 013 brought a fist down across her chin. Ratty fell through the slick, tired of fighting, refusing to let the wound rebuild itself.

"C'mon..." The possum croaked, struggling to regain her footing on the wet concrete. "Fucking look at me."

Another strike, and Ratty was on her back. She struggled to swallow the rising guilt as the woman she failed to save stared blankly down at her.

Sett flinched behind the nearest cement wall as the last of their paranormals lowered each other into the portal. Dying wasn't an issue, but getting shot would hurt, and being sent back to Hell would be a layer of complication that they didn't need right now.

"Where's Ratty?" They asked, pulling a pair of needles from subspace and preparing for the inevitable advance of gunfire. Angel stared blankly for a half-second, responding only after a relatively harmless bullet through the silicon chest kicked her into gear:

"Just around the corner, middle of the office courtyard." Fern's voice came from the robot's mouth. She was too annoyed at her own inaction to be annoyed at Fern. Instead of snapping, she picked up a metal piece of the barricade and pulled Sett around her back, hobbling down the hall as fast as her stiffened legs would take her.

"I would like to have a conversation about boundaries, Fern." Angel's mouth finally caught up with her head. Sett almost toppled the deer as she stopped in her tracks, her front leg apparently frozen.

"You're okay." Sett murmured, ducking under Angel's arm and taking the piece of metal from her hands. "Here, hold on. I have you the rest of the way." Angel complied, limping along with one functional leg, using Sett's as their surrogate.

And there she was, right where Fern said she would be: backing her way through the concrete risers of an underground corporate courtyard, her fists clenched at her sides as 013 repeatedly brought their hammer of a fist down across her jaw.

In a sudden burst of energy, Angel picked Sett up by the collar of their near-ruined pant-suit and charged, throwing a portal behind 013 and checking her into it. She put a protective arm around Ratty as the foundations of the building began to rumble.

"What are you doing, I could have—" The shock wave from the collapsing building cut Ratty off, rattling the windows of her apartment building as it sent a rolling cloud of dust over the city. Ratty had lost track of where she was for just long enough to be dragged home.

"Ratty, was that—" Fern threw down their headset. They stood, silhouetted in a freeze frame of the deer on their monitors.

"She will be fine, Ratty." Angel cut them off. Did her best to rest a comforting hand on the possum's shoulder.

"Why not- I could have saved her." Ratty pleaded, furious with the drone.

"No, Hanratty." Something twitched behind Angel's visor, an emotion unhidden by the over engineered façade. "You couldn't have." she said.

Sett, now released from the robot's grip, gently pushed their way under Angel's arm and pulled Ratty's eyes to their own. All over again, those same tired eyes. The goat wrapped her arms around the possum, and in that moment, her spirit broke.

And she just knelt there, small, numb, until she was numb enough to stand again.

# 1992 — 20█
# Wrong Place

"What do you mean it's on two tapes?"

"What do you mean, 'what do I mean'?" Alfonzo Redic flipped through his sleeve of Commodore 64 tapes "It's a long fuckin' game, it could be on fuckin' thirty tapes."

"All these fucking tapes, how're you supposed to find it?" Alfonzo's friend Phil poked, gently kicking another sleeve of tapes next to his foot.

"Don't—" The pair jumped as a knock came at the door. "Fucking c'mon. Again?"

"Where's the tape?"

"Man, shut the fuck up. How come it's always when you come over that I get noise complaints?"

Alf was used to being kicked around by some trumped-up mall-cop looking shithead with a flashlight instead of a gun. In all likelihood, America's finest was here to tell him that his neighbours had called, and that his music was too loud, and that it smelled like weed. He would raise his eyebrows like he had any power, say something that sounded more like a threat than a warning, and go jack off to the thought of beating Alf to death.

He might have asked Alf if he knew anything about the riots going on outside. He might have pictured dragging Alf to a police station, receiving a pat on the back from some real cops, and spending the rest of his life telling that story at parties.

What he would not do — and in fact did not do — was be an eight-year-old, and not an apartment cop. Which was odd, because Alf could have sworn that the cop thing was more likely. Her hair was matted at the ends from where she had been chewing on it, hand still raised as the cheap MDF door swung open. She transitioned effortlessly into a handshake, her paw absolutely dwarfed by Alf's. He was probably a little too careful, but it had been long enough since he interacted with an eight-year-old that accidentally pulling her arm off was not out of the question.

"My name is ███████, but my friends call me El'." she started, completely unprompted, her voice incredibly casual. "I like your music."

Alf had seen this kid before: her mother worked at the community centre. The kid sat with her, usually kicking her little sneakers against the inside of the front desk. Phil stood to look over Alf, dumbstruck for a moment, staring down at this stranger's kid.

"That your new girlfriend, Alf?." Phil had no idea how to keep his mouth shut.

Alfonzo spun, snapping through gritted teeth: "Man, shut the fuck up. That's a kid. Get your act together."

"Man, my act?" Phil clicked his teeth, apparently amused by the situation. "You're the one inviting kids over."

"Phil, get off this. Swear to god.'

"Fuck. Fine"

"Hey, and don't cuss either. It is *literally a kid*."

"That's okay," El' spoke up, her thin voice cutting through the two baritones. "I know 'fuck.'"

"Okay, well, you shouldn't. Don't you tell your mom we said cuss words in front of you, alright?" Alf stood up straight, finally getting a handle on the situation as the enthusiastic child in his foyer finished up with her handshake.

"Okay." El' smiled. "What's your name?"

"I'm Alf, like the alien. You like Biggie?"

"Oh! Yeah... he's my favourite." The little rabbit bluffed. At the turn of the decade, you didn't have to be a child not to know about The Notorious B.I.G. "I heard him through the floor and I thought it would be cool if I came and listened to some. There was one like- uh—" El' tried to beat box it out. Alf laughed.

"You mean like:" He tried to match her beat: a scratched warbling slap bass that was hard to reproduce with a normal person's mouth.

"Yeah." Even that pathetic attempt got her chin moving. "Can I listen to that one?"

"Sounds like you already heard it." Alf teased.

"Yeah but like, I only heard it through the floor."

"Oh..." Alf nodded. "For sure then. C'mon."

Alf brought El' back into the apartment, helping her up onto the cleanest section of the couch as Phil balked.

"Phil, put the fucking weed away."

"Shit, like you meant an actual child."

"Man, what did I fucking say?"

"I dunno dude, who the fuck brings a kid into this kind of situation?"

"He ain't never heard Biggie before."

"Nobody heard of Biggie. The kid's like 18. Just 'cus he's got a mix tape out doesn't make him like — a person people should'a heard of." Phil ribbed.

"Well." Alf helped El' up onto the couch after watching her legs kick for a few moments. "Me and El' both like him."

He grunted as he bent down below the coffee table, fiddling with the controls of a cassette player and starting the tape from the beginning, letting the blinking "LOAD TAPE 2" at the bottom of his computer screen slip from his mind.

The three of them went through Alf's entire collection that night, Phil doing his best to focus on Super Space Invaders. For him, any high at all was too much to be anything but thoroughly uncomfortable with this intrusion.

Alf had a few staples: a completely unworn copy Licensed to Ill, a copy of Straight Outta Compton that had started to flutter in places, a few clearly pirated Public Enemy singles, but mostly his collection was made up of other people's demo tapes. Some autographed, some vandalized with red marker by some angry studio exec, all very lovingly kept.

El' sat still for most of it, asking questions as they popped into her head, making conversation as best she could with a man three times her age. It was easy to tell what she liked: she would stop abruptly in the middle of a sentence, a slow smile dawned on her face, and she rocked back and forth to the beat. Every time it happened Alf made a quick note of which tape and what the number on the counter.

Alf's collection grew thin as late night stretched into early morning. Before he knew it, Phil was asleep, and they were down to the only box in the collection that had accumulated any dust, labelled 'weird shit from quebec.' It was halfway through an annoying French chorus that another knock came at the door.

"Hi, I'm so sorry to knock this early but—" El's mom started as soon as the latch clicked. "I just woke up, and I can't find my son and—" She froze as she spotted El' over Alf's shoulder.

"███████ Elijah Sloth-Bunny Jr!" The older rabbit roared, charging through Alf and towering over her daughter. "What the fuck do you think you're doing walking out in the middle of the night? There are riots in the streets! What the fuck is wrong with you?"

El' looked up at her mother, a blank confusion on her face. "Alf and me were talking about music." El's mom glared down at her before turning her ire on Alf, burrowing him into the drywall as he gave an awkward smile.

"It's all cool, he's safe with us. We've really just been talking about music."

"Did you know about hip-hop, mama?" El' asked, knocking her mother out of rage and into confusion.

"Wh— yes I know about hip-hop, ███████. C'mon, we're going."

El' gave a weak "Okay" as her mother dragged her out by the wrist. "I'll see you later Alf."

"See you around silly rabbit."

---

The newly installed phone on El's beside table rattled in her grip as she struggled to catch her breath. She could hear her uncle Alf's phone in the apartment below, felt her breath catch in her throat as the creak of his floor groaned up through their shared wall.

Click.

"Alf speaking."

"Alf, it's El'."

The old dog let out a long sigh.

"El', it's fuckin' four in the morning. What the fuck do you want?"

"You know the like, queer thing that happened today? Or, yesterday..."

"Yeah, the fag march. What about it?"

"So like..." El' started, running through all the ways to come out in her mind like a Rolodex. "What's a transgender?"

148

Alf let that one sit for a moment, mulling it over. Another creak from the rapidly aging apartment building pushed both of them through that silence.

"Man, I don't fuckin' know. It's 4 a.m." Alf repeated.

"Didn't you date one of them once?"

"Nah El' I just— that's not— that's nothing. Why couldn't this wait?"

"Do you still have her number?"

"El' why the fuck— What is going on?"

"I think I might be one." The words fell out of her mouth like vomit as nausea took over her body. Her heart kicked at the walls of the chest as the background hiss of the call r se to a roar. Time stretched on as—

"Real shit?" Alf asked.

"Yes, dude." El' replied. She was comfortable in the silence now, having overwritten the last thing sh said.

"So like," Alf started cautio sly. "You got a w name or something?"

"Yeah... I'm thinking lea or."

" lright. Tight. Go the f k to sleep Eleanor." Alf h up, s ing one last volley of c t ro h the ceiling as h b d back in o bed.

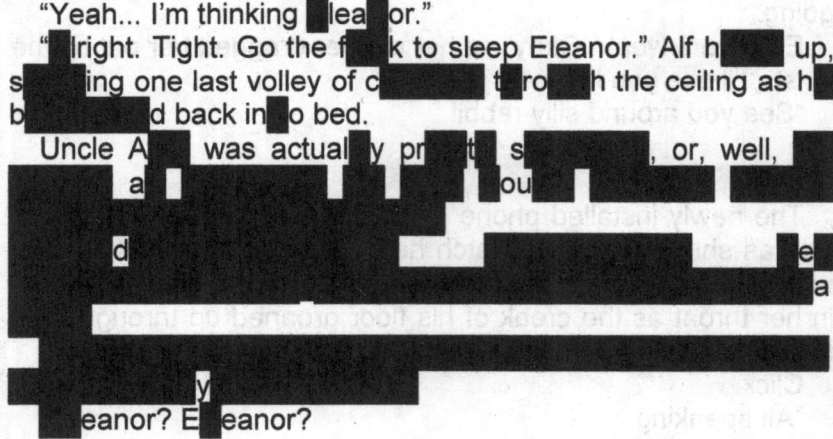

Uncle A was actual y pr t s , or, well,
a ou
d e
a
y
eanor? E eanor?

---

"Eleanor. C'mon. Wake up, we're leaving." The blurry image of her panicked mother came into focus as Eleanor blinked the sleep from her eyes. She watched, dazed as the older woman stood on tiptoes to pull a spare backpack from the top shelf of her closet.

"Wh— what?" Mom dropped the backpack on the bed, stuffing it with a recent pile of either done or not-done laundry by the fistful.

"We're going on vacation." Her mother said, not making eye contact.

"What? No, I have like- class to go to."

"It's fine, I already called the school. It's fine, okay?" A familiar annoyance rose in her mother's voice as she rolled out of bed.

"What about— me and Uncle A were supposed to—"

"He's busy."

"What do you mean, we've been—"

"Eleanor. He's busy." she snapped. An awful an▮iety rose in the rabbit's chest with the panicked confusion.

"Mom, can you please just tell me what the fuck is ▮

"So, Eleanor." the neatly disguised voice of a god began with all the politeness of a talk-show host. "Can you tell us why you want to work for Warner Brothers?"

"Well, I've ▮

Fuck.

This isn't working like this.

Hold on.

---

"Next stop, Olive and Warner Bros 1."

[The bus's brakes squeal as it stops.]
[Its doors hiss open.]

"Thanks."

[Eleanor's shoes thump down onto the curb.]
[She takes a deep breath, then begins to jog.]
[She struggles to breathe as she arrives at the security checkpoint.]

150

"You're late."

[A voice inside the security booth says.]

"I know I'm late. It was the bus. Buzz me in."

[Beat.]
[Buzzer.]

"Thank you."

---

[Clipboards clatter in and out of a plastic organizer.]
[Eleanor gives a long sigh.]

"Who's... Ellie! Where are you? You have my clipboard again."
"Here! Sorry."

[Ellie holds her breath as they trade clipboards.]
[Eleanor clicks her tongue, annoyed.]

"I don't— Eleanor, Ellie. They're different names. Look—"

[Paper rustles as Eleanor shows Ellie her clipboard.]

"You're up in the booth today. You shouldn't even be here."
"You shouldn't have headphones on."

[Ellie struggles to get a foothold in the conversation.]

"First of all, I have one headphone on. Second, you tell your supervisor and I'm sure she'll let me know."

[Beat.]

"I don't wanna be a prick. Just next time: Eleanor, Ellie, okay?"
"Alright."
"Okay. Good job yesterday by the way— I saw that cover. That was quick work."

"Thank you."

[The music in Eleanor's ear dims with a pop as she drops her right headphone.]

"Okay. Big smile. Pretty bunny."

[She psyches herself up before entering a door labelled "Green 1"]
[Inside, a quiet conversation between a mother and father stops abruptly.]
[Their child holds his breath.]

"Hi everyone! My name is Eleanor, I'm gonna be looking after you until Ellen gets a second, okay?"

[The silence is broken by the son's cough.]
[Beat.]

"And you must be our special guest. Are you a big fan of Ms. DeGenerous?"

[The father clears his throat.]

"We just came to make an appeal."

[The mother's breath hitches in her throat.]
[It becomes clear that everyone in this family is holding back some emotion.]
[Beat.]
[Beat.]
[Beat.]

"Some water would be nice."
"For sure. I'll be right back."

[Eleanor goes to leave, then stops as she checks her clipboard.]
[She has long since learned to hide her feelings at work.]

"I might be just one second. Gotta make sure my team is doing what they should."

[Eleanor's music comes back to its full volume.]
[A team of two men strain to hoist a wooden crate into the air.]

"What are you guys doing?"
"Hoisting the thing."
"Masks."
"What? Why? These go by the door. Who told you to do that?"
"Ellen."

[Beat.]
"Did she tell you why?"
"Nope."
"Well there's—"

[Eleanor strains.]
[She ties rope around an anchor.]

"There's no time to bring it down now. We'll give them out at first break."

[One of the men sighs, frustrated.]

"If you wanna question her, go right ahead."
"I'm on my way to her dressing room right now, dude, and I'm sorry, who's your supervisor?"
"I answer to a higher power than you."
"Not on my set you don't."

[Beat.]

"She's not in her dressing room. She's in hair and makeup."
"Thank you."

[Eleanor stops as she hears the rope strains again.]
[She snaps her fingers.]

"I said leave that."
"Go talk to her!"

---

[Eleanor stops at the door to hair and makeup.]

"Where's the fucking— did someone take the gum bowl?"

[She takes her own pack of chewing gum from her pocket and pops two pieces before knocking]

"Hi, Ms. DeGenerous?"
"Hi! Ellen, right?"
"It's actually Eleanor, Eleanor Sloth-Bunny."

[Eleanor laughs nervously.]
[Ellen laughs genuinely.]

"Of course. How could I forget? I love that scent by the way!"
"Thank you, I always keep a pack on me."
"I know! Y'know, that's really considerate of you. Don't tell anyone else, but I think you're destined for great things after this show."
"Thank you. I—"
"I don't think we run half this smoothly on days where you're not here."
"Thank you."

[Beat.]

"The uh, mask box, for the picture thing."
"Right! Of course."
"Evan said you told—"
"I did!"

[Ellen laughs.]

"I have some special plans for it. I just want it to be out of the way. It'll come down before the show starts."

154

"Alright. You let me know when."
"You'll be the first to know! I hate to go over your head but no one could find you."
"I was late. The—"
"The bus!"

[Ellen laughs.]

"Of course... Did you meet Devin yet? Lovely kid. Such a shame."
"I did. I'm actually supposed to be getting them water."
"Oh! I'm so sorry I didn't realize you were on an errand. You can go, so sorry to keep you."

[Beat.]
[Beat.]
[Beat.]

"Are you going to give them time?"
"Oh!"

[Ellen laughs.]

"It's not as easy as it looks. We have to find some to give first."
"I hope you find some."
"I'm sure we will."

[Ellen laughs.]

"Good."
"Good! Hey, why don't you come see me after the show?"
"If I have time, of course."
"I'm sure you will."

[Beat.]

"Well get going! I'm sure poor Devin and his parents are parched by now!"

"What did she say?"
"Leave it up."
"Told you."
"Whatever."

[Eleanor's walkie talkie drowns out her music.]

"Talent moving. We're on in five."
"Go get your make-a-wish kid seated."
"Sorry, again, who's supervising who?"

---

"Hey folks! We're running a little behind so we'll have someone bring you those waters once you're already seated, okay?"
"Alright."
"Cool, cool. We've got you right in the front row. If you look really close you might even be able to see me behind the scenes, running the show."

[Beat.]
[The son coughs.]

"Alright! Let's get moving!"

---

"Family seated."
"Eleanor? Could I get you over here real quick?"
"Sure. Hold on."

[The front of stage façade gives a hollow thump.]
[Eleanor strains, then hops to her feet.]

"What's up?"
"Ellen just wanted to see you uh, over here."
"Here?"
"Yeah, she was very specific about... right here. I'll go get her."
"Okay."

[Eleanor waits a few moments before turning her music on on low.]

156

[She taps her toe, more out of impatience than rhythm.]

"C'mon..."

[Her walkie beeps.]

"Talent moving."
"I hate this."

[Eleanor is momentarily distracted as she hears the rope strain above her head.]

"That's comforting..."

[Eleanor's walkie beeps.]
[A distant voice asks:]

"Could I see that for a second?"

[Ellen speaks directly into the walkie.]

"Hi Eleanor! I'll be right over, okay?"

[Click.]

"Yes ma'am."

[Click.]
[Beat.]

"What is she doing over there?"

[Eleanor is once again distracted as the rope strains above her head.]
[Her walkie beeps again, startling her.]

"Can we get the light test guys over here?"

[Beat.]

"Is she… Okay, yeah. Hi? What is she looking at?"

[Eleanor's walkie beeps.]
[Crackles and static.]

"I'm looking at you, Eleanor!"

[Ellen laughs.]
[Eleanor does not laugh.]
[The rope strains.]
[Beat.]
[The son coughs.]
[Her walkie beeps.]

"You shouldn't take your eyes off me, Eleanor."

[Ellen laughs.]
[Eleanor does not laugh.]
[The rope snaps.]
[Eleanor's head is

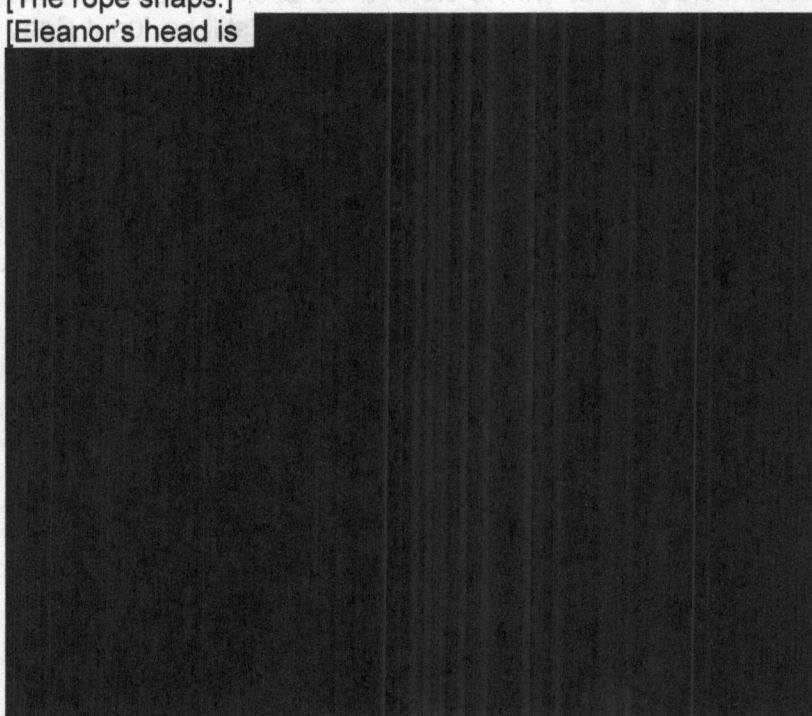

# 2004
# Reunion

Ratty circled slowly around a glass display case in the Royal Ontario Museum's *Earth's Treasures* section, more fascinated with the way her thoughts reflected off the sharp black curves of the stone than the actual beauty of it. She wasn't explicitly brought here to do anything illegal today, but museums had insurance, and royal museums — when they couldn't be fucked to display paranormal artifacts properly — preferred payouts to dead patrons.

It was easier to be a paranormal criminal than a paranormal courier. True, most crimes were a lot easier when one was incredibly hard to kill, but it would probably still be fun if Ratty could die. She was not, for the foreseeable future, getting her degree back. The skills that underlay that degree, however, still existed. She was still good at connecting with people — at least on a surface level. That skill was just not accredited.

Sett had warned her not to do anything explicitly death-defying several times before that point. She had two years to kick the habit before YouTube came into being and shot all chances of "Possum Survives Falling Off Building" going by quietly. That would be the end of her career.

Of course, there would be no career in the first place without the possum who could dive off a six story building or charge through a hail of gunfire. The people who hired her did so because they knew a Ratty job was a job that got done no matter what.

"You sure I can't convince you to part with it?" She did her best impression of a disappointed collector; insurance claims were about theatre. The curator huffed, glaring at the possum. They were never happy to work together. She refused to play the part. That kind of thing could get you in trouble with your insurance company if you weren't careful, and it was also a fucking downer.

It was business: the curator cared about history, the courier cared about feeding her rapidly growing family of rejects and freaks. Neither of them thought about insurance until they had to.

"Isn't there something you could do? 'Enchanted glass' or something of that tone..." The curator drawled. Ratty stopped circling, leaning in so her face was almost flush against the glass. The stone's curse licked at her cheeks, struggling to interface with the collection of supernatural ailments she had accrued over her years in the field. It was a hungry energy. Anyone who touched it had either retired early or aged out in a matter of minutes.

"I mean... it's a rock." Ratty stood, her curiosity now satisfied enough to keep her well away from the evil little thing. "The only thing that makes it special is that it's got a charm, and it occasionally kills people." Ratty turned to the rest of the cases. The same could be said for any of Earth's treasures that had its own display case.

"And it's history." The curator was incapable of not huffing every word she spoke.

"No, yeah—" Ratty peeled a white card off the side of the displaced case, showing it to the curator. "I read it. For sure. If you wanted someone to uh— fact check your history... I'm 20th century, actually— real quick, can you—" She stuck the white card to the glass, blocking the curators line of sight. "Tell me what's behind the card."

"It's a stone."

Ratty nodded, then peeled the card back off. "And one more time?"

"It's a priceless, one-of-a-kind, gemstone."

"See, charm." She tossed the card aside, focusing instead on the drywall divider between this and the next-door storage room, tapping along it until she found a decent gap between two studs.

"You only like it because it's telling you to like it. Plus, and I don't wanna be rude, but—" Then to the entrance, she knelt to go through her duffle bag and slipped a pair of thick, black, elbow length gloves. "For one thing, you guys pay like shit and have no expertise. Did y'all know that the last time my partner

was here, y'all made them fucking cry? Little goth thing—
trillion years old? They went home and cried."

She slipped on the other glove as she fumed. "Oh, and that's
not to mention—" Ratty pushed past the curator and pointed
out the massive black totem pole that ran up the centre of the
stairwell. "—THAT is a near constant-barrage on the spiritual
immune systems of everyone who comes near this building. I'm
no expert in indigenous stuff, and this is definitely a tangent,
but building your museum around a monument to like, an
ongoing cultural genocide is..." Ratty sucked air through her
teeth, trying to cool off with the stale air. Even dressed
"professionally" she stood out when compared to the kind of
person who belonged in a blocked off museum wing. Some of
the regulars had clustered around the entrance to stare.

"Anyway..." she stammered, returning to the centre of the
room and placing her palm flat on the side of the glass display
case. The curator's impatience turned to frustration, attempting
to glare the soul out of the possum she realized what Ratty was
about to do. "...here's what I'm willing to do for you."

Ratty tipped the display case, shattering it across the floor
like a dropped bag of marbles. "I'm gonna steal this..." She
scooped up the stone, centring it in the thickest part of the
glove, "and then, uh, leave."

The three — Ratty, the curator, her guard — stood in
stunned silence for just a moment as a few extra patrons
gathered at the door to see what kind of glass was broken.

And then, as though responding to a starting pistol, everyone
moved at once.

Ratty charged headlong directly into the weakest part of the
drywall. She winced as something heavy and metal on the
other side stopped her motion.

"Y'know what I just remembered, actually—" Her voice
caught in her now broken and dust-filled nose as she attempted
to yank herself loose. The curator's personal guard advanced
to corner her. "I actually — and thank you for pointing this out
— totally forgot my bag." She dug the toe of her boot into the
remaining drywall and hopped up over the guard, scooping the
black duffle by the handle and backing out of the room.

A cloud of curious museum-goers had blocked the way to the
stairs, a few of them even trying to play hero with their

wingspan, and the only other option was the adjacent hall where she would have to try her luck with more drywall...

There was also a balcony...

A careful person could survive a 20 foot drop onto marble, probably.

She backed up as close as she could get to the stone half-wall of the rotunda. Then, throwing up a quick sign-of-the-horns, toppled herself over the edge in a perfect stage-dive. Her tail mostly broke her fall. Not enough to completely avoid a definitely-audible crack when she hit the ground, but enough to justify a minor limp as she rolled back to her feet.

Someone shot. Someone else screamed something like "are you insane?" Ratty felt a dull pain in her shoulder.

Whatever shook itself out of her spine pulled itself back into alignment as she limped towards the west exit. A pair of cops had already responded to the alarm, both bewildered, one holding a half open ticket-book. He dropped it and pulled his gun from its holster as full function returned to the possum's legs.

Someone shot. Someone else screamed, wordlessly this time. Ratty felt a dull pain in her shoulder.

North exit, then. The price of admission kept the front hall largely empty. No one here to stand between her and gunfire, which — she needed to clarify internally — was a good thing.

The limited number of museum guards on staff barricaded the entrance, supported in part by a swarm of Toronto's finest on the other side of the glass barrier. Somehow, exactly two people had thought to cover the exit to the ground-floor gift shop.

Ratty once again chose to forget that she was practising pretending to be mortal as she tossed herself through the glass, through a pile of plush toys, and back to her feet.

"Sorry!" She felt a pang of guilt at the clerk's face: a combination of 'oh shit there's a robbery going on' and 'man, I just fucking stacked those.' She shattered her third piece of glass in the past several minutes pushing through the front door. In a moment of pure convenience, the now-free push-bar dropped into her hands. She swung blindly at the pair of awaiting cops.

Police officers were unlike everyone she had ever fought in

one key way: they were cowards. The kind that — even after watching her trip and fall all the way over the hood of a taxi — were deterred enough by a door handle to keep back if they couldn't be absolutely assured the balance of power was in their favour.

"Sorry!" Ratty waved at the driver, turned, dropped her weapon, and sprinted across the rest of the street.

That was another thing she was very good at doing: disappearing.

She ducked down an alleyway, pulling the pin from a tear gas canister and dropping it at the entryway. The few curious pedestrians that'd huddled around to gawk scattered as the burn hit their throat. That was a few seconds of privacy.

She stripped off her gloves, turning the left one inside out to conceal the rock, then the right one over that, finishing the protection by the entire arrangement into her duffle. She then tossed the bag a few feet in front of her, used the moment it took to catch up to it to remove her blazer and undo enough buttons to turn professional into slutty, then pulled a ball cap and sunglasses from the duffle as she slung it back over her shoulder. She stuffed her hair through the hole in the back of her cap, and ducked into a restaurant's side entrance.

"You said 'maybe'!" the woman behind the counter screamed. The disguise would be enough to walk home with after some heat died down. Before that happened, she needed to get out of sight.

"I did say 'maybe.'" Ratty took a deep breath, something sticky jamming and unjamming the mechanism that moved her lungs. "Maybe means 'maybe yes.' Where's my food?"

The woman sighed, affronted, and ducked under the bar. "What did you have?"

"The uh— it was the small bulgogi." A paper bag hopped up to the ledge, the words 'SM BUL' scribbled on the side with black marker. Ratty grabbed it.

"We are even." the woman said.

"We're more than even! I absolutely owe you, you perfect angel." Ratty started backing towards the ladder.

"Alright, fine. Go up to the roof." She flicked her hand at the intruder.

Ratty stuffed the lip of the bag into her mouth. Up the ladder, through a window at the top, out onto the fire escape, up metal stairs, and into the roof. Gravel shifting under her feet, she poked her head over the side just long enough to see the front entrance swarmed with police.

She stood back, put her hands on her knees, and tried not to breathe too loudly. The owner would shut and lock the door just in front of the ladder. It was made out of the same wood siding as the walls for this exact purpose. It used to be for employees of the museum, lying low whenever a collector — or entire culture — that'd been stolen from got angry. That ladder was supposed to go down, though.

"Fuck." The little bag of Korean beef and rice dropped between her boots as she panted.

She picked it back up, gripping it as tightly as she could in one hand. She took off sprinting at the edge of the roof opposite the museum. She had tried this trick as a kid and never gotten much luck out of it, but she had also changed significantly since dying.

There were pieces of ductwork on the roof of her own building that were as far apart as this roof and the next. She paced it out, late one night, when someone could measure the width of a street without being hit.

The depth didn't matter, just the distance.

She jumped, held her breath, and jammed her eyes shut in the silence. Her ears fluttered in the gentle breeze, the only thing passing through the completely still air. Her stomach did not drop. She opened her eyes halfway across, still roughly level with where she had started.

No idea why this worked. Didn't matter, just did.

No time for gravity to pull her down, she figured. That was napkin math.

Another cough crept in under her tongue. She let go of the held breath, and rolled onto the opposite roof. The gravel burrowed itself into her forearms as she tried to force a stop. No time to waste. She pulled the cover off a fake air conditioning unit and climbed inside.

There would be another bus in 14 minutes that she would have to miss. Probably the two that came after that one, too. In about 45 minutes, it would go from active search to passive investigation. There would be a bus showing up around that time, too.

She opened her food, the smell masked by the other myriad restaurant smells leaking from other rooftop vents, and the smidge of teargas in her throat, and also the fact that she couldn't breathe. The lazy fan spinning above her head wasn't helping much.

At least she got away with it..

---

It took Sett one look at the stone to recognize it. They spent a half-hour cross-checking it with the relevant historical texts, looking for some excuse not to track down the creature who made it. Now, following at the back of a pack of tourists, they dreaded the moment at which their guide would ask the goat if they wanted to pose next to a sun bleached cardboard standee of the god of Decay.

"No thank you," they mouthed, getting closer to the front of the pack. "No thank you."

Angel, thankfully, took over when it was actually time to speak. The goat hated TV studios. The corporatization of performance turned art into mechanism in the worst way possible, begging to be greased with the blood of the worker. Low effort talk-shows were the worst of this: people's lives condensed into timber, hammered together to prop up a soulless figurehead, an icon of other people's hard work.

If it were up to them they would never appear even remotely close to a TV studio. On those rare occasions they wanted to perform, hollow floors that boomed when their audience stomped were more than satisfying.

All of this to avoid thinking about *The Ellen DeGenerous Show*.

They broke off after the photo-op, taking advantage of the huddle around an ancient printing kiosk to escape detection. Ratty had shown them how to walk with the straight back of someone who looked like they were supposed to be there. A woman who frequently startled people in public standing still regularly earned the right to brag about "getting in anywhere" with a pair of black headphones and a confident stride.

A half-minute of weaving through a traffic jam of producers, various stagehands, and other TV etcetera landed the pair at the door to Ellen's dressing room. The cheap drywall construction just barely dammed a familiar energy: hungry, dark, tendrils licking at their cheeks, the whole tired act. Sett wondered how many the elder god sitting comfortably on the other side had killed.

The lesser demon gripped and un-gripped the doorknob, failing to calm their nerves. Their heart froze in their chest as the metal clipped the end of their claws on its dive into the room. The star-marked door in front of them had swung open. In its place was the god's grotesque, hairless face, contorted into a wide, toothy smile. Sett's stomach churned further as they took in the odd, stump of a snout in the centre of her face, the strange, monkey-like ear flaps, its brilliantly white soulless eyes.

The creature had called itself *human* when it first manifested here: the first of its kind. For some reason, TV audiences really got a kick out of that.

"Well don't just stand out there! Come in!"

There was no trusting an elder god. In mortal realms their otherworldly foresight allowed them to play a few steps ahead of almost everyone else. Still, Sett was here to talk, and talking over the door frame wasn't going to get them far, so — against their better judgment — Sett followed Ellen back into her dressing room.

It was cushy; real in the same way that a third floor office with no windows was real. A revolting combination of medical brightness and claustrophobia, topped off with the outdated trappings of Hollywoodian Americana.

Beautiful, isn't it?

Sett turned to check the corners they had not yet seen. Like any point in the studio not visible to roving tourists, the reverse wall was decorated with framed covers of magazines and newspapers. Among a healthy dose of scandal — there really is no such thing as bad press — above the door, pride of place, the host knelt in a black jumpsuit next to three red words.

Beautiful, isn't it?

Not those words, of course. Ellen understands that we are not going to fight over control of this narrative. She makes the decision, without coaxing, to stay within the bounds of regular speech for the foreseeable future, because she understands the concept of turf.

"Beautiful, isn't it?" Her peppy drawl cut through the silence of the dressing room, now isolated from the rest of the building. "Bland! Very 'Earth'." She smiled, taking a beat to savour her next move. "How is Hell, by the way?"

Sett caught Ellen's stylist's eye for a moment, content to ignore everything said between the pair as they returned to perfectly dishevelling the god's hair. Sett swallowed their rising anxiety.

"I left, actually."

"Right, of course. You'll have to forgive me, these kinds of things just tend to slip my mind." That was an outright lie, and Ellen made no attempt to cover it up. "Awfully boring though, last time you were there, wasn't it?" This was cat and mouse for her.

"I'm here for a reason, Ellen." Sett said, their voice taking on a rare sharp edge.

"Oh c'mon. Play with me." The god whined.

"Ellen."

"Okay, yes, fine. Let's skip ahead: you and I banter a bit, you show me a photo, I act surprised: 'Oh it's my [whatever] of [whatever]! Wherever did you find it?' as though I don't know. Yes, it's mine, no it can't be neutralized, put it in an arcane-proofed safe and hope nobody ever finds out about it." Ellen lectured, annoyed enough with the goat's impatience that she forgot to pretend to breathe. She also did not get away with saying "[" or "]" and therefore said "square bracket" out loud like a fucking dolt.

"Now, c'mon... How did you find Hell?" Ellen pressed. Sett sighed, taking their hand out of their purse and abandoning the PDA they had been cradling.

"Fine. Last time I was in Hell it was—" Sett started.

"Oh do please be specific." Ellen cut them off.

"Yes. Fine. A prison in the middle, experience machine, border camps, big wall." They did their best to keep the imagery out of their mind. Ellen's toothy smile turned smug as she steepled her fingers, holding one string of Sett's tied around each.

"What about John? How's John?" She was just teasing now. Even with the god-like ability to warp reality, she couldn't conceal the knowledge of John's fate behind her eyes. Truly, she just liked watching the goat squirm.

"John has been... removed from his former position." Sett said, matter of fact.

"Oh yes! I know! Isn't it fantastic? And they — I mean the damned — they still don't suspect anything?" Ellen prodded.

That threw Sett completely off their composure.

"Pardon me?" They stuttered.

"Oh— oh, isn't that rich." Ellen's voice crackled in her throat: the low tones of a predator catching their sharp edges on the smooth surface of reality. "No, nothing. I just thought — you of all demons would know what Hell *really* looked like."

What Hell *really* looked like?

The latter portion of their stay was admittedly better than the first, but they had made a deal with the devil. That's how it's supposed to be: you compromise your morals in a way that makes you feel better in the short term, and worse in the long term.

What Hell *really* looked like?

It was primitive, sure. More sinners meant less time for each individual one. There was miles of blue sky between a really shitty prison and *No Exit*, but John was never one to waste time on fancy torture. Pain worked.

What Hell *really* looked like?

Pain worked.

An ache formed behind Sett's eyes as they tried to push Decay's poison out of their brain. She could tell the little goat was aching not to cry in front of her, sucking up every moment as they ran over this internal turmoil.

What Hell *really* looked like?

And then the door opened behind them.

"Boss?" A rabbit poked her head through, snapping the situation like the latex skin of a sterile rubber glove. "Curtains in five, we need you for lighting."

"Oh, yes, of course." Ellen smiled, dropping the previous conversation. "Eleanor, would you actually come in for just a moment? This is Sett—" the elder god gestured. "—we used to work together."

Eleanor nodded impatiently at the goat. "How's it going?"

"Never so bad it couldn't be worse." Sett gave a weak smile, taking some comfort in the way their voice parroted their partner's in this moment.

"Sett and I were just talking about you, actually." Ellen lied. It was pointless to argue: she had an agenda, and Eleanor had so far acted smart enough to avoid trusting a single thing her boss said. The four let the silence hang after that, Angel not at all breaking from form as she continued to stand motionless in her corner.

"Okay... Well... Curtains in five." Eleanor said, clearly trying to keep annoyance out of her voice.

"I look forward to seeing you then!" Ellen grinned, waving cheerfully as the rabbit left. That was fucking weird.

"Such a bright rising star, Sapph. You're really going to want to watch that one." Ellen smiled.

"I don't watch your show." Sett snapped back, cold and curt.

"Oh no, I know, but I mean you're really going to— eh-heh." Ellen cut herself off, stifling a giggle as something jumped into her mind.

Don't touch that dial, Sett. You're really going to want to see how this plays out.

With that, the elder god stood, crossed the room, and stopped deliberately on the threshold.

"Was there anything you needed?" Ellen asked, both feet over the line.

"What did you mean about Hell?" Sett asked, dropping their pride for a shot at reassurance.

"Hm! So sorry, that's all the time we have for today." Ellen stood stock still in the doorway as if to emphasize: I have plenty of time, I just want to keep fucking with you. "Oh! and thank you so much for the whole — I mean I know it's been YEARS at this point, but the Angelcorp breakout has been really good for me. I'm almost certain we were up for the same job there, and your little girlfriend really toed my audition up over the line." She winked. "See you around."

And with that, she was gone, leaving Sett to contemplate in stunned silence. They jumped for the second time in a quarter hour as Angel set a gentle hand on them from behind. "Jesus Christ, Angel," they snapped, moving a hand to their chest in an effort to slow their heart.

"Would you like to go home now?" The drone asked,

unfazed.

"Wh— where's Ratty?" Sett asked.

"She's at home, talking to Fern about your shared anni—" Angel stopped herself, a white progress bar flashing across her visor.

Angel had been several hundred years out of date when she had travelled back from the 2900s. She was several hundred years older now, living rough, far out of range of anyone who could put her back together in the intended way.

"She is talking to Ms. Jozwiak about a fascinating new open-source operating system she has just completed." She corrected herself.

"Can you— can you call her?" Sett stammered.

"Of course."

---

"Ratty speaking" The possum mouthed a silent apology at Fern, flashing a blank phone screen at the borzoi by way of explanation. Caller ID was one of the things she missed most about the future. Fern, having had the concept explained to them before, nodded and went back to their work.

"Ratty." Sett's voice held a clear note of slow-burning panic, obvious enough to make Fern hunch their shoulders over their keyboard from several meters away.

"What's up, hun?" Ratty asked.

"If we were still in Hell, you would tell me." Sett said, telling instead of asking, and in so doing willing it to be true.

"Sett— what?" Ratty stammered, caught completely off guard.

"I mean— I know you love me, I know. And, I've been a really good partner to you, and this is a really long con if—" the goat's breath hitched in their throat as panic overtook them. "Are we still in Hell?" They begged.

Ratty turned it over in her mind for just a second, stopping short of a quick no.

It wouldn't be convincing, and it wasn't like Ratty had any proof to the contrary. Earth was Hell in its own way, even outside the paranormal sector.

Bush was president, Harper was coming up as PM, Angel Computers had effectively put a surveillance device in every home. Two of those three were making more money than god off the global war on terror, having orchestrated the flash point themselves.

To be honest, Earth might just be Hell.

"I mean, are you—"

"No, Sett. I'm your partner. I was born in Toronto General Hospital in 1998. I grew up just south of Etobicoke and spent almost every summer in a small town outside Bobcaygeon. I have never loved anyone like I love you." Ratty said, her voice firm and caring as it spilled out of her. "If you are in Hell, then we are in Hell together, and I am as willing as ever to bust out with you."

"I—" Sett paused, steadying themself again as they came back down ever so slowly from their panic attack. Deep breaths. Deep breaths. Of course Ratty wasn't a demon, of course she wasn't a double agent from Hell. Their relationship had not been perfect, but then again, wouldn't a demon want to make it perfect and save themself the trouble?

"Decay got in your head, I'm guessing?" Ratty asked.

"Yeah, sorry." Sett said, "She mentioned something about- we were up for the same job?"

The line sat silent for a few seconds.

"As in, Angelcorp?"

"I think so."

They listened to the ambient hum of the other room, rising to fill the gap where Ratty's voice was as she processed that.

"Do you still want to do date night?" she asked, finally.

"Can I pick the spot?" "The spot" was very likely to be a stress-free meal they could bring home with them.

"Yeah, for sure."

"And after that?" Physical affection was a well known treatment for anxiety.

"Whatever you want." The possum's voice wrapped Sett like a blanket, even through the crackling speakers of their cell phone.

---

They struggled to hang up, spending most of their energy on anxiety-quelling breathing exercises. The room had pulled away for a moment, leaving Sett in a blank void, accompanied only — now more often than not during a panic attack — by their reflection in rich tones of black and grey.

They had forgotten where they were for just a moment. No big deal. Angel, the dressing room, the stylist desperately trying not to look the little goat in the eyes.

"I— I'm sorry about that." Sett stammered, gripping their cell phone like the single free pole on a packed subway, no less anxious than if they were at risk of being tossed to the floor and trampled at the next station.

The stylist waved their hand, still not meeting Sett's gaze. "Not the worst thing I've uh— worked through." They shrugged.

That really was all there was to be done here. As shitty as Ellen was, "It's my [whatever] of [whatever]!" and "Yes it's mine, no it can't be neutralized, put it in an arcane-proofed safe and hope nobody ever finds out about it." was really all Sett had come to California for. They really hated the weather: a dry and constant reminder of the arrogance of plastic capitalism. It was a small blessing that Ellen was so short.

"So... Angel..." Sett turned to their mechanical friend. "Portal? Uh, my bedroom, if you could." They wanted to have some time alone to think. Ratty would be working for another half-hour trying to find a place in their safe where the stone wouldn't react with anything else, and they wanted to be comfortable.

Angel nodded, pulling a slow-to-populate gold ring from the wall and having to physically hold it open with her shaking arms as Sett stepped through.

"Might want to have Fern or Steph look at that, huh?" they asked.

"Yes." Angel nodded, letting the portal close, leaving Sett to their thoughts.

They sat on the edge of their bed, staring at the ripples in the aging carpet as their mind continued to race. Time sped along, kept them busy, kept them tired. There was a new kind of anguish in their eyes: they had rarely kept up with Earth affairs, but they had been through eternity enough times to know how this world played out. What they were doing to help was minuscule.

They checked their watch, and when their arm fell back down, their grey reflection was there, hovering over them, little more than a pair of hoof-prints in the carpet. It was always when they were emptiest that the other Sett showed up. They rarely did anything, just stood, sometimes sat, always watched.

The original opened the top drawer of their bedside table, full of empty tobacco tins, and fumbled for a full one with no luck. They threw themself back into the duvet.

Ratty never made the bed; Sett didn't see the point in it either. They picked up Ratty's pillow, burying their snout in the soft fabric and taking a deep inhale of her scent. Demons did not smell like Ratty smelled. Demons, Sett thought, smelled like sulphur, fire and brimstone, all that. Ratty — or at least her pillow — smelled like... oily hair.

Sett rolled over, catching the lower half of their squashed face in the mirror. They wondered if they smelled like fire and brimstone and sulphur, and whether they had just gotten too used to it to be able to tell. Ratty would have told her. She could be mean like that, without thinking. A demon wouldn't accidentally blurt out the kinds of things Ratty blurted out. The goat avoided moving anything but their eyes as the possum poked her head into the room. A demon would have been able to see the other Sett.

"Hey! There you are." She smiled, same as ever. "Sorry, is it alone time?"

Would a demon ask? Would a demon, knowing that they were on the verge of being found out, pretend to be nicer than they actually were. Would a possum, understanding that her partner was in a shitty place, turn up all of the things they loved about her?

She didn't look like a demon. Sett's eyes flitted back to the mirror: a reminder of what a demon looked like.

"No, I think I'm done." Sett said, a solemn note creeping into their voice. They relinquished Ratty's pillow as the possum plopped down on the bed next to them.

"I just wanted to say — and then I'll be done with work talk — but that was insane. I send you a picture of a weird black rock and you're immediately in the books like— anyway." Ratty dove into her duffle bag. To Sett's relief, she came up with a plush bat, more faux-taxidermy than children's toy. They let themself be pulled the pair closer with the possum's tail.

"I brought you a friend." Ratty smiled, ducking behind the

creature and wiggling its arms with her fingers. The bag went onto the floor, where Ratty would later kick it under their bed.

"Your nose is broken." Sett noticed, now examining the crook of it up close.

"You're not even going to say hi?" Ratty teased. Sett rolled their eyes, then got down on the plush's eyeline.

"Hello." Sett bounced softly in place, a mix of pedantic, quietly delighted, and still trailing melancholy. "What's your name?" They asked.

"I dunno!" Ratty said, the falsetto she put on completely fitting of the tiny creature. "Ratty didn't think of one while she was stealing me!"

Ratty sat up, twisting her wrists so she could still puppet the plush and look it in the eyes. She glared down at the bat, miming a little bit of shame into the stiff felt. "We said we weren't going to tell them about the stealing." Ratty scolded the black plastic eyes. Sett snatched the creature from Ratty, taking on a faux protective stance as they plopped it into their lap.

Sett looked down at the gift in their lap as they stroked its bristly little head. They stopped, took Ratty's chin in their hand, and pulled her lips against theirs.

This probably wasn't Hell. Horns hit chest and Ratty toppled over, settling into her groove in the bed. They smiled down at Ratty, their eyes damp from the stress of the day. Ratty smiled back. Deep breaths.

The fabric of her cheap shirt dragged along the underside of Sett's claws as they crept under her jacket. They stopped at the possum's chest, waiting to feel her heart thrum to life under their palm. They felt the stiff edges of a pair of frayed holes through the front. Ratty grabbed her partner's wrist a few moments too late, eyes flicking to the ceiling fan as Sett found her out.

"What do you want to do for dinner tonight?" She tried desperately to change the subject.

"Are these bullet holes?" Sett asked.

"They're— yeah. Great shot grouping, though. Very sexy, I think I look like— like a 'last girl' kinda thing, y'know?"

"Ratty!" the goat whined, pulling back and stripping the jacket back far enough to see her blood stains. They turned her over to look at the entry-wound, shocked by how visibly out of shape her spine was. "Your back too?"

"Hey, it's okay!" She grunted through the second word as the goat pushed an upper vertebra back into place. Her hand went over her shoulder, gently guiding the goat's wrist up into her hair, letting it go on the comforting cluster of nerves where her skull met her neck. "It was an accident."

It barely hurt to forgive her this time. If they didn't, it would have been an argument. They didn't need that today. It wasn't impossible to believe that two shots and a bad fall could be had as part of an accident.

If left alone, it would defuse itself. Sett collapsed slowly against the possum's back, careful not to hurt her or move their hand from its place.

"Fine." they muttered into their pillow. "Okay."

They shut their eyes and let that sit.

"Can we order in?"

"Yeah," God, the possum was so warm. "For sure."

"For sure." Sett parroted.

There's a bar just outside Toronto, and there's no telling if it existed in 2004, but they had this deal where you can get 60 wings for 30 bucks. Sett ate roughly once a month. While they were very rarely actually 'hungry' in the way a mortal would define it, they either picked at whatever Ratty made — enjoying its taste more than relying on it to fill them up — or ate a lot.

That was date night, and it was comfortable.

Sett's mouth bled profusely, tingeing everything they swallowed with a stinging edge of copper. It made it hard to go out for dinner, waiters would pass them over, kitchen staff would huddle at the door, just watching. It was embarrassing.

So, 60 chicken wings, a half-pound of weed, whatever was cheap and microwaveable at the nearest convenience store, sweatpants, and a "nothing movie" was as close to a perfect date as Sett ever needed.

They sat, fascinatedly picking chicken from a bone as though performing brain surgery, a near-dead blunt hanging off their lip.

"I think they changed the recipe." Ratty said, scrutinizing her own wing.

"You think?" Sett turned, barely noticing as a clump of ash went tumbling down the front of their chest and between the couch cushions.

"Yeah, it tastes more like ketchup this time." Ratty nodded, the clear and clinical tone of a non-partisan third party taking over from wherever in her brain her journalism training was stored.

"Ketchup..." Sett turned back to their own wing. "Huh. I don't actually taste any ketchup at all." They tossed the now completely clean bone into a pile with its siblings, wiping their claws on their cheap, light grey sweatpants. They froze half way through, realizing what they had done.

"Aw fuck, your pants." Ratty pointed, her paw formed into a weird spider-claw to keep three of her five fingers clean.

"It's uh, fine." Sett shrugged, slipping them off and taking with it the remaining sauce, thoroughly soiling the ball of fabric. "I was done with them anyway."

"Nice butt, babe." Ratty snatched the pants and tossed them directly into their shared laundry pile.

"Yes, thank you." Sett gave a mock bow. "I grew it myself."

"Well, excellent work." Ratty teased, worming a finger into one of the leg-holes of their underwear and giving it a teasing snap. Sett's bow deepened until the tip of their elbow touched the floor, where they tipped right over it and fell.

"You're all the way out there, eh kid?" Ratty asked, eliciting a short eruption of giggles from her partner's crumpled form.

"Yeah..." They nodded, staring down at the possum's paws. "Can you... turn off the movie?"

"Sure." Ratty stepped over Sett, hitting the red light on the plug-strip that powered everything in their TV cabinet. Sett shot up behind her, crossing to the kitchen and flicking on the radio that hung from the bottom of the cabinets.

"Rrrrrradio time." Sett grumbled, dragging out the R. "It's time for radio." They wandered dizzily back to the living room and tripped over a folded piece of carpet directly into her partner's arms.

"Whoa, there." Ratty said, suddenly taking on her partner's entire weight. They looked up into Ratty's eyes, their own a massive pair of quivering half-moons.

"Ratty Vermin, you're my hero." They said, injecting all the faux-reverence they had ever received into their voice at once.

"Okay, buddy." Ratty smiled, doing her best not to laugh.

"You need to get more high so I'm not— I'm not being a silly goat." Sett said, pressing their face into Ratty's chest.

"I would, but if I take my hands off of you you're gonna fall." Ratty said.

"Easy solution." Sett slumped over, just barely able to reach Ratty's almost untouched joint with the tips of their claws. They came back up, honestly astonished when Ratty stood firm. "You're strong." They said, perching the joint on her lips and lighting it with a bundle of threads.

Ratty sucked it back, still not quite sure how to properly smoke weed after something like 80 years of experience, and came up coughing.

"Wow, fuck." She shimmied a free hand away from her partner and plucked the joint from her lips, taking a second to try and read whatever she had written on the filter. It was Headband: the strain of weed that when smoked, makes you feel like you're wearing a headband.

"Go on, Ratty." Sett teased, trying to nudge Ratty along.

"'Go on' what?" Ratty asked.

"Make some of those noises you make when weed hits you good." Sett said, gently nudging the possum's wrist with their fist.

"What are you talking about?"

"Y'know, like—"

"Like you want me to do some crowd-work here? 'What'd they make antidepressants for when there's weed and goats already?' like I'm Robird Williams?"

"No, no, like—" Sett stood up to their full height, clearing their throat like a true thespian, their weak vocal chords coiling in preparation for the loudest sound they had ever attempted before. "Ahem."

"SEEEEEWIE!" They hog-called, throwing their head back before snapping to attention in time to finish: "I'll tell you what, that's some good— some good— pfft." They broke down laughing mid-sentence.

"And what if it doesn't hit me good, madame?" Ratty prodded. "What if I'm having one of my crazy li'l scheming highs?"

"Oh please! Please do one! Just for me?" Their bloodshot moon-eyes pleaded up into the possum's.

"Alright, uh—" Ratty started. "Fuckin'ay! That'll knock you right over and put you back up with your head on the floor," she rambled, the curvature of the sentence resting perfectly in her northern drawl. Sett choked on their laughter, burying their face back in Ratty's chest.

"That'll— ooo-ee. That'll put your therapist out of a job." The goat's laughter turned into a wordless scream, just barely broken up by hitches of delight as they stomped their hooves.

"You gotta stop. I'm gonna pee." Sett managed, out of breath between fits.

"That'll—" Ratty started, barely able to contain her own laughter at this point. "That'll make your partner pee."

"RATTY!" The goat's voice snapped, leaving only the quiet squeak of the floorboards under their bouncing hooves as their psychic voice took over again. The pair let the laughter die naturally, Ratty trying to wave it out of their face while Sett shuddered quietly into her chest.

The radio returned gently as it faded, something slow-dance-y, accepting the silence as a gift as the possum began to rock, guiding the goat in a simple waltz.

"This is nice." Sett said, listening more to their fiancée's heartbeat than the music going on behind them. Sett had always had poor circulation: an odd thing for a creature constructed to perfection. Ratty's temperature varied wildly by the seasons. On a cool summer evening, rated cold-handed by other mortals, she was like a warm and airy blanket to Sett. She was incredibly comfortable to slow dance with.

"I'm glad this is like... a thing." Ratty mumbled into the top of Sett's head.

"We could just do this." Sett ventured. "We have savings."

"We don't... have that much, Sett." Ratty said.

"We could sell the tea shop."

"You want to retire?" Ratty turned the possibility over in her mind. Sett was more than old enough for it.

"I want you to retire. Or change jobs— you could—" They stopped, realizing as their fiancée did that their master's degree would not exist until at least 2023. It would actually not likely exist at all, if the new Ratty didn't start making the same waves as the original.

There was no telling exactly how unkillable the possum actually was. It was reckless to keep putting herself in harm's way. Any one of the near-death experiences they had gone through together — or any of the ones Ratty had faced alone — could have been the last: the fall that caught her neck exactly right, the randomly enchanted artifact that overwrote whatever power she had gained from her connection to Sett, not to mention fates worse than death.

There had been times where an unsatisfied employer of the courier had threatened throwing her into the lake, letting her drown and come back to life over and over again until she was found. Granted, that employer had since been replaced, and nobody quite so cruel had shown up since, but it left its mark. Ratty would sometimes refuse to shower because of it. When she swam, she would hold her breath for as long as possible, just to see how much time she would have to escape.

Ratty, Sett thought, had been through enough. In the less-than-humble opinion of one lower caste demon, Ratty had "made good." She — of course — disagreed. Every good thing she had tried to do in her time back on Earth had failed. Sett was a totem of their goodness, and until at least they could live comfortably, it would have been wrong for Ratty to rest.

Something akin to guilt shot through the goat as Ratty tensed up in their arms.

"Sorry." They offered meekly.

"No, it's okay. I want you to talk to me when—" Ratty started, realizing too late that she was doing her diplomat voice. "Do you think we would be happy like that?" she asked.

"I would be happy if I knew you were safe."

"Is that all?" Ratty pulled back, flashing her overconfident grin and eagerly turning onto the first exit from this line of thought. "It takes a hell of a lot to kill me. It took a bomb going off in my chest the first time, and that was before I was soul-bound to the whole... whatever keeps you alive."

It wasn't about the fall, really. It was the sudden stop that changed Sett's mood. It just felt bad. That was the only word for it. The undead spent a surprising amount of time thinking about death, and it sat in Sett's gut like a curling stone.

"I don't—" Ratty choked on her words, bringing Sett back from their thoughts, realizing only now that their fiancée had started to shudder. "I don't feel good when I slow down." She had gone through the same thought process in reverse. Her options were to give up or leave Sett in a constant state of panic. That didn't sit too well either. "I don't know what else to do."

"We can — let's talk about this when we're sober." Sett said.

"Yeah." Ratty sighed, a weight lifted off their chest for the time being. "Sorry. This— this is the only difference I can make."

"Are you and Fern still—"

"No, we haven't had a lead in..." the possum trailed off, eyes growing ever tired. "I'm sorry." she repeated.

"What about Angelcorp? Any leads there?"

"No, Sett." The drug in her system made it hard to hide how hard that was to answer. "We're... we aren't doing that anymore." She swallowed hard. "It's whatever. We kicked them hard. That's more than most people ever do in their lives. I'm giving up, okay?"

That was not the kind of decision to be made in this state.

"I— I don't know." She walked it back almost immediately. "I'm sorry. Can we just talk about this when we're sober?"

"Yes, we should. I apologize."

"It's okay, when we're sober."

"When we're sober." The goat nodded.

They re-embraced, each content to forget about it for the time being and just sway as the drug in their system pulled their thoughts along the current. Soon enough, it had slipped completely from either of their minds, now only present in the memories of the walls around them.

Sett dropped slowly, their exhaustion getting the better of them as they decided suddenly to sit on the ground. They snatched the little card that had come with the weed off the coffee table, turning it over in their claws.

"This is supposed to be a sativa?" They asked, their head rolling around on the limits of their neck.

"Apparently." Ratty smiled down at the blasted little goat, "You're really in and out of it here, huh Settler?"

"Heh. *Settler*." Sett repeated, reaching up to play with the hem of Ratty's boxers. "Why are you still wearing pants?"

"I— these are my boxers." Ratty said, her face suddenly flushed.

"And?" Sett prodded, their long tongue rolling out of their still bleeding mouth. Ratty's face rumpled, pushing the gloss out of her eyes, having already forgotten why it was there to begin with.

"You are such a pervert." Ratty stammered, entirely unable to keep up a façade while this high.

"And?" the goat repeated, reaching up the back of her leg and tugging a pinch-full of butt furs. "Take 'em off." They commanded, her usual god-domme tone replaced with the tight growl of an inebriated pervert.

"We are in a state where I don't think that would be right." Ratty said, gently nudging Sett's hand away from her genitals. She had the gentlest ways of turning down sex.

"Fair." Sett waved the thought away, slurping their tongue back into their mouth. "Then, my banjo, and a tall black coffee, Hanratty."

"Oh, yes ma'am." The possum curtseyed sarcastically as she made her way to the bedroom. "We gonna get soul-of-the-south-Sett tonight?" she called, struggling with the clasp that held Sett's banjo to its stand.

"You know it, baby!" Sett shouted, the quiet thrum of their tail against the floor more fitting for the lead singer of a hair-metal band than a tiny goat about to pluck out some melancholy about the real devil being capitalism. They brought the instrument to their lap, fumbling clumsily into a sloppy rhythm. "Can you— can you make me a tea too?"

"Sure, hun." Ratty went straight to the kitchen, setting the coffee maker going and watching the near-black fluid swirl around the cloudy pot. She suddenly found herself absent from her surroundings, snapped into her own head with the click of the plastic switch on their kettle.

Sett didn't get it.

Ratty wasn't going to tell them that, but giving up now would be fatalist. This was it, for the rest of her life, until it killed her. The idea that she had "made good" already or that she ever would was stupid. She wasn't so chauvinistic as to believe Sett needed protection, but Ratty knew she would die one day, she planned on dying one day, and before that happened the world needed to be better.

She ended up in Hell for a reason. She was a bad person. Despite everything she had done before being nabbed by Angelcorp — her teaching, her reporting, every single thing that ran her fingers raw — she was at least firm in the knowledge that her good deeds were buried under 13 feet of dead bodies.

It wasn't as simple as doing a story, or stealing a rock, or whatever. She had come to the understanding that writing a story never actually changed anything. Unless you were the first person to find something out, there were a hundred other more talented college graduates willing to do her job for less.

You hurt them when you told one of their secrets. You hurt them when you blew up their R&D campus. Opportunities like that were once in a lifetime. By her count, she had had three or four big ones by this point.

She was a machine trending towards death.

That was a stupid and far too extreme understanding of the things she was feeling. She resolved instead to feel about a tenth of that now, as not to ruin the evening.

She didn't know where to hit. It was hard to find another spot.

It wasn't fair, but then again, that was life.

Ratty returned to the kitchen as the kettle began to whistle. In the living room, she set the kettle down on a coaster next to a strainer full of dried green tea. She had, without realizing, dumped a few tablespoons of hot chocolate powder into a second mug and left it in the kitchen. Coffee pot and straw in the other hand, she raised it to Sett's lips, still hanging open, muttering something about a "little plush goat..." and still with a little sauce in one corner. They took a deep sip of coffee, relishing in the way it tore at their throat.

"You still hungry?" Ratty asked, setting the coffee down on the coffee table, thus fulfilling its purpose.

"Little bit, but I want to play right now." they said, a sudden stride of confidence taking over their hands.

For a moment, Ratty just watched. Her eyes stopped along the individual grey furs that crossed the border around Sett's snout, glowing in the moonlight of their eyes.

"Mind if I vamp?" Lyrics to the tune had begun to bubble in the back of Ratty's mind.

"Sing, my angel, sing." Sett replied, morphing around the slow little bluegrass standard they had started with.

Ratty began to rock with the tempo, every gritty folk song she had ever heard bubbling to the front of her mind as words began to assemble themselves in her mouth:

"Okay, uh..." She started simple. Amateurish lyrics about the devil's thumb, fingers numb, etcetera. Running away, being set free, feeling shackles. All hallmarks of this kind of music. She stopped. This sounded silly said out loud.

"I can't—"

"Keep going. Keep going." Sett pushed.

"You sure?"

"I'm sure."

"Alright, I gotta find a spot to jump back in."

"Here... here." Sett punctuated the start of each bar.

"Babe if you're saying 'here', then I can't jump in."

"Okay, well, then... I will be quiet, I guess."

"Don't stop playing, though..." And again, a little better this time. About a dead creature she saw come back to life. About a smile wider than she had ever seen before. Sett's head began to bounce as they drummed out a supporting beat on the body of their banjo.

"Keep it going." they muttered.

"Oh, you couldn't stop me with a concrete wall." The devil followed them to Earth, tried to tear them apart, was both a metaphor for capitalism and a literal guy who just existed. All very cliche in Ratty's mind. Well trodden, unoriginal, etcetera. Sett failed to notice. Her tone shifted after that bar, slowing the tempo for a more melodic section. She pulled the lyrics and melody whole-cloth from somewhere else.

"You didn't write that part, did you?"

"No, it's from an old World War II song."

She veered into darkness, the sight shifting from behind her eyes. She spoke the plan as it was made in her head: too high at that point to stick to Sett in any meaningful way. Something about money, and death. These were the mainstays of this kind of music. It was perfectly normal at the time. Now overpowered, the radio just sat and listened, playing for no one.

At some point, after it had been cleared for broadcast, the midnight DJ announced that, in distant, sunny California, a stagehand by the name of Eleanor Sloth-Bunny Jr. had been crushed to death on the set of *the Ellen DeGenerous Show*.

# 202█-2009
# Television

"This podcast has language some might find offensive.

"It was fall 2004. Eleanor Sloth-Bunny Jr. had just been promoted to production editor on *the Ellen DeGenerous Show*, having shown early promise as an intern at Warner Brothers.

"She was aware of the show's reputation around trans women, according to a diary released by her mother, but she thought she might be the exception to the rule. She thought maybe the rumours she heard had been greatly exaggerated.

"She was wrong.

"In her fourth week as production editor, Eleanor Sloth-Bunny Jr. was crushed to death when a piece of the set fell from above the stage.

"It was the first Ellen Show death to make national headlines.

"But, why? Why was every other death so easily covered up? And how did Warner Brothers keep getting away with these 'accidents?'

"For *MICE Magazine* in partnership with the Bedel Corporation, I'm Hanratty Vermington. This is *The Dark Side*, season three."

---

"So is it a podcast or a documentary?"

"The podcast is a tie-in with the documentary"

"I like it." Glen's tired eyes hung lazily over the grey placeholder cover on his podcast player. He turned the phone over, eyes flicking up to meet those of an excited, young Hanratty Vermington. The kid had talent, there was no denying that, but this pitch had landed on Dan's desk at least a hundred times at this point, and it was either going to end with a green-light, or Vermington pitching it to another outlet. There was just one problem.

"Listen, I trust you as a reporter, and I'm glad I'm not hearing it in this one so far, but you cannot do the ghost shit." Ratty's excited grin faltered just long enough for a seasoned journalist to pick up. She noticed that he noticed, and so dropped the façade entirely, searching for something in the pockets of her mind that she hadn't shown her editor.

"You watched the clips I sent you from that last broadcast before the hiatus, right?" Ratty asked.

"Yeah, it's a scary looking glitch Ratty. They get them all the time on Ellen."

"The fact that it happens often enough for you to say that it is a thing that just happens on Ellen is exactly why we should be investigating it."

Dan chewed his lip, closed the phone and handed it back to the possum.

"You know I took a risk in hiring you, right?"

"I know. I appreciate—"

"The kind of people you hang around,"

"They're good people, Glen— good sources—"

"You have a reputation. People think you're a broken clock —"

"When was the last time I was badly wrong?"

"You do good work, I'm not denying that. One of these days though, Ratty, one of your little conspiracy theories isn't gonna pan out the way you think, and you'll end up either blacklisted or dead in a ditch, depending on who you piss off." It was as angry as the tired old man was capable of. "The thugs you choose to write about will turn their backs on you as soon as we publish something they don't like." That was blatantly untrue.

The tabby took last month's magazine out of a desk drawer and slapped it down between the two of them. "We make news, Ratty. If you want to make *Ghost Adventures*, or *Former Bank Robber Tells All!* go to *BuzzFeed.*"

Ratty stopped hiding her disappointment. "Fine, no ghosts."

"It's insensitive." Glen said. "Sloth-Bunny's family lives a few hours north, I don't want them knocking on my door, telling me they heard a ghost story about their daughter. There are plenty of other angles, take a different one."

"Yeah, okay." Ratty struggled to hide her annoyance. She

thought she could trust him with this. She had built her way up to ghosts with a half-decade of solid reporting— it wasn't like she was some ghost-obsessed lunatic, her job was to write down what she saw and speak coherently into a microphone about it. Despite every job opportunity to fly over her head, every pitch email to go unread, she valued what those professors who couldn't set aside their morals for the industry bullshit had taught her.

Granted, not letting her cover a ghost story was not the greatest example of how the business of journalism was broken, but it was in roughly the same category.

She planned, while she was in California, to do the ghost angle anyway, sacrifice her free time in exchange for a better story. If push came to shove, her 1,400 or so Twitter followers would eat that shit up.

She never got that chance. As soon as she clicked shut the cover on an international SIM card she was informed by a slew of emails and texts that Warner Brothers had bought, and subsequently spiked the project while she was going through security in Toronto. Every employee, former-employee, and family member of the victims she had spent months scouting out had left her a voicemail rescinding their commitment to be interviewed.

She spent a week in her hotel room while the magazine's money people figured out how to pay for a flight home, chain-smoking something semi-legal and screaming into cheap, scratchy linens. They left her there for months, not bothering to assign her stories while her paycheck got smaller and smaller. Her work visa ran out. In a conversation mediated by a too-polite ICE agent, MICE agreed to fly her home. She had had a date that night. The girl had teased Ratty about cancelling. She was going to have to.

Her job was gone by the time she got back to Toronto. Maybe it was time for her to go back to school. She had always wanted to.

A flashlight was just about useless in combating the thick dust of the abandoned halls of Warner Brother's abandoned maintenance trenches. After *the Ellen DeGenerous Show* moved out of Studio 11 and the trench-side entrance had just up and vanished, an entire wing of the loop had been left to rot. Such waste was typical underground in the land of the permanent sun.

Something was — and had been — fucking with the geometry of this place. The affected part of the maintenance trenches ran in a loop around the entire lot. Ratty and Sett had circled, on foot, three times so far. Moving backwards didn't work: going clockwise, Studio 12 came directly after Studio 10. Counterclockwise, Studio 12 was followed by Studio 12, which was in turn followed by Studio 12, and so on. While wide enough to accommodate a few lanes of golf-carts, it was devoid of working ones.

The pair's absent conversation had become tense with frustration, not wanting to miss the studio for a fourth time: "What're the odds it's an actual ghost?" Ratty asked, slowing to a crawl as they passed Studio 9.

"Not sure." Sett mused. "one in six?"

"One in six?" The possum turned, incredulous.

"What's wrong with one in six?"

"I dunno, one in six is like, the way they do dentists in commercials," she teased.

"I don't know if there is really any other way to do odds." Sett cocked an eyebrow, a little offended at being so thoroughly called out for their dentist-style odds-calling.

"You could say it as like, 12 per cent." Ratty said, running the math completely wrong in her head.

"Maybe," the goat muttered, distracted enough trying to figure out just how far behind them Studio 10 was.

"Wild how one in six is only two percent off one in ten." Ratty chose not to re-run the math as she mentally found more and more flaws in whatever had brought her to $\frac{1}{6} = 12\%$. It didn't matter, really. Other things to worry about — mainly this flashlight. On top of going exactly six inches through the dust, it had begun to flicker, and—

"Wait!" Sett grabbed Ratty by the front of her sweater, both strangling and scaring the shit out of her as she fell through the dust. They turned, shining the beam of their flashlight on a pair of white painted numerals denoting the end of Studio 10's section of the tunnel. Ratty, on the other hand, saw 12.

"Fuck. Did we go too far again?"

"No, I think..." Sett yanked on Ratty's hood, pulling her back through the threshold. Studio 12's sign tessellated itself infinitely across her eyes in the instant before she hit the ground, accompanied by a single segment of some rapper's deep, booming voice repeating and overlapping for the second and a half it took to drag Ratty back to the Studio 10 side of the barrier.

"Shit, sorry." Sett winced as their partner's elbow cracked off the cement floor.

"It's fine. I think it's like..." She reached out with her unaffected arm as her opposite elbow began to knit itself back together. Her hand stopped on the surface of the divide, like putting a flat palm against water.

It was obvious as soon as their eyes adjusted to looking at something barely-there. Dust clung to it in layers, thinnest in the several person-shaped outlines they had punched through the surface in the last hour. The edges of those cutouts now wobbled where Ratty's dropped flashlight highlighted them. "...It's there. See it?"

"Oh, yes. Yes I do." Sett knelt, curious. They placed their own palm against it, surprised as it pushed back against their weight. "This is... fascinating. How do you think we break it?" their eyes wandered up the wall.

They closed their fist through the gelatin, attempting to grab any fistful of threads that might be running through it. No dice. The goat then slipped down to their knees, running their eyes along the line where the barrier met the ceiling, then down the wall and across the floor. The possum's legs appeared at a weird angle where they were stuck through the barrier, like a straw poking out of a glass.

Hm.

"May I see your flashlight?" Sett asked.

"You may." Ratty mimicked her partner's tone reflexively. Sett took it, then switched both of their lights in unison.

"Oh, wow, okay. Did not know you were going to do that." Ratty said, just barely panicking as her eyes locked onto Sett's. From the corner of their vision, they watched the possum calm down as her eyes adjusted. Sett knelt forward with their own light, pushing it lamp-side-up into the wall. It was even more obvious on such a small scale: like someone sawed out the middle inch of the flashlight and tried to glue it back together. They pushed until the little round bulb disappeared completely between the barrier.

Sett pressed their thumb into the rubber button, then a click, a crack like a piece of wood snapping, and a baritone voice echoing through the trench.

"I got it!" Sett beamed, their tail thrumming with sudden excitement. They were doing that more, Ratty had noticed. That was nice.

"You got it!" She smiled back. Her ears perked up. "Is that Biggie Smalls?"

"You would know better than I would." Sett shrugged to their feet.

"Yeah. That's Biggie. How have you never— we've been here for like, 30 years at this point."

"The Notorious B.I.G has only been around for 15 of them." Sett said. "When you were doing that story, did anything come up to suggest that uh... any of the victims might like Biggie?" The goat was struck by the sudden practical empathy of that fact. People like things, dead people also like things.

"Oh yeah, totally. One of the moms — I think it was Eleanor Sloth-Bunny's? Anyway she let me copy this mixtape she made." Ratty said, leading the way into the studio.

"Are we going to assume it's Eleanor Sloth-Bunny, then?"

"Might as well be." She braced herself against the stuck entrance door, doing her best to push it open quietly. Something on the other side had it jammed closed, so in lieu of the silent approach, Ratty took a half-step back, braced herself on the interior of the hallway, and kicked the door off its hinges.

That was pretty hot, Sett thought. Sett didn't want that kind of behaviour to be attractive to them, but it was.

"It certainly smells like a ghost in here." They said, pushing past Ratty with an eager curiosity as their snout was assailed by the stench.

"What do ghosts smell like?"

"Well, uh— like this." They were too preoccupied rubbing the smell of mildew out of their nose to explain further. It smelled disconcertingly like a regular abandoned building. Then again, almost all of the American continent was deeply haunted. Most places probably had a ghost or two.

The stage was in an incredibly advanced state of decay for the amount of time it had sat empty. The walls that hadn't collapsed under the weight of their own rot were coated in peeling flakes of uncared for drywall paint. The scaffolding that held up the stage lights had long since settled into their position, having crashed through the stage's thin vinyl veneer.

Below the X where they crossed, the ghost sat with her legs folded on a pile of torn up seat-cushions. It had been a long time since Ratty had spent her nights poring over every scrap of information on Eleanor Sloth-Bunny Jr., but this was almost certainly her.

The ghost took a deep hitching breath as Biggie's backup singers faded into silence, crying softly as she waited for her voice to be drowned out by the next song from her digitally hissing, barely-held-together CD player.

"Time to get to work." Ratty rolled up her sleeves and gave her partner a quick nod and a half-bow, signalling — perhaps unnecessarily — *after you.* They gave a short curtsy in response, enjoying the little rituals they shared.

Sett straightened their collar on approach, bumping their shoulders just enough to fill their pile of sweaters with air. A lot of people liked to see something cuddly when they weren't expecting visitors.

"Hello, Eleanor." They kept back a good couple feet. It was better to be safe than sorry, considering how many ways things could break bad. The ghost jumped, startled by what must've been her first visitors since the studio was abandoned. She turned slowly, staring over her shoulder with the same care and anxiety as a frightened animal. Heavy, rotting brown tear tracks burrowed through her ethereal fur, most obvious against the sickly white of her piebald pattern. Everywhere but her lazy left eye and the tips of her ears and fingers, the rabbit's ashy purple-black masked the stains of time. Her frizzy, white hair fell in a pair of bangs that just barely hid a pair of deep black, terrified eyes.

"My name is Sett, this is my fiancée, Ratty." They pointed, struggling socially as the ghost barely reacted to their words. She turned, her fear beginning a slow gradient towards curiosity. Her eyes weren't actually black on closer inspection, they were hollow; empty sockets held open with a pair of massive invisible marbles.

"Are you able to speak?" They asked.

The ghost shook her head slowly, shuttering like a mechanical doll.

"Not a problem. Are you Eleanor?"

The ghost didn't respond to this. Her eyes remained empty, her expression blank.

"That's... also not a problem. My fiancée and I run a centre — a home, even — for displaced paranormal entities. We were hoping you might like to come live—" The ghost stopped them with a finger, lifting a spectral chain in her hand, giving it a tug as if to illustrate:

"You're stuck." Ratty stepped in, hopping up onto the stage and startling her up onto her haunches with the sudden approach. The ghost nodded as their composure returned, stabilizing the crouch with the tips of their fingers.

"I bet I could just..." Ratty stomped the floorboard where the ghost's chain slipped below the stage, cracking it and spooking the two others. The ghosts form began to shake, tearing in horizontal lines, getting less and less *person* with each echo. Her fingers slipped from the ground as tension built in the back of her calves.

Ratty lifted her foot again.

"Ratty, wait!" Sett shouted a half-second too late. The boot came down, the floorboards came up, and a laminated piece of paper sprung from the gap. It shot directly to the ghost's face as though attached to the other end of a rubber band. She yelped as it slapped against her cheek, pulling the chain with it as it fell from the stage.

She transformed in an instant; the tension in her calves tearing through her spectral clothing before snapping and launching her from her position. Her eyes tore two long holes across her skull, dragging down past her chin as they gulped for sense data.

Ratty rolled out of the way as it lunged, missing her by a few feet thudding against the back wall of the stage. Against everyone's better judgment but her own, she fell on instinct into a fighting stance, completely unprepared for what the creature could have actually done.

Sett watched as their fiancée prepared to tackle a ghost, apparently having only one mode of dealing with danger. "Hey!" They called, waving their hands over their head. Once again the ghost turned, a heightened version of it's smaller form's automaton-like shuddering.

"It's okay, Eleanor, we're—" They were cut off as it rushed them. Sett raised their flashlight in a moment of artificially inflated fear, and anticipated the worst.

They blinked slowly as the rush of blood through their ears gave way to a low, rumbling hiss. It was caught in the beam, struggling against its seizing muscles to cover its eyes. Sett took a cautious half-step back, focusing the beam until Eleanor was small enough to be called Eleanor again, then clicking it off.

Eleanor stared at Sett for a moment, then turned back to Ratty, and — in another half-second — took off running.

"Oh, shit." Sett murmured, watching the ring of off-white purple retreat down the dark hall.

"It's okay." Ratty dropped down off the stage, starting a half-run down the aisle. "We can catch her."

"Wait. No." Sett stopped Ratty for a half-second, considering their options. They stared down at their flashlight, pulled a length of glowing rope from subspace to examine, then back down the hall. "Make a trap, I'll route her back here."

"Babe, there's like— I don't know how to make a ghost trap!" Ratty stammered, mentally flipping through the catalogue of garbage populating the trash-heap of a studio.

"And? You used to work in a studio like this, right? Her music thing is still working, there has to be something to work with!" Sett said, backing towards the door. "Work some magic!"

Ratty stood, stunned at being left to "work some magic" on equipment at once a decade older and several thousand dollars more expensive than anything she had ever used. She turned slowly, her eyes tracing over what was left of *The Ellen DeGenerous Show*. As though taunting her, her eyes stuck on the cross between the two of the racks of fallen lights.

Yeah, those might still work.

Tracking the ghost was easy. Not only was she trailing the

now bright spectral chain and accompanying slip of paper, and not only did she glow bright enough in her panicked state to be seen above the beige studio buildings, but she was also tearing at the walls of the main corridor, leaving a perfect trail of black ectoplasmic streaks against the concrete.

Sett paused at the exit to Studio 11, tying a thread to an exposed piece of the gas line and making a barrier that gave anyone with any reason to avoid light cause to duck into the studio rather than face it. They did this to the rest of the nearest intersection before heading into the main corridor, creating a net to catch their ghost.

They started east, careful to keep flat against the soundstages each time the beam of a guard's flashlight swept through the perpendicular corridors. They tied off each one as they went. Most mortals didn't bother to look directly at the way their universe was constructed, content to let their eyes slip over the things that sat right in front of them. The night guards could have just as well tripped over the string, and only stare back in anger for long enough to confirm how stupid they felt.

They ran out of rope a few crossings short of the end of the corridor. The end of their line thudded at the end of its spool, yanking way above Sett's centre of mass and almost toppling them over. That would be far enough, so long as they could walk the ghost for a few blocks.

At the end of the aisle sat a block of outdoor sets. The tall windows and marble architecture of Parisian-style condos sat opposite to a replica of one of Radio City Music Hall's less ostentatious (and likely less copyrighted) marquees with the serial numbers filed off. Centre to that was the steps and marble pillars of a courthouse with one presumed Eleanor Sloth-Bunny Jr. glaring desperately through the glass front door. She had yet to notice the hollow warehouse beyond the two meter cube of "office."

"Eleanor." Sett risked raising their voice. "It's okay, I'm sorry we startled you."

The ghost turned, their massive hollow eyes now held open by panic, shuttering — even while standing still — hard enough to rattle the fake door.

"It's okay. We're here to help." They took a step closer, reaching out with an open palm. The ghost stared at it blankly,

194

the slowness of their fall from panic reflected in their creep down the marble steps. She stayed ready to bolt if need be up until the very instant she set her hand in Sett's.

"It's okay." Sett repeated, resting a gentle — though not trapping — thumb over the back of the ghost's palm. "It's okay." They then took the chain in their free hand, pulling the laminated sheet of paper towards them. On it was printed the hollow-eyed face of Ellen DeGenerous.

The ghost avoided looking at the card stock cutout, choosing instead to stare at Sett's hand as they led her back to Studio 11. If everything went well, they would collect their things, find a motel for the night, and figure out how to communicate in the comfort of flower pattern sheets.

That would be, of course, if some trumped-up pseudo-cop had not shouted: "HEY!" at the top of his lungs. The ghost bolted, tried a few side roads as she went, and found each blocked off.

Sett allowed themself a light fist pump before confronting the guard. "You're not supposed to be here," his voice snapped as the little demon glared, completely unfazed by his only weapon: a threateningly large flashlight.

"You just saw a ghost, and your first reaction—" Sett let the honest bewilderment come through their voice as they advanced on the guard, slipping their belt off as they went. "Your first reaction is to try and arrest it, with a flashlight." In one fluid move, they slipped under the guard's arm, tied the belt around his neck, and pulled.

"Close your eyes, you'll wake up in the hospital." They toed the line between *you don't have to be nice to cops* and *being nice feels good, especially when you're strangling someone expertly.*

"Yeah, right, work some magic. Because it's that easy." Ratty grumbled through a mouthful of torn up wire jacket as she successfully completed the task that required magic working. It was surprisingly easy, not something she was going to admit to anyone, let alone herself.

The lights had torn their power lines from the ceiling when they fell, and the ghost had wired her Discman into a power line running through the wall of the adjacent studio 4.

The Discman was held together in places by a torn up piece of label. Reassembled (mentally, as not to damage the machine), it read 'ELEANORS DISCMAN.' The ghost was probably Eleanor. Ratty decided to stop pussyfooting around that.

In reality, all there was left to do was organize the torn-out cables and steal enough power from next door without shocking herself.

Or, well...

"Without shocking herself" was generous. She shocked herself several times, each time far more annoyed than hurt. Ratty had spent a lot of her free time basement-engineering, and every zap made her feel more and more like an amateur.

That annoyance faded just slightly as she tied off the last cable, thrumming the final light to life. She clambered up the scaffold and — using her hoodie's sleeves like gloves — twisted the light so it crossed with the rest of the beams in a central trap zone. She let go unceremoniously, falling to the ground with a hollow thud.

Stomping like that before was a stupid idea. It was shitty not to think about how it could have scared this complete stranger, one who was already on edge, not to mention needlessly self-destructive. Even as her leg stitched itself back together, she could feel the ache the femur-shattering left behind.

She ignored the aches most of the time. Before she died she had been able to ignore the half-hundred times she had been stabbed. Help was always there, she very rarely lost so badly that she couldn't stand up and keep moving. She ignored the several times she had fallen farther than any living creature should have been able to. She ignored it all.

Ratty ignored pain. That was what made sense to do. It was how she was brought up, and how she lived her life. It was probably why she had been told to hang back: Sett loved her, and there was no guarantee the possum wouldn't needlessly throw herself into danger again.

Now, the river Styx behind her, she had yet to find an upper limit to how much her body could take. She had not been killed yet. Statistically, she couldn't be. She could get away with infinite attempts at suicide, an incredible catharsis.

196

That was not what Eleanor needed.

Oh well.

Ratty sat up, bored of introspection. This was the first, and most likely the last, chance she would get to poke around the old Ellen stage.

The broken board was first on the menu. She picked away at what was left of it, creeped out when a small fortune of paper masks of Ellen DeGenerous with cut out eyes stared back at her.

Shit.

That was fucking disturbing.

She picked up the largest piece of cracked wood. It was barely smaller than the hole, and roughly the same size as one of the masks. Some distant ancestral pack rat instinct told her to pocket it, and she did.

The vinyl around the hole had also started to chip in a weird pattern, having bloomed a slightly lighter shade of black by what must've been heat. Ratty followed it about a quarter of the way along before realizing that yeah, okay, it was just some weird sigil.

Sett had taught her a few runes, just the ones she was most likely to see. Among the thousands of little characters, she picked out *Decay* once, then followed the sentence along. *Decay* again, then the unique shape of a name, busy with information. More *Decay,* some *death* and *binding.* Certainly nothing cheerful.

The frankly mundane realization was interrupted as Eleanor came whipping around the corner with her eyes behind her. More concerned with what was chasing her than where she was going, she flew directly into the centre of the beams.

She froze in place for a moment, slamming into the light like a wall, before falling to the stage. Ratty dove forward, catching her out of the air just before she hit the ground.

"Gotcha." She grinned. Eleanor's head lulled around as she recovered from the impact, too dizzy to do anything but stare as her eyes met Ratty's. Sett brought up the rear, looping her belt back through their pants.

"You get her?" They asked, panting.

"I got her." Ratty replied.

"Good." They sighed. "The... lights..." they pointed, pausing to catch their breath. "You do that?"

"Yeah." Ratty nodded.

"They look nice."

Ratty smiled, looking up at her creation just in time to see one of the lights sag out of alignment with a sad little creak. She looked down into the ghost's panicked eyes and let go of her. She propped herself up into a sitting position and shimmied back into a bubble of personal space.

"So, your name is Eleanor" She yanked the electrical assembly, pulling the Discman over and plunging them back into darkness in one movement. The words "ELEANORS DISCMAN" caught the light of the ghost's faint glow as the little machine was presented to her. She was grateful for the darkness, but — once she had acclimated to her comfort — stared at the black marker with the same blankness as before. The possum stared into her eyes for a moment, searching, before she was struck with an idea.

"Actually..." she said, looking through Eleanor at Sett. "Can I try something?"

"Sure." The goat had already started to pack up.

"Hand me that mask." Ratty put her hand out for it. Sett stopped, put down the flashlights, and fished it back out of the bag. She lifted the piece of paper, blank side to Eleanor's face, pausing mid-move as she caught the rabbit's eyes again. "Do you mind if we try and put this on you?" she asked. Eleanor's face remained neutral. "Okay..."

Ratty perched the mask on the tip of Eleanor's flat snout. It bounced back, setting into a hover a half an inch from her cheeks.

There was not much colour to return to her purple-grey fur, her hair stayed the same over-bleached shade of white. The only major change came in the form of a deep, dry maroon that spread from the top of her head, down over her neck, and soaked into her t-shirt.

She was quiet for a moment, moving her chest in a way that would suggest struggling to breathe as she remembered she was supposed to. Behind the mask, a sudden agency turned over in her hollow eyes: a switch from fear to consciousness.

It was like she had to remember what being a consciousness was like, because... she kind of did.

"You there, Eleanor?" Ratty prodded gently, after having left the requisite gap for soul-searching. Eleanor stayed silent for just a few more moments before...

"I *really* don't know if I'm Eleanor," she said, her voice thin, struggling to recover some deeper resonance after years and years of silence.

"That's okay." Sett hopped up onto the stage next to the rabbit, now more fascinated with the talking ghost than their bag full of flashlights. They hovered a caring hand just above her knee and met her eyes for a nod. They scooted closer once they got it, doing their best to make comforting contact against the incorporeal. "Let's start with what you do know. Do you remember anything about your before-life?"

Eleanor screwed up her face as she searched her memory. "I used to work here..."

"As a production manager, right?" Ratty asked, calling on her own before-life. "How did your face get messed up—"

"Ratty." Sett snapped. Eleanor was already too stuck into the first question to notice the second.

"Yeah. Yeah that makes sense..." Eleanor murmured "...and Ellen, dropped something on my head... She was like, sacrificing people? For views? Or..."

Ratty caught Sett's eye. "The talk-show host?" she asked.

"She's also an elder god," the goat explained.

"I mean, yeah—" Ratty started, clearly flustered by information she was supposed to know, but didn't. "But like, don't you think she would pick one?"

"This— Ratty, did you think that every time I visited Decay, that she just also happened to live in the Ellen studio?" Sett asked, too incredulous to keep their therapist-like tone. Ratty's embarrassment rose in the silence as Eleanor took a break from her own soul-searching to stare — a little bewildered — at the possum she had just met.

"Yeah, maybe." Ratty replied.

"At no moment, based on context clues, did you—"

"I don't want to talk about this anymore." Ratty murmured, leaving the trio in silence.

Eleanor stared for a few more moments, feeling pain creep up behind her eyes. She groaned as it took over her senses. She shuddered, rubbing some soreness out of her slower eye socket. "Fuck. My head..."

"Right, yes, of course. That's okay. This is actually a really good start, Eleanor. The more we can learn about you, the more likely you are to stay like, on this plane." Sett explained.

"Let's get you somewhere comfortable." Ratty ducked suddenly under Eleanor's armpit and hoisted the taller woman. Sett's look told her how strange that was.

"It's cool, thank you." Eleanor had evidently also caught that look. She buried her snout in Ratty's neck to drown out the light before realizing that she was the light, leaving it there for the cool comfort of her damp fur against her forehead. "Where're y'all from?"

"We don't sound like Californians?" Ratty teased, guiding Eleanor step-by-step down from the stage.

"Nah, I mean the goat sounds fine, but you talk like a farmer." Eleanor's voice was muffled by possum fur.

"I do *not* talk like a farmer." Ratty grumbled.

"Oh, hun. You totally do." Sett chose to betray their fiancée in this, her hour of need.

"Well, fuck." she mumbled, annoyed. "I'm from Ontario, Sett is from Hell."

"Oh, uh, cool. Tight, I guess." Cus like, some nights are just — why not, y'know?

It took a few hours for Eleanor's memory to plateau at a stable level.

What came back was an outline: structure without substance, the fact that she had been alive at some point, with scarce actual facts about that life. The few details that came back — annoyingly — were largely centred around *the Ellen DeGenerous show*, and all coloured by the shame of having participated in it.

Explaining it to Ratty and Sett helped. Each had their own history of participating in an institution they now found incontrovertibly evil.

"So, essentially, we would get these branding deals, right? Everyone in the audience gets a free kitchen mixer and the company gets like, some advertising. It's like a trade, essentially. The thing is, though, is that we didn't just do that with kitchen mixers. What really brought in the views was when Ellen like, brought in some dying kid on and like, 'paid' for them to not die or whatever." Eleanor explained.

"We kind of hand-waved it to be like, 'oh, we paid their hospital bills' or something, but in reality it's more like Ellen would use her godhood to take the years that that child would lose to sickness from someone else."

Still, there was nothing to explain why she was the only ghost out of the presumed hundreds that would die between the show's inception and Ellen's eventual death. If the mask was anything, it was just something that was nearby when Eleanor's soul needed something to cling to, no more than a Halloween episode tie-in that never panned out.

All of this came back as Eleanor lay on a motel bed, the first bed she remembered seeing in this version of her memories, waiting for someone named Angel to come pick the three of them up and whisk them off to Toronto, Canada. Here was no better than there, she thought, thoroughly detached from it all.

"Do you guys like, charge rent? I have money."

"Keep it for yourself," the goat smiled, "we're just here to help."

"And if I want to like... pass on," she asked, once Ratty had left to get food. "Could I do that?"

"I could certainly help you with that, if that is what you really want." Sett said. Eleanor thumbed idly at the edge of her mask, wondering if she would ever be able to take it off without risking a return to instinct purgatory.

"What about this?" she asked, pressing the nose of the mask to her own with a finger. "Can I take it off eventually?"

"I would have to check a spectrology textbook, but I assume the worst case scenario would be something like, you dissipate, get sent back to the uh... 'ghostzone'... and whatever progress you've made to constructing this form is reset," they explained from the opposite bed.

That memory was really going to need some work. What little the rabbit retained of non-existence was something akin to a collective, thoroughly nasty, feverish wet dream. A never ending rave where one could never get tired, just bored and confused and higher and higher before peaking just above the clouds that constructed the barrier between realities.

"I should mention though, that it would not be permanent." Sett said, doing their best to be encouraging as they scooted to the very edge of the bed and rested a comforting hand on/in Eleanor's semi-corporeal shoulder. "The people back home are good at this kind of thing. Working together, we could find a way to bring you back in no time at all."

It was Sett who was good at this kind of thing— matters of life and death. Stephanie and Fern covered matters of one and zero. Angel, here and there. Ratty, built and ruined. Sett had life and death.

Eleanor stood, walking through Sett and exasperatedly throwing her weightless form down on the motel's dusty-smelling couch with a completely inaudible *flumf*. She stared up at the motionless ceiling fan through the mask's tiny eyes, somehow more comfortable on the old leather than on the cheap sheets.

"It's annoying." The rabbit said.

"I can imagine." Sett got up from their spot and sat back down on the arm of the chair.

"It feels like shit to have to wear the face of the woman who killed me."

"That I cannot imagine."

"It's like, metaphorically fucked up too, right? Having to wear someone else's face to stay alive."

That Sett had not encountered before, a unique facet of Eleanor's relationship with Decay, most likely. "Absolutely." They nodded.

"And we're not even entirely sure I need it."

"We—" The goat paused, not having said that. "No, we are not sure that you need it."

"Alright then, fuck it." Eleanor grabbed the paper face by its chin and whipped it off, slapping it down on her lap. It went easily, not clinging to her face, as though completely within her control: it would stay when told to stay, and come off when told to come off. Some of the substance drained from Eleanor's form, but otherwise, she was still entirely there.

"How do you feel?" Sett asked, recovering from that sudden spike in anxiety.

"I still feel weird that putting her face on is what made me 'come back.'" She was still talking too.

"It is very fucked up, and probably an intentional piece of abuse on her part." Sett guessed. "Can you give me a rating out of ten?"

"Seven."

"Are you still with us?"

"Mostly, yeah. I would say... yeah." For whatever reason, less of a body was actually more comfortable. Less places to ache, Eleanor guessed, as she rolled over onto her side and sunk into the couch.

"Do you feel like you're gonna stay at seven out of ten?" Sett asked, standing to take in the rest of the rabbit. She was staying.

"Yeah... probably." Eleanor murmured, a sudden exhaustion taking over her voice as she got comfortable. "Can you— can you save me if I start to look too far gone?"

"Yes, I can." Sett said. "Are you going to sleep now?"

"Mhmm."

"Ah, well. Okay. Good. Sleep well, Eleanor." With that, Sett got up, flicked off the lights, and slipped out to wait at the door. They would warn Ratty that Eleanor had finally found a spot alone to rest properly.

# 2010
# Ready

"Hey, Eleanor, Right?" Her neighbours were overly friendly to say the least. A small, dark-haired kirin and his boyfriend, both of whom looked like they had known exactly what the word *homeless* meant since their early teens.

Eleanor nodded back silently, popping one headphone out to listen, finding — as was often the case — her voice stuck in her throat.

"We uh— there's an anarchist book club tonight, we were wondering if—"

Eleanor shook her head, again silently. "S-s-sorry." she stammered.

"Oh, no worries. Maybe—" The kirin was cut off as Eleanor slipped into her apartment and shut the door. It was unclear whether that stutter was a result of her time spent alone. For the few months between her death and the studio's abandonment, the audience could not see her. It was during these days that she found Ellen's — or Decay's, she guessed — most in"human" qualities. She did not ignore Eleanor. It was that her ears were not used for hearing, and that her eyes could not see.

She took a deep breath, once again disappointed when her lungs stayed tight and shrivelled. The worst part about not being able to breathe, at least right now, was not the obvious terror of suffocation. It was not being allowed the catharsis of a long sigh.

It would have been nice to get out some. The book club would have been a good opportunity to do that. Running miscellaneous errands for the people she already knew was the baby-step on the way to getting involved with a club.

Her mask hung low in the collar of her loose-fitting sweater as she went about her chores. Sett had suggested giving herself a reason to get out of bed in the morning; this was as good as any.

She set spinning a copy of The Notorious B.I.G.'s *Ready to Die* on her record player, a gift from Ratty that likely would have been weird if she hadn't prefaced it with, "This is the only Biggie album I have on vinyl."

And it was a good album. No complaints.

Her plants were next. Sitting under a constantly buzzing bulb was a countertop filthy with flora. In the cold, Canadian winter, the only thing keeping them green was the heat from this bulb and a few spritzes of water each day. Eleanor didn't mind. She slept in the living room on a pull-out couch, and the constant glow was comforting, an anchor to pull herself back to when her nightmares got too intense.

She took a step back when she was done. It was hardly fair to call that *chores,* but it was reason enough to go around the corner for plant food.

Sigh...

Maybe a shower would make her feel better. She dragged one of the speakers through into her bathroom, having specifically set it up with a ridiculously long cord for just that reason. She pulled off her sweater and stared into the mirror, the paper face of Ellen DeGenerous caught in one of the cups of her bra.

Cool.

She took it off, set it down on the bathroom counter, and stepped into the shower.

It was cold water that sent Eleanor back to the ghostzone for the first time. Tired, standing under the shower head, she forgot about her "sensitivity" and just flipped it on as normal. Like a snap, the cold bore her chest out, giving her only a half-second to register the hole through her chin and the rest of her body before she was completely gone.

It was strange to experience death again with a full consciousness. A lot of falling, really. Eleanor had gotten used to floating most of where she went — not that she needed the extra couple inches it afforded — but death cared very little how much you could float.

It was boring, really. Just falling. Falling... falling... falling... No 2001-style flashing lights, no great revolution, no crossing of an incredible boundary between life and death. Just... fucking... falling. Ratty had said the other day that she didn't remember her first time dying, and it was clear why. It was about as memorable as an amusement park queue show.

And then she blinked, and in that instant trees came up around her, already too tall to see the tops of. Another blink and she could feel the gravity of the ground that formed below her. With a thud she hit the supernatural floor of this strange forest, its rootless trees rising like lamp posts, shifting in colour as she turned her back on each one as though repainting themself each time her vision blurred between head movements.

"What the fuck..." she murmured.

And the forest spoke back: "What the fuck?"

Great. Cool fucking forest.

Not one to waste time, or maybe just not today, or maybe just not under these circumstances Eleanor picked a direction and started walking. She ignored the colour shifting trees, ignored the tempo with which the leaves crunched under her paws, chose to focus on the small miracle that the afterlife had chosen to at least give her something to wear.

It looked like her work uniform. It probably was her work uniform. There was no reason why what she was forced to wear in purgatory would be anything but consistent. They probably didn't get a lot of repeat guests.

Her claws looked stark white under the dead grass, the hard black of her shirt.

"Fuckin' weird ass place..." she spoke, or thought, or something.

"Fuckin' weird ass place..." The forest repeated, now mostly behind her.

"You get used to it." Came a voice from above. Eleanor's eyes shot up from the ground. Somewhere under the crunch of the leaves the soft earth below turned to the cracked tar of her old street. She found the lamp posts of the wilderness now making orderly rows down Harrison street, toothpicks sandwiched between a valley of blank beige mid-rises.

"Up here, El'." The voice repeated. "Yo! Hello? Eleanor Sloth-Bunny Jr."

Uncle Alf.

206

His face suddenly snapping into sharp focus from a blur of memories.

"Uncle Alf?"

"Nah El', it's the fucking tooth fairy." he teased, presiding over the gap between buildings like a king addressing his court.

"You're dead?" Eleanor asked.

"Yeah, I guess so." he replied.

"Sucks."

"S'whatever. Come let me get a look at you. Elevator's still broken."

---

"Well..." Sett stood back from their work, folding shut the ancient tome of ghostzone mechanics on Eleanor's bathroom counter. It was a mess, but it was better than nothing. The paper mask had been metaphysically torn open like a manhole cover. Sett had tied a rope to a fixed point in space above it and fed it down through the drain. Nothing particularly complicated, but something to climb out with at the very least. "That's the best we can do for now." They said.

Ratty stared at the shimmering tangle required to keep the rope suspended, another possibility forming at the back of her mind. She bit down on the gnarled end of a pen, the little end-stop coming loose in her mouth.

"What if one of us went in there?" she asked. Sett blinked once as they processed this, turned to stare at their fiancée, and blinked again — even more bewildered — when her face gave away no hint of irony.

"Well, Ratty..." They started, their tone not dissimilar to that of a lecture on the dangers of forks and electrical sockets. "One of us would have to die."

"Well, okay, cool then. I'll just die temporarily and then when I'm ready to come back you can put me back together."

"That's— no, actually. That's not a good idea, Ratty." Sett stammered, now completely lost as Ratty pushed past them, out of the bathroom, out of the apartment. "Where are you going?" They asked, struggling to keep up with her as she skipped every few feet.

"Storage." She turned around for a half-second to reply, not slowing down.

"Why?"

"Find something that kills me." She looked almost excited at the possibility.

"Again." Sett snapped, their voice now reverberating across the concrete walls of the stairwell. "That is not a good idea."

"She's gonna need someone to help her get back to that rope." Ratty explained, already rummaging through the plastic crate closest to the door.

"What has gotten into you?" Sett stared at the cold pallor that had taken over their fiancée's face, an almost plastic-looking sheen of sweat dulling her fur as she searched. The pen had exploded in her mouth, leaving a smear of black across her lips and up her cheek. Her eyes had glossed over, mouth hanging open in a breathless grin. She looked like a mortician's first day on the job.

"I'm— I'm trying to help."

"You're not helping. Eleanor is going to be fine." Sett reached out, their hand entirely ignored by the frenzied possum.

"What if she's not?" Ratty went back to her search, tipping over boxes and cracking arcane safes that had been sealed for years. Sett watched as an unidentifiable silver urn rolled from one, just a few inches from being stepped on. They scooped it up and placed it gently on its base, still struggling to keep pace with Ratty.

"You're going to break something!" Their voice shook, straining under a now tipping-tower of arcane encyclopedias and the weight of their growing anxiety in equal measure.

"Good idea." Ratty's head popped out of the box, foam packing peanuts freezing in mid-air around her head. She had clearly progressed beyond being able to listen. "Where's the stone?"

And for a moment, Sett froze. As slowly as they could, they let a subspace needle slip from inside the wrist of their sweater. Ratty was too far gone to notice, staring into space and indexing her memory. "Oh, y'know what, I think it's still in my bag, actually."

She was too fast. In the instant Sett realized the possum had moved, she was already half way back upstairs, time hitching in her favour.

"Ratty, stop." They were pleading now, the idea of physical

force elbowing its way out of the front of their mind, holding this last volley of begging by the hair as it positioned a knife at its throat. "Let's at least talk about this."

"Nothing to talk about."

"What is wrong with you?"

"I just want to help, Sett. Only I can help."

"There's nothing you can do right now! You go in there, your regeneration stops working. You don't come back."

"Here—"

It's unclear whether Ratty actually touches it. There is a moment in which Sett's hand — with nothing but perfect intentions — clamps down painfully around Ratty's shoul

Stop.

An Irregularity has been detected. This product will not operate when connected to a system which makes unauthorized copies or modifications to the original program. Ple

Stop.

An Irregularity has been detected. This product will not operate when connected to a system which makes unauthorized copies or modifications to the original program. Please consult your user manual for more instr

[Ratty drops a handful of blue and white pills as her father drags her off of the living room floor.]

[Ratty yelps as her head slams into the upper-edge of the door to a police cruiser.]

[Ratty's heart stops as Handler Smith sets a hand on her shoulder.]

There is a long stretch of unconscious ███, void in all dimensions except time. A man sits down at a console. This man is ████ ███. He doesn't waste time on his excitement. He knows not how much he will get.

Where to start... there's some music playing, Sinatra I think. One of those men with sweet voices from the prohibition era. You know. I wonder if Sinatra knew he would still be listened to in 2025.

The music stopped, or... will stop. The music stops, leaving the canteen in a state of hushed conversation. Around 13 of them, if memory serves. One gets up on stage: a goat, brown fur, black horns. She looks like your wife, Hanratty.

She speaks in a language they all think you cannot understand: "Ladies and gentlemen, we need you all to move out, right now. We have just received word that there is a soldier from the United States here."

You do not react to this. Good little soldier.

Some people run. Others put their hands on their weapons. D██ ██orry, you'll d██al with the runners later. ████ ████ that night.

They realize it's you when you continue not to reac██ ████████████████ on your feet, the barrel of an assault ri████ ██████████ush it out of your face in sl██

██████████ick the man holding the gun in the stomach, he pulls the trigger again████████ ████████out of his hands and spin it, ████████

Who else...

████████ardly exciting... if you ask me.

Maybe this will help:

█ are covered in blood... Kneeling in a puddle of it. It dries in a █████ film on your fingers. Your first thought is how that's going to affect you tactically. You have been trained well.

Blood and guts, all over the place.

This is hard.

█promise I'll be more prepared next time.

It seems as though I'm losin█ ██ou, Hanratty. Sh██me. ████

████ one more b█fore y█u go,

You he██████████ing: crying ██████nder the stage.

Oh, you know what? That's funny.

██'ve got the world on a ██████████████████████████

████████████nny. Don't ██████████'s funny, Hanratty?

In any case...

You ████████████████████, your boots crackling as the tacky blood peels from the concrete with each step. You pull back the slide on your rifle: ██████und left.

You kneel to see a crouching goat trembling below the stage. ██████████eally excellent co██idence ██████████ope you kn██ that.

██████████████ by the ankle, dragging her through the slick ████████████████████anything can be said about your m██████████clinical.

You put a boot on her ch█st.

You l█ne up the barrel of your firearm.

████bright golden eyes████████████████ They are familiar, aren't they?

██████████████████████████████████████████████████████

presses the hard metal through the flaking bloo███ finds its ███████ releases the hammer, and ████████

██████████████████████████████████████████████████████

STOP.

---

"*Stop*." Ratty hit the present moment like an 80-mile-an-hour wreck. The carpet, her hands: slick with something warm and wet that she was far too disoriented to identify as sweat.

Shaking and sore from where she hit the ground, she begged, suddenly feeling very broken: "Don't touch me."

It took a lot of effort to push the images of those memories left behind out of her head, keeping the events of her before-life in too much pain to move. To animate for those memories would have been tantamount to a corpse directing their own funeral, and yet all it took to break down the walls she had constructed with bleeding nail-beds stubs was one moment of supernatural stress.

She pushed out into the darkness, found nothing, and pushed further. There was fear in the unknown. It could only get worse until she understood it all. Knowing that, the blank in her memory refused to yield.

Sett stood back, staring down at the hand that had triggered Ratty's attack, waves of guilt emanating from the palm in a deep, unyielding ache. They froze in the chilling surf, their mind running through all the ways they could have acted differently, hours of possibilities flashing behind their eyes in moments, each with their own wave.

*Don't touch me* was the hardest thing in the world when the brash, cocky, loudmouthed possum who took on Hell and won stifled her sobs with the coarse fur of the carpet. The floodgates were now open. Curious as she was, terrified at how small and how gruesome the picture she received was, she pushed at the edges of the memory, begging the pain for salvation.

---

It had been too long since Eleanor had actually, properly smoked. Mortal weed was passable, but considering how hard it was to inhale, it took a lot of effort and a lot of waste to actually get her high. The ghostzone had its own weed, and it was fucking excellent. She silently thanked the brave marijuana plants that had to die so she could have this meal.

"So like—" she started, now de-stressed enough to talk about life with her dead uncle. "How did you die?" She offered the joint. Alf stared down at it for a moment, shook his head, and pushed it back to Eleanor. You don't stop taking the medicine when it starts working.

"How does anyone die in Oakland?" he joked, leaving the c-word unsaid. It was surreal, almost, to hear those words said from beyond the grave. Alf had been making those same jokes since before death was his immediate reality.

"Fuckin' asshole." Eleanor murmured around another drag. Alf paused, staring at the plume of smoke, changed his mind, and gestured for the joint.

"How did you die?" he asked.

"Workplace accident." Eleanor simplified for the sake of not saying "I joined a Hollywood cult by complete accident and became blood for the blood god."

"Did your mom get comp or anything?"

"I dunno, I didn't know I had a mom 'til you said that."

"You brain damaged?" Memory loss wasn't a normal part of dying, in spite of a pair of cases that proved the opposite.

"Yeah, I got hit on the head, man, look at me." Eleanor gestured to the part of her face she knew to be a frozen façade of what was once there. Alf stared for a moment, then shrugged.

"I don't see anything." he said. Eleanor turned to the window, the only reflective surface in the room, and stared at herself. She could see an almost rubber seam between the part of her skull that had been caved in and the rest of it. A few experimental faces reaffirmed what she knew: a half-second lag between the left and right sides of her face.

"So you gonna stay?" Alf asked, snapping Eleanor out of her examination. It took a slight delay to process the question, and a few seconds more to come up with an answer. She settled with:

"I don't know. I'm kinda struggling to integrate upstairs." She went back to her reflection, searching her own hollow eyes. "Have you been to Toronto?"

"Nope."

"It's a weird city. There's not like — *places* there. Does that make any sense? Their places are like... a Pizza Pizza across from a department store. Not real places."

"What's a Pizza Pizza?"

"It's like Domino's but in Canada."

"Weird." Alf went to take another drag, then, thinking better of it, set the joint down in his ashtray. It went out almost immediately. "Maybe you're not giving them a chance to be real 'cus you miss Cali."

"I don't even fucking remember 'Cali.'" She mimicked her uncle's tone.

"Sucks." Alf kicked his head back to stare at the ceiling fan, watching the smoke rise up through the vents. "Cali was sweet."

Eleanor took a deep breath, relieved of the constant suffocation of the mortal realm by the fact that this was technically where she belonged. The Pharcyde took over their dull conversation as she stared through at the adjacent, equally beige building. It was familiar and distant at once. It was comfortable here, watching the natural deep purple return to her fur. The only ache here was her memory, and the fact that she was not alive.

"Can you tell me who I was?" Eleanor turned, now looking at her uncle. Surely if someone knew her, it was him. Alf stared back, empty of recognition, with the kind of pity in his eyes that only comes from people who hate pity. Eleanor had grown up without him.

"Honestly, I don't know. We weren't like that. You only told me important shit, and like, I died when you were in the tenth grade," he said. "You're clearly not that person anymore."

"Huh." Eleanor sat in the empty silence, staring at the grey carpet. Though not surprising, it was still disappointing. Her choice was clear: never find out who she once was and stay here (if that was possible), or go back to the land of the living and maybe find some way to become whole again. "That sucks."

"Actually..." Alf stood, drawing Eleanor's gaze up from the floor. "Hold on." He crossed to his closet and, after a few short moments of searching, turned back around with two armfuls of cassette bags, roughly 300 across six bags. "This is what you and me had together. When you go, you should take these with you."

When you go...

That was what Alf thought was best. He was probably right.

She unzipped one of the tacky zebra-print cases, releasing a plume of plastic scented dust. Again, distant and familiar. She clicked the tip of her finger across the combination of professionally printed and handwritten labels, stopping at the first one that jumped out in her mind:

"Chris Wallace. 1991 demo." Alf read. "I remember that."

The two shared a quick moment, a thread not materializing, but just becoming apparent between the two. Alf's smile faltered as his next thought came up, embarrassed at the show of emotion.

"I wasn't a great uncle, but I remember what was important to you. Maybe— maybe this could help you remember that, too."

Eleanor stood and hugged the old dog in one motion. Content in this insubstantial memory, they stood in that embrace like both had somehow found their family again, like there was no one actually gone. For a moment she had the privilege of knowing some part of herself.

And in a cruel moment, that feeling was gone. She caught her uncle's eye as the living realm pulled at the back of her sweater, scared and alone all over again.

"Aw man, looks like they aren't going to give you a choice." Alf spoke, choking back a rising feeling in a way only his closest friends would have been able to recognize as even being there.

"Uncle A, are you sure about these?" Eleanor scooped up the bags in her arms even as they began to disappear.

"Yeah dude, I have an iPod now." Alf grinned, his eyes glassy. "Do me a favour actually. The cop who shot me— his name is—"

And she was gone.

Standing in the shower, water turned off, a paper mask floating on a puddle where the floor dipped below level, the bags full of tape still securely cradled in her arms.

This was a start.

As she stepped out of the shower and set her bags down on the toilet, her fur settled again against her skin, kicking off some of the eternal dust as it did. A richer colour in the bathroom mirror, everywhere but the white impact mark over her eye.

"Eleanor?" Sett's harsh whisper jumped Eleanor out of her reverie. "Oh thank god you're alright." They fell into a hug that was a little too tight for their level of friendship at that point. She wrapped the little goat in her spectral arms all the same: she could tell they had both had an emotionally draining day.

"Hey, uh— Sett." Eleanor muttered, unable to keep the discomfort from their voice. Sett looked up, realized what they were doing, and stepped back.

"Sorry, yes." they said, now back to curt. "Ratty is asleep on the couch, just so you know."

"In— in my apartment?" Eleanor asked, poking her head out of the bathroom. Sure enough, there was Ratty.

"It's a long and really very stressful story. Could you please just try not to wake her?"

"Yeah, sure." She was cool enough to let sleep on the couch. Eleanor slipped quietly into the living room and sat on the edge of her pull-out couch, across from Ratty, curled up in a loveseat. She watched for just a moment, wondered what nightmare had scrunched up her snout, and turned to Sett.

They had already forgotten Eleanor, their eyes locked on their fiancée's crumpled form as they nervously chewed at the tips of their claws.

Huh.

Long day.

---

Ratty woke up sore too, her head swimming with a blurry swirl of water-ruined ink-prints of her life before death. What a stupid thing to do.

Eleanor lay on the adjacent couch, comfortable, glowing softly, completely at peace for the first time Ratty had seen. She was the future, the possum thought. Proof that some amount of what she put herself through was worth it.

"Ratty?" Sett's voice washed the ache from behind Ratty's eyes. Fully alert, she turned to stare at her partner. They looked like they had been on the verge of tears for a while, and were about to let it go as soon as they could affirm Ratty was okay. She couldn't move for a moment, frozen in the goat's gaze, bright golden yellow and full of fear.

"Hey Sett." Ratty said, her voice raw and quiet.

"I'm sorry." Sett said, now letting tears spill down their cheeks.

"No, not your fault." Ratty stood, starting towards her partner. She stopped a few feet shy, taken over once again by the force that held her on the couch a moment ago. Sett knew, or maybe they didn't, but the fear of losing a loved one, of seeing them in pain, looks a lot like the fear of death.

They were scared. Not scared of their fiancée, but of losing them, and if they talked about it, Ratty would have been able to figure that out...

"Are we going to—" Sett hiccuped. "Are we going to talk about this?"

The question scared Ratty. The memory contained nothing of substance. There was nothing to tell. A singular question occupied her mind: was Sett scared of her?

Of course, it was a question she could never have answered. If they were, they would say no. People lie to the people they're afraid of on instinct. If they weren't, they would say no, and Ratty would have to live with the fact that someone was either afraid for her, or too afraid to tell her the truth.

There was nothing to talk about. The possum stammered through a few "I—"s before Sett took over again.

"It's okay." Sett's breath caught in their throat. "I'm sorry. I didn't know—"

"No, it's not your fault." Ratty took another step forward, her eyes working overtime for any uptick in Sett's outward show of fear. They continued to shake, damp tear tracks darkening the fur of their cheeks, but they were tentatively drawn into their partner's arms.

In a moment of rushed judgment, Ratty wrapped her arms around Sett. Sett wrapped her arms around Ratty, and felt ever so slightly better. Ratty's skin crawled. This was stupid. Sett would come to hate her for it.

# 2012
# Courier

She was awake. For an hour before the hour she was supposed to wake up, Ratty clicked her phone on and off, keeping herself awake figuring out how much time she could have slept if she just fell asleep right now. She's awake. She's leaving the building.

Sleeping pills were too much. She could get trapped in her dreams, getting up to turn the lights on over and over again until she gave up and just started kicking shit.

"Morning, Ratty." Coming out of her office into an occupied common area always startled her. Fern and Steph were here last night, it just never made sense that they would stay as long as she did. Fern didn't even live here.

The common area — probably intended for use as some open-concept meeting zone when the building was built — had undergone significant renovations since Steph moved in. That always kind of irked Ratty — the fox had *patents*, she still got income from Angelcorp, still got them delivered to a PO box down the street. She didn't technically need to be living in free housing.

Then again, she didn't technically need to be contributing so much to the food pot. She didn't need to stock their coffee cart with the hot chocolate Ratty liked or to leave one out on days she knew Ratty was working. She didn't need to finance community STEM programs out of their little building either. She probably should have vacuumed up the drywall dust that running cables kicked up, though.

"Morning, Fern." Ratty responded specifically to the borzoi. "Morning, Angel." She sat in a nest of blankets, a few panels hanging open. "Why are you—"

"Good morning, Ratty." Steph spoke up, glaring at the possum.

"Good morning, Stephanie." Ratty sneered into her mug. "Why is Angel in pieces?"

"We're—" Fern started.

Steph cut them off. "We're working on a way to offload some of Angel's internal processes onto more current hardware, in the event that she stops functioning before suitable replacements are invented."

"Good morning, Ratty. Good morning, Ms. Jozwiak." Angel caught up to the conversation. "My wrist is broken." She held up the arm to demonstrate, her hand flopping over, fingers still wiggling.

"Yeah." Ratty nodded. "Absolutely true."

"The part we keep printing is too fragile to hold for any longer than a couple of days." Fern explained.

"Can I take a look at it?" Ratty knelt next to Angel.

"That's her decision."

"You may." Angel set her wrist in Ratty's hand. Behind an unnecessarily complex forest of actuators, two pieces of blue plastic hung from metal hooks.

"It's just a stupid size." Fern said. Almost the same size and shape as...

Ratty unpinned one of the safety pins from her jacket. She would wear it up until she had to meet with someone, swap it with the blazer in her bag, and switch back on the way home. *Peacocking* was the wrong word for it. Ratty didn't know that.

"Can I get a pair of pliers over here?"

"Sure." Steph rifled through a drawer, tossed them, and missed by several feet. Ratty stared at them for a second, then at the fox. She shuffled over far enough to pick them up, never breaking eye contact with the orange head of shame trying to recede behind her glasses.

The plastic crushed easily between the metal jaws, dropping out into Ratty's waiting palm. She put one of them between her teeth, tossing the other away.

"Are we still on for this weekend, by the way?" Steph had recovered quickly from their horrible throw.

"Hold on, Steph." Ratty positioned the safety pin between the pliers, hooking it between the two tiny catches and smushing it shut. "Try that, Angel." She sat back. The robot lifted her hand, not immediately shattering the connection. It swivelled, clicking loudly as the replacement part ran up against something.

"It works!" She struggled to modulate her excitement. "Thank you, Ratty."

That was weird. Ratty froze in place. It was a calculation, probably: someone does something nice for you, and you say thank you. Not something she needed to accept as legitimate. Not something she needed to process.

"Sure." She nodded. The robot did not notice her synthetic hair being ruffled as the possum got up.

"So, are we still on for... the... thing... this weekend?" God, she could never fucking shut up.

"Oh, yeah, no, I'm gonna have to cancel." Ratty answered, starting towards the elevator.

"What? why?" The 3D printed plastic part shattered into its layers in the possum's mouth.

"Cus, Steph, I have a disease in my brain that makes me feel bad all the time. Touching people I don't like especially makes my brain feel bad, okay? Can I not just say no?" she snapped. She picked the ribbon-ified part from her tongue and stuffed it in a back pocket to be forgotten about.

Steph bit her tongue for once.

"I'm sorry, I—"

"Are you two fucking?" Fern interrupted, as full of excited curiosity as their monotone could go without losing its flat top. Oh yeah, Fern's here. That's actually really funny. That's about as good a mood as Ratty was willing to be in right now. The fox radiated heat, head working overtime to explain what just happened.

"Don't say anything," she demanded, watching a suppressed grin creep across the possum's face.

"Does Sett know?" Fern asked.

"Sett does know." Ratty confirmed. They didn't know specifically about Steph. Hatefucking was one of those things the goat didn't like knowing about, but they didn't ask for an itemized list of all the possum's hookups, so...

"I'll text you about it." Ratty held up her phone to illustrate.

"You better."

"Nobody is texting anyone." Steph butted in.

"Goodbye, Stephanie." The possum's faux-flirting came out more sour than she intended.

220

"Can I at least get my panties back?"
"Nope, mine now! Bye!"

---

The girls who worked here liked Ratty well enough. She came in the early morning, usually around the time the majority of their shifts ended. That's how she could tell: at the end of the night, usually draped in a massive piece of comfortable clothing and counting their tips, one or two would invite her into their booth to talk.

She would lean against the padded wall, ignoring the pole in the foreground of her vision, and have polite, underclass conversations with half-naked women until their shared boss showed up.

"I still need your number, by the way," one of them had asked at some point. "I brought my phone from my locker, so —"

"Yeah, here. Tell me when you're ready."

"This isn't like— I'm not gonna 'call you,' I just— it feels safe, y'know?"

"For sure." No one there knew exactly what she did. They knew she came in bruised sometimes. They knew Mr. Liu paid her anyway.

"Alright, here." She handed the phone over. Ratty smirked at the words briefcase seller in the name field. She filled out the rest.

"Ratty!" There he was. Everyone wanted to startle her this morning. "C'mon, you spend any more time in there and I'm gonna ask you for an audition!" He flashed a set of keys, ready to unshackle her from his package. She handed the phone back, gave the woman a final nod for the night, and met her boss for the day at the bar.

"That's alright, sir." She set it on the counter, presenting her wrist to be unlocked. Liu pinched the cuff specifically, careful not to touch her fur, and popped it open. Then the case, specially designed — according to the man who handed it to her — to cradle whatever she had been carrying. Liu stood up to his tiptoes to look straight down at it.

"This is why I love you, Ratty. My god, I could cry." His hands hovered a few inches from the open case, thought better of it, and retrieved some silk gloves from under the counter. Ratty tried not to be noticed leaning over the counter, curious what she was protecting.

The gloved hands lifted a small, semi-translucent piece of green stone, carved into the figure of a woman, mounted on a red stained wooden base.

"Beautiful, don't you think?" he asked. She recognized it from the bounty that'd been put out for its return: significantly less than was paid for its delivery. It was an ostentatious display of wealth, but better off here than in some underground private collection. Liu didn't wait for an answer. "Only woman I know who could get on the bus with a beautiful piece like this and get back off, and dressed like that, too."

His eyes drifted down the rumbled shoulder of her blazer, a compliment to the tune of *a secondhand jacket can't stop bullets.* The bus had never given her any trouble before.

"Do you have any idea how much work I put into getting this out of the hands of those—" He came close to indicting himself in the rapture of turning it in his fingers. Those people, whoever they were, were evidently too good for anything but shiny black SUVs.

"In any case," he popped open a glass panel behind the bar, a far cry from the climate controlled vault it was used to. This would not be a closely loved piece, but a dare. "Come and take it from me," Ratty could have sworn he said.

He unlooped his watch on the return trip.

"I just got this from a friend, you want it? I hate how it looks on me." This was his attempt at a generous tip. Watches like that didn't just go missing, though. Anything worth more than a few thousand became a totem of paranoia for anyone who might be interested in buying it. She would be lucky to get a tenth of what it was worth at a pawn shop.

"Not something I would wear." She burrowed her fist deeper into her jacket pocket, hiding the rubber-banded Casio the drug store down the street sold her for 11 dollars. Liu noticed, then laughed.

"Of course, I apologize." In its place, he bumped open the cash register and slid out a few brown bills. "To reappropriation." There was at least that to be proud of, at least to the degree that people could see it again.

Ratty stared down at the hundreds.

"More?" He laughed, slipping one, then two more bills from the register.

Again, Ratty stared at the money, not entirely sure why.

She took it — "Thank you." — and turned to leave.

"Actually... I was hoping you would do me a quick favour on your way home? Not for me— some mom from up north called, said her son's been arrested." She stopped halfway to the booth. "He's in a holding cell. It's on your way."

The rest of her day was clear.

"Yeah, alright."

___

You had to dress nice to report a crime. Cops wouldn't let you past the lobby otherwise. You couldn't be carrying anything either, not after 9/11 anyway. You also couldn't just stash your bag somewhere nearby, or the entire bomb squad would be called out to put it under one of those thick metal bowls and sublimate it against the concrete.

Fern's shop was nearby, though. She left it by the front door.

Passing all those checks, she sidled up to the front desk, and spoke to the man at the front desk. "Fill out these papers and —"

"I actually—" She raised her hands, Letting go of the control it took to keep them from shaking. "I actually can't write on my own, I'm so sorry. I was hoping to speak to—"

"One moment." He stood up abruptly, talked to someone else behind the bulletproof glass, pointed in her direction, and slapped him on the back. He walked out of the back of the office and came around to guide her through the security doors.

"I actually— I'm really sorry." She waited until they latched closed behind her. "I really need to pee. Is that still possible?"

The officer rolled his eyes. "This way."

He stood outside while she pretended to pee. She scrolled through her phone in the relative quiet, popping in an earbud and playing something loud.

Wednesday, June 13, 2012. Legally, she could have used the women's restroom. It wouldn't have been a great look, though, a trans person using the correct bathroom on the exact day it was legalized, the same hour as what would probably be written up as a terrorist attack.

She shut her eyes with her back against the stall door, took a few long, deep breaths, and then held the last one. Outside, across the hall, and halfway up the stairwell. She had been in this building before. The camera halfway up only covered everything below it, and the camera on the landing above didn't cover the corner underneath.

She vaulted off the handrail at the landing camera, yanking it out of its moorings. With that gone, she let go of her breath and pressed against the wall nearest the upstairs door.

Whoever came through to check why it went dark would think that they had tripped. That suspicion would subside once they woke up in their underwear. The door clicked, Ratty froze time, grabbed the collar, and threw him to the ground.

Out cold, nobody the wiser. She stripped off his uniform and kept moving. Smaller precincts like this usually had a two-man system. Man number two — impatient as he was — had already gotten up to check on his friend. Ratty left him passed out in an empty office.

Her lungs started to ache at the threshold of the security office, throat spasming as she pulled the plug on the camera system. She stood up and let it out, coughing a few times to normalize her breathing.

"Yo! I didn't know they hired magicians here." The rabbit started as soon as her hand slapped the countertop. She struggled to stand to her full height with the ache in her chest. "How'd you do that?"

That was their charge. "White rabbit, dirty-blonde hair, kiwi accent," Liu had told her. She took an earbud out to focus on the terminal, ticking a line of checkboxes and watching their corresponding doors slide open.

"Oh, you're here to bust me out!" he began to bounce in his seat. "Hell yeah! Prison break. Gotta love it." Liu hadn't mentioned how energetic he was. That wouldn't be great for the disguise.

"Why are you like that?" she asked, stepping into the cell.

"Like what?"

"All jittery."

The rabbit looked Ratty up and down.

"Same reason you don't know that's rude to say." he

answered. "You're scary looking."

"Yeah, sorry. I have a lot of curses." She picked one up from just about every paranormal adjacent job. "What'd you do?"

"Oh shit, you're an undercover. Very sneaky. I like that. You guys are smart. I gotta hand that to you."

"Do I look like a cop?" All of this was exhausting. Ratty had very little energy these days to begin with. His eyes traced their way up her cheap collar, around the back of the hood billowing from the top, over her mop of curly hair.

"Is that a wig?"

"Do you want to pull on it?"

The rabbit considered that, stood up and reached out slowly, and gave it a gentle tug. One of her ringlets erupted into a frizzy collection of knots. "Go on." she offered. "Little harder." Another tug, hard enough to make her wince, and he sat back down.

"Sorry— are they contagious?" He went back to the curses.

"No." She couldn't be sure of that, but this was the least exhausting answer.

"I still didn't do anything. Some cop was talking shit and I talked shit back. Then he started talking about my family. Talking shit about my mom, and she's a good person, too. I really like her. She's a lesbian— I got two moms, actually, but one of them is my stepmom. Her name is Eleanor." He couldn't stop himself now that there was someone trustable in the room.

Two rabbits named Eleanor in the same province was not an especially pressing coincidence.

"What's your name?"

"Casey Rabbit."

"Did you tell them that?"

"No, do I look stupid?"

Two rabbits named Elanor in the same province, both with animal names, was a little closer to something that warranted looking into.

"Is it a requirement that all rabbit families have the word rabbit or bunny or some shit in their name?"

"What's your name?"

He's got you there, "Hanratty."

"Is it a requirement that—"

"I'm not a rat, I'm an opossum." She dropped the uniform in

his lap to cut him off. "Put this on and walk me out of the building."

She let him get as far as the hallway before stopping him. "Hang on."

This much commotion would warrant an extensive investigation, even in a tiny shithole precinct. If half the precinct was gone, though...

This jacket had a lighter in it. She broke from Casey and back into the security office. There was— which desk was it under? A wastepaper basket full of crumpled up scrap. She took a piece, lit it on fire, and dropped it back into the basket.

Probably the wrong order to do things in, actually. She picked it up — already a little warm to the touch — and set it under the camera's backup. Temp servers like this were small enough to keep off the ground. The desk had probably been prefabricated with the intent to sit in a basement office, where it was liable to flood.

She pulled a small pill bottle from the same pocket, popped the top, and sprinkled the ash within across the paper. There was still enough unfried terpenes in the stub of her joint to stink up the room.

"What're you doing?"

"I use this to snuff out joints, right? So it's got a bunch of ash in it." She backed into her explanation. "Desk protects the fire from the sprinklers. Fire's going to burn the tape of us getting out. Fire alarm is going to help us do it. The investigators are going to want to know where the fire started, and when they find the ash..." She left the rest unsaid. That would explain why two officers were found in weird places outside their station, one of them without clothes. "Marijuana is a very dangerous drug, Casey."

Occam's razor would be their Achilles' heel here. That was stupid. As soon as it *might* be something bad, everyone involved would be fired, and the investigation would be shuttered. Journalists would submit FOIA requests about it and create stories that no sane news operation in the GTA would pick up.

"That's some fucking Sherlock Holmes shit." Casey said.

Ratty didn't need the compliment. It wasn't clever. Ratty wasn't clever. It was stupid luck. She hadn't planned to show up today with exactly the tools to ruin some evidence. It was luck. Sherlock Holmes was smart. He earned the fact that he was an asshole. MacGyver still had to be nice to people on the off chance he didn't have anything to work with.

"God, I hope not." She would have to kill herself if she ever became smart enough to justify acting like an asshole.

"We should team up." The possum stood up and offered her arm. Casey took it, no better at pretending to be a cop than the people who got stuck with camera duty. "You and me, Hanratty and Casey."

"Quiet down," she whispered in his ear the entire way to the foyer, taking the back stairwell and crossing the edge of the little bullpen. She stopped him just outside the foyer.

"What're you—"

"Shut up." It was a slow day. There were empty terminals. One of them had been left logged on. "Take me over there. Pretend like you're booking me or something."

"What, why? We're right here."

"Just do it." She kicked a foot towards the desk. Casey walked her to the swivel chair, dropped her into it, and cut around the desk to sit in his own.

"I want to go on record as saying I hate this part of the plan."

"Good to know. Go to the desktop, open 'My Computer'" Thank god the rabbit looked young enough to be tech savvy. Breathing this hard, anything in the air started to smell like it was right under your nose. Ratty smelled smoke. "What's there?"

"There's—"

"There should be a subheading like 'Network Drives' or—"

"Network Locations?"

"Yeah. How many are there?" Something should have gone off by now. She used to throw baby powder at sprinklers to get them to go off. They were sensitive little devices.

"Two. One is called network and the other one is called—"

The possum looked down at the desk, and at the gold name plaque that sat finger-smudged on the thick wood. She picked it up and held it up to Casey. "Pick the one that doesn't have this guy's name on it."

"Okay, okay." You couldn't mistake the bouncy little rabbit for a cop even if you wanted to. He was too excited. "This is insane. This is fucking crazy."

"Shut the fuck up. Hit the search box and type Cane. C-A-N-E." She stood up, kicked the rolling chair out from under her. The smoke had started to attract people's attention to the upstairs balcony. Someone ducked into the back stairwell to check on it. She tipped the tower over as softly as she could and undid the two latches on the side.

"There's 128 results. 24 with an active criminal record."

"Any of them Marshall?"

"Two."

"Copy them both to a local drive."

"What does that—"

"Drag them—" she turned the monitor to look at it and pointed from the network folder to the desktop. "from here, to here. If someone asks you, I'm an IT specialist."

"You don't look like—"

"I know I don't." The fact that nothing had gone off yet was a miracle. She could hear a fire extinguisher puffing in the upstairs room. The lid came off the case and presented a nice, fat Angelcorp logo, just sitting on the motherboard.

It looked like it hadn't expected to run into anyone it knew today.

"Couple seconds." Casey says.

"Excuse me?" Both heads snap around to see the name on the desk replicated in miniature on an officer's chest. His hand is already on his gun. "Can I ask what you two are doing? There's a fire, we're—"

"She's from IT. I wasn't— I couldn't log in, so I thought—"

"Probably couldn't log in because you're sitting at *my desk*."

"Oh, well that makes sense, then." The rabbit put on a pretty convincing fake laugh and stood up away from the computer. He raised his hands slowly: apologetically at first, then up towards surrender as the button on the officer's holster clicked open.

"Can I get your badge number, buddy."

"I—"

Ratty watched the little built-in speaker rattle its cage as the machine finally chimed. In the next several seconds, alarms went off, followed by sprinklers and an automated man's voice shouting 'FIRE.'

Ratty tipped the tower off the desk, yanking the local drive free and stuffing it into a pocket in one motion.

"Shit." The officer hadn't noticed. Whoever was manning the fire extinguisher had failed to extinguish the fire. It hit something pressurized in the wall and made something bang. That woke the sprinkler system up. "You two stay put." The officer made his way towards the north stairwell.

"Start walking towards the exit and give me your name tag." All quick thinking today, huh, Ratty? Casey reached into his shirt and undid the pin, handing it over. Ratty scraped through her shaking palm with the sharp edge and held the cut to her forehead, letting the blood drip down over her eye. She hunched over and started coughing as they approached the lobby.

"I can't breathe!" she sobbed, dramatically. "I can't breathe." She let the blood drip all over the white marble, making sure to smear it with her boots.

"Shit, get her out of here." A taller detective pushed them towards the door before darting into the back.

Ratty stopped sobbing, tracked through the still-wet grass lawn, clearing the blood off her boots, then took Casey by the arm and ran down the rest of the block. The rabbit had not stopped freaking out since they were confronted.

"How the fuck did you—"

"Keep it down, keep walking. Take all the identifying markers off your clothes and undo all the buttons." She licked the hole in her hand, effectively doing nothing but cleaning up what blood was there.

She took out her phone and texted Fern, her eyes flicking every so often to the reflection of the street behind them in a car windscreen.

✉ 5:31pm: **New Message** — Ratty:

"got you a present"

She sent a picture, making sure to get both the Angelcorp and Toronto Police Department logos in the light. Fern expected her to text. It only took a few seconds for them to start typing.

✉ 5:31pm: **New Message** — Fern:
    "Shrimp..."
✉ 5:31pm: **New Message** — Ratty:
    "??? shrimp :?c"

"Your stepmom's name is Eleanor?" She started a parallel conversation for no other reason than to avoid being rude.

✉ 5:31pm: **New Message** — Fern:
    "yah like shrimpteresting"
✉ 5:31pm: **New Message** — Ratty:
    "ok leaving it at your shop"

She put her phone away, trying to ignore the way the glass screen clicked up against the metal hard-disk.

"Yeah." Casey answered.

"What's her maiden name?"

"What's it to you?"

"I also happen to know a rabbit named Eleanor."

"Who said she was a rabbit?"

"I—" Well, no one said that.

"Nah, sorry. I'm just fucking with you. It's Sloth-Bunny." Casey answered.

No fucking way.

"Eleanor Sloth-Bunny Senior?"

"Yeah, how'd you know?"

No shit...

---

The possum knelt to unco her boots as her front door shut behind her. Sett's jacket, their boots, and the etcetera they brought with them through the door was missing, suggesting the goat was out at the moment. Still...

230

"Sett?" Her voice probed the stillness. After a few seconds of nothing she resumed her normal routines. The zipper on her left boot had been giving her some trouble staying up. In the early winter, and with the constant possibility of needing to take off running, she had wrapped a leather choker around the part of the boot just above the curve. This kept the zipper mostly up, and had the added benefit of a little extra punk flare.

Still, every time they needed to come off, the possum had to loosen the small buckle and pass the zipper under the strap.

She stepped clumsily out of her boots, toeing one off with the other and kicking both onto the plastic mat in her foyer. She walked backwards into the kitchen on her toes, watching the warm collection of condensation ovals her socks left behind on the tile disappear.

She popped up onto the counter, fumbling blindly in the cupboard behind her head for... somewhere... there. A box, pushed towards the back, of granola bars. She took one, automatically resisting the urge to have two, and peeled the wrapper off, dinner to go with her show.

Sett didn't need her like this.

Bored with the dots as they plateaued at near-opaque, she opened her mp3 player, not all that different to the one she had had as a kid, scrolled past the few folders of Eleanor's recommendations, and failed to pick anything out of her library. She wondered, chewing on the grainy, artificial peanut butter, if she had fucked up the timeline enough for "music as a service" to never come about.

Unable to decide, she hit shuffle and set the device down on the kitchen counter. Something melancholy, a little whiny, Priests, maybe? Didn't matter.

From the kitchen to the bedroom she stripped off her socks and belt, tossing the pair into the *hers* side of a vandalized *(t)h(e)i(r)s and hers* laundry basket, and hanging the other in the same piece of plastic it always ended up on. She stopped as her hand fell from the hook, catching her reflection in the open bathroom door.

She rolled her shoulders back, watching the way the spikes pulled themselves into alignment as the back sides pressed more tightly against the sweater underneath. She straightened the collar next, and Hanratty Vermington stared back at her.

The jacket came off next, hung over the belt on the edge of the closet door, then the pants, left where they fell. Folding her work coat for long enough to get home creased it, but it couldn't look much worse.

She circled the bed, keeping focus on the mirror.

Even her nice hoodies had started to blow out at the sleeves. All the same brand. Black, plain, and clean was about as much as she could get away with with comfortable clothes, thanks in part to the chic of owning her own business.

They had to be tight around the wrists; they were liable to be grabbed otherwise.

She turned on both taps and pulled the mechanism that plugged the drain, watching it fill for only a few seconds to confirm it was working. She pulled her "nice" sweater off over her head, careful not to snag it on the sharp parts of her horns, and hung it on the back of the door.

There she stood: Hanratty Vermington.

Someone split her lip a few weeks ago. Healing in the cold, dry air had left behind a bright red mark. Her tight, clean ringlets had been all but annihilated by the dry winter air, leaving behind the more typical half-curly mess of frizz and flyaways. She pulled it out of the way of the darker patch that tagged her shoulder, tracing it from the bottom of her neck on the left down to the top of her upper arm with her finger, aware for as long as she would allow it of how wrong the slope looked against the rest of her form.

The bald scar across one side of her stomach stood out against the darker parts of her pattern.

Sett didn't need her like this.

The hand went to her back, popped her bra strap, and let it dangle down the length of her arms. Starting where it crossed her birthmark, she traced the groove the over-tight bands had carved through her fur throughout the day. Skipping across the softer parts of her chest, she thumbed down the pair of converging lines carved into her ribs, wincing at the sting as each downy strand folded itself back into place.

She wrapped her fingers around the lip of the sink, leaning in as close as she could without leaving the floor. The makeup around her eyes — she rarely put on more than that — had become smudged throughout the day by virtue of the imperceptible and unstoppable habit of touching her face.

The discolouration around her eyes stood out even through the smudged fistful of black liner, sinking her eyes into their sockets. The whites, where they could be seen, had begun to go bloodshot.

There were features no one else noticed until they were pointed out. The ridge above her brow, for example, came at such an angle that it made her face look sewn on in the right light. That line continued almost all the way around, completing the effect.

Her eyes drifted out of focus as the lukewarm water began to lap gently at her fingertips. There were the eight indentations her nails had carved in the soft faux-porcelain, pressed into by the tips of her fingers.

Quietly, her eyes refocused on the gap between the faucet and the edge of the sink.

Drowned out by the hollow noise of the runoff drain, her mp3 player switched to a new song.

She blinked once at the rough surface, then plunged her face into the water.

It's calming at first, gently cupping her cheeks in a cool full-face embrace, making rings where her whiskers meet the surface. It's quiet. Even with her ears above the water the rushing of the faucet drowns out anything more than a meter away.

A few small bubbles trickle out of her nose, filling it with water. Her throat gets tight first, starting at the top of her chest. Trying to distract herself, she pays closer attention to the way the water rocks back and forth against her face.

Her thoughts start to race, *why am I doing this* coupled with images of her head getting stuck under the tap coupled with the most mundane things. The pressure is most obvious where her chest rests against the countertop, moving down through the centre of her torso and branching out like heavy roots.

She lets out a little bit of air and regrets it immediately. Following that moment her chest gets exponentially tighter each second. It becomes exponentially harder to force herself to stay under. Her legs buckle slightly, the solution to that being a few kicks against the cold, hard tile.

She thinks about the faucet again.

She starts to feel like coughing, comes to understand that she cannot, and starts to feel her eyes water.

She becomes frustrated with her temptation to come up so soon. She thinks about the times she hasn't had the option to pop back up for air. She thinks about how long she's been under and realizes she's fucked herself. As soon as she asks that her brain catches up with her lungs.

She hits and then passes a mental wall. Her nails scrape against the sink as though it was against the inside of her own eardrums. Her hand moves from the interior of the sink to the edge of the counter, struggling to keep balance as her one leg kicks harder.

Her lungs start to suck involuntarily at the inside of her mouth, swallowing spit and ash. A portion of her brain sets itself aside to keep her nose blocked off, flexing a muscle that must get used by normal people once or twice in a lifetime.

She begins to search along the ground with her kicks, looking for the grout between tiles. It's rougher, it hurts more, it's more distracting.

At this point the ache in her lungs has plateaued. It becomes less about breathing and more about trying not to breathe. The counter creaks through the water as her arms strain against it. It would hurt so much more if her lungs filled with water.

It has been roughly 45 seconds.

Her throat starts to make a sobbing motion. With everything in her body clamped firmly shut it manifests as little more than an anguished, sucking cough, made completely impotent by the fact that no air can enter her body.

Her arms are shaking. She is cold and alone, straining against her instincts. The smear of blood dripping from her toe-knuckle dragged through the grout is the warm little centre of the universe.

And then she came back up. Not a relief. Her nose at that point was so full of cold water that what didn't shoot back into her throat dripped pathetically down her chest. Her breathing struggled to settle, and her eyes followed the droplets down the front of the counter to the smear of blood between the tiles. It was now so obviously small.

Sett didn't need her like this.

She pulled over a bath-mat from the shower's exit to cover the stain, pulled her loose-fitting college hoodie from the back of the door, and slumped to a sitting position against the counter.

"Hey phone!" she called through the silence. The automated assistant chimed from inside her jeans pocket. "What time is it?"

A half-second, then "It's 2:41pm."

She let out one final sigh, forcing it to settle her lungs, and got back up. From there, she trudged the five-or-so feet between the bathroom counter and her bed, fell into it, and wrapped herself in the duvet.

---

Ratty got told off a lot of tapping her toe when she was a kid. It was impolite, or something. She worked out a system: tap twice as much when she couldn't be seen waiting, and then stop whenever someone looks at her.

The floors here were too thin, though. If someone walked too heavily, the whole building shook under their feet. Everyone got used to that. You couldn't file a noise complaint in a building you didn't pay to live in.

She stared down at the most recently sent message on her phone, waiting for a reply.

✉ 6:09pm: **New Message** — RV🐉:
"hey im at your door can i come in"

That was rude too, probably. No one ever clarified. Usually when someone asks you why you do something, they're actually telling you to stop. It depended on the tone of voice and some other arcane factors.

The music leaking through Eleanor's door reminded her that she needed to talk to Eleanor, so she stopped. People never accepted the simplest answer.

✉ 6:10pm: **New Message** — Eleanor SB Jr. 🐱:
"b my guest."

She was still getting up from her pull-out couch when Ratty pushed through the door, her pouchy stomach hanging over a pair of bright red y-front underwear. "Oh, you meant like literally —"

"Sorry!" Ratty turned to the wall. The underwear was the only thing Eleanor was wearing.

"It's chill, hang on."

Ratty idly examined the black pedestal installed in Eleanor's entryway instead. Somewhere, a few inches below a slot in the top, some arcane mechanics tugged on the thread that kept Eleanor's mask bound to her, and tied on enough slack for her to wander around most of the building without it.

"Sett do this?" Ratty asked, too quietly to actually get an answer. Sett was the only one who could have done this. "This is cool."

She put her hand down on the smooth black surface, surprised when a bubble of pressure pushed back against her palm. It grew and vibrated in time with Eleanor's music.

"That is so cool. It's like a subwoofer." She watched her hand rise and fall from the shiny black surface.

"What?" Eleanor asked, the word vibrating against Ratty's palm.

"Like a subwoofer—" Eleanor had thrown a brown and mustard yellow hoodie over their head, abandoning the thought of putting on any more clothing. It almost covered the bottom-most part of her underwear. Ratty remembered she wasn't supposed to be looking.

"Sorry!" She turned back to the pedestal.

"It's fine, this is as dressed as I was planning on getting. What are you talking about?" Eleanor stood at Ratty's side, a few inches taller even in her bare paws.

"Are you sure? I can—"

"I don't like, remember how to flirt."

"Oh…" Wait, what? "Oh!"

Wait, really? Even the possum's worst plan was better than standing next to someone with their pants off.

Well—

Whatever.

Tall, dark, and good looking. Ratty had no complaints.

"It's like a subwoofer for your brain." Ratty explained. "Every time you talk- here." She took Eleanor's hand and set it down in the same spot hers had just been. It was immediately apparent. When she tried to breathe, the vibration mimicked what would have been her in-and-out, her weak ethereal heartbeat. When she focused on the buzzing synthesizer and simple snare behind them, the bass abided by DOOM's lopsided tempo.

When Ratty took her hand just then... she hoped it wasn't too loud.

"Cute undies, by the way." She had stopped trying to be polite about staring.

"Too hot for pants." Eleanor shrugged. Ratty blinked, leaning to look behind Eleanor's back and counting at least six space heaters, all plugged into the same less-than-solid power strip. That — in conjunction with the obelisk, made her just about opaque.

"Yeah." She nodded. "It would be." Eleanor turned to follow her line of sight, then blushed.

"Sorry— I— they make me feel real." She turned away abruptly, the red still visible on the tips of her ears. "It's good for the plants, too— I'm sorry, this isn't anything, right?" She threw herself down on the couch, kicking the record player on her floor and burying her face in her elbow. The tonearm picked itself up and set itself down in its cradle.

"What 'isn't anything'?" Ratty sat down on the arm of the couch, intentionally positioning herself so that her and Eleanor's fur was touching. Eleanor — evidently — had no idea about her soft spot for massive dorks. Eleanor groaned quietly into the muffling fabric of her sweater in false confidence that it would completely silence her.

"What was that before?" Ratty — sensing a plea for mercy — changed the subject.

"I don't remember." She uncovered her mouth. "Can you put something on?

"Do you have anything in mind?"

"You pick something." With that, Eleanor turned over and buried her face in the pull-out mattress, somehow less muffled by that than her arm. Ratty knelt next to the coffee table, sweeping aside a pile of cassettes half way through their reels and pulling one of the plastic-smelling cases towards her.

She tapped along the tops of tapes until she found what

must have been the only piece of punk-rock in Eleanor's collection: an almost untouched pirate tape of These Monsters Are Real. She rolled back on her haunches and shut her eyes as the song picked up, her fangs poking through as a gentle smile touched her lips.

God that was cute. Eleanor hoped silently that she couldn't be seen staring. "You like this?" she asked.

"Love it." Ratty muttered, flicking her hands in time with the beat. "Do you always have to be playing something?"

"Yeah, sorry."

"Always hip-hop?"

"No, I uh— I like the Beatles?"

"Well, don't be stupid, Rigby. Everyone likes the Beatles."

"Sixties British rock more broadly, then, I guess— these aren't my tapes— is it annoying?" Eleanor asked, suddenly feeling a little tight in her chest.

"Not at all, I'm just..." Ratty met Eleanor's poorly hidden gaze. "...curious about you," she said, a subtle wink in her voice. It came out of her mouth lopsided, a little weird.

One of the fortunate things about being a ghost was that a certain level of blush plateaued above what could be seen in her translucent form. What it could not hide was the goofy, scrunched up smirk Sloth-Bunny was now all too conscious of pulling.

"You a fag or something?" Eleanor teased, trying to recover.

"You probably get a lot of fags here, so..." Ratty doubled down, throwing up a quick hand-horns as though to accent her sharp edge. Eleanor froze, trying and failing to come up with a comeback for long enough to phase slightly through her mattress.

She settled on a shaky "Shut up, oh my god. Why are you here?" with a sarcastic lilt in the last word.

This was flirting for Eleanor. That realization immediately crumpled the possum's façade. For the third time, she turned back to the black pedestal in the foyer, this time spinning all the way around to hide her face.

"You good?"

"I am so good." Ratty answered, putting a palm over her snout to cover the hot rush of blood. "I— uh— found your family." A flawless and not at all abrupt change of subject.

"What?" The rabbit's blood ran cold. She sat in stunned silence as Ratty popped up onto her feet, not noticing the rabbit's struggle to scrape up any scrap memories that didn't consist of smug shit-shooting with her Uncle Alf.

"I uh, broke your step-brother out of prison." Ratty said this as if it was the simplest possible thing. "Angel is gonna come up and portal us over, and I am going to leave so you can put pants on, I guess."

"Well, wait. Hold on." Eleanor grabbed the possum's wrist, shooting a spike of ice up into her chest. "We should dri— are you okay?" Ratty had flinched hard enough to have to stabilize herself on the opposite wall. She stood shaking, glaring down at Eleanor's hand.

"Yeah, sorry, just don't—" she started, her heart still racing as she tried her best to get back to normal. Eleanor pulled back, debating re-changing the subject and scrambling for an excuse. "You said Angel's thing has been, like, messing up or something, right?" Eleanor forced a grin, struggling to hold down a rising bile. Something about the combination of anxiety and tone clicked in Ratty's mind, letting a silent 'oh...' cross her lips.

"It is within driving distance," she said, nodding slowly, choosing to focus on Eleanor's anxiety over her own.

"Yeah, see, cool."

"And we could get the big van out of storage."

"See, absolutely, big van road trip."

"Alright, cool." Ratty clapped, backing out of the room. "Big van road trip."

# 2013
# Road Trip

The van rolled to a stop after a few hours on a coastal road edging the South end of Hudson Bay. Angel — a few loose wires disappearing into the cracked panels of the dashboard — went into hibernation immediately, her head tipping forward as she tried to diagnose what had actually gone wrong.

"Is that normal?" Eleanor asked.

"Yeah, she uh— yeah," Ratty only bothered to look up for a half-second.

This early in March — year-round, honestly — it was too cold for Eleanor to swim without a risk of dissipation. While Sett and Ratty made their way down the frigid beach, she floated to the roof of the van and smoked.

It wasn't perfect, but the hot smoke made her throat and trachea solid enough to carry about 40% of whatever she inhaled through it. Bongs made that harder. By the time it reached their mouth smoking through a bong, the smoke had already cooled off enough to float up through the roof of their mouth and into the air.

It helped with the anxiety.

The temperature did not stop Sett, slowly backing into the shallow with Ratty's hands in their own. The possum's toes refused to cross the white edge of frigid surf as she bent further and further over to avoid the drag.

She shook her head, hair clearly bouncing back and forth even from this distance.

Sett fell back, keeping their hands firmly around the possum's and dragging her in. She could sometimes get loud when she talked. This was not that kind of loud. Ratty screamed, a wordless single note that sent both Sett and Eleanor's spines straight.

Sett hands hovered over Ratty as she stood, careful not to

get too close. Ratty pointed, and Sett put their hands up apologetically. Ratty took a moment and let her hand drop. Sett offered their hands, Ratty stared down at them. She took one. They talked, all too distant to hear.

Sett pointed up the beach, drawing a circle around an abandoned fire pit with their finger. Ratty shook her head and let go, flopping backwards into the water and startling the goat. She floated a little ways into the deep.

Eleanor's cheeks lit up as Sett stripped off their soaked sweater — too far in the middle of nowhere for anyone but her to notice. A fire would have been nice right now. It might have even brought her up to 60%, but it was close enough to intervene if Ratty stopped floating. Better not to get in-between that. Wrapped in a blanket, the goat sat and dripped dry.

Ratty spent another half-hour soaking, staring up at the sky. Every few minutes she would put her arms at her sides and sink just deep enough to cover her snout. Sett would anxiously watch the bubbles for a little over 45 seconds, and then Ratty would bob back up as though nothing had happened.

She got out, either too bored or too cold to continue, and slogged her way up the beach to stand shivering by her partner. It was weird seeing them from this far away. Ratty wasn't good with contact; she had this way of keeping her distance whenever she had to talk to someone she didn't like. There was usually some softness in her posture when she talked to Sett, like she was ready to collapse into a hug at any point, but despite her hiding it well, the same façade that became obvious around strangers radiated from the possum. There was something wrong between them.

After a few minutes of back and forth — the goat never dropping out of their apologetic posture — Ratty bent over to set a kiss on her partner's forehead, trying and failing not to drip on them. From there, she turned tail and trekked the rest of the way back to the motorhome. Her mostly untied boots hung loose around her ankles as they stomped through the brush and stopped on the gravel curb.

"Hey Rigby." She forced a smile, exhausted, up at the sloth-bunny's rooftop perch.

"Hey Ratty." Eleanor nodded. "Sorry for making you swim in like, negative degrees."

"You didn't make me do anything." Her voice rang hollow, muffled by the corrugated aluminum just long enough to pull a towel from a compartment inside the door and wrap herself in it.

The frayed ends of the towel danced in the ambient light as she shivered, waiting for something.

"Mind if I come up?"

"Oh, yeah. Be my guest." Eleanor scooted away from the ladder, guessing that that was what she wanted. Ratty took a half-step back and jumped, rocking the van as she dug the toe of her boot into the corrugated metal siding.

"There's a— there's a ladder." Eleanor watched the possum shake as she pushed herself the rest of the way up.

"Did you use the ladder?" There was less mirth in her voice than Eleanor would have hoped for. "What're we listening to?" Ratty scooched in closer and held out her hand for an earbud. Her eyes remained blank. Eleanor handed over her spare, turning the music down enough to talk over. It was filler. Not complex or something she listened to by name, just simple piano and simple drums. Just filler.

Still, Ratty rocked to the tempo, shaking the van under them. Her hands raised from their fixed position on her lap, almost imperceptibly air-drumming along. Something about that prodded a blank spot in Eleanor's memory, only a few synapses away from her mutism.

"Are they okay?" Eleanor asked, nodding to Sett after a few quiet moments.

"I— yeah..."

"Did you want to tell me about..."

Ratty disappeared from behind her eyes as the rabbit trailed off. "They can't swim." she said, filling the silence on instinct.

"I didn't know that." Eleanor said.

"Yeah, me neither." Ratty murmured, drawn back to reality if only slightly. She clamped her eyes shut, threw the towel over her face and scrubbed water out of the top of her snout. The sound failed to hide her long sigh. Even if it hadn't, Eleanor would still have felt her go tense.

"I shouldn't have freaked out like that." Her voice crumpled. She caught Eleanor's eye, faltering as she noticed a legitimate twinge of concern.

"You have like… a water thing?" Eleanor asked.

"Like a phobia?"

The ghost nodded.

"No, no. I'm not afraid of anything." That clearly wasn't true.

Eleanor watched as Ratty's eyes tried to refocus on the distant goat, squinting too hard to make it worth it. Her blank expression dissolved into some kind of melancholy as she sat back. The pair let the next few songs pass. She closed her eyes during a particularly interesting little melody, as though the music had convinced her to meditate.

"So…" Ratty pivoted. "You nervous?"

"What?"

"To meet your mom, I mean."

"I dunno, I mean—" The rabbit took a deep breath. Where even to start with that? She stayed silent, turning it over in her head.

"It's okay if you don't want to—"

"She moved away and changed her number," Eleanor stared down at the gravel below, stuck between not wanting to make everything all about her and having already opened her mouth. Ratty — by way of encouragement — wrapped her tail around Eleanor's back and pulled her in a little closer. There was tension in this little show of intimacy, but it was better than being alone right now.

"I had these texts— 'can you get milk on your way home' or 'happy birthday' or whatever, and I never thought I'd actually get to meet—" Eleanor sniffed. "She's a stranger! She's straight up a—" Eleanor choked, trying to pull air into her non-existent lungs. She stopped as her voice, now bricked over with anxiety, refused to come out of her mouth. It took a second of frantic, amateurish sign-spelling to get the point across.

"I am so sorry, El', I don't— I'm sorry, I don't know sign language." Ratty sat back to try and read the hands anyway. That was fine. What Eleanor knew was not fit to replace this kind of conversation. She instead settled for pulling the possum back in, feeling the drops of water on her fur fizzle against her form.

Cold and empty, Eleanor clung to Ratty, waiting for her voice to come back. She hated how pathetic that made her feel, their only tether to the outside world equally tethered. The both of them hovered above it all, grasping at the tips of lampposts and utility poles to try and drag themselves back down.

Sett probably felt the same way.

"S-s-sorry about t-t—." Eleanor stammered, words coming back before thoughts.

"What? Today? What about it?"

"Grab—"

"Oh, El', don't worry about it, okay?" Ratty smiled softly, letting the ghost's heart sink into normalcy for just a moment. This particular non-incident was not worth forcing herself through a massive panic attack for.

At least the possum had weight. Short of being able to come down, she could thrash. She had enough control to pull them through the air, sometimes down.

They sat like that for a moment, a different kind of silence sitting between the two of them. Ratty was incredibly comfortable to sit with and for a moment. With a sudden brick wall of guilt, Eleanor imagined how much more comfortable they could get together if she just— no. Stop.

She traced the cold oval of wet where their arms overlapped, up Ratty's arm, across her throat, up into her eyes.

There was still too much she didn't understand. There was not enough Eleanor.

It was almost distracting enough, the way the possum's eyes explored her own.

Eleanor pooled in her feet, in the tips of her fingers, barely enough to slosh from one limb to another when she moved.

Distracting enough was the tip of Ratty's tail resting gently against her opposite thigh.

Ratty hadn't noticed how little there was.

Distracting enough was — in spite of herself — the gentle way the crook of her snout led into her lips. She quietly hoped her eyes were dark enough not to be seen.

"It's going to go well." Ratty said, her low-tone voice taking on a slight crackle as she hovered just above a whisper. "I know it will."

The voice drew Eleanor's eyes to the possum's lips, staying parted for just a half-second longer than usual as she finished speaking. Eleanor — secure in the knowledge that her heart was not going to start or stop racing — leant in slowly, watching

Ratty's eyes for any small change. She was not going to kiss Ratty. Ratty did not want to kiss her. It was the weed, probably. Anyone as energetic as Ratty should not be giving recommendations on weed to smoke for anxiety. She would ask Sett next time.

She was getting closer, though.

Both of them jumped out of their skin as Angel smacked the sunroof to the edge of its hinges limits. "Ratty. The spare battery doesn't have enough charge to finish the journey. I will walk to the nearest garage and find a replacement. You will have to sleep here."

Ratty took a moment to compose herself, the hand on Eleanor's thigh turning from flirtatious to protective as her wheezing slowed.

"Alright, sounds good." Ratty said, swallowing the gravel in her voice. "Is there anything in the new one?"

"There is enough for you to be able to run the heater and the radio. You might be able to charge a cell phone, but it would interfere with everything else."

"Cool." Something cracked as the possum dropped, heavy, off the roof. "I'm gonna, uh, sleep — fill Sett in for me?"

Eleanor nodded, too stunned by the sudden change to do anything else. It would have been bad timing either way.

She let her eyes defocus as Ratty went inside, listening to the heater thrum to life behind her. Another few minutes to collect her thoughts and bring herself down, then a hop down to the curb.

---

Sett had left an empty spot next to them on their driftwood bench. They smiled tiredly up at Eleanor, scooting over after a few quiet seconds to make sure the rabbit was comfortable.

"Evening, Eleanor." Sett said, their quiet voice all-consuming in the silence, eyes fixed on the steam rising from their sweater.

"Hey, Angel says we're gonna be stuck overnight."

"I figured as much, have a seat." Eleanor complied, trying her best to act like the goat had not just watched her become familiar with their fiancée's personal space. Eleanor didn't know much about them at that point. Sett was smart, and that was it.

They intended to take advantage of that for as long as it lasted.

Their fur had puffed up in the process of drying, leaving them looking significantly more like a plush doll than they preferred. They had tried and failed to slick their fur back down around their cheeks, leaving it frizzled in one uniform direction and giving off the appearance of mutton chops.

"We should talk more," they said.

"Yeah. We should— I really appreciate all the, uh, like arcane—"

"We have something very important in common." Sett cut her off, the hint of mischief creeping into their voice, their eyes twinkling under their usual glow. Around their wrist, Ratty's watch ticked over to 1:00 a.m. They were not going to be able to keep up this air of mystique.

"What— uh— what's that?" Eleanor asked.

"Similar taste in women." Sett smirked. That gave it away.

"I—" Eleanor stammered. "Shut up, no way. No way, no way, no way."

"It's fine, Eleanor," Sett said, trying to wave away their quiet laughter. "I'm only teasing."

"How did you—"

"Oh, don't act coy. I know what it looks like when my fiancée flirts with another," Sett teased, deflating Eleanor's ego just a tad.

"I'm not— it was her— she started it." the rabbit stammered.

"Calm down, dear, Ratty and I have been engaged for sixty years. I can definitely understand the appeal." There had so rarely been good times, but they weathered the bad expertly. Something about that made them smile, raising a hand to hide their rumpled snout.

They loved Ratty. It would have been stupid to try and deny that. They were waiting for a return on that investment.

That wasn't fair, actually.

Eleanor could be good for her. She could be good for Eleanor.

They closed a hand over the watch.

"The two of us are very secure in our union, Eleanor," they said. "You may do what you wish." They watched the flecks of orange rise from their fire.

The moment passed as both of them focused in on the last

embers of the fire, still warm enough to force gravity into Eleanor's body. It occurred to both of them that, if she were to be stabbed, a knife would actually stick into her.

Again, the next little while passed in silence, interrupted only by Eleanor's phone buzzing to let her know she had 15% of her battery left. Sett stood silently once the fire had gone out, smiled sleepily at Eleanor, and made their way back to the motorhome without breaking the silence.

---

The rabbit watched smoke rise from the still-warm coals, taking their time to flicker and die as she cranked her music. It did very little to drown out her thoughts.

It was also hard to tell whether there was a legitimate attraction between her and Ratty, or just that her brain — devoid of the context from the rest of her life — just latched onto any pretty girl that was nice to her. Sett was pretty and nice, and there wasn't really anything there.

She wondered if things between them were always kind of tense. Before she came back from the ghostzone, everything felt pretty much fine. The limited time Eleanor had to observe the two had only dipped into the red whenever Ratty injured herself: Sett would get frustrated, Ratty would throw herself over her partner, apologize profusely — either sarcastically or genuinely depending on the situation — and things would be resolved.

She hoped quietly that she wasn't coming between them — they were like, what, a hundred and a million years old respectively? It was conceivable that she was the first new friend they had in a few decades.

Memories had come to her in flashes. The feeling of being excited to sit in the front seat, forgetting about how aggressively she had been buckled in. A small apartment. Screaming next door. Rough carpet against her face as she listened to heavy bass tones in the room below.

Her conversation with Uncle A hadn't helped either. The best it did was help to put a name to a song that some piracy program had mislabelled as *1syWDI7H013.mp3* in her phone. She remembered a few moments from her childhood scrubbing through the collection: learning to navigate an iPod with a nonfunctioning screen, getting an earful from her mother on more than one occasion, seeing her downstairs neighbour's apartment cordoned off with yellow tape.

She remembered a uniquely woeful note in her mother's voice as junior fought a vacation for all the responsibility she had. A swimming pool at a small New Zealand hotel. A bartender with white fur and red eyes, having a sleepover with her kids while their mom had a sleepover with hers.

"My mom's a lesbian." Eleanor figured this out out loud, solving the memory like a puzzle. Of course she was. There was a family structure in her head: Mom, the bartender, the bartender's kids, and her. After spending so much time avoiding thinking about her past, there was an exhilaration in finally confronting it...

...Until her music died. A curtain of black fog dropped in a foot-wide ring as her chest tightened. The fire had gone out, it's blackened logs visible only in the light from the barely waning moon. She stood, panicked, and turned in the direction she assumed the motorhome to be. There was nothing there but black. Ratty and Sett had probably gone to sleep, they probably also turned the lights out.

Eleanor walked. The walk turned into a jog, which turned into a run, which turned into a painful bang as she ran headlong into a corrugated metal wall. She braced herself against it, felt the cabin's radiator just on the other side, took a moment to recognize how lucky she was to have buzzed herself off the only part of the van that she wouldn't just go right through.

Sett was lying on the couch, just barely awake as Eleanor floated up through the door.

"Everything okay?" they asked, their glowing eyes squinting through the dark.

"My— my music died." It sounded stupid once Eleanor said it out loud.

"Oh, I'm sorry. Is the radio loud enough?" Eleanor took a moment to focus in on what was already playing, it was hard to decipher, not necessarily complex, but alien. Radio friendly alt-rock, maybe. She shook her head.

"I need *my* music."

"Of course." Sett reached up above the couch and clicked the radio off. They motioned Eleanor over, ducking so she had room to plug her phone into the cigarette lighter. The heater dimmed slightly as the screen lit up and in a second, the cabin was filled with the same slow, soft hip-hop as before.

"I'm sorry." Eleanor said, taking stock of her actions in her unsteady peace.

"It's okay. We all have our things." Sett said, turning back over and burrowing into the couch.

"Wait, why are you on the couch?" she whispered, realizing Ratty was still asleep on the bed at the back of the trailer. The goat mumbled inaudibly into their cushions before falling back asleep.

A new, calm kind of panic set in at the back of her mind as she took stock of her options: She could sit in the navigator's seat and wake up aching, or she could take up the extra room in Ratty's bed. Her body made the decision for her, trying its best not to creep as she prepared to climb into bed with a sleeping woman.

Ratty came up to just about eye level with Eleanor, standing on the first step up to the bunk. She lay there, eyes phasing between shut and screwed shut, chewing holes into the collar of a worn-out grey hoodie. It was only for one night. If Ratty got mad she could just say she didn't want to wake Sett up. It was a big bed too, she could have very easily just taken the other side.

Eleanor focused on the beat as she very carefully hoisted herself onto the little loft, hovering slightly as she tried to climb over Ratty without touching her, and nestled under the blankets. The bed creaked loudly as Ratty rolled over, her snout settling just inches from Eleanor's. Something flickered over her snout in the ghost's glow. Either behind or in front of her, a pair of runic languages unspelled themselves as they collided.

This was such a bad idea.

The possum opened one eye and jumped, banging her head on the roof of the cabin.

"Oh my god, I'm so sorry, I—"

"It's okay. It's okay." Ratty pulled her breathing back under control, rubbing some of the soreness out of the base of her horn and staring curiously at the dent it had left in the metal. "What're you—"

For the first time in her life, Eleanor's anxiety forced her to speak. "Just, Sett was on the couch, and I—"

Something changed in the possum's face as she met Eleanor's eye. The understanding that she was being shown affection spread under her fur in a light red blush, highlighted in the ghost's shadow.

"I can leave if—"

"No, please." She scooted back to make room. "Stay."

"Are you sure?"

"I promise it's okay, Eleanor." She slouched back down under the sheets, rolling over once more to slot herself neatly into the taller woman. A chill went up Eleanor's spine as Ratty wove her tail between their legs, wrapping it neatly around her ankles. It took an awkward moment to settle in, Eleanor's hands hovering — afraid to trigger the possum's PTSD — until Ratty took them and held them close to her heart. The smaller woman's lungs rose and fell through her own chest, and for a moment, it almost felt like she was breathing again.

---

Sett was gone when Eleanor woke up. They left a note on the couch: *went for coffee, back soon.*

It was permission, if anything, to relax. Ratty's snout lay in the same foam groove as Eleanor climbed over her, a heavy enough sleeper just to be watched for a few minutes while the rabbit waited for the goat. Angel was nowhere to be found, probably still looking for a compatible battery.

It startled Eleanor when Sett dropped down on the adjacent wheel well. The goat had somehow entered silently with both hands full of coffee cups.

"I didn't know what you like," they whispered, "so I got—" They opened their purse, revealing what must've been an entire Tims' worth of cream and sugar packets. Eleanor also didn't know what she liked, and so took the cheap, bitter, basically-water plain, adding to it as she got a feel for the flavor.

"Should we move?" Eleanor asked, tilting their head towards the sleeping possum.

"She won't wake up." Sett raised the cup to where their lips ought to be and drank absorbing it through their fur like a sponge. "How are your plants?" they asked.

"They're okay." She pushed at the edges of her memory, searching for a past affinity that would explain how the cheap little hardware store ivy had flourished. "I dunno if I ever like, did that before, if that makes sense."

"Your memory is getting better too. That's exciting." Sett confirmed. "You should bring them to group some time."

That wasn't exactly the most attractive idea. Eleanor had felt a certain way about exposing herself to strangers for as long as she could remember.

"Do people do show and tell?"

"Mhmm. We treat it more like a little theatre, really. I read some poetry or play a song, sometimes Ratty shows up to sing with me." Sett smiled down into their coffee. The whole thing was a little bit silly to them. "Small venues only, of course. Friends and parties and all that."

"You do music?" Eleanor asked.

"I do."

"How do you manage with the..." the rabbit trailed off, letting a quiet trace across her lips explain for her.

"Oh, have I never shown you this before?" Sett asked, a quiet excitement flashing behind their eyes.

They took Eleanor's moment of silence as an invitation to explain, shifted their jaw with their hands as though rubbing some soreness out of it and, with one eye jammed shut in concentration, opened their mouth wide and tore the skin that covered it like a zipper. Behind it was a row of normal-looking teeth, an upper gum, tongue, throat, and all the other fixings of a regular jaw.

"This is what my real voice sounds like." The words hissed from their throat, barely audible.

"Okay. That's sickening." Eleanor said, trying her best to convey *no offence* with tone. "Please put it back."

"Does it make you uncomfortable?" they asked, their telepathy taking back over as they produced a glowing needle and thread from the air. They went to work patching up the hole, keeping their eyes on Eleanor as the wound disappeared.

"It just looks really painful."

"I promise it's not." The goat smiled. It had already healed over, the only lingering evidence of its existence a few flecks of blood on the white tip of their snout. They turned ever so slightly, noticing for the first time that Ratty had been watching them.

"You're really beautiful," the possum murmured, not a trace of irony in her voice. Her eyes flicked to the mattress as Sett's locked on. Eleanor followed the interaction, stopping on Sett when it became clear that they had noticed.

"Hey... Ratty." Eleanor prodded. The possum's eyes screwed shut against the light for an extra half-second before she turned over, centring the ghost in her vision.

"Hi El'." She squinted against the rabbit.

"Are we good on uh, last night?"

"So good," Ratty replied, her eyes lulling closed. "Good as Gandhi, silly rabbit."

"Oh, hun, Gandhi sucked." Sett dropped themself back into the conversation, scooting a little closer to the edge of the wheel well.

"I kinda know, I just thought maybe I could say that and get away with it. Indiana Jones my way under the slowly descending stone door of my partner telling me which historical figures secretly suck," she explained, blindly sliding the back of her hand along the top of the mattress to illustrate.

"Dude, Gandhi did not secretly suck. It was like, in books and stuff."

"Eleanor is right, and I simply can't stay engaged to a woman who refuses to append a historical callout to her riffs."

"Yeah Ratty, that was kind of fucked up of you." Eleanor piled on.

"Oh fuck, I'm being exiled." The possum buried her head under the duvet. "I just woke up and I'm getting Romeo'd out of Stratford on Avon," she said, her voice trapped in the down.

"Romeo wasn't—" Sett started.

"Fuck! You're right!" Ratty growled into the blanket.

"Who was— what're we talking about?"

"Romeo was from Verona, Shakespeare was from Stratford on Avon," again muffled by the soft down.

"Shakespeare?" Sett said, the corner of a laughing fit edging into their voice. Ratty's snout poked out from under her nest, eyes glowing through the tiny gap. "I barely—" They cut themself off as they caught Ratty's expression.

"I need this from you." The rust of sleep had started to kick itself off her voice.

"I—"

"I need you to finish this." She advanced a little further, duvet now barely holding her ears by the tips.

"I barely—" They stopped again, waving away a fit of giggles.

"Please. I need this from you, you sweet beautiful shining star of my life." Her melancholy had completely melted, now entirely focused on Sett. The goat cleared their throat and straightened their back, putting on a very convincing serious face.

"Shake spear?" Their voice shook with the effort of keeping it together. "I barely know her."

Which was just about worth it.

Alright, this was it.

Eleanor wove her fingers through a length of glowing gold thread. Burning bright against her knuckles, it kept her grounded and corporeal, belligerently refusing the cool morning air's threat to shatter her. Despite the long, almost completely ephemeral leash, Sett stood clearly just behind her. The gentle excitement emanating from the pair behind her likely would have been noticeable even without the string.

It was hard to know what she herself was feeling.

Nervous, probably.

No use putting it off. She raised her hand, the thread making it just physical enough to hit the wooden door, took a deep breath, and knocked.

Energy built in the soles of her shoes as she waited, listening to something on the other side of the door as it shuffled closer. The something stopped, leaving a few seconds of silence and a final moment to run before the lock clicked and the door thunked open against its chain.

"You had better have a damn good reason for—" Something wooden and hollow-sounding clattered to the floor on the other side as the woman recognized her daughter's face.

There she was; Eleanor Sloth-Bunny Sr., her namesake. She was shorter than expected, the strands of grey in her dark purple-brown fur and tied back pom-pom-tight black curls

highlighted in the subtle glow of Eleanor Jr. Same colour,
different shades. Sr. had none of Jr.'s patterning; death had not
brought the same chalky overtone to her fur.

"Junie?" The older woman's voice shook.

"Hey, Ma'." Eleanor responded, not missing a beat. She had
just come home from work, like her mother had put the chain
across without realizing she was still out. She raised a
trembling hand to her lips, tears welling up in her eyes.

"Hey, baby." The door shut for just a moment before
swinging wide and crashing into the metal fence that edged the
small landing. Eleanor Sr. stood, stunned as her daughter
pulled her in. She was still for just a moment before throwing
her arms up around Eleanor Jr. her shaking arms trying to
crush the life back into her daughter.

"Missed you." Eleanor murmured into the top of her mother's
head.

"I missed you too, baby."

---

There was something weird about not remembering her own
car, about it being the second most valuable thing most people
ever own and simultaneously just not existing in her memory.

All of this was so distant. She had never stood in this house
before, decorated with all the trappings of a home, a few
scattered photos of her in the corners of rooms where they
weren't easily encountered. The moment Eleanor Sr.
understood that her daughter was, and was going to keep
being, dead, something changed.

It was a nice car though— a wrecked and gutted Camaro RS
from before her time. There were memories in this car: picking
out the boxy silhouette of its headlights against the orange light
of a scrapyard at night, sprinting home and begging Uncle Alf
to beg a friend to beg another friend who owned a towing
business to pick it up for her, the summer afternoons spent with
her nose in repair guides, sneaking back into the scrapyard for
parts.

It was really a wonder her mom had dragged it all the way
here from Oakland. It was a compromise — she explained — in
return for not being able to keep her daughter's collection of
rare plants alive.

254

The engine staunchly refused to turn over, the undercarriage had started to rust out, and the passenger seat was just gone — not like it had been removed, the entire structure that would indicate there ever had been a passenger seat was non-existent.

Apparently, this was her baby.

Stranger still was the sensation of wandering out to the garage, taking a chest of tools from the trunk, and setting to work on instinct as though she had never put it down.

She couldn't sleep, not like this: the disappointed look in her mother's eyes, the barely hidden tone as though she was in trouble for dying, taking turns on repeat in her mind as though having come back from the dead in any form was somehow not good enough for her.

This particular anxiety was not conducive to sleep.

She smacked her head off the underside of the hood of the car as the sound of the garage opening behind her overpowered her headphones. She spun with her wrench in her hand, too spooked to understand what she planned to do with it.

Ratty, paranoid eyes half-lidded, ducked under the rising door. She held a steel baton, dressed in her usual sleep clothes: bright red boxer shorts and a baggy college logo hoodie.

"...scared the shit out of me, El'," she finished as the rabbit slipped off her headphones, her soft morning grumble tinged with annoyance. "Saw the garage light and..." She trailed off, setting her baton on the nearest shelf.

"Nice, uh... underwear." Eleanor turned back to her work as her heart settled.

Ratty pulled up a stool and watched, occasionally handing her tools and becoming tiredly fascinated with a smudge of grease that somehow found its way onto the back of her hand.

"So, you do cars?" she asked once the stain had gotten boring.

"Apparently." The rabbit fell to her haunches and wiped her brow.

"Mind if I sit in it?"

"You gonna spin the wheel and make driving noises?" Eleanor teased.

"Only if you want me to." Ratty teased back, in a more flirty tone than sitting in a car and pretending to drive warranted.

"Alright," Eleanor wiped her brow, satisfied with her work, and slowly slipping back into a non-distracted state. "I think I need a break now anyway." She followed Ratty into the bench back-seat, stretching out in the extra legroom afforded by the missing passenger seat and cornering the possum in.

"No fair." Ratty said.

"I'm taller, this is what makes sense."

"I am also tall! Here..." She shimmied over, close enough to make Eleanor self conscious of her work-stench, and crossed over her legs in the void. She smelled too: lake water, sweat, and a little bit of weed. She paused to think.

"So... Why did you come sleep with me last night?" the possum nudged.

"Oh god, I'm sorry. Was that crossing a line?"

"Nope. I just wanna know." Eleanor's brain whirred, trying to remember why she actually did it.

"Sett was on the—"

"Eleanor." the mischievous little marsupial drawled, the low baritone of her voice metaphorically rattling the windows. "Is that the only reason?" Her eyes searched the ghost, the trapping gaze of an examiner.

Eleanor turned it over in her mind, opening her mouth as soon as cohesive thoughts started forming: "I'm really, like, kind of lonely right now, and I think Sett like, figured that out. And you've been really nice to me — you and them both — and—"

"I getcha." Ratty interrupted. "You've spent the past couple years cooped up in your apartment, and like— living forever still feels like a long time 'cause you've just started doing it, so... uh... yeah." She trailed off again. "Sorry, your mom has good shit and I'm like, struggling to keep a train of thought, lol," she explained, actually saying "lol" out loud.

"What's it like to be alive passing?" Eleanor asked, struggling not to be jealous. The possum snorted at the turn of phrase.

"What's it like to be cis passing?" Ratty shot back.

"You pass," the rabbit groaned, tipping her head back.

Ratty spent the next few minutes getting increasingly comfortable against the ghost, wiggling and burrowing a few inches into her body. Her fur glowed in places where it touched

Eleanor; a florescent pink afterimage of her nocturnal ancestors.

"I'm gonna shotgun you," she started suddenly.

"You are so high!" Eleanor scurried back into the corner of the seat.

"Listen!" Ratty commanded.

"Yeah! I'm listening."

"If you wanna—" Ratty rolled over, straddling the rabbit and groggily playing with the collar of her shirt. "If you want to fuck me, all you have to do is ask."

"Uh—" Eleanor's voice caught in her throat.

"I mean— okay, wait." She pulled back, dropping out of this new persona in an instant. "If that is what you want, obviously. I don't— I need you to understand that like, I'm not going to kick you out or stop buying you stuff if you say no."

"R- R—" Eleanor stuttered.

"And I'm also not going to stop being your friend."

"Ratty." She spat the word out, more firm than she had intended.

"Hm?"

"I'm f-flattered, and like— absolutely yes at some point, but right now I have a lot on my mind, feel me?" Eleanor explained. Left unsaid was the fact that her breath smelled intensely of marijuana, bordering on self-destructive levels. Left unsaid was the fact that — regardless of what Eleanor wanted — Ratty clearly didn't. Left unsaid was the fact that cheap self-worth was worthless.

"Yeah for sure— I'm sorry, I realized as soon as I saw your face that I misread that, I just didn't like— it's always the first time for me, y'know?"

"You're good. I just— actually, do you mind if I talk at you for a minute?"

"Go ahead." Ratty rolled back off, lying across Eleanor's lap. "This good?"

"Yeah." Eleanor absentmindedly wove her fingers through Ratty's curls. "So, was your mom scared of you when she saw you?"

"Yeah, I think at first that came with the territory of like, having been almost killed again and meeting her in the middle of the woods, covered in blood, when she was searching for a spree killer, but I think it got worse when I told her about... uh, like... being undead."

"I think my mom is feeling that." Eleanor glossed over the rest of whatever that was.

"I noticed that." Ratty nodded, her eyes lulling closed. "I— the thing that I learned, is that— people want you to always be the way that you always were. Even if she's cool about trans stuff, everybody- everybody has their breaking point, y'know?"

"Yeah."

"No one wants anyone to like— 'have a character arc.'" She threw up some misplaced air-quotes. "It's unfortunate, 'cause a lot of the time, the times when we change are the times when we need the most help."

"Weed makes you smart, huh?" Eleanor said, trying to push some light into the conversation.

"Thanks! I'm *so* pretty *and* smart!" The possum snapped back.

"You are pretty!" Eleanor tipped her head against Ratty's.

"Nuh uh. No way," the possum sniffled. "It'll probably go back to normal eventually, but it's not something you can force. In the meantime, you got me, you got Sett, we're gonna start doing community nights at the, uh, place, again, so there's that too. Plus! You've got siblings you ain't even met yet. It's all— it's all gonna be good, buddy, I promise."

"Thanks, buddy." Eleanor let that slip into her lexicon as her eyes lulled closed, trying to focus on how close Ratty was, and trying to put out of her mind how distant she was from her own family.

# 2016
# Separation Anxiety

Sett woke up alone again. That was fine, just disappointing.

They rolled out of bed, tossing the duvet back into place and staring as it settled into the pair of divots where they usually slept with Ratty. They needed a new mattress. A few small piles of books had started to form around their bedside.

Clutter got out of control quickly when Sett had no one to clean up for. Ratty never tripped, never complained in the bouts where Sett's mess had taken over their entire apartment, but the goat sometimes worried that she might, and so...

They cut a small hole in their lips through which to brush their teeth, barely conscious as they rinsed the scalpel that lived next to their toothbrush. A few brown spots refused to wash out. That was an infection risk. They needed a new one of those too.

Their phone buzzed in their pocket. It would be Pokey, this early in the morning. There was something... they needed to buy new chairs for the common area. The ones they had were falling apart.

Before resealing their mouth, they popped a tab of Lexapro and a tab of amoxicillin and swallowed them dry. Hardly worth it to pretend they still hurt going down. A discarded bottle of hairspray caught their eye as they stitched over the hole. That would also need replacing. Funny how everything always needed replacing at the same time.

They meandered out to the kitchen, choosing on instinct to pick up the duvet they had just flattened and huddle themself in it. It was a weekend day, probably. They could afford to fall back asleep on the couch. They could ignore the centre for one day.

With their eyes closed against the mix of morning light and harsh fluorescent, they fumbled for their kettle, blinking through the burn as they found nothing was in its place. Their tea kit had been laid out on a clean dish towel, the nicer kettle they had bought as a treat for themself already half-full on the stove.

Sett took stock of the apartment. Ratty's jacket was missing, as usual. She had probably set this out before heading off. They stared at the meticulously prepared tea bag as they waited for the hot water, their eyes dragging along the clumsy creases. It would hold the tea together, that was all that really mattered.

It was good to know that she was at least alright.

It was good to know, too, that she wanted Sett to know she was alright.

She had come to hover in their bedroom a few nights over the past four or so weeks, just watching them sleep. Sett pretended to sleep, cherishing what had come to feel like the odd intimacy of their distant fiancée.

Sett shelved their favourite mug in favour of a steel traveller, set the messy tea bag at the bottom, and poured the water over it just before it tipped over its boiling point. They tore the little paper tab Ratty had affixed to the end of the steeping string, stopping above the recycling bin as they caught a smear of black against the white.

*Good morning,* it said, accompanied by a careful drawing of a butterfly. Sett stared at it for a moment, then slipped it into the pocket of their pyjama pants. They sat down on the old, smelly couch and dragged five special threads from subspace. Once they were firmly in their grasp, they tugged, and their banjo materialized on their lap.

They took a half-second to light a cigarette — Ratty had suggested some years ago that they roll a bunch at the beginning of the week. The banjo was not exactly the instrument for morning music, but it was still helpful. A creative outlet mostly. A fine excuse to make their wrists hurt, too. They began to play, their head hung low to accommodate the weight of the duvet.

"Where is your partner, Sett?" the music asked of them.

"Why doesn't she come home anymore?" it pressed as the melody darkened.

Ratty had been gone for a while. She had started to pull away ages ago. Or, at least what felt like ages ago. Sett struggled not to blame Eleanor, because it really wasn't Eleanor's fault, it just started around the same time they showed up.

Then again, that could be chalked up to the flashback she had while Eleanor was in the ghostzone. The years between Eleanor coming home with them and that happening were pretty normal for Ratty's standards. It was so hard to keep track of time on Earth.

All of this to distract from the obvious.

"You know why she doesn't come home anymore." the angry twang spoke. "She has stopped loving you." They stood, refusing to give this line of thought its day in court as her banjo twanged its way back into subspace.

No. Ratty was somewhere. Someone knew where.

They slung their oversized coat around their shoulders as they stomped down to the parking garage. The big van hummed quietly with the several kilojoules of electricity it took to keep Angel alive in her old age. Sett slammed the door open, given the time between floors to get frustrated.

"Angel?" they asked the dark interior. The robot turned, more intimidating as the light from their visor shone through the dust.

"Hello..." A bar flashed across her visor. "...Sett." The goat had started to feel guilty about the tone with which she stormed in on this elderly android.

"Hi, uh— do you know where Ratty is?" they asked, throwing out their original accusatory tone in favour of something lighter. Another loading bar flashed across her visor.

"Miami." she said, the edges of her voice crushed against the strain.

"Miami?" Sett stammered. "What is she doing in Miami?"

"Cocaine, probably." Sett stared for a moment, trying and failing to decode the layers of whatever went into that response. Angel stared back, her chin falling as her joke flopped. Something clicked in her neck, and her range of motion went from *child's birthday party animatronic* to *almost living*. "Not the best time for jokes, I gather." She reveled in her renewed ability to form complete sentences.

"Not really. Do you want me to have Fern take another look at you?"

"Is that something we can afford?"

"We've helped Fern in the past, I'm sure they would be fine with helping us."

"Then yes. I would like that."

"Okay. Good." Sett made a mental note to reach out. "Do you know what Ratty is doing in Miami?"

"I do not. She says she had courier work. I don't believe her."

"You asked her?"

"I was curious." Angel said, something like pride stuck behind her motionless face. Sett blinked, realizing what just happened.

"You can get curious again?" they asked.

"It seems that way."

"That's really fantastic Angel, good for you." They smiled, temporarily forgetting their mission.

Then it came time to ask the awkward question. There was no easy or non-stalkerish way to ask. Suddenly withdrawing affection without warning was one form of abuse according to some people, so... 'an eye for an eye' is what Sett told themself.

"Can you— do you know where her cell phone is?" A threaded needle way to ask to have someone tracked down. Angel sat up straight, taking just a moment to calculate before pointing off in an arbitrary direction.

"Angel, that's not helpful. I need—"

"It's right there." She pointed more firmly. Sett followed the line of Angel's arm, then followed a bright orange charging cable out of the side of the glove box and into the van's cigarette lighter.

Okay.

So what the fuck?

Ratty barely registered the crack in her metacarpal as one of the worst punches of her life connected with her assailant's chin. She snatched the knife — blade first — from his now dead-stopped swing. It fit naturally into the barrel of the shotgun ready to discharge into the back of her head. She pushed up on the knife, putting the first shot in the ceiling and yanking the firearm out of her other assailants now shaking hands. She braced the barrel of the gun against her shoulder, pointed the butt at his chin, and let a shot off, propelling the mass of wood into his nose.

Number one groaned behind her as number two fell like a sack of hammers, fully unconscious.

"Go home. Bring your friend with you." she growled, only realizing the damage she had sustained as she pointed with the jagged stump at her wrist. She stared at it as the still conscious young man struggled to hoist his partner in crime. A hand was a complex thing to rebuild. It was hardly worth the energy.

She stopped weighing the pros and cons as a bullet tore through her eye. She threw her coat up over her face to hide the wound, fearing the kind of extreme measures some people found access to when they were dealing with something paranormal.

The possum charged the hallway blind, bullets punching holes in the black denim over her face. The actual missing eye was of almost no consequence in the dark. She tackled the person she thought was the gunman and knocked him out with a quick and clinical punch. A volley of shots then tore through the back of her shoulder, and she realized her mistake. The mass of flesh slumped off like melting candle wax as she stood, jamming the top of her skull into her attackers chin.

"Go home!" she repeated, now — understandably — a little more frustrated. The amount of energy it would take to heal would be more than she could muster, and so she just pressed on.

---

Sett stepped down off the bus in one of Ratty's two hometowns. It would have been a nice place to retire, if the rampant class disparity could be ignored. Then again, everywhere was like that nowadays.

The buses here were pretty nice though, so thorough that two different buses took them within a few blocks of their destination. Two portals for Angel in her current state was two too many, and it was calming to watch the snow whiz by on the combination of public transit it took to get here, so best not to risk it, really.

Sett shut their eyes against the cold as warm vapour whistled through their nose. They had always liked winter. It felt to them like the whole world was taking a quick break, a 45 minute nap so they could be energized for the new year.

Ratty liked winter too, for completely different reasons. As a kid, she spent her winters with her mother in the shadow of the city, and her summers with her father in the middle of nowhere, an hour walk to the nearest town.

Sett crushed the intrusive question of how much Ratty would remember about their past with a fantasy of traipsing back through layers of public transit together with her, visiting Ratty's mom for a holiday dinner, or her birthday, or the kind of thing normal people did. Instead, for the second time in their strained relationship, Sett had to ask Ratty's mom to help sleuth out where her missing daughter might have gotten off to.

The Vermington household edged on the high side of humble. A stout green bungalow that — from the outside — didn't look as though it could have more than three rooms. That was heavily compensated for by the massive garden space in the front lot, currently grey and rotting under a thin layer of snow.

Sett knocked, taking an instinctive step back as they always did. A bubble of anxiety rose through their chest, popping as the lock screeched through its strike plate. Tilde Vermington opened the door, shooing her cats away with the heel of her slipper.

"Just a second, Han," she called into the house. Sett winced. Ratty went through her childhood named after both a fed and a Star Wars character. That must've been rough. "Hi, I'm sorry—" The older woman stopped dead in her tracks as she locked eyes with Sett. She never liked them. The paranormal in general had left a bad taste in her mouth.

"Hi, Tilde. I'm sorry to—" Sett started.

"It's Miss Vermington, please." She stepped out, her slippers browning in the snow as she forcefully closed the door behind her. Sett wondered if all in-laws were this bad, and reveled in that moment of normalcy.

"Of course, we're sorry." the goat spoke softly, immediately put on their back foot. "We need— Ratty is— She's not missing, but—" they stammered to try and find a normal way of communicating what they were trying to do. "She ran off, and we know she's okay, but we haven't seen her in, weeks, I think... We think she's avoiding us and... I don't know, you're her mother, and I thought you might have some insight."

Tilde stared for a moment, having made a decent living off stalkers in their past life. With her miniature vendetta, she was really looking for a reason not to like Sett. This screamed *concerned partner* louder than it screamed *malicious creep,* and to be honest, the fact that Sett hadn't aged a day since they met in Tilde's early 20s signalled that — if this goat wanted someone found — a 'mere mortal' wasn't going to stop them.

"'We' as in 'you,' right?" Plus, who doesn't like an adultery case? "When did it start?" Tilde asked, putting no effort into keeping the eye-roll out of her voice.

"She had a— I'm not sure what you would call it, like a PTSD attack the other day, and—"

Hang on. That's not right. That was six years ago. Sett didn't notice. They stopped mid-sentence, but they didn't understand why or what about what they just said was wrong.

"She's just been getting more and more distant ever since," they finished, keeping it simple.

"Oh, okay." Tilde lit a cigarette, taking advantage of the moment away from her kids. "Easy. Something in that episode reminded her of you and now she's avoiding you because she doesn't want to be reminded of that part of herself." There was no blow-softening in her tone: a tone perfect 'Detective Overconfident' cliche with no real revelation.

"I—" Sett stammered, their eyes drifting out of focus as they processed the information.

"Jesus, don't cry. Look." Tilde stomped their cigarette, already having finished it, and drew out another. If offered, Sett wouldn't have taken one, but it would have been nice to be asked. "She get violent? Scream-y and twitchy and whatever?"

"She didn't— hit me, or anything."

"Kinda collapse in on herself, though?"

"Yes." They remembered the shivering pile that'd replaced their fiancée, not days, but years ago.

"She's afraid of hurting you."

"Ah, um—" That was... marginally better. "So how do I—" Tilde jumped as the door opened behind her, dropping her cigarette and kicking it into a puddle. She tried to flap the excess fumes away as both her and Sett turned to look at their guest: a tiny Ratty.

"Mom— can you—" she started, stopping as she caught Sett's eye. There was something adorable about seeing her big, tired eyes in such a tiny skull.

"Go back inside, Han." Tilde snapped. immediately annoyed at the interruption. Little Ratty ignored her and stepped — in her socks — out into a puddle of slush. One of the house's cats slipped by in the commotion and went tearing across the lawn, tearing Tilde away for a few moments.

"Hi, I'm Ishmael. What's your name?" she asked. Sett crouched, getting eye level with the little possum and managing the best smile they could without a mouth.

"Hi Ishmael, I'm Sett." They beamed. "I thought your name was Hanratty?"

"Ishmael's my middle name. It's way cooler. Do you wanna see the movie I'm working on?" she asked, taking the goat by the hand instinctively and beginning to lead them into the house.

Hanratty Ishmael Vermington. H.I.V. Three strikes for the possum's shitty name. Four, if she had ever been bullied for having an animal name.

"We—" Sett stammered, looking over their shoulder and immediately being burned alive by Tilde's glare. "I don't think your mom would be okay with that."

"Oh, okay." Ratty dropped Sett's hand and — not sure what else to do — went back inside of her own accord.

"You stay away from my son." Tilde growled, throwing the cat over the threshold and slamming the door.

"She looks really young for—" Sett started, bewildered at a Ratty — born in 1998 — that looked no older than 12 in 2016. They were cut off as Tilde dragged them off the porch and down the lane.

"I would actually really prefer if you left *him* alone. This is a Christian household, and I don't want any of your Satanic business corrupting my child. Now..." With a final half-shove, Sett was off their mother-in-law's property. "...please leave." They froze in the driveway for a moment, processing a lot at once.

"Can I ask, how old is Han?" Sett asked, deliberately using

her first name to avoid misgendering her.

"No, leave."

"Right, of course, we're sorry." Sett stepped down the curb, now more confused than defeated.

"Alright, everybody out." Ratty dragged open the ridged red door of a shipping container with the stump of her wrist. Inside, a huddle of foxes shielded their eyes against the new light. They looked cold and underfed, the scraps of burlap left to them by accident doing nothing to hide their ribs, their sallow stomachs. "There's a van outside, it'll take you somewhere safe, we're gonna try and get your lives back on track."

They were intimidated by the half corpse, each giving her a wide berth as they slunk out of captivity. Only one stopped to speak, their fur stained black around their lips, nose and eyes.

"You're going to die," she said. Ratty looked down at the puddle she was standing in, the leaky roof doing no favours to any of these women. One eye missing, the other half swollen shut. No hands, one arm, and a limp from putting her leg through a rotting stair.

"Okay." She shrugged. The fox stared for a moment, then joined her fellow escapees on their way out of the building.

Time to deliver a package.

Ratty flipped the top off her messenger bag with what was left of her arm, a rumpled cardboard box with a quick scrawl of the building's floor-plan sitting alone in the darkness. Boss's office was up ahead.

She tipped it out on the desk, sitting down on the window sill and watching everyone file out. This wasn't a 'bring the building down' bomb. It was more of a 'we can get to you anywhere' bomb. Designed to scare, not to do too much damage. Still, it was good to make sure everyone who mattered was safe.

She examined the blood on the lighter parts of her remaining fur, watching the subtle edge of the stain flicker in and out of existence as it was turned in the blacklight. A tacky office like this would not be missed.

She heard the box chirp as the last woman — the one that told Ratty she was going to die — climbed into the back of a moving van. Her contact had forgotten about her. That was fine, ten seconds was enough to get out.

Or, it would have been if the door wasn't stuck.

That was fine too, Ratty thought. She had long since avoided the universe where she died. She would get lucky, everything but what was vital to her regeneration would be destroyed, and then those things would grow back. Psychopaths believed in quantum immortality. Ratty just hadn't died yet.

She elbowed a hole in the window, dropped her somehow barely-scathed jacket to the street below, and sat back to wait for it to go off. A blurry cluster of muted orange bodies huddled around the van that brought her here. These were good people. This would be justice.

The bomb blew her out and across the street, throwing her spine against the curb and her head — horns first — against the grey pavement. They cracked off, leaving unevenly shaped stumps. With what little energy she could muster, she turned her head to watch them roll to a stop on the sidewalk next to her. That was fine. They would grow back.

"Shit! Ratty are you—"

"Yeah." she gurgled, her throat too far forward in her mouth. "Call Angel."

---

Their horn clicked, vibrating against the train window and buzzing through their thoughts. Sett chose to focus on the incongruity of little Ratty looking and acting half her age. The first mystery they set out to solve this morning was more or less put to bed from the start. Tilde hadn't told Sett anything they didn't already know. Some extreme time dilation — despite the metaphysical implications — was far more approachable.

Sett sat up and looked around the car. A red cap of hair bobbed quietly in one corner behind them, in and out of sleep. Other than that, they were completely alone. They scooted into the centre row, pulling up the music player on their phone and scrolling past their rarely listened-to collection of random folk punk, alt-rock, and midwest emo, down to a file titled *our song*.

Ratty's voice came first, energized as Sett warmed up.

"Ready?" she asked. There was a pause where the recorded Sett nodded. "When was the last time we did this?" They remembered Ratty rocking back and forth in her seat, the dull thrum of their own tail whipping the floor.

"Not sure," the recording said, tuning in their first note. The pair of voices held a thick veneer of love. A little hard to listen to, honestly. Sett shut their eyes, gently tossing their switchspace form through the seat behind them. It was easier to leave their body when there was something physical to push the two apart.

They could feel the strings underneath their back, underneath their hooves as they got up. A gentle, ever-present thrumming that drew lines between people and their controllers. The metaphysical world was run on cables buried in the ground. Their breath was amplified to fill the silence. For a few moments of white noise, Sett waited.

The first notes lit up subspace like a single flash of a broken streetlamp, then another, and another, until the entire hidden world was lit in the golden orange hue of neglect. They kept their stance spread, staying upright against the gentle rocking of the train they left behind.

The deep black above was lit by what they now recognized as pin-sized pillars of pain, shooting up into the sky to be eaten by an entity beyond their perception. Somewhere behind the goat's corporeal form, a weak chain tied a standing figure with very little ambient pain to someone whose anguish was enough to shield their eyes against. Someone was being fined for not paying their fare.

Sightseeing was not what they came for today.

Ratty's voice started just off beat, the quiet sound of paper being set aside taking its place as they ditched written lyrics in favour of improvisation. With that, the jade plane of time flickered through the floor below, as though colouring in-between the orange lines.

And it was too fast, or too slow, depending on how they looked at it. Black blades of grass raced to try and keep up with their colour. Sparse scenery behaved almost confused, bending and shearing out of shape to keep pace before jumping ahead, further out of sync with the rest of its plane.

On a hunch, Sett unplugged their headphones, stopped *our song*, and held their breath as the intimidating thud of Hell's material plane crashed through her chest. It roared in the manufactured silence, cutting through subspace with a screeching grind. Sett, shielding their ears from it, turned to the source of the sound: Hell cut perpendicular to the path of the train, and roughly 500 kilometres to the South-East, Hell's Kitchen was burning.

Three unique energies stood in the centre of the blaze: the other end of a broken chain, now limping through his afterlife; the sucking black-hole of the elder god Decay; and the soulless ambition of one Director Eden Ross.

Oh, yes, that made sense. Decay and Angelcorp had bored a hole in the material plane to mine energy from Hell. How incredibly obvious, why didn't anyone think of that sooner. They stepped out towards it for a better look.

A fare inspector tapped Sett on the shoulder. In an instant, subspace was gone, the plane of time was gone, Hell was gone.

"Ma'am, we really prefer if you stay seated while the train is moving." Sett's head whipped around the car for as long as it took to take stock of their situation: they stood in the middle of the aisle, spinning with their arms outstretched. They flattened their clothes back down, hiding their face in the collar, avoiding eye contact as they wordlessly tapped their transit pass against the inspectors ticket checker.

A green check mark and a mumbled "Have a nice day," and he was on his way again, leaving Sett to stare out the southeast window.

---

Ratty focused on her breathing as her spine pulled itself back into alignment against the cold faux-porcelain of her bathtub. After a long fall, lungs were always what she prioritized.

After that was whichever hand had sustained the least damage. Today, it was her right hand. A lucky break. She fished one of the nigh-indestructible generations of mp3 player out of her pocket, and went to click on some public radio recording. She didn't like to listen to podcasts. She *thought* she liked podcasts, but they bored her easily, even when she had to lie still to pull herself back into alignment.

Today was only slightly different. The black highlight bar jittered back and forth on a song it refused to move on from. The bloodied and cracked wheel of her player refused to accept an input that put her below *our song.mp3* and its accidental copy, *oursong.mp3*. She stared at it for a few minutes before dropping it to the tile below. Back to breathing...

She barely moved as the door clicked, Angel lurching into the room with the possum's cell in her hand. Ratty propped herself up to grab for it, grimly satisfied to find she had an elbow with which to do so again. She sunk back down as soon as soon as the mass of soft tissue closed around it, wincing as her back crackled under the weight.

📞 10:04am:          **Missed Call** (13) —    ♥🐫

✉ Yesterday:          **New Message** —      Unknown number:
       "Ms. Vermington,"

✉ Yesterday:          **New Message** —      Unknown number:
       "We're choosing not to press ch...

✉ Yesterday:          **New Message** —      Unknown number:
       "We look forward to wor...

✉ 10:05am:          **New Message** —      ♥🐫:
       "Hope you're okay."

✉ 2:56pm:          **New Message** —      ♥🐫:
       "Ratty, theres something we need to talk abo...

✉ 2:56pm:          **New Message** —      ♥🐫:
       "I don't know whats going on with us but thi...

And, what she was actually looking for:

🏦 3:08pm:    Tap here to accept your **NetBank**™ E-Transfer from Jane ...

Her retainer covered food for the month. After other expenses, food for the unemployed folks in the building, etc., she would be able to put away another thousand or so dollars. She let out a sigh as her head lulled back, throat finally sealed against the rest of her neck guts. She shut her eyes against Angel's glare. Just breathe, there's money in the bank.

"Your horns are broken." Angel cut through the peace. She wasn't actually capable of glaring.

"Yeah." Ratty replied, doing her best to say 'go away' without actually saying it.

"You should talk to Sett." Angel continued.

"I can't move," as if to say, "I'm probably going to have to."

The robot took a step forward, keeping their eyes locked, silently watching her charge bleed down the drain.

"Don't touch the tap."

"I'm not going to."

"I know, just— don't, please." Ratty said, her gaze flipping back and forth between the silver valve handle and Angel's visor. She settled on Angel after a few seconds of mild panic, understanding suddenly that she had some brain damage to repair as well.

"Fern has finished processing the data you retrieved on Doctor Cane."

"Okay."

Something in Angel's body clicked quietly. An improperly secured hard-disk threw itself against its cage a few times as she processed the possum in front of her. If she was capable of emoting annoyance, she probably would have been doing it.

"You and I are similarly motivated, Hanratty," she began. "I like to be useful."

"Everyone likes to be useful."

"This is not useful. You feel as though your life is finite, and the faster you use it up, the more useful you will have been."

"Okay." Ratty slumped deeper into the tub. "Thanks."

"You're not listening to me."

"No," Ratty turned over, opened her phone, and hit play on whatever was loud and room-filling. The curvature of the tub deafened her against anything on the outside. "I'm not."

---

"Customs office, New York, New York. How can I help you?" Sett fumbled for something to say to another demon again after all this time. Becca was a demon, and she and Sett spoke just about every day, but the ones who were still "in it" had a certain way of speaking, like everything was okay and that the credit for that should rest squarely on their shoulders.

"Yes, hi. I was just calling to see if— sorry—" Sett shielded their phone against the sound of downtown traffic. Incredibly annoying how one of the busiest parts of the city rose up around their quiet little corner. "I was just calling to see if passage is open right now?"

"Oh, yeah. Passage is actually always open. You should have gotten a newsletter about it, we're actually under new management." Sett knew about "new management" already.

"Uh-huh," they said, half sprinting through a slim gap in traffic, giving a polite wave as they went. "Angelcorp, right?" The voice on the other end went silent for a moment.

"I'm sorry, who is this?" she asked.

"I'm Sett."

"Sett?"

"Just Sett."

"Oh! Icon of Chaos Sett!" she hooted. The goat winced as they pictured John — likely in the same building if he was in New York at all — hearing their name and the random cluster of words used to ID them said out loud. They hoped he knew not to fuck with them. "Yeah, sorry about that, I just— y'know, they really drill into you like 'don't talk to journalists' so... I just had to make sure. Yeah, it's Angelcorp. You should come see actually," the desk demon went on, content to monologue now that she assumed it was safe. "It's changed a lot since you got out. They have these big fuck-off cables going through the mouth like, at all times. I don't even think they run elevators anymore. It's crazy."

"How are they keeping it open?" Sett asked, crossing the threshold of their building, heart racing.

"That's the even crazier part! You know Decay? Like, the elder god? It's all her. She's been doing some crazy shit to it, like making it rot. It smells like a fucking septic wound in here all the time, and the time dilation! I mean they warned us about it but like, I mean it feels like it's worse than downstairs! Which side of this thing is supposed to be Hell again, am I right?" The demon laughed. "Anyway, where are you living now? We should get—"

Sett hung up, bracing their back against the door and slipping to the ground. Becca stood up to see over her desk as Sett sunk out of sight.

"Everything alright?" she asked.

"I... Maybe."

Sett let their eyes fall closed. Filling their lungs with air took some of the weight off their back, and they stood again.

Ignoring the ache in their chest, they pressed on to the elevator.

"Okay." Becca nodded politely and sat back down.

Elevator. Tense.

Hallway. Tense.

Keys. Tense.

Sett hung their coat behind the door and made a beeline for the bathroom, desperate to wash the feeling of grime from their hands. They screamed hard enough to throw their blood into their head, putting black circles in their vision, as they locked eyes with Ratty's half reformed corpse.

The possum jumped, dropping her phone into the tub and snapping more than one part of her body in the sudden terrified scramble. The pair stared at each other as that shock wore off, each painfully aware of the gruesome scene. Sett hated the way bile rose in their throat at the sight of their partner's mulched corpse.

"Good news!" Angel's interruption re-startled Sett. "Ratty is home!"

"Yes, I can see that." How hadn't they noticed the music?

Ratty sat far enough upright to look Sett in the eye. "Hey babe," she sighed. That was close to the only option.

"Why are you bleeding?" Sett asked. Ratty stared down at herself, still mostly not there.

"I dunno. 'Lotta effort to stop."

"Right, of course." Sett had already knelt, already pulled a needle from switchspace, and only realized when they found Ratty's skin harder to puncture than usual. It bounced back as the first stitch punched through. She was incapable of processing Sett's discovery.

"Where have you been?" they asked. They didn't want to be doing this. They didn't want to do any more of this. They spent the entire day focusing on someone who hadn't given them a second thought.

"I— I've just been working."

"We're supposed to be a team." they murmured. No response. This was just self-harm. Whatever had taken over Ratty during her attack, it was just making her hurt herself. Any wound at all in the kind of possum that could literally freeze time on command was self-harm by omission.

They weren't going to talk about Hell today.

Ratty would do something stupid.

"Do you ever think about what would happen to me if you didn't come home?" Sett rolled back on their haunches. Ratty stared at the ceiling for a moment, her lips searching for the first word in her response.

"We have savings. You would be fine—"

"That's not what I'm asking." Another moment passed. The goat dropped their tools and turned on the fan, pulling some of the stench of rot out of the room.

"No, I don't." Ratty said plainly. Sett stood stunned for a moment, then pulled their tools back into subspace.

"People depend on me." Their voice started low, intense. "I am sick and tired of thinking you might be dead somewhere. I am tired of worrying about you, Ratty. Do you have any idea how smart I am? This—" They produced a length of subspace thread. "I invented this. I was the first working caste demon to touch subspace and I did it on my own in my apartment by accident. I cannot stand the thought that all that power has gone into following you around and keeping you from killing yourself." It stopped being possible not to raise their voice. "You think dying will make you great, Ratty? Is that what you think?"

"You never told me about subspace." A missed opportunity to be proud of them, if anything.

"I— I don't know... I don't like bragging." Their claws dug into the palms of their hands. The pain grounded them, stopped tears from welling over, kept them angry enough to finish the thought. "I get it. You can't fight giants anymore and I understand that. I prefer that, actually. But now? What's it all for now?"

Their chin fell to their chest. They would not let this break them. "You just want to hurt yourself. You're not even pretending to help people anymore."

"I helped people today."

"*You*—" Flecks of blood flew with their spit as their vocal chords crashed on takeoff. The ache bent them over, their entire body pointed at the new source of their anger. Their psychic voice took over again. "You are skilled. You are extremely, measurably lucky. After knowing you for several weeks, scattered across lucky weekends, you and I broke out of Hell together. You're telling me— who did this to you."

Ratty waited as long as she could to admit it. "A couple of guys."

"'A couple of guys' turned you into pulp." They seethed at the possum until that energy dissipated. What it left behind was hollow guilt. This is what Ratty did. This is what she had done since the day they met. They stared into the tired eyes, blinking sadly, understanding what hurt she had done.

"Can you heal this yourself?" They fixated on the dripping wound hung over one side of the tub when they couldn't take eye contact anymore.

"Yeah, probably."

"Okay. I'm going to stay at my shop for the night." And with that, they turned and left.

# 2017
# Breach

"Pickup for uh, Sloth-Bunny, Sett and Vermington." Eleanor popped an earbud out as she approached the counter, doing her best to minimize her time spent having to exist in the world outside her music. Being in public, talking, and at the front of a line compounded her nerves into a dense puck of existential ache. Every second of space she took up she felt like an unwelcome intrusion. The good people of Toronto would turn on her at any moment if she held the line.

"Address?" the pharmacist asked, already rummaging through the S and V drawers.

"They're all the same. 212 Dundas. It'll— sorry." Eleanor leant over the counter. "I don't know why, but mine is always filed under B for Bunny."

"Uh-huh." the pharmacist muttered, not bothering to take his nose out of the S drawer. "Just give me one quick second here."

"No rush." the rabbit sighed, preparing herself for the same delay, the same surprised "ah!" The same, "It's so weird, Sloth-Bunny was under B." The smaller pharmacy around the corner closed down half a year ago and she had yet to find one that was both locally owned and not terrified of the paranormal. People stared here. Some combination of the fact that she was six feet tall, noticeably transgender, and obviously undead eroded the social contract and turned Eleanor into an icon of the unknowably different.

It was hard to see the world through black eyes, eyes that couldn't be seen to be staring back.

"This is so weird—" The pharmacist popped up, dropping an armload of nine different little paper bags on the table and zapping through them. "Sloth-Bunny was filed under B."

"Crazy." Eleanor watched as each prescription popped up on

the monitor:

Ratty's estrace.

Ratty's spiro.

Ratty's Lexapro — which would sit on until it expired.

Sett's Lexapro — which would not.

Ratty's inhaler — which Eleanor had never seen her use.

Sett's amoxicillin.

Eleanor's estrace.

Eleanor's spiro.

Eleanor's Lexapro.

It helped — or at the very least was distracting — to count them. It would have been a lie to say putting them in eight separate bags was odd, this pharmacy had never done what would have been convenient.

"Can I get a plastic bag to put these all in?" Eleanor asked.

"Bags are five cents." The pharmacist glared, annoyed, down at the pin pad as though either giving away one five cent bag or cancelling the pin pad to add five cents to Eleanor's total was tantamount to stopping and restarting his own heart.

"Wh— why are bags five cents?"

"I dunno. Environment. probably."

"Well, you could have just like, put them all in one paper bag, considering they're part of the same order."

"Sorry sir, company policy."

"Sir? Really? I'm walking away with— you can read my name!" She picked up one of the estrogen bags and held it up next to her face, pointing back and forth between her name — Eleanor — and her incredulous expression. Eleanor did not do or say any of that. She wished she could.

The pharmacist waited impatiently through the few silent moments, leaning to glance around the ghost as if to say, "Now who's failing the social contract?" She stuffed the paper bags into her pocket as a hot rush of shame shot up from the back of the line and took her over.

She missed Dr. Shepherd from the walk-in, missed — even though they had annoyed her at first — the little bible verse cards he put in the bottom of each bag. There was safety in a small, under-performing business, but that kind of thing didn't last downtown for long.

"You still—" the pharmacist started.

"Yeah, I know. I still have to pay for it. No shit." She took a zip-top bag full of change out of her pocket. With the pharmacist paid by the company and the actual product paid for by the government, these fees — coming out of her laundry budget — were essentially paying for nothing, which made the fact she would have to empty her change bag to cover it worse.

Worse still when she began to feel the eyes on her back, heard the subtle tapping of a rubber-soled shoe. She wanted to turn and scream, that — if there was literally any other choice — she would not be wasting anyone's time. She needed her medicine, the sooner she could roll herself up in her covers, put on some music, and fall asleep, the better for everyone.

She turned to leave, picturing the soft down of her duvet, jumping as someone tapped low on her shoulder.

"Sorry, Miss." She turned, ready to burst into tears at the smallest inconvenience, and came face to face with sunglasses, an upturned collar, and a duck bill, all badly hidden under an oversized trench coat. "You dropped this." The coat held out a paper bag.

"Oh... thanks." That was less shitty than expected. She took it, nodded as graciously as she could muster, and left.

Pills rattling in her pockets, she took off due east, practically begging to get home as quickly as possible. The bus ran on a 15 minute schedule, she could power-walk the same distance in seven.

There was no way of telling whether that was what it was like in Oakland, but fuck. It was a wonder anyone in this city held down a job with the amount of time they just spent gawking at strangers. Most people were curious, sure, but there would be times — looking for a seat on the streetcar, waiting in line, doing the most mundane shit — that people would glare like they wanted to kill her, as though she could get any more dead.

She wished she was dead-er, honestly. Outside people were scary, the people at home were scary, Ratty — Eleanor's only friend, essentially — had started acting scary. It was difficult to communicate. Difficult to make friends.

Distant scary turned into immediate scary as Eleanor caught something behind her in a mirrored window: sunglasses, trench coat, duck bill was following her. Fucking great.

She folded her tape player shut, stuffing whatever she had

been switching between into her pockets. She dialed Ratty on instinct, checking windows each block and becoming progressively more certain that, yeah, she was being followed.

"Ratty speaking."

"Hey, it's Eleanor. Someone is following me." No use beating around the bush.

The line went silent for a few seconds while Ratty planned around that. "Where are you?" she asked.

"I'm just crossing Church."

"Okay, turn left. I'll meet you at the university. Don't hang up. Make small talk." Right, of course, small talk. What did people small talk about? Ratty took the burden of answering that off Eleanor: "How's your day been?"

"Good." she said on pure, cordial instinct. "Uh, well, wait. Not great actually."

"No, yeah, I imagine not."

"What about you?"

"I'm fine... they wanted me to come consult on this— okay, actually, can I rant?"

"Please, go ahead." There was something calming in the normalcy of the possum's voice.

"Not that it matters, but I feel like any time that I'm like, called in on my academic merits anywhere its because someone has like, already died, and they're worried that the fucking X-files unit is gonna come down on their head..." Eleanor stopped at the curb, using the cover of looking both ways while crossing to check. Sunglasses was still about a block behind her. "...and it's like, your priorities are so fuckin' out there that— like nobody would be dead if you just called me to begin with, y'know? We used to call it parachute journalism — I guess they do it in universities now too — where you get just any guy who's on hand to jump in and jump out of a subject for a quick story."

"Is that— is there really an X-files unit?" Eleanor had gotten hung up on that part of the monologue.

"What? No? It's a TV show. I mean, like Angelcorp, I guess? The FBI has it's Unexplained Phenomena department — they actually just got a bump in their funding... plus, I mean, the freelance scene..."

"Okay, cool. Thank you, Ratty. Really setting me at ease

when I am literally being followed home by a *men in black*."

"You asked!"

"I expected you to say no!"

"Hang on, I see you." Ratty waved from across the street. "Is that the guy?"

"Don't stare."

"I'm not staring. Hold on." Ratty hung up, her posture changing from tense concern to open excitement. "Oh my god! Eleanor? Is that you?" She pranced across the street, exaggerating the amount she had to get on her tiptoes to come to eye level with the ghost. She watched as the stalker, suddenly panicked, ducked down an alley and disappeared.

"Is he gone?" Eleanor asked.

"Yeah." Ratty let go of Eleanor, looking up at her friend, each letting a silent moment of *how about that, the life of an undead transgender* pass between them. "Thank you for calling me." Ratty said.

"Thanks for picking up." Eleanor smiled, however weakly.

"Wanna get a burg?" Ratty prodded, looking for a way to cheer Eleanor up.

"Yeah, sure. That'd be cool."

---

"I mean, it's not like we keep this stuff a secret! They literally just don't care." Ratty finished through a mouth full of wet bread and recently unfrozen ground beef. Eleanor watched as the possum — cursed by her species with an unsophisticated mouth — struggled to keep the mess between her teeth. She sucked quietly on her own milkshake, enjoying the taste even as the chill tested the corporeality of her throat.

It was worth it. Lactose intolerant people sometimes drank milkshakes, there was no reason that the same reckless disregard for what your body can handle couldn't apply to her as well. Plus, no real risk of an upset tummy. Her worst case scenario was spending an afternoon with her uncle.

"This is really good." Her throat waved as it struggled to stick to this plane of existence. "I love food that's just like, soft and wet."

"Five soft wet dudes made me this hamburger and I am going to cherish it for the rest of my life." Ratty smiled in spite of the day. That was rare nowadays. Even now, there was more than her usual tiredness behind her eyes. Eleanor chose to ignore it, instead choosing to let the moment sit for the time being.

"Amen," she sighed, sucking back the last dregs of peanut butter ice cream and whipped milk. She stared down into the empty cup, running over the day's events in her mind as the parts of the medium-brown slurry too fine to be sucked up by her straw swirled around the bottom.

Their chest ached through the cold, a dull reminder of the slush-covered street on the other side of the glass. Something gnawed at her. Ratty had been too quick with her plan. She happened to be only a few streets away when Eleanor called. Probably nothing, but... "Do you... worry about me?" she asked.

"I— you can take care of yourself." Ratty put her food down, meeting Eleanor's eyes. "I would come looking for you if you didn't come home a couple nights in a row without saying anything, but you're smart."

Cool. So that probably wasn't it. She tried again: "How are things with Sett?"

"Oh, I dunno." It wasn't uncommon for Ratty to break a gaze like that. It offered no clues as to what was going on inside her head. "They've been really weird lately. I haven't seen them." An inaccurate way of saying something that was technically true.

"I'm not... pulling you two apart at all?" Surely, if something was wrong, it had to be her fault.

"I want to spend time with you, El'." Ratty smiled, her eyes remaining hollow and sad. "We— me and Sett have been engaged for like, what, 60 years now? I'm sure they're fine with my little girlfriend."

Girlfriend was a new word. Eleanor wished it had cropped up under less disappointing circumstances. Coupled with the word *little* it was kind of diminutive, but it was new, and it didn't feel terrible. Eleanor wanted Ratty to be in a healthier mindset, or at the very least understood why she wasn't.

"Okay." Eleanor sighed. "I just like them and I like, don't want to be a problem for you two, y'know?"

"Yeah, nah. If there's a problem, it's not sitting at this table."

That was an inaccurate way to say something completely flat out false.

"Okay," Eleanor said, a few tense moments passing between the two before Ratty — always uncomfortable with silences — rose to speak again.

"I'm not avoiding them or anything." There was an undercurrent of frustration in her voice, the dark circles under her eyes growing darker as her expression shifted to shadow them.

"That's— really none of my business, actually." Eleanor watched for a moment as Ratty processed what she just said, her eyes flickering with stress and confusion. "You really kinda tipped your hand there, huh bud?"

"I— no? I literally am saying that I'm not."

"Did something happen between you two?"

"No? I don't know what would make you think something like that."

"Okay." Eleanor tried to bring the situation back down as her throat began to clog. "Sorry I brought it up."

"I'm with you right now because I don't want to think about Sett."

A few more seconds passed in silence, Eleanor no less anxious than when she had started down this path, wondering if Ratty would take it as a personal offence if she got up to throw out her milkshake cup. She chanced it, and was pleasantly unsurprised when the possum kept staring at her half eaten burger.

She popped the top off, put the plastic straw and lid into one container, then dropped the paper cup into another. She stood there for just a moment, took a deep breath, and went to sit back down.

"Just, stay out of my—"

"You are being a huge bitch right now." Eleanor cut her off.

"What are you talking about?"

"I'm just— I just want to chill, y'know?" The chill fled out from Eleanor's throat, knew the weather outside wouldn't help as her fur prickled. She sat, feeling it stand up on end as the static of the plastic bench clung to it. "Either you want to talk about Sett or you don't. I'm not interrogating you."

"I don't!" Ratty snapped.

"Well good!" Eleanor snapped back. With a bang unfit for and louder than the outburst, every light in the restaurant went out, leaving Eleanor as the sole source of light in the dark. She didn't have to open her eyes to know she had made herself the sudden centre of attention.

Ratty turned, a sudden cold wash extinguishing her anger as she took in Eleanor's face: on the verge of tears, eyes jammed shut spilling over. She opened them on the possum, the only way to avoid the fact that everyone was staring at her.

"I'm getting more and more afraid of days like this one," she choked. "I don't want to fuck up my friendship with you because you and Sett are the only people I feel even close to safe around."

"I'm— I'm sorry."

Eleanor didn't respond on her way out.

---

Ratty struggled to keep her eyes focused on Angel's nest, using a few of the robot's sharp edges to keep awake in the dark. Her antlers and the supplemental hands at her waist flickered on and back off at long intervals, whatever internal mechanism that controlled them stumbling occasionally into working correctly.

They waited, together, for the next job. Work had become significantly scarcer, not being able to use Angel to travel. It was simpler to wait here and sleep in her desk chair when she needed to, rather than getting up to move from bed to desk and back each day. Nothing about that hurt.

She dozed off to the sound of quiet conversation and occasional laughter echoing up through the vents. Below, Sett's group clumped up into pre-support-circle cliques, catching up before they had to spill their guts. That was good. Ratty stayed up here, they stayed down there, the whole system worked as long as everyone got what they needed.

It was not the first time her phone woke her up in this room. She blinked awake slowly, ignoring the ache in her back, and neck, and face, as she squinted against the bright white notification. It was an automated ping from downstairs: Fern — who had to be put away for the night — had breached containment.

The possum got out of her chair, shrugging off the borrowed winter coat that kept her warm in this uninsulated part of the building.

"You should get some help." Angel spoke up as Ratty passed her on the way to the stairwell. She stopped, let her chin drop.

"Are you gonna help?" Angel probably couldn't process flippancy at this stage in her life, no use pretending to be nice.

"Sett is available." she said.

"Sett is in group." Ratty corrected. A progress bar flashed across the drone's face.

"Fern is available." she said.

"No, they are not." Ratty corrected. Another progress bar, a few seconds of silence.

"I am available." Some mechanism in her lower half whined and clicked as she tried to stand.

"Forget about it, Angel."

"Okay." The robot watched Ratty disappear into the frigid stairwell.

She didn't need to check to know her keys were in the other jacket. Still, the hard parts of her hands probed her pockets, touching nothing but the grainy dust that built up in the bottoms. That wasn't a problem. She usually ended up jamming the basement door with a brick anyway.

Fern struggled to do anything but get mad in the cramped hallway, too big for it in a way that made it hard to move without methodically thinking out each limb.

"Hey!" Ratty whistled and clicked her tongue, an old move of instinct from when the dog was manageable. "It's bedtime. C'mon, Fern." She had meant to practice with them. It was an awkward thing to talk about unprompted: "Hey, do you mind if I clicker-train you with my mouth?" No, not necessary. It was Fern's idea when they were kids, she would let it be Fern's idea again.

The mass of parts organized itself around its sight line on the possum, more mobile now that it had prey to pounce on. Ratty sighed, rolling some of the ache out of her shoulder and breaking into as much of a sprint as she cared to. Fern was always the same. They went for the throat, Ratty went low, tackle up and into the chest, and then—

Actually, not this time, Ratty.

Fern braced up against the ceiling as the possum's full weight tried to kick them back. They stalled upright on their hind legs, in almost total control of their own body. They took Ratty in their teeth, thrashing like a predator with a dying-but-not-dead meal. The possum kicked against the tearing sensation in the back of her neck, teeth cracking under the pressure of her composure.

"Fucking stop!" It came out sounding like the pathetic last yelp of a dying animal. Fern threw Ratty to the ground and abandoned her. A brick ground against the concrete just far enough to escape the door-jam, and a heavy metal door slammed shut behind the borzoi. Fern had left, and locked Ratty in their basement cell.

"Huh." Her voice stopped dead in the tight hallway. "Well, fuck."

She checked her phone: a solid zero bars under six feet of concrete foundation.

Fern probably wouldn't get far before someone else stopped them.

This was still fine.

This would have been a good time to reflect. Maybe if she wasn't needlessly self-destructive this wouldn't have happened. Maybe her self flagellation did more harm than good. Did any of that occur to Ratty?

No, why would it?

Ratty felt bad and chose not to think about it. She sat down on the cold concrete and stared at the door.

Someone in the building was making breakfast for dinner. You could smell it through the vents. Someone was banging on the floor. When someone was having a bad night, you could feel it all throughout the shaky little construction. Sett tried not to think about the fact that the land they owned was now worth in excess of 200 dollars per square foot.

Things like that bothered them more when they were tired. They spent the night before chain-smoking in the little apartment above their shop. Even that little space could have sold for a couple hundred thousand. It weighed on them to leave it empty. They wanted to just get rid of it.

Then there wouldn't be the option. Ratty would have nowhere to sleep when she wanted to sleep alone. There were other apartments in the building — empty apartments — but Sett didn't think about that.

The commute over exhausted them. They couldn't remember if this was normal. It almost certainly wasn't. The dry mouth, the headache, everything about them right was the product of a bad choice.

They folded and unfolded a scrap of paper in their hands. The support group had evolved over the years: plucky friendless teenagers would bring in a book or a poem or something to talk about or recite. The book club usually met before in one corner of the room, hovering far off from the snack table. The poetry became a mainstay of the group itself.

Whatever they had written came out muted anyway. They specifically left Ellen's name — anything that could hint at her existence — stuck in the wrist of their writing hand. It was repetitive anyway, too formal to be called poetry, a prosed out angry letter to the editor.

Sett was there to support, not to be supported.

They stuffed the paper into their pocket, folded into a little flower by their pointer claw. Last night's tobacco weighed on their lungs as they turned to start the circle. Pokey caught them by their shoulders.

"Whoa." She was gentle, but firm, worried the goat might fall over if she let go. It was awful of them not to see something was wrong. Pokey had aged five years in the past thirty. She decided in a half-second of looking into the goat's eyes not to move on. "Everything okay, Sett?"

Another deep breath, another long sigh. Pokey asked something like "Where's your scary looking girlfriend?" and that was enough to tip them over the edge. The toothpicks that propped up their face buckled. A log thudded into place in their chest when they saw Pokey wince. "Okay, bad question, sorry. I was just thinking—" She held all the subtlety of someone raised primarily by a middle school social studies teacher. "I was thinking I could lead the group tonight, if that would be okay with you."

Sett blinked up at the lizard. Sett bit their tongue, swallowed their pride, and nodded. With that out of the way, they dragged the shrink-wrapped tears across their cheek with the back of their wrist, a child failing to act brave.

"Sure." It came out too loud when they finally spoke. They corrected, and said again: "sure. Thank you, Pokey."

"For sure." She held them for a few more seconds. "You are okay though, right?"

Sett swallowed the greasy lump of smoke in their throat.

"Yes. Yeah, I'm just tired."

They had no memory of a support group that'd gone well. All that stuck out to them was the first one: how embarrassed they must've been to run out crying. They didn't remember the feeling. They sat down next to Pokey. The log in their chest rolled over. They noticed for the first time that the youngest generation — all in their approximate mid-teens — ranged from having been born in 2002 to as far back as 1979. Prisha, who sat next to Pokey in the goat's periphery, should have been pushing forty.

They let their eyes drift out of focus as Pokey began to speak. "Okay everyone! We're going to — uh — do things just a little differently today." Davy coughed the word differently into their hand, lifted their sneaker, and stomped once. "Sett is just going to supervise, and I'm gonna try and lead group today, sound good?"

Murmurs and quiet conversation turned to white noise as the goat's eyes disappeared into their skull. Their mirror self flickered into existence in the middle of the circle of chairs. Their grey fur and black tipped muzzle, their single, quiet eye — the pair of them existed from the outside in, instinct wrapped around nothing.

Davy stood first, as he always did. With a list of participants and where they would sit, Sett could have pulled a string around each chair in the exact order the group would proceed in. They had no idea how that knowledge built itself.

What did Hell really look like? Was it finding someone to love after spending a non-figurative eternity in regimented isolation? Having that person — and by extension the goat themself — grasp a better version of themself and let go over and over again? Was Hell the bare minimum of not being actively suicidal?

Their shoulder-blades ached against the cheap metal chair, sitting there, absent of what they had once thought to be their life's work. Maybe other people had callings. It was like this every time: the connectors in the back of their eyes went loose, and they had to deal with the fact that they would never see the world in full colour again. Then something bumped them just right, and they forgot all about the black and white.

"Sett?" Pokey nudged the goat. It was supposed to be her turn. They had switched roles. It was Sett's turn. "Did you want to talk?" *Talk* was the word they always used. It was specific. When people heard *go* they thought about leaving. When they were offered to *take their turn* they felt talked down to. *Speak* was too formal, so... talk.

The goat's eyes fell to the floor while they composed themself.

"I don't know what I'm doing with my life. I thought it was this." She met the eyes of a few of the longest-standing members, of an older gentleman who they had never seen before, of the semi-strangers who came only when they needed it. "I guess having started this could have been a lifetime achievement, but I never felt like I did it well." They had seen him before. He hadn't aged since— was it the third meeting?

"I never felt like I even did good enough... as good as a person would do it, I mean." Even now, it felt pathetic to explain. The depth of their feelings had become unhitched from their source, pulling trouble in paradise and general aimlessness in the same category of millennia spent holed up and helpless in the underworld.

"I don't feel like a person." It took time to admit that to themself. "I look in the mirror and I still see a lower caste demon. I see a creature that wasn't designed to make anything of themself, was designed to help exactly as they were told, and I'm wondering if that will ever stop."

No one knew what to say to that. For a long few seconds, everyone came to grips with the fact that the most put-together person they knew was just as much a wreck as them.

"Sett." It was clear when the older gentleman spoke that he had been alive almost as long. Quiet, cracked by time, something Germanic... "I know how you feel."

That was it. He stood, brushed off his lap, and stepped out.
Air pushed some of the soot from the goat's chest. They
nodded, mostly to themself, and sat back in their chair.

---

[The faded tile of an apartment building's lobby whizzes by
below a pair of oversized dress shoes.]
[The view tilts up, barely crossing the floor level trim as the
operator of this hidden camera attempts to film the room.]

"I—"

[A voice pants from out of frame.]

"I am- this is a special episode of the Dark Side Podcast. I
am... in the office... of Canada's... real life X-files department,
V Logistics."
"Hi, sorry, can I help you?"

[The frame whips around and centres Becca, sitting at her
desk.]

"MA'AM"

[The off-camera voice is startled.]

"IS IT TRUE THAT THIS FACILITY HOUSES CREATURES
OF A PARANORMAL NATURE?"

"Uh, yes... We prefer if you don't ... film... actually."

[The frame goes dark as a hand covers the lens]
[The off-camera voice whispers directly into the microphone.]

"It appears that the receptionist has some variety of mind-
reading augmentation."
"No, it's just not that good of a hidden camera. You really can't
—"

[A chair screeches against the tile.]

[The off-camera voice yelps.]
[Oversized dress shoes clap down a hallway.]

"Hey! C'mon, kid. You can't—"

[The slam of a metal door reverberates up a stairwell.]
[Oversized dress shoes click up concrete steps.]
[Through leaking headphones a man's low voice can be heard.]
[A purple glow appears on camera, projected against a cement wall.]

"It's the— the spectral form from this morning's report." A weedy little voice cut through Eleanor's cheap headphones. The stairwells in this building were cold and wet in the winter, and almost too steep to climb if you actually weighed anything. Covering her eyes on the way in, she hadn't run into anyone but Becca, who was fantastic at keeping her nose out of other people's business.

And of course— of fucking course it had to be the creep with the sunglasses.

Her heart would race if it wasn't completely dormant. As is, it rose into her throat, completely halting any pantomime of breathing she had gotten used to.

"Stop fucking following me!" The words came out lopsided, her tendency to clam up overwritten by rage.

She blew through the nearest door into the second floor common area. Eleanor was not the first to interrupt Sett's meeting.

The lizard — Pokey? Maybe? She stood sentinel over a huddled mass of support group attendees. Hunched into a defensive stance, their eyes stayed locked on the massive ball of dull, oxygen deprived fur in the middle of the room.

Sett wrestled with a crackling length of rope at the other end of her glare, thrown against the creature's back and parts of the drywall interior as they fought to keep it tight around Fern's snout.

"Hi, Eleanor!" Sett called, forcing themself to greet her warmly. Their hooves lifted from the old carpet with a thrash. "I need—" Fern flung their head backwards, sending Sett rolling across the room as their ropes snapped. "Would you help me with this, please?"

"Yeah that's not—" All the ways Fern could tear her apart flashed behind Eleanor's eyes in sequence, ignoring for a moment the fact that she wasn't solid enough for that to actually happen. Sett backed towards the creature, waiting for Eleanor's answer. "That's not in my wheelhouse, I don't think." She reversed into the stairwell, only noticing as the duck-billed stalker passed through her lower chest. Frustrated but short on time to argue, Sett turned and ran at Fern, jamming a rope through their maw like a bridle.

"They can't hurt you." Fern snapped their jaw, failing to slip free as Sett repositioned and took them by the neck.

"N— no, yeah—" The rabbit's blood drowned out her headphones, crossing the threshold where keeping it together was at all possible. Tears floated away from her eyes as she blinked, blurring her vision. Each eye went dark in sequence, plunging her into the rot of her former home as a new level of panicked hell overtook her body. The scaffold that held up her stage lights crashed through the stage's thin vinyl. Below X where they crossed the white noise Eleanor had spent so much time cleaning from her memory began to settle again. Mouth moving on instinct, she tried desperately to form anything but a wordless stammering, the first and last bastion of being Eleanor.

Sett slid to a stop at Eleanor's feet, the stink of carpet burn only adding to Eleanor's panic as the two locked eyes. "It's okay, Eleanor."

"I— I c-c-can't br-breathe."

"It's okay." They got to their knees, trying to shortcut what could have been an hour of gentle coaxing in the short seconds available between Fern's moves. "It's okay—" they started, their eyes flicking between their back and the ghost's eyes, "You're here. Your name is Eleanor Sloth-Bunny Jr. You— where's your music?"

As though on cue, the half-second of hissing silence between the compressed voice of Ted Taylor gave way to a hard snare, and she was back.

Some recognition flashed behind Sett's eyes. They gave a short "good job" nod and stood. Dust fell from their sweater, and they charged back at Fern.

Actually...

It's not like the dog could actually hurt her.

The stalker stepped forward into the void, her hidden camera now functionally identical to a regular camera. In that single moment of hyper-clarity, Eleanor grabbed the duck by the back of her trench coat and tossed her back into the concrete shelter of the stairwell.

"What the fuck are you doing?" she snapped. "Don't be fucking stupid."

"This is fascinating. I've never—" The two were cut off as a thud put cracks in the cement above their heads. Eleanor stuck her head through the wall in time to watch Sett, body clenched, climb out of the plaster. "Two telepaths, a fully formed spectre, some variety of dog-beast-hybrid. This is fantastic! This is the best day of my life! What is this place?"

"This place is fucking— not a tourist attraction, is what it is." Eleanor finally squared up her stalker. The trench coat hung loose around her wrists, dirty in places where it had dragged along the dusty edge of the staircase. Splattered across the chest was an extensive collection of *I WANT TO BELIEVE* style patches and buttons, now not hidden by the duck's raised arms. Eleanor snatched the sunglasses off her face; she looked barely old enough to be let out of the house alone, too short to see over most counters, a set of green-banded braces slurring her speech.

Just a kid, familiar in her wide eyed fascination.

"You look like a creep with the sunglasses—" was the first thing to come to mind.

"Eleanor!" Sett shouted from across the room. The rabbit turned to see Fern charging at the stairwell door, the full force of their fangs ready to strike. Shit.

Eleanor — her heart pounding, actually pounding — flinched as the lights snapped off around her. She shifted in an instant, her soul suddenly filling the room, stretching-to-breaking her soft sweat-suit. She blinked away tears and her eyes dragged themselves across her face on the return. The tension throughout her body snapped, launching her from the walls to the centre.

Fern stopped just shy of the duck as they crashed into the smaller rabbit, half-growling half-whining as the ghost phased through them and took their throat by the interior. She dropped with the dog's neck in her hands, bracing for the slam against the floor. Instead, Fern's back cracked the plywood underneath, and Eleanor continued through into the lobby. Her hands were lost on the other side of the ceiling.

The creature choked and gagged as its body recovered from the equivalent of a hard jab in the throat. Eleanor's hands fumbled around on the carpet for something solid to pull herself back up by, eventually re-finding Fern and pulling herself up by the dog's fur. The ghost's eyes locked onto her stalker when she was sure the ball of fur below them wouldn't move.

"Pokey! The thing!" The words had barely left Sett's mouth before a light yellow syringe had left the lizards hand and landed in theirs. They jabbed it into Fern's neck, their rapid breathing falling in tandem as the drug worked its way through the creature's system. The room fell to a tense normal, and they let out a long sigh.

"You did it." They fell to their side.

"Yeah, for sure." She let go of herself, letting the ache in her limbs press her into the floor.

"Okay—" Sett sat up between breaths. "Who's hurt?"

---

To her credit, Ratty had endeavoured to make the staunch refusal to perform any kind of introspection marginally more interesting. Now, not only had she spent a stupid amount of time staring at the door, but she was currently exploring endeavours in staring at the ceiling.

There was something going on upstairs. She could hear the building settling and resettling, vents creaking against each other as somewhere, a few floors up, the old floor bowed and unbowed. Perhaps coincidentally, Ratty could no longer hear Fern fucking around in the stairwell.

She desperately wished for the cement walls around her to turn to their usual black tile. Held her breath, waited, stared up at the medium grey.

So, c'mon Ratty.

Let's talk.

She stood up and paced the length of the hallway. Even in the tight space she felt small.

Was, *why did I let this happen?* even the right place to start? No. She knew why she let this happen. There was a very clear line of motivation stretching back to the core belief that Sett either hated her or should hate her.

If, from the moment she woke up in her office, the universe gave her 1000 different opportunities to repeat tonight with her memory wiped, there was no random component that would have intervened and made anything but this happen. It wasn't as though Ratty had let it happen. It had happened, and would always have happened.

So why did it happen?

"There's never an amount of self sacrifice I should be able to do that doesn't solve the problem. There is infinite Ratty, ergo, there should be enough Ratty to be burned to fix anything — everything, even," she said aloud, inviting the room to queer that line of thought.

The most obvious, but least interesting flaw was that there was not "infinite Ratty."

"I don't know how to fix things without hurting myself." She tried. Not quite.

"There's something wrong with me." That was the core of that thought. "Is that my fault?"

She woke up one day in the middle of the desert with a head full of someone else's memories. The cop out answer would be to say that she was doomed to misery from that moment, but she had had so much joy in her afterlife, even with the spectre of guilt hovering over her.

She had only seen her father once past age 18, at her younger sister's wedding. She contextualized that day through one terse interaction, wherein the man had berated her for some "lifestyle choices."

In one moment, everyone is laughing at you for your temper tantrum, and how weak you are, and how you could never hurt anything. In the next second you smash a glass Tupperware over your father's head and everyone hates you.

He was probably even older now.

Not that any of that had actually happened. That Hanratty Vermington did not exist. All the work she had put into her network, and her journalism, and her students, all existed outside the scope of her life.

Ratty fell onto her back, cushioned slightly by the nest of torn sheets. She tongued at the cut in her lip, still there after so long.

There was a small window. She could probably break it if there was anything around hard enough.

Her sister's wedding would be coming up soon, actually. The fall of 2024, delayed only slightly by that year's pandemic.

It would have been, at least. That sister was never born. Something about the relationship between the new Ratty and her parents never produced a second child. Something stopped the new Ratty from wanting what this Ratty wanted. There were so many people who had never met her here. Old universe friends were new universe strangers.

Ratty sat up abruptly as a clump of dust fell into her eye, the tremors back again.

"Fucking— god damn it." She jammed the heel of her palm into the socket.

Sett was handling it. They would have been able to get out of this room. It was more likely that Sett wouldn't have gotten stuck in the first place.

She began to rub the other eye, telling herself it was another clump of dust. She stopped abruptly, just letting the sting sit, letting the tears well up and roll down her cheeks, hating herself for every one.

"Fucking... hate this," she said, the sticky urge not to sob clinging to her voice like a tumour. Every second of alone time she had had, for her entire life — before and after — all she had ever done when the universe left her alone was think about how much she fucking sucked.

She let the silence hang, sat up, stared around blankly, as though she could see the absence of sound, as though waiting for someone to speak.

This was fine.

Sett didn't need her anymore.

Eleanor wouldn't need her, soon enough.

Better this way. It had happened with Fern in the old universe. When she felt the end of a relationship coming, she burned it.

Better that no one miss Ratty Vermington.

When that didn't work — and there were times with Sett

where it hadn't worked — her paranoia worked against her.

Better to be aware of her cycles than live in fear of them.

No one here to see those thoughts. Just Ratty, miserable, alone, too stubborn to face anything any way but by herself. It was fate that put her through Hell. It was Ratty who decided she deserved it.

God, what a fucking mess.

The drywall beaded up around the holes left by Fern's claws, wide enough for the possum to put her fingers through. She gripped the cheap plaster, the cold metal of an aluminum stud holding her in place. She pulled, taking a white chunk out of the wall and launching it towards the exit. It shattered on the cement floor, throwing dust into the air.

"FUCK," she screamed, hand buzzing. She swung at the hole, feeling something in her wrist crack as she hit the aluminum stud. Hollow ringing pressed into her ears. She wove both hands together and dragged that ball of flesh through the drywall. Sett didn't do this. Sett wasn't like this. A piece of black tile chipped off the wall.

"Fucking finally!" She picked it up, the high pitched metallic whine of the building pressing into her chest as it crumbled between her fingers. "No, come on!" The force of her voice scattered what was left of the black dust. "Come the fuck on." Something pathetic lodged itself in amongst the noise.

Dust caught her eye. She dragged a balled fist across her face and smeared more drywall into the wound. The ringing in her chest pushed the air out of her lungs. She stared at the grey concrete, the exposed slating and loose wires behind the walls, and slid down the opposite wall.

"Come on." she coughed. "I need it."

No black tile.

"I deserve to be miserable." It sounded so ridiculous when she said it aloud. It wasn't about *deserve,* it was the result of a lifetime spent making only choices she thought were good. She hurt people. With the best intentions and best available information, she still made choices that hurt people.

*Miserable* was predetermined. There were unchangeable false positives she held about herself and the world. Without letting those go, she would be trapped in *miserable.* If there really was nothing she could do, then the only thing that hated her more than she hated herself was fate. That was stupid.

Fuck that. She stood up. Window. Something hard. All of her staring had paid off in the form of a perfect image of the door, its handle barely hanging on. Fate could go fuck itself. All it would take is one good kick and—

It swung open.

"Oh. Huh."

She swallowed a mouthful of dust, spitting out what she couldn't get rid of, then held her breath and ran upstairs.

Most obvious was Fern, lying unconscious in the middle of the room. In the corner nearest the door, Pokey presided over minor wounds, bandaging the cuts and scrapes that had resulted more from fleeing than from the actual creature.

Prisha followed closely behind a duck Ratty had never met before, circling Fern's unconscious form, frozen in the middle of a flinch from a slap on the hand they had just received.

Miss Nelly, woken up by the commotion, still in her pyjamas, towered over Sett, deferring in posture to the goat's orders.

And Sett.

Ratty let out her breath and all at once the chaos resumed.

"Sett!" The goat jumped as their partner snapped into existence from thin air.

"Ratty." They composed themself quickly enough not to fuck up their delicate stitch-work. The possum stopped at their side, realizing on the in-stroke that her airway was still coated with dust.

"I— sorry, I wanted to say, I never made you important to me." she managed to cough up through laboured breaths.

"No, you didn't." Sett finished up the wound, sealing it up and moving on to the next identical claw mark. "You're doing great, by the way." they told their patient. One of the neighbours — that kid who lived one door down — he temporarily un-bit the ream of printer paper he had been biting into for stability and offered a weak "thank you" grunt in response.

"I want to fix that," she said.

"Good." Sett turned away from their work for a moment, met Ratty's gaze for a split second to confirm that this was exactly the kind of conversation they had wanted for years now, and resumed their stitch-work. "Let's talk about it later."

"Yeah, absolutely." Giddied excitement took over Ratty's

voice. "For sure."

"Right now, go grab the big first aid kit from my— our bedroom and come back with it."

Ratty nodded, turned to take off, and choked on the rough fabric of her shirt's collar as it dug into her throat. She turned back, her chin landing neatly in Sett's palm. "Hang on." Their eyes scrutinized hers, flicking to her lips as she struggled not to cough a mouthful of drywall into their face. They rocked up onto the tips of their hooves and pressed the cover of their lips against Ratty's.

"Thank you." Sett let go of Ratty.

"For sure."

"I love you." They brushed drywall dust off their sleeve.

"I love you too."

"Alright, go."

———

Sett sat carefully on their shared couch, a slightly overflowing mug of green tea in one hand, a small bowl of sugar in the other. Usually they didn't like to sully the flavor, but today was a long day. A little treat wouldn't hurt anyone. They had spent the past few minutes searching for the tiny porcelain scoop that went along with the dish, then gave up and settled on dumping a few seconds worth of sugar into the blend.

"So…" they began. "What's, um… what is up?"

Ratty sat up, pulling the sleeves of an old college hoodie over her cold fingers. *Old* wasn't accurate. She had waited for her undergrad school to stock the hoodie she wore for most of her freshman year, then bought one on a trip to that part of the city. It was a comforting ounce of normalcy, even as the new fabric required she grind the burrs off on the lap of her jeans.

She took a deep breath, and began:

"When I had that flashback… like a month ago… I saw some of this… just horrible shit." She looked empty. In spite of all the work she did to keep it suppressed, keeping the vision from flickering behind her eyes entirely was impossible. From the corner of her eye she was struggling to keep eye contact through, the goat she had executed aligned itself with Sett, stopping dead her pathetic attempt to hold a gaze. "There was this goat, and I didn't know their name, I— they just looked so much like you. And I think, what I thought, was that— I was worried that you weren't safe around me, or..."

That wasn't it.

"I— none of this to say you should feel bad for me. I just, for a long time — I guess I still do— I want you to hate me. I wanted you to feel nothing when I died. I picked up every job that came in for the courier, and I don't know if I was going to kill myself at some point, or I had just hoped that it would happen eventually, but my plan was to just to leave you with guilt-free money."

Ratty stared at her paws, her shoulders bunched as she let that admission settle. She hadn't noticed when she started crying, catching wise and hiding her face from Sett only as she watched something wet drop into the carpet.

Every thought that crossed through Sett's throat, waiting to be spoken, lived for barely long enough to earn a first word. Their eyes changed position, back and forth between the ground and the waning edge of their partner's face.

"I am... I think I'm mad at you?" they said, speaking it into reality more to ask the question than to actually make an accusation.

"That's understandable." Ratty let her concentration lapse, allowing herself to turn around, indulging in the comfort of watching Sett's hands in exchange for showing some outward vulnerability. It was less a latent machismo and more a guilt over the balance of pain. Sett was the one who had been wronged.

"I'm sorry, this is quite tense, but I really don't know what to say to that."

"That's— I also, wouldn't."

"You put a lot of people in danger tonight."

"I know."

"Fern could have been shot if they decided to leave."

"I know."

At least she knew.

"I am glad that you're not dead." Sett nodded, using this as a mental anchor to build out from. "Is it selfish if I say that if you ever chose to kill yourself, that's not something I would want you to decide without me?"

"I don't think so. I think that's reasonable."

"God... I wonder if anyone has ever felt this before." They raised their chin to the ceiling as if to use gravity to keep their emotions from welling over.

At least she knew.

They let out a short, cough of a laugh. "What you said was funny."

"Was it?"

"I mean— you know, it's so... just... odd how little control I have over my feelings right now. My actual, most powerful emotion — or maybe the one I'm processing the most clearly — is that—" The goat laughed again, taking a long sniff to stabilize themself as they turned down to meet Ratty's eye line. "I'm a little upset that you thought you could kill me." Both sets were glazed with tears.

"Oh, okay." Ratty grinned through her dry anguish. "If anyone could, it would be me."

"You— absolute fucking idiot." The goat smiled. "How could you possibly think I could do anything but love you."

"I tr—" The possum stopped herself as a sob caught in her throat. "I tried my hardest." She let it out, hidden under another cough-laugh.

Sett broke the barrier between the two, clinging to Ratty like she had already died. They head-butted her chest, listening to the hollow *thunk* of her rattling lungs. Again, at a different point in her cycle, and the noise changed. Her hand had grown back wrong. There was a clear shift in colour, delineated by a balding patch of scar tissue around her wrist.

Ratty dragged Sett into her body, pressing her own ache into the goat, themself trying to convey through the hug a simultaneous anguish at almost losing their best friend and gratitude that they had not.

"I am an entire person, Hanratty Vermington. If I ever hate you, it will be for my own reasons." Sett pressed their forehead against the side, feeling the side of the jagged tip of Ratty's broken horn against their cheek.

"Can you—" There was a light pressure against the base of her horn, accidentally scratching her partner's chin as she turned to look up at them. "Can you help me repair these, by the way?"

"I can't, actually. They have to grow back on their own."

That was unfortunate. Ratty let out a long sigh, struggling not to cough through the middle of it. She reached up to touch the jagged break. "At least help me file them down?"

The goat nodded. They used the change in position to take their turn as the embraced, rather than the embracer, and waited for that thought to pass.

They tucked under ratty's chin, her prickly fur gently scratching the corner of their forehead. "When was the last time you brushed?" Sett asked.

"Oh I'm suddenly the only tran who can't rock some stubble?" Ratty teased back. They had nothing to say to that, and once again let the moment pass.

"I want to do couples therapy," they muttered into their partner's chest.

"You don't want to get married?"

"Nope. That'll be something for you to stick around for. Just couples therapy for now."

"I thought that was a given."

"Yes, well. Good." The pair sat in silence after that, getting acclimated once again the way their bodies fit together. It took almost no time at all for Ratty's tired eyes to flutter closed, her half sleeping mind nesting deeper into them on instinct alone.

"You know I don't want to go on without you, right?" Sett asked.

"I know."

"And I know you feel the same way about me. And so..." The goat wove their claws through their fiancée's hair, lost in the mess of dark curls and cheap conditioner. "For the time being, I'm not going to. We're sticking around."

"Yeah, for sure." Ratty smiled.

"Good."

"Good."

## 2017
# The Ellen DeGenerous Show

She woke to Sett's eyes, glowing half-moons hanging tiredly over her face.

"Did you just wake up?" Ratty asked.

"I've been up for a bit." Sett answered. "I don't know if you got my text." It had been on their mind.

"The other night when you went to sleep at the tea shop?"

"Yes." A little awkward to have kept it this long, knowing that — in the explanation — Ratty would come to understand that it'd actually been a lot longer than a couple nights. "So, that wasn't the other night."

"Oh, I know." Oh, she knew? "I've been feeling the time dilation." Well, that was easier than expected.

"You didn't think to mention anything?" Sett asked.

"I didn't think it was supernatural, time naturally changes speeds when shit gets worse."

"Have you always been able to—"

"Yeah, I just have a pretty good sense of time. I could tell you exactly what time it is right now without even looking."

"Without looking, what time is it right now?"

"Like... 4:35 in the morning." Ratty said, her eyes still shut. Sett checked their watch, barely moving as to preserve the comfort. Sure enough: 4:34 a.m. "So... we kill Ellen DeGenerous?" She didn't wait to be told she was right. She didn't wait to be told the rest of the story.

"Yes, that is probably what we are going to have to do." Sett nodded.

"Cool." Ratty muttered, using her last act before falling back asleep to throw up a pair of horns with her free hand, completely unseen by anyone.

The floor thudded as Ratty dropped a stack of file-boxes of old research onto Eleanor's coffee table. "Okay!" She spread out Sett's research — the entire several-volume collection they held on Decay and its mechanics — across the section closest to where they knelt. She pulled up a drum stool, popped the top off her own stack of papers on the Ellen murders, and pushed towards Eleanor the background research she had done while first working on the story.

"So, we have basically until Steph and Fern can get Angel up and running to figure out what we're doing." Several among them were still referring to 2004 as "the other day"; better to finish this as soon as possible.

Sett picked out a tome from the centre of their stack, unfolded it, thumbed dust off the pages, and began to study and speak at the same time.

"There is something here which I think we are going to be able to exploit." They took brainpower out of putting colour in their voice to devote to searching. "How is Fern?" They hadn't gotten a chance to ask.

"They're okay," Ratty said, given the duty of checking on the borzoi as payment for letting them out in the first place. "They're mad at me, but they always used to bounce back pretty quick. Did you want to talk about—" The possum turned to Eleanor, who shook her head into the aging magazine in her hands.

"Not right now."

"Okay, smart. Whenever you feel like it, I am emotionally open for business."

"Good to know." It was hard not to let a note of annoyance step into her voice.

"Here we go." Sett pushed the book into the centre of the table, as though either Eleanor or Ratty could read ancient gods' cant. "So the way her foresight works, there would be a window of opportunity after her vessel is destroyed where she wouldn't be able to predict our actions."

"How long?" Ratty tried anyway. Eleanor picked up another story about her death.

"I'm not sure, the language this is written in has a different base counting system."

"Wouldn't it be impossible to destroy the vessel if she could see it coming?"

"Maybe. She would have to..." Sett trailed off, trying to figure out the conversion to minutes, or hours? Maybe? Trying to figure out the conversion to parsable time in their head. Eleanor stood up to look down into the box, pushed a stack of papers to one wall, and pulled a Time cover from the very bottom. 1997, "Yep, I'm gay" printed in block red letters.

"Where did you get all this?" Eleanor asked, unfolding the empty jacket.

"There's a whole corner of storage that's just dedicated to Ratty's collection of old newspapers."

"We have the space." She was defensive about that. "There could be something useful."

"Is this useful?" Eleanor turned a newspaper headline to the other two. A 1998 paper with the other two fragments of the date worn off, and *Ellen DeGenerous cleared of all charges* in ink blurred by time.

"Oh shit, yeah." Ratty took it, fumbled at the top of her head like she was searching for glasses, and squinted at the small print when she found none. "I don't know if I remember this."

It wasn't a block in her memory so much as it was something she hadn't heard about. When she wanted to be tortured by guilt, she read Wikipedia articles about the other girls Ellen killed. Most of them did not have men's names.

"It was— I think— do you remember the guy's name, Sett?"

That was enough to get them going. The first book was pushed off to one side as another, far wider text became the centre of their attention. They thumbed quickly through the pages of *Tracking Lineages of Godhood,* the same copy with the same scribbled-out name had found its way to Earth. The tip of their finger dragged along the top of the quick-reference table until the word *Decay,* then down... down... down... Decay was a mantle that passed by blood.

"Was it... Aleksey Brusilov?"

"The Russian General?"

"Yeah, like he—"

"Faked his death in 1926, I know." Ratty's attempt to speed the point along resulted instead in the goat blinking up at them for several silent seconds. Incredulous, she said, "I'm still a professor—"

"That doesn't explain how you know he faked—"

"So wait," Eleanor stepped in. "Ellen has only been a god at this point for like, twenty years?" Eleanor paused to turn that over. "What're the odds she hasn't lost her first vessel yet?"

"She wouldn't know what it felt like." Ratty said.

"It's a possibility." Sett watched Eleanor abandon that line of thought as a name on the edge of a file caught her eye.

"What about this?" she asked, pulling a fat stack of bulging manila folders onto her lap.

"Oh! That is the background research I did on the original Ellen murders. I had my mom pull them out of storage when we came looking for you," Ratty explained. Eleanor stopped to process what was wrong with that.

"In 2009?"

"Yeah,"

"So you would have been like, 11?"

"Yeah."

"And in another universe?"

"Yeah."

"So that research— are you not seeing anything wrong with this?"

"I dunno, like, you would have to ask my mom. She just had them." Ratty shrugged. Fuck, fine. No time to finish that conversation. Ratty could be belligerent when she didn't know something.

Eleanor flipped open her own file. The address of her old apartment building wrote itself into her mind from the page. Names of friends, family members, old co-workers. The final group's names had been highlighted when they were one of the ones to turn up missing, each with little notes in possum-scratch.

"Do you think they'd be in the ghostzone?"

"It's more than likely." Sett said. "Without something to link themselves to, it would be hard to actually bring them out."

"What if we bring Ellen in?"

Sett stopped to think that over.

Ratty watched Sett think it over.

Eleanor watched them both.

"She would be powerless." Eleanor suggested.

"She... would be." Sett took an extra pause to make sure

they weren't missing something. Hearing that, Eleanor got up, hovered through the wall into her foyer, and came back with the talk-show host's false face.

"Hold onto this." She handed the cardstock to Sett. "I'll be right back." and she vanished into the ghostzone.

---

"Pokey!" Ratty stopped the lizard in the stairwell, catching a thick bundle of cables as Pokey tripped into her arms.

"Sorry, heavy." She got up and kept dragging it.

"What's going on?" Ratty asked, picking up the weight of the slack.

"We're— Angel is going to teleport the van, I think."

"Oh? Whose idea was that?"

"Hers. She says it would be easier to do one big thing than four little things."

"Okay, yeah. Smart." Ratty nodded, stumbling into the garage behind Pokey. "Is she doing okay?"

"She's powering through, c'mon." The lizard gave a firm yank, pulling Ratty all the way off her feet and across the floor of the garage. She got up, opened the van's door, and disengaged the parking brake.

"Hello, Ratty," Angel said, sitting in the driver's seat.

"Hey, buddy." She went around the front of the van and braced against the grill, inching it backwards. "Here, Pokey, make it easy." Someone unseen joined her in pushing, crossing the last few feet between the van and the wall.

Pokey dragged the cable up through the side door, through the headrest for a little extra stability, and jacked it into the back of Angel's neck.

"Watch this." She raised a hand to get Ratty's attention, and dropped it to signal Pokey. Pokey hit the call button next to Fern's name on her cell. The lights overhead dimmed, and the glow that'd spent the past several years ebbing out of Angel surged back. Ratty shielded her eyes against the robot's light.

"Jesus." Her voice came muffled through the windshield. "Were you always this bright?"

"Yes." Angel answered flatly. "I am ready whenever you are."

The van rocked as Sett tossed their duffle bag into the back, a few pieces of light reading weighing it down. They put

Eleanor's mask in an outside pocket, weak enough to rip if the ghost came back with mass.

Ratty followed, not sure where to look when a vehicle wasn't moving forward. The dim lights closest to them surged suddenly, popping in a ring around the van as a metallic smelling smoke leaked from Angel's joints. This would probably be the last gate/portal/whatever she ever conjured. What finally fried whatever part of Angel allowed her to pull points in space together like rubber, was moving a big, beige van from Toronto to Burbank, California.

And it got stuck. The van, thudded slowly into a digital facsimile of subspace as though sinking to the bottom of a river, rocking gently back and forth as though being brought across the gap by ferry. It took a few seconds to recognize the gilded seam between the darkened garage and wherever they had ended up.

"Is this— are we okay?" Ratty leant forward to search the front window.

"This is normal. It is usually much faster than this, but yes." The same general process as before, just slower. It was difficult to see with one's eyes smoking, but what lay ahead was functionally identical to what Angel's advanced senses were used to. "We will end up in range of Burbank within three to four hours. There will be time to correct once I start to see parts of the world form around us."

Ratty, trying to be mindful about being mean, took a moment to think over her next question. It came out wrong anyway. "If we were just gonna be teleporting for four hours, why didn't we just get a plane ticket?" Ratty leant over the driver's seat, distracted from examining the source of Angel's smoke by a full view of the tar-like ropes of wire that surrounded them.

"Yes, Ratty." Angel turned, the extra power relieved from her teleportation subsystem bolstering her lifelike movement. A quick progress bar flashed across their eyes, illuminating the haze for a moment. "Let's — four people with very little money — get same day plane tickets to California, on New Years Eve, on a time limit. Then, we will get a hotel room in Burbank California, on New Years Eve, with — again — no money."

Ratty glared, incredulous at the robot for a moment. "Alright, you don't have to be a shit about it."

"I didn't know, is your answer." Angel turned to single out the goat in the back. "Sett thought what I said was funny."

"That's not fair!" they protested. "I was trying very hard to hide that."

"Are we— are you guys not too tense for jokes, right now?" Ratty asked.

"Please! When have *you* ever been too tense for jokes?" Sett answered.

"I'm going through character development! I'm figuring out if it's still okay to goof off when our lives are in danger."

"Yes. It's always going to be okay."

"Okay, well, good." The possum stuck her tongue out at Angel and started towards the back of the van. "I'm gonna nap or some shit. Sett, I love you. Tell Eleanor I also love her when she wakes up," she said, staring pointedly at Angel as she backed into the darkness.

"Aw, I love you too, grump." Sett teased, flumphing into the couch with Eleanor's mask on their chest. "I'll wake you up so we can finalize when she gets back."

"I love you also, Ratty." Angel said, turning back to the wheel and staring — blank — out the inky blackness of the front window.

"For sure." Ratty's voice came from the bedroom just before the curtain slid shut.

---

Eleanor made her way back from the ghostzone in record time. While the overworld missed her for a little less than half an hour, she was exhausted when she came up to breathe, and quietly asked Sett not to wake Ratty. There would be plenty of time to brief her, and she needed some quiet time with her girlfriend's partner.

The pair watched as — like stars — flecks of passing townships and cities shot past the windows: bright little flecks of people's lives.

The ghost slipped through the door once holes in the metal siding became too small to see through, hovering above the rushing current below and staring up and letting the weightlessness of their body hold them like the soft curve of a grassy hill under the false sky. She turned as Sett sat down on the stairs, doing their best to see up past the lip of the van.

"Sorry for freaking out the other day," she said.

"It was justified. You saved lives." The coat smiled up at their friend.

"Yeah... I feel like, whatever that was kinda like... unblocked my mental sinuses, and now if I push at the edge of a memory it just kinda, like— it's less invisible wall and more fog-of-war, y'know?"

"What kind of memories?" Sett prodded, dropping down another step and cautiously poking their hooves into the current below. Eleanor's eye shifted, now more into the back of her own head than the sky above.

"I had a girlfriend in high school. I was out, and popular, and I used to fix teacher's cars," she started, just following a train of thought until it dropped off. No matter, it would come back if it was important. There was a comfort to being able to remember at one's leisure, not fighting for every scrap of biography.

"What else... what else.... There was this little greenhouse I used to go to like, once a week. The owner's name was Rick Black, he had six kids in college at once. I think he offered to pay for me too. He taught me— oh *FUCK*—" Eleanor's arms shot up in the air, startling Sett and sending her spinning. "I have a like, a notebook full of shit about my old plants! I couldn't find it when we were there because the little door was stuck but if I— I—" She worked herself up with excitement, fumbling over her words as they came up too fast to say.

"That's exciting! Ratty has been talking about building a greenhouse on the roof, you two could—" Sett bit their metaphysical tongue as the rabbit stopped spinning. They let out a soft, "Ah." Eleanor hadn't gotten her closure yet. She had only barely overheard their conversation after the containment breach and probably hadn't spoken to Ratty since.

"What's, uh... can you fill me in on her deal?" Eleanor asked, doing her best to phrase it as neutrally as possible.

"You..." Sett sighed. "You met Ratty at a very weird time in her life, to say the least. She was trying very hard to kill herself, and I think— I mean, I actually don't know why. Not yet. We're doing therapy together to try and figure that out."

Eleanor nodded, chewing her next question. "So was I like... am I..."

"Like a fling?" Sett asked, receiving a cautious nod from Eleanor. "No, Eleanor. Ratty has had more than her fair share of flings, and if she didn't care about you she would have just cut you off. She was a bad partner for a moment there, I can't imagine how garbage of a girlfriend she must've been, but you're definitely not a fling."

"Cool." Eleanor nodded, going back to her stargazing. "Cool..."

"You can... go talk to her... if you want?" Sett poked.

"I might do that later."

"Good. Good."

Eleanor took a moment to push out on another memory that'd been troubling her: her mother. There wasn't a lot there. Iffy around trans stuff, pushy, kind of selfish. Sr. wasn't the kind of person Jr. was going to reconnect with, and that was fine, but it also left her feeling — well, to be frank — incredibly lonely. She had to secure the few people she did have in her life.

"Do you hate me, Sett?" she asked.

"No, Eleanor. I don't hate you." The goat's eyes conveyed a genuine eagerness to answer that question, something few people ever did. "I really like you, actually. I've been thinking about— I used to grow my own tea leaves and I would love to get your help. I would say you're one of my closer friends."

"Yeah?" Eleanor pantomimed a deep breath, held it for a moment, then let it out. "What are you having trouble with?"

"It's the climate. Too cold, can't afford to heat a greenhouse year-round, as far as I know..."

The goat slid off the bottom stair tentatively, satisfied as their hoof found solid ground below the river. It ran dry around their ankles, a gentle push towards the front of the van. They watched the ghost's shimmering reflection as it intermingled with their own, then — in a moment of instinct — looked up and told Eleanor, "I love you."

"I love you too, Sett." The ghost smiled, only a half-second of happy silence behind.

"I don't think people tell their friends that they love them enough, and so I'm going to start doing that." They nodded as if to lock in their resolve.

"Fuck yes. I can absolutely get behind that." The ghost

touched down in the stream, now relatively sure it was safe, shocked as her glow infected the world around her. Every fluid cable she touched lit up a bright blue, sending power through the rest of the system.

"Oh, wow." Sett mused, running their claws through the stream. They spent the next moments quietly listening to the music of their environment, watching the stream react to different paranormal phenomena, to their presence, to unknowable forces as parts of their destination threaded themselves onto the wires like beads.

It took a few tries to get it right, but the goat was able to hook the strings of their banjo, pulling it to their lap through subspace.

"Does Ratty ever tell you stories about what we were like before you met us?" they asked, ignoring the stars and beginning to tune up.

"Nope."

"Mm. That's in character."

"I would like to hear about that kind of thing, though." Eleanor prodded. The goat smiled, scraping the rotting walls of their mind, watching memories curl off like rings of dried mud. What a weird metaphor. Sett cupped a few amber grounds of tobacco in the hollow of their claw as they simultaneously prepared a paper cone and rummaged through the memories.

"Give me a theme." they said, pinching, rolling and lighting in one smooth motion. "Any theme, and I can tell you about a Rett adventure."

"Rett?"

"Yeah like, Ratty and Sett."

They spent the rest of that hour telling stories, each with their own warm and weightless hue of memory. Each somehow conveyed the feeling directly opposite to carrying a stake through ones chest.

---

"Hey. Hey, Ratty." Eleanor nudged the possum with the tips of her fingers, toeing the line between waking her up and not startling her. She turned over, blinking as her eyes faced the full force glow of her girlfriend. "Sorry." Eleanor said reflexively.

"It's chill," the possum yawned. "What's up?"

"Can we talk?" As if waking someone up out of the blue after they had apparently stormed off faux-angry wasn't tense enough.

"Yeah, we should probably get you caught up on the—"

"No, I mean... not about that." There was a whole catalogue of knowledge on how to approach this kind of thing behind Eleanor's wall. A person learned to be a person through doing, and when the experience of doing wasn't one you remembered it was hard to index an approach to—

"Oh, okay." Ratty's smile put a small dent in that atmosphere. "Shoot, Tex."

Eleanor nodded, rocking on the balls of her feet with her hands in her jeans' pockets.

"So..." she started, "this whole thing sure is wild." Okay. C'mon Jr., you can do better than that.

"Yeah, for sure." Ratty posted her own air ball. She sat, equally awkward, trying to hide how tightly her shoulders were bunched. "Your eye's gotten better."

"Yeah," she laughed, "I don't even remember like, how long ago that was... How long do you think we've actually known each other at this point?" Eleanor asked.

"I really couldn't tell you." Ratty rolled to one side to make room for Eleanor. "Does this feel like a ten year long friendship?"

"No." Eleanor stared down at the empty spot. "I mean no offence, but like, for sure not."

"Yeah, no, I agree. Six months tops."

"Okay." She dropped onto the thin mattress, a weak crackle rising up from the wood beneath. "I mean like, a pretty decent six months, but..." She loosened her core, lying back across the foam and watching Ratty's eyes lull slowly open and closed.

"I'm not gonna fall asleep," she said.

"I didn't expect you to." Eleanor ribbed.

"No, watch." Ratty rolled over, propped herself up against the side of the van, and — for good measure — shook whatever sleep was left out of her head. She tossed her legs over Eleanor's lap for a little extra comfort, then snapped her eyes open, fully awake.

"So..."

"So?" Her fangs popped out from below her smile. For what could have functionally been the first time, Eleanor felt herself zeroed in the trained observer's eyes. While it could be comforting at times to know she was capable of listening, it was unnerving when she — without malice — chose to listen well.

"Do you remember at my mom's place, you were high and you—"

"Oh god, yeah." She could already see where this was going. "I'm sorry, that was—"

"No, I know it wasn't— like, I believe you now, that you wouldn't have kicked me out or whatever."

"Did I say that?" Ratty winced.

"You said I could say no and you wouldn't kick me out."

"That's a fucking awful thing to bring up, I'm sorry—"

"Can I finish?" Eleanor cut her off. Ratty stayed silent, her eyes focused. "Sorry. I just really didn't want to be alone again, and I liked you, and it really scared me that I might lose whatever we had." Eleanor paused, chose her next words carefully. "So what are we?" Eleanor asked the version of the question that was least likely to have a painful answer.

"I dunno, Eleanor, what are we?" The possum had a confrontational way of speaking when she was curious that survived the several careful filters she set up in front of it. Her gaze was the same, if a little hopeful. Eleanor held it for as long as she could, trying to read the perfect answer out of her friend's eyes. When nothing came, she stared up at the ceiling, a broken push-lamp she had never seen before, and chewed the question in her mind.

What were they?

"Remember when you called me your girlfriend?" Eleanor asked. Ratty nodded, unseen. "Like at the burger place, I mean. It would be cool to have you do that when you're not angry at your other partner."

Ratty nodded, breaking her gaze to stare down at her boots and just ponder. She held still, her chest rising and falling more and more slowly as the detritus of guilt settled on her in layers. "I really kind of did some weird shit to you, eh?"

"A little bit." Eleanor nodded, letting her head slump back to stare at the beige ceiling. "Things have been kind of weird. I guess like, I don't know if I blame you. I just think like — I don't want to just be the things you can't get from Sett."

"Yeah." Ratty nodded. "Okay." That was everything she had to say. Eleanor sat up, only now noticing how close Ratty had pulled herself in. She had wrapped her tail around Eleanor, helping the rabbit stay upright. When all was settled, only a few inches of air remained between their faces. "It's— it's gonna start getting better, though. We're gonna take a break from all of this, I think. Once we stop the world from ending—" she turned to face Eleanor. "It's fuckin' vacation time."

"What comes after this?"

"You wanna get burgers?"

"No, I mean like... we kill Ellen DeGenerous. Cool. Job Done. What's life after revenge?

"Oh! Yeah, I still don't know. I haven't really gotten revenge yet. I will say that uh— for Sett at least it is kind of comfortable? Little aimless? I guess the thing about Angelcorp is that— I mean, especially after we kick their ass here, they're the kind of arch nemesis that you can really put down and pick up. They're like, bigger than Apple at this point, so it's not like I'm ever really going to stop them, I kind of just get the opportunity to stop some of their more dastardly schemes."

Dastardly schemes. What a fucking dork. Such a fucking dork that it made what Eleanor was about to do all the more unlikely, but fuck it. People don't always make sense. She sat forward abruptly and set a gentle kiss on Ratty's lips. The possum sat stunned for a moment, processed it, and tried to force down the shivering blush that rose on her cheeks.

"I'm— uh— more used to being the forward one."

"Shut the fuck up, nerd." Eleanor bumped the possum. "That was an advance on healthy Rattily."

"Rattily?"

"Yeah, like Eleanor and Ratty as a gay thing."

"Oh, rock on. Cool." Ratty nodded down at her feet, then — never be outdone — kissed Eleanor, shifting her weight so the spectre could feel her warmth.

"Couldn't let that one hang, huh?" the rabbit giggled against the possum's lips.

"Nope." Ratty grinned, bumping their foreheads together. Ratty was pretty cool, all things considered. It was going to get better.

In the live TV game it was almost too easy to get thirty seconds confused with thirty minutes and vice versa. Not for Ellen, of course, but for her drove of anguish-pollinating worker bees. Her top down view of everything gave her minute control down to the very smallest decimal point. DeGenerous was the worst boss ever in a way very few people could actually articulate.

And that was so much fun.

Fun too was the oncoming surprise. So rarely did she look to the future with anything but bored disinterest. Assassination attempts came and went, the summation of some great conquest for most, braggarts who couldn't help but make their presence known and died of old age within moments of meeting her.

Today, there was going to be a surprise: precious little Eleanor would pay them a visit this afternoon, then something would happen to interrupt their foresight. She could hardly wait to have a real conversation again.

Sett was also there. Sett's girlfriend was not.

"Where's your other friend, Eleanor? The sick one..." It was so fun to ask questions she didn't know the answer to. A rush of adrenaline, almost.

"Ratty's not coming." The little demon stepped forward. Right, of course. They were the de facto leader. That wasn't going to change, no use fighting it.

"Well, okay!" The god gave a cold smile. "Weird to cripple yourself for the big bad, and y'know— I really hate to cheat, but I don't remember not seeing her..." She spun on her heels. "Surely she must be SOMEWHERE!"

She had made her audience a little more than uncomfortable at this point. Most people that go in for a live taping of *The Ellen DeGenerous Show* end up coming back obsessively if they could afford it, or in therapy if they couldn't, but this was shaping up to be a very special New Years Eve.

Ellen stood from her expensive little host couch, probably better maintained and more expensive per-month than the homes of most of her fans, and handed today's production schedule off to her doting personal assistant— another rabbit, funnily enough.

"Could you push back my meeting with Eden, it doesn't really need to be too long," she said, creating a moment of privacy on the stage; the kind of politeness expressly designed to isolate. Ellen's assistant nodded tersely and took the excuse to power-walk out of the god's aura of influence.

"I really thought it would be nice— I mean it doesn't matter, but Eden is coming down to watch the show today, talk about the fruits of our labour." The god was disappointed when her surprise stayed silent. "Come on, are we fighting? I—"

Ah, that was what that flash was. The possum, the bright red steel of her axe. Odd — everyone in attendance thought in exact unison — how similarly a head and a bowling ball sounded when dropped.

And then, silence.

A complete lack of reaction, as though every single member of the audience simultaneously constructed and ran through their own flow-chart of where exactly they got off on the stages of grief.

Presumably, if you made the effort to get all the way out to *The Ellen DeGenerous Show,* your favourite host just got beheaded in front of you. You were deathly uncomfortable up until this point, but you figured it was just pre-show jitters... now... what the fuck do you think?

If you're a stagehand, you have to be crossing your fingers. That was a brutal chop, and Ellen has talked about Eleanor before... Maybe her friends are the ones to finally kill the tyrant that has monopolized your work-week grief... and if they aren't...

If you're one of the three people in on the operation, even, after enough silence you're starting to wonder if that actually worked. You're starting to do the math on how much planning went to waste, you start to ask your partner: "Is that—"

"So good to finally meet you, Hanratty." And of course that's not it. The head began to laugh, flapping its jaw hard enough to roll back over. Enough to glare through tears at Sett, now gripping a sharpened shard of subspace in their claw. And Eleanor... poor, scared Eleanor.

"I bet this was your plan, wasn't it, Sett? That was really clever. I don't mean to be patronizing, but you were always really smart, honey. You should have been leading the charge this whole time, honestly. And I totally get it too! You're dead..." The god's old body flung an arm towards Sett, a marionette's cruel mockery of a point. "And you're dead too." The arm flung at Eleanor. "And— actually I can't— could someone turn me over?"

That— yeah, no.

"Never mind, you're right. It's alright." The head's last action was to grin as it's voice slipped loose from its moorings. "You three are all dead, you think you're bringing me down to your level, is what I'm saying... which is actually... really cute."

Like a hat slipping off the top of an invisible head, Ellen's corpse stirred its last, giving rise instead to the god's true form. Its arms materialized only as they pressed up on the hollow stage, coated in the blood of it's former shell.

Decay — the true elder god, no longer contained by the rotting sack of meat I had inhabited for 20 years — stood up to my full height. I was formless, taking shape only in the drips of blood that traced their way down my limbs. Ratty shielded her eyes as she struggled to get a read on me, like the absence of light, sucking in the same way staring into the sun pushed at the back of one's eyes.

The few audience members who had not fled had now either passed out or died in my presence, and I smiled. Anyone who could have said to have seen me would have said I was smiling.

I'm excited to show you what real death looks like. My voice is unchanged.

Each trail of red dove first towards Eleanor, the flat drips of blood transforming into thick, meat-like ropes, veins building from the inside out as they pierced the rabbit.

In that moment it invented what creatures of that nature did to show confusion, noticed its weapon coated in a thin layer of a black and lavender in a paint-like veneer.

Unable to resist a gloat as Sett tightened a snare around its wrists, Eleanor flicked on the sound booth's reading light as her apparition dissolved around Decay. She tapped on the glass when she was sure the rope was tight and spoke. "Hi, Ellen. You missed me." She had earned that right. Decay was trapped, having accomplished nothing. It glared up at the

318

booth, made too solid by Sett's abilities to lash out.

Sett kept a tight hold on the rope as the creature bucked. Their partner moved completely in subtime, vaulting off the now ribbonified chair, unseen by what free limbs Decay had left as the heel of her boot clung to the back.

She put a second pair of hands on the rope, followed in quick succession by a third as Eleanor darted through the wall and wrapped her wrists in it. She caught Sett's eye first, emboldened by their resolute glare. Then Ratty, whose legs were purpose built for this kind of balance. She gave a confident thumbs up.

Then, all at once, Sett and Ratty let go, and Eleanor dragged her former boss into the ghostzone.

# 2018
# Decay

Decay's breath stuck in its chest as it thudded to the grassy floor of the expansive forest of the ghostzone, landing face up in a cage of subspace rope. Halfway between their corporeal form and the incomprehensible form of a god, ghostzone was no man's land. No god, God or demon had more power here than the average spirit.

So, not a great one, huh, Decay? Why don't you try to take over the narrative, buddy. Black out some of this page, why don't you? Fuckin jackass. Get bent, loser.

Miles of glowing string kept it trapped and subdued, far too much to have come from one demon. Its mind raced through the stages of grief associated with the suspicion that more than one member of the afterlife hierarchy was conspiring against them before they actually touched the rope. Again, a substanceless cloud.

"Do you like it?" Sett's — or maybe the possum's — voice rattled around the treetops. That was, of course, impossible. It was illusory, like the rest of the god's cage.

"I don't have a problem with you thinking that." Definitely the possum. Her voice called Decay's gaze to a treetop, her feet swinging idly as she watched.

"I painted it myself. The other one, too."

"Explain how you're here."

"Dunno. Always been somewhere in between." She fell from the treetop into a pile of green leaves, popping the pile as though it had been spread out over a sharp updraft, and disappearing into it. Decay winced as the disgusting, overpowering stench of the forest began to suffocate it.

"That was your great plan? Expose me to plants? How terrible, I suppose I'll just keel over and *die*!" It growled. "You think I give a ▮▮▮▮ about a little pain? I INVENTED PAIN." It stood, swiping furiously at the illusory walls of its cage.

Its neck snapped around as a whistle caught it's ear. "Over here!" the construct of the possum waved from another treetop. Decay stared for a half-second, processed what she was doing, and spun in the complete opposite direction.

Sett, or a construct of Sett, stared back, carrying two half-barrels of the leaves. They stood, frozen, for only a moment before charging, throwing one barrel to blind the god, and disappearing. In the scuffle of turning away the soft soil below Decay's feet turned to gravel, and as it wiped the poison from its eyes it found the trees and its cage replaced with beige buildings, equally imposing in their infinity. On the edge of the rooftop — silhouetted by the sunset — sat a very familiar rabbit, bouncing on her haunches, gently nodding along to a cassette.

"Oh, hey, Ellen." Eleanor smiled, popped out one earbud, and gave a gentle smile. Her eyes fell to the god's feet as they strained against the universe, trying to charge at her. "It's— this is my city. It's not going to let you come any closer if you plan on hurting me."

The ghost was almost sorry for this, responding to the god's unsaid *really?* with a shrugged *yeah.*

Decay, in response to the understanding that it had at least temporarily been put on the back foot, stood upright, gathered itself, and told itself not to kill her.

The roof released its legs, and it sat down next to Eleanor on the edge.

"There we go." Eleanor smiled sadly into her former boss's eyes. There was always something sad about the ghostzone. "Y'know, it's funny." She spoke softly for someone with the full blunt force of everything that's ever rotted hibernating a few inches from her ear. "I grew up around a lot of crime. Not-so-safe neighbourhood, y'know?"

Her eyes fell to the street, her head turning along the dashed line in the centre as the sun shifted colour over the bay. "I like this place. People here have such a passion for life. They don't want to leave yet. See, what I figured out recently... It wasn't any of these people that made me afraid to go out at night."

"Well, I mean, a few of them were straight creeps, I'm not gonna lie to you, but the creep ones were just like you. People like you, with so much that they prey on the weak to get their kicks. You're the kind of person who made it dangerous to go out at night. It all comes back to you."

She stared out over the broken city, the wistful happiness of missing home passing over the pair like a cold breeze.

"There's this pizza place just down that way, run by two folks who came here from Afghanistan— Well, okay, not *here* here. Actually, I don't know if it's still *there* either. Anyway, every morning I used to walk past to get to the bus route, and every morning they would bake this like, beautiful smelling sweet bread kinda deal. It was beautiful! I used to treasure that part of my morning every single time."

She pointed south, and Decay's eye followed. "And there, just down there. My uncle Alf's friend let me keep this scrap-heap of a car in his buddy's tow place for fucking *months* while I tried to rebuild it. Right next door, there was a gym where I learned to box. I didn't even know there was a garage there until I needed it. Isn't that crazy?"

Then north, and in the blur between the movement of the god's eyes, the beige was replaced with rust red rows of Victorian homes, a needle rising up through glass towers. "I haven't actually been to the CN Tower yet. I don't think like— I mean it's not close to the top of my priorities list... what's here, what's here, what's here... I'm starting to learn what's here. Ratty likes the bulgogi at this little basement spot down that way, near the museum. Sett's tea shop is like, a few miles west... There used to be this nice pharmacy... what else... Oh! There's this bookstore in Chinatown that's run by this super hot werewolf chick. I mean they're hot but they're also smart, you know what I mean. Tall as hell, too. Really cool."

The god grew bored with the trappings of simple life, staring at blank buildings. It was a museum of someone else's history, fascinating only as a distant curiosity, not to be explained by someone who had loved it. And so the god asked, "Why are you telling me all this?"

"Oh, I'm mostly stalling, actually. Look." The rabbit pointed straight down into a crowd of 18 pairs of black eyes, and in the blur of refocusing, the city of Toronto gave way to the original Ellen stage. Studio 11, in an even more advanced state of decay, quietly rotting away with the god's victims huddled below.

Ah. That was what this had all been leading up to. They felt nothing as they took in each individual face, some less focusable than others. The only thing approaching emotion in the god was the indignant need to explain to their lesser why her sacrifice was necessary, and so they asked the second honest question of the night. "You know why I did this, don't you?"

"Maybe." Eleanor shrugged. "Maybe you were a decent person who had a bad thing happen to them, someone handed you power, you let it corrupt you." It was impossible not to catch snippets of its victims' conversation. "I think you were looking for someone who would let it corrupt them in the same way, because maybe some part of you regretted becoming part of what you hated."

"What makes you think that?"

"Everyone wants to die, Ellen." The rabbit's voice took on a quiet melancholy. "It wasn't that long ago that you and I had the same reasons."

"I wanted a worthy successor. I— just look at this."

Absent of a change in setting, Ellen's eyes sparkled with rows of twinkling lights, of blinding spotlights, of a blinding pastiche so all consuming that it could only be described by its god: "Our past can disappear in the glow of an eternal present, Eleanor. That's what I wanted for you."

"It feels a lot like you just wanted someone to feel like you did. C'mon, let's say hi." With that, the scaffolding collapsed below them, the rabbit's springy legs far more prepared for the drop than Decay's. They fell into the centre of the crowd, surrounded by her 18 dead. Their lives, their sacrifice still as worthless as they were the day they died. It felt dirty to be in their presence again.

"Go on." Eleanor nudged. "Say hi."

Panic returned to Decay in waves, as though each locked gaze piled on another layer. Its heart raced, thrumming through its chest, glowing red in spite of its body's tendency to suck in light. In a panicked instant, it turned on Eleanor, driving a woven fist into her chest and pumping wave after wave of decay into the ghost's body, dumping its ability to burn into the spectral form like a river of hot slag.

And the form stopped, frozen as its voice rose from behind

Decay:

"Oh, Ellen..." Muffled as it rattled against the laminated paper of a mask, legitimate pity in her tone. "I really didn't expect you to fall for that twice." The rabbit stepped out from behind the 18, dropping her mask to the string around her neck and staring at the spot where Decay connected to the fake Eleanor. It crawled up its arm like creeping vines, slowly digested by the rabbit's will to live, by the lives that would have been if it had not cut them short.

It fell to its knees in the embrace of the illusory Eleanor as the women that it took watched it be taken back. Some turned away, disgusted by the gore, too polite to watch a creature who heartily deserved it finally breathe its last. Others fell into the pile, as though pantomiming the process of reclaiming what was lost would somehow make it so.

Eleanor got bored of watching in time, turned away when she had had her fill, and left the ghostzone for what she hoped would be the last time.

---

It was a long drive from California to Toronto. In spite of her apparent disrepair, Angel insisted on driving, keeping the moon above them for forty straight hours. It came in waves: quiet celebration, followed by boredom, followed by the intimacy that boredom often bred, and again by boredom as the excitement of the day was allowed to ebb back into the group's normalcy.

Eleanor was the first to sleep, then Ratty, who had not planned on falling asleep across Sett's lap. In that silence, another Sett flickered in and out of darkened existence in the opposite seat. Sett watched, used now to their inter-dimensional stalker.

Stalker wasn't the right word.

Watcher.. Follower, maybe.

Hard to say.

The rope burns around their wrists shimmered in the black, barely visible were it not for the pure moonlight filling the cabin.

"Angel," Sett mused quietly, intent on leaving Ratty undisturbed. "Do you see her?" The goat pointed.

"I don't see anyone there, no." Angel replied, not taking her eyes off the road.

324

"I thought not."

The pair of goats sat in silent conversation for a few minutes, each studying the other. It was the other Sett that spoke first:

"I'm not a threat to you. I will be forced to take your place soon. You should prepare for that eventuality."

They let that sit, having delivered the entirety of their message with still minutes left until they had to disappear. Their eyes drifted down to Ratty, her tired eyes closed against the streetlights. She looked peaceful.

"You have no idea how lucky you are," they said. Sett blinked as the other goat's eye popped out of existence, as the burns around their wrist went from deep gold to shimmering red below their fur. Sett left the air still for as long as they could manage, not wanting to trample the weak voice.

"I am very lucky," they said, finally. The other goat nodded, and with that slipped through the air before disappearing altogether.

# 2018
# Therapy

Ratty watched as the curves of a glass frog statue speckled the inside of her partner's rope-burned palm with light, scattering the border between brown and black. She listened politely as the *talking frog* was explained by a kindly late-in-life couples counsellor — where she got it from, what it meant when someone was holding it.

They had never had a problem with interrupting each other, never reached screaming until a few weeks prior; theirs was a quiet simmer, but the way it made light dance was enough to justify its stay.

"So, are we all clear on the rules?" The elder grizzly smiled. Ratty nodded, turned to Sett, watched them nod. "Well, good. Sett, since you're already holding the frog, why don't you go first?"

Sett nodded, staring down at the lump of glass. They started with a weak psychic croak. Having spent the morning waiting anxiously for this moment, having run through everything they planned on saying, they now had no idea where to start. Conscious of each passing second, they picked a random point and dropped their spade there.

"The other day, when you were— we were on our way home and you were lying across my lap, and I had the thought that — before that point — I couldn't remember the last time we woke up together." They took a deep breath, shuddering as the anxiety of holding it in left their body. "And I thought, I know the difference between being given space, and being left alone." Another deep breath, another moment of twiddling the glass frog between their claws. "I never want to feel alone like that again. You were so far gone and I felt completely powerless to do anything but lose you, and you're my best friend, and I missed you, and I still miss you. I just— I want to stop missing you."

Sett set the frog down on the table between them, staring at it for a moment and then looking expectantly up at their fiancée. Ratty cast her gaze to the door trim as she processed, blinking back tears. She had hurt Sett.

She picked up the frog, staring into its little glass eyes as she spoke. "I don't know— um— I don't know how to reconcile the fact that you love me with the way I feel about myself, and... uh... I actually don't remember where I was going with this, I'm sorry—" She moved to set down the frog, found her hand cupped gently by their counsellor.

"Hold on, how do you feel about yourself, Ratty?" she asked. The possum met her partner's eye, then the counsellor's, then back to Sett's.

"I wasn't wronged, though? Shouldn't we be talking about how Sett feels?"

"I'm sure we'll get to that, but I think they also want to know how you feel." Ratty took a moment to read a *yes* out of Sett's expression, then another to compose her thoughts. She had never been given time to figure out who she was or what she was feeling. It was difficult to talk at length because of that, and so she just let whatever thoughts were shaken loose come out in order.

"Okay, well, I mean I don't really want to get all, 'woe is me.' I guess, after all this time I feel like I'm taking advantage of you? Almost? That doesn't make sense." She bit her tongue, shaking that line of thought out of her head. "It's more like, I'm just bad. De facto bad..." She took a deep breath. "I just hurt people, and I hurt you, and I knew I was doing it, and I couldn't stop."

There was a short moment of silence, the counsellor asked for their frog back, then handed it to Sett.

"We don't— I don't know if we need the frog." Ratty interjected, doing her best to defuse what she just said. "We've never really had a problem with that kind of—"

"Well, Ratty, for one: no couple has a problem until they have a problem, and for two: you don't have the frog, so—"

"No, but I feel like you're kind of interrupting the flow with this frog thing."

"Ratty." Sett interjected, the edge of a smile peeking out from under the grey cloud in their voice. "You don't have the frog."

they teased. It broke them out of therapy mode for a second.

Just a second, though.

"Fuck... I'm a frogless loser..." That earned a tone-breaking snort.

"Sett..." the counsellor started.

"Yes?"

"Do you feel like Ratty is a bad person?" she asked.

Sett took a long breath, letting the last scraps of frog humour out as they turned the questions over in their mind, confronted with the fact that they were, in fact, there for therapy. "No, I don't. Can be selfish, and dumb — not dumb, sorry," They caught Ratty's gaze. "Neither of those, actually. Not even like, thoughtless. I just don't really know what you're thinking a lot of the time, I don't know why you make some of the choices you make..." They turned back to their counsellor. "...I trust that she makes them for the right reasons, though. She's not bad, and I want her to be a part of my life."

"How does it make you feel that Ratty thinks she's evil?"

"I... I really don't get it. We've all done things. I think, out of a lot of the people we know with similar trauma she had almost the least choice, I don't know if anyone has really sacrificed more to correct for that." Another deep breath, another pause, maybe a shift in weight.

"I feel like, somewhere along the way — Ratty — maybe you got some wires crossed in your head, to where getting hurt makes your good deeds better? And that scares me, because — I want to be a part of this world, and I don't want do that without you. I don't want to if I don't have to. I will be utterly alone if you die."

"I don't want to die." Something thick caught in the possum's throat. "I'm sorry, I cut you off."

"Don't be sorry Ratty, that's a good step." The counsellor set a massive paw on Ratty's knee. "I want to ask you something. Do you think of Sett as your hero?"

Ratty laughed at this, then — aware that it wasn't immediately apparent — stopped to make her position clear: "Obviously."

"Sett, do you think you could come to think of Ratty as good?"

"Ratty is capable of goodness." The phrase *frogless loser*

328

had set the two of them in a joking mood. "Yes, Ratty is good." they clarified.

"I think, Ratty, if you need to be specifically *heroic*, maybe one thing you could do is be there for the person who needs you in their life."

"God, that's so cheesy." The possum tipped her head back, staring, exasperated, at the ceiling fan.

"It's going to get cheesier. I want you to tell me that doing that will make you good enough."

Ratty stayed still for a few moments following that request. She re-seated herself, cautious against slipping out of the chair, and checked the pair of faces for a way out. Her eyes stopped over the individual threads of fur that poked across the grey-brown border around their snout. It could have been a joke, or something optional, or— well, no.

"Staying alive is good enough." She spoke firmly.

"Good! That's a really good promise, Ratty."

"All thanks to the frog." Sett gave a sniff at their little joke.

"And I'm not gonna run off anymore, because I know how that scares you." Ratty said, on a roll with making promises.

"Good! Two!" The counsellor clapped again.

"I don't know if I need all that." Sett smiled, a little overwhelmed getting more than everything they wanted. "We lead dangerous lives. I understand that. Just, be careful and keep your cell phone on you."

"I can do that. I can definitely do that."

"And maybe take a self defence class."

"Only if you take it with me."

Sett let out a held breath with a huff. Probably high time they learn to fight in a way that didn't depend on their demonic supremacy.

"Sure," they said.

---

The various sounds and smells of cooking caught Eleanor off guard as she crossed the threshold of her apartment. Something like barbecue, or hot oil, or— actually, it was easier just to look around the corner into her kitchen than to guess. Ratty stood at her stove, tending to a pot of round little dough balls, a fat slab of black-crusted beef resting on the counter.

"You're in my kitchen." The rabbit blinked against her confusion.

"Hi Eleanor!" Ratty smiled, deafened by the rattling of the cheap overhead fan.

"Yeah, hey!" She gave an awkward wave as she pulled her mask from under her shirt and set it down into her obelisk. She popped her headphones out and draped them around her neck, catching a glimpse of Sett kneeling in front of a menorah as she shed the trappings' outsideness. "You guys are doing Hanukkah... in my apartment... several weeks late."

Sett nodded as though there was nothing abnormal going on.

"Cool, why here?"

"Well..." Ratty let a steaming dough-ball fall out of her mouth and back into the hot oil, eliciting a crackle as her spit sublimated below the surface. "I— your mom called and was like 'what did y'all do for Hanukkah?' and we were like, oh fuck we didn't do Hanukkah! And so now we... are!"

"Are you two... Jewish?" Eleanor asked. Sett was literally from a kind of non-denominational freelance Hell — something she was pretty sure Jewish people didn't have — and Ratty, short of having never talked about her religion, clearly had no practice with the whole Hanukkah thing.

"Nah El'!" Ratty scoffed. "You're Jewish!"

"I'm— I'm Jewish?" Eleanor blinked.

"Yeah babes!" Ratty raised her arm, dropping a hot ball of perfectly cooked doughnut on the floor. "We got brisket! We got some doughnuts and the latkes- we got the Menorah! Sett sent me some readings which I did NOT do, except for the recipes obviously." She picked Eleanor's recipe book from a wire cookbook stand and wiggled it in the air, demonstrating its existence. "I like— it's cultural osmosis. I asked Fern about it. Y'get it."

"We didn't get everything, because we are still very much broke, and also didn't know if this would be something you wanted to do, but... we managed quite a bit." Sett picked the menorah up from where they were kneeling and set it precariously on the edge of Eleanor's TV stand between a bunch of salvaged equipment.

"Here—" Ratty concentrated for a moment on snatching one of the cooked doughnuts from the hot oil, then offered it to

Eleanor on the end of a fork. She stopped as she noticed Eleanor crying, forcing a smile through the tears. "Whoa, whoa. What's wrong?"

Another doughnut took a dive as Eleanor shook her head, trying to clear up the overwhelming surge of emotion. "It's—" the rabbit hiccuped. "You guys are just really nice." Eleanor collapsed in on herself as her friends dropped what they were doing to hold her.

She was so small for someone so tall. Even as she continued to push out into being, more and more extant by the day, the gaps in her body and mind fit perfectly into the support structures of her friends. Sett's tiny shoulder and Ratty's firm grip propped her up, fill in the blanks of her self-image like a puzzle piece.

The rough wave of emotion cleared slowly, ebbing into a gentle stream of contentment.

And then presents. Ratty hung behind to wipe the spilled oil from Eleanor's stove as Sett led her to a small pile of newspaper-wrapped boxes.

"The big one is yours." Sett pointed. Eleanor sat down and waited, stuck in the awkward phase of being told that a present is yours and not being able to open it.

"Oh my *god!*" Ratty shouted, taking a quick break to watch with a formerly-white rag hanging out of her mouth. "Don't fucking wait for me, you nerd!" Eleanor turned to Sett for approval, and — upon the goat's short nod — dove in, tossing the financial section aside.

A tape player. Beautifully polished brushed silver front, wooden body with just barely chipped corners.

"We found it at a thrift store." Sett explained. "Ratty looked it up on her phone, apparently it's a really good one, and it only needed some minor fixing, so..." the goat trailed off.

Eleanor's smile was almost reverent as her eyes traced the machined corners. It was familiar more than anything. Old and new to her, but unmistakably polished in every sense of the word.

"I know you already have a little one, but we thought you might—"

"It's perfect." Eleanor stood, teetering the menorah as she cleared a spot on her TV stand and slotted it in neatly. Each wire sat waiting, matched perfectly to the back of the box without even the fuss of rerouting, as though her setup had expected that core element.

The rabbit took a step back to admire it, then without skipping a beat dove under the couch for one of the bags of ethereal tapes she had stashed there. It took a few moments to find something that fit the mood, but soon enough the warmest and most comfortable jams in her collection were running between the play head and pinch roller.

"It's really perfect." Eleanor stepped back and took another long look at the somehow chaotic and organized pile of audio equipment.

"Mine next!" Ratty hopped over the counter with a mouthful of doughnut.

"Wow, okay." Eleanor turned to smirk at the possum.

"No I mean — we did like a round robin, so I meant — mine for Sett."

"Oh!" Sett shifted in their seat. "Yes, of course." It was clear which one had been wrapped by Ratty: such intense care had been put into preparing it, and yet an entire fucking mess. A little ring box, again, wrapped in newspaper. Sett shook it, smiling as it let out a series of jangles.

"You're not going to propose to me, are you, Ratty?" the goat teased.

"I — do you want me to?" the possum asked, reconsidering her decision not to when she was out gift shopping.

"Maybe later." Sett laughed. They tore it open, not quite so aggressively as Eleanor, but still with an amount of fervour. Inside: a small, brass set of keys hanging off a varnished possum skull key chain.

"So, I had um — this one requires a little explanation." Ratty started as the other two watched the keys spin gently on their ring. "I called in a favour, installed some bookshelves in the storage room, organized our— your collection, and uh— I also put a lock on the door." Sett's eyes jumped from the keys to Ratty. "If there's anything in the world that can kill me... it's probably in that room, and you have the only two keys."

Ratty smiled at her partner. "Plus, I mean, there's a desk in there now. It sounds like a lot but I really just had some guys help me move a bunch of shit from the empty apartments."

Sett swallowed, considering the gift. It was — in essence — a private library built from spare parts. How very Ratty...

"Thank you." How perfect: a signal that this new Ratty wouldn't need constant attention, that they could devote time to their study again.

"For sure."

The goat slipped off their necklace, tied the end around the key ring, down next to their sigil, and tied it back around their neck.

"Ironically, mine is also in the same vein of um— well— keeping you alive." Sett handed Ratty her gift as she sat, setting a tray of steaming doughnuts on the coffee table. Which, by the way, were damn near perfect. Lest anyone forget that Ratty is a kitchen legend.

"I mean, mine is... I basically sorted books for you so— lots of reading."

"Yes, okay, fair enough."

"We should put some carpets in there, actually. Keep your hooves warm."

"That's an idea." The goat smiled at her scatterbrained fiancée. "Open your gift." The possum took a half-second to remember that she was, in fact, supposed to be opening a present. She unfolded the wrapping carefully, doing her best to preserve the paper, because despite being a little nerd, she was also a massive dork.

It was a harness, a small winched clip, hook, and a length of rope.

"I noticed you really like throwing yourself off of things, and so... this is a safe way to do that."

The possum's eyes lit up as she took in the mess of nylon straps, clambering into it with all the style and grace of anyone trying to tie themselves into a secondhand mountain-climbing kit with no instructions. "Fuck yeah," she whispered. "Fuck yeah!" and again, louder this time.

"Race y'all to the roof!" She took off as soon as the harness could be called any semblance of secure.

"No, Ratty— its not—" Sett rushed after her, grabbing the harness as the possum's upper body tipped over the lip. "Babe, it's not a—" they couldn't help but laugh. Eleanor joined the pair at the window as Sett began to slip, slipping through the wall

333

and attempting to prop Ratty up from the outside.

It is impossible to know what year it is.

Two young queers desperately try to explain to a third that she should not jump out of a window. All three are laughing, there is a black spot in each of their memories, but at the present moment, all they can think about is each other.

They hover above the snow-dusted streets of a busy city, all too concerned with their own business to look up.

There are others here. The reanimated corpse of an opossum brought back from the dead, the spectral remains of a rabbit whose life was cut short and was now beginning anew, and a demon who — trillions of years old — is now getting their first opportunity to be a dumb 20-something.

This moment is seared into their memories.

As the wheels of time shudder and screech and do their best to realign themselves, this moment is given a short chance to last forever.

And then it moves on.

Because it has to.

If it were to end happily, it would end here.

Here's everything you missed:

The year is 1991.

In a dusty motel in the middle of nowhere, New Mexico, Marshall Cane doses himself with a life-extending smart virus, gifted to him by an old co-worker. Somewhere in a nearby radio station, the comedic hand of fate pushes the DJ — the only man in the building — to play one of his favourite songs: "Every Breath You Take," by The Police.

Made paranoid by years on the run, Cane stares at the ancient machine, and contemplates suicide.

The year is 1992.

An eccentric billionaire from Dubai stumbles upon a heavily augmented, still breathing deer carcass while out for a weekend of dune-riding with his friends. He brings her home, nurses her back to health, and is massacred by the reactivated

Angelcorp drone for his passing resemblance to 017.

013 begins planning her return to Toronto.

---

The year is 2022.

Warner Brothers Studios has quietly replaced Ellen DeGenerous with a lookalike after what they call an *unplanned hiatus.* The show's ratings tank, and it is taken off the air after several years on life support.

Netflix produces a cheap documentary the same year, talking to everyone who was in the audience when she was beheaded. Poor journalism work creates a few holes in the story, and the truth about paranormals is largely regarded as an off colour joke.

The Warner Brothers lot in Burbank, California is bought by the Bedel corporation, and all assets relating to *The Ellen DeGenerous show* disappear without a trace.

---

The year is 2018.

John — after what amounts to a particularly eventful afternoon on his timescale — goes back to ruling Hell's largest population centre. He becomes nihilistic, and phones it in for several trillion years before being voted out.

You're surprised to read that Hell is a democracy, but that surprise fades a little when you realize they only hold mayoral elections every several trillion years.

The year is 2018.

The new Elder God of Decay, Alfonzo Redic, is spotted leaving the home of the police officer who ended his first life. The officer's body is not found. A nearby garden flourishes. Similar sightings are made across North America.

The pantheon of the gods decides not to intervene.

---

The year is 2019.

Director Eden Ross has worked themself up into a panic following the forced closure of the New York customs office.

For what is not the first time, they berate Handler Smith for firing Marshall Cane, and believe that — without his engineering — the drone program will fall through, and the Angel Corporation will inevitably go under.

Handler Smith assures Eden that, while Angelcorp may go under, the company is no longer limited to one universe. By way of explanation, Smith shows Eden a pet project that has recently come to fruition.

---

The year is 2019.

Pokey — in the midst of applying to study astrophysics in British Columbia — hears her younger sister scream from her bedroom. Prisha runs out, jamming the screen of her phone into Pokey's face. On it are five text messages from Ducky Smooth. Despite her nickname, the texts read as follows:

✉ 8:08pm: **New Message** — 🦆:
  "do you want to start a band"
✉ 8:08pm: **New Message** — 🦆:
  "like you and me"
✉ 8:12pm: **New Message** — 🦆:
  "also maybe go out some time as like a thing"
✉ 8:12pm: **New Message** — 🦆:
  "like I know ur technically 40 or whatever but like,,"
✉ 8:13pm: **New Message** — 🦆:
  "w/e"

---

The year is 2020

Pokey switches majors into something more focused on community development. She will be the first person at the centre who actually knows what the fuck she's doing.

The year is 2019

Fern... I mean Fern just keeps running their bookstore? Their story didn't change much. There's a lot of people for whom life just kinda goes on.

They start to dig into Marshall Cane's files. It seems like the right thing to do on Ratty's behalf. They wonder what the other universe's Fern was like, how they met, how things were different.

They would never be that Fern, but completing this investigation was probably a good way to show Ratty that they could be friends.

---

The year is 2019.

Eleanor's family misses her dearly, but not dearly enough to invite her home for Passover.

---

The year is 2018.

Hanratty Vermington buys a "for parts" failed streetfighter bike from Kijiji. Eleanor and her bond over repairing it. She rides it to her first cognitive behavioural therapy appointment two months later. At the behest of her therapist, she admits to Sett that she hasn't been taking her Lexapro. It was never something that worked for her, but she says she'll try again. Her therapist recommends Zoloft instead.

With the advent of better mental health, and Fern's help, she begins to track down Marshall Cane. The occasional side-mystery crops up, a literal or figurative ghost to be put to rest; and of course there's the courier business to keep up with, but they get close.

She also keeps an eye on Angelcorp, but — at least from the outside — they seem content to make consumer electronics for a while after getting kicked out of Hell.

---

The year is 2018.

Sett passes ownership of the community centre down to Miss Nelly and focuses on building their library.

After several months of their tea shop sitting mostly empty, a young cat with dyed green fur wanders in on a perfect day looking for a job. Sett, now manning the counter more out of obligation than joy, passes the store on to them without condition. They continue to do the book-keeping and save the upstairs apartment for themself, but otherwise take their hands off and let the cat rake in the profits.

They're not a landlord, just so we're clear.

---

The year is 2019.

At Ratty's suggestion, Eleanor also starts going to therapy. She talks about her family, her depression, her history and how out of place she feels. Her therapist suggests she starts writing, so she does. With Sett's help, she finds a poetic style that fits with her experiences.

In about a month, she performs at a small poetry slam at the university around the corner from the centre. Her poem gets a 7.3 out of 10, and she's absolutely ecstatic. She keeps performing, moving away from tiny school shows to Toronto's actual slam scene. Sett's reputation gives her a minor leg up, but she quickly surpasses her mentor.

She makes some friends. All is good.

The year is 2020.

Angel takes a bad fall, badly damaging her central processor.

Fern and Steph implement the equivalent replacement for a CPU from the distant future: an entire room of high powered servers, designed in part based on repair schematics found on Angel's hard drive. Angel's mind effectively takes over Ratty's office and the surrounding bullpen. Ratty — despite the occasional spat with Angel — doesn't mind, so long as the android has a window to look out of.

Now, let's move on.

# 2020
# Future

The process of time unfolding, flattening out its crinkles, had gone unnoticed these past two years. It was just about done, throwing a few nightmares into those who paid special attention as it finished its instigated tantrum.

Detective Dick Reckard was just about the only woman in the FBI with her snout in this supernatural business. An opossum with a sharp, crooked nose and a keen wit, what had seemed to everyone else like a regular car accident stuck out to her like a flashing red tail light. The driver's jacket, shirt — Hell, their entire outfit had been left sitting in the driver's seat, as though their body had disappeared right out of it. Dr. F. Jones had not punctured her airbag and decided to go streaking.

The radio had been left between channels, along with a cell phone, a purse, and a wallet. Far beyond courtesy, Reckard switched on the phone, gently navigating the cracked screen as not to cut her thumb against the damaged surface. These disappearances had something in common, and if Reckard could find one more—

Under the GPS application, the most recent search read "V Logistics."

It was a tiny courier service, involved mostly in moving around the kinds of things no one was ever supposed to touch. Breath passed her lips in a scoff. Predictable. The detective opened her own phone, jotted down the doctor's details, and—

"Detective Reckard?" She stood bold upright, smacked her horns off the inside of the car door, and dropped both phones into the seat. She picked up her own before it was noticed. "You should probably be wearing gloves."

"Yeah, uh-huh, for sure." She nodded curtly, fumbling through the pocket of her hoodie for her inhaler. The momentary shock subsided as her lungs opened back up, giving way to a dull ache that spread from the top of her forehead. The cop— officer, fellow... law member, guy. The person who had asked for her attention stared with an eyebrow cocked as she pocketed her phone.

"Did you hear me, detective?" he asked.

"Yep. For sure. I actually have everything I need anyway, so —"

Another cop, just out of her field of view spoke up. "Hey boss, is there a reason uh— the detective's bike doesn't have a license plate?" he asked. He stood, tapping the bike's tires with the toe of his boot.

"It's a motorcycle. It doesn't need a license." That, according to just about every reaction within earshot, was not actually correct.

"No, detective you— why is there paint on your jacket?" Even on her nicest piece of clothing, a small splotch of green paint marked the sleeve. "Are you wearing sweatpants?" She didn't have to check to confirm that.

"It's—" She singled out one of the cops farthest from her bike. "If you— I gave that guy my badge, so—" the one she pointed to shook his head violently. His face went out of focus as her hands began to tremble.

Well...

Worth a shot, right Ratty?

"Angel!" the possum grunted into her headset as she checked the nearest cop, going straight for his gun. "We've been made!" She dropped the mag and kicked it away. It ended up under another cop's foot, tripping him and putting him under his buddy. She flung the other part of the gun a half-block away.

A third cop drew and fired in a single motion, hitting Ratty square in the shoulder.

"*Fuck,* dude. That *fucking hurt!*" she whined, turning and charging into him. That'd taken some practice— like a person with self esteem issues saying nice things about themselves (which Ratty had still yet to master), saying the words *that hurt* out loud made it easier to understand than to avoid. Pain was an evolutionary response to danger. Somewhere along the way that link got broken. No harm in manually putting it back together.

Her baton hit his throat, his head hit a wall before he could get a second shot off, knocking him out cold. Again, Ratty scattered the pieces of the gun.

"Should I start—" Angel started.

"In a second, don't execute yet." Cops one and two grabbed the possum from behind, de-tenting number three from inside her jacket. He got to his feet in time to join the cluster of Toronto's finest pinning her to the side of a squad car. "Hey — hold on!" She struggled not to smirk as the fragmented slug in her chest tinked off the hood. "Freedom of the press! Freedom of the press!" That rarely worked, but it was fun to rile them up. They pulled her mask down over her chin, trying to straighten her face as they spun her around. "Social distancing! I'm infected!" She made a big show out of a fake coughing fit. She was almost certain at this point that she couldn't get sick, but... good to set a good example... good to cover her chin, too... not her favourite part.

"Shut the fuck up. Look at the scanner." An arm, disembodied by the struggle, gripped her chin, pointing her face at a T-shaped camera, two bright lights on both arms.

"Augh! I'm wounded! You gotta—" She burst out laughing at the thought. "You gotta take me to a hospital!" There was no amount of struggling to make this whole thing look believable anymore. Grinning, she stared into the Angelcorp logo between the two lights, giving the little lens above it a perfect scan of her face.

A flash, and a half-mile away in the depths of 40 College St.'s data-centre, Eleanor Sloth-Bunny Jr. stared into the cracked screen of a disposable scrap-top, built from spare parts. It was hot enough in the centre of a column of servers to actually have to prop herself up, her sneakers shaking against some fragile bundle of connectors. Her body stalled at death, leaving her with the better-than-average physique of a stagehand for her entire afterlife.

For the few moments after hearing the scanner click through her headset, she bit her tongue, waiting for— there it was. Ratty's name blinked through the database. Eleanor caught it and set her program running: a learning project headed by Angelcorp's own former head of computing. She slotted the machine into a free void between servers, and sat back.

"Got it, Ratty," she murmured, staring up the vent.

"Fuck yes." The possum's voice came, strained, from her headset. Unseen, Ratty's TOPS file flicked across the screen, branching out to her known associates, and their associates, and etc.. "Are you okay to get out?" Ratty asked.

"I'm—" A cable snapped under Eleanor's sneaker, dropping her a few feet further than was comfortable. "Fuck. I'm stuck, actually." the access hatch was a few racks above her.

"Could you- ow, fuck. Hold on." Inside the door of almost every cop car, below the panel with the window controls, whatever company was in charge of refitting almost always left the attached wires hanging. With teeth like hers, it was easy to strip off a few inches of rubber and pinch them together. What was less easy was not gloating about it. She had made it halfway out the window before someone saw. "Alright, yeah Angel, it's time." Her bike's engine kicked from idle to full boar, slipping neatly between the cops and their car, directly under the possum.

"Gents," What a smug prick. "It has been a sincere plea—" Angel didn't let her finish that one. The bike snagged her collar, stronger than either the cops or the possum, and dragged her out of their grasp. She sat up just enough to watch the muffled thud of a paint bomb coat the car's interior.

"Was that sexy? I feel like that was pretty alright. Angel, check this out." She worked around the handcuffs, pushing herself up backwards on the saddle. The bike swayed under her as she rose one boot to the poorly attached sheet, and on came a vision of the future:

Having failed to jump through her handcuffs like an adventure serial protagonist, her face would smear itself across the bright pink letters below her wheels. She would be found hours later, sitting in a police station with a road burn all the way up her right side, and would have ruined the entire operation.

"Never mind, actually." She pulled the back of her nice coat up over her hands, searching for the safety pin she had stuck through the lining. Better to stick with what she had planned. Handcuff locks were usually simple to deal with, too. "I need a —" She spun right-way-around as sirens followed her around the corner. "Find a long alleyway where I can change without being seen."

"Bashful, are we?"

"When did you turn into a night rider car? Stop having a sense of humour."

Sitting in a pile of blankets, arranged into the perfect nest. Aging duvets had been piled not to interrupt airflow around the life support servers that kept her going, while still comforting the rapidly aging synthetic fur that coated her body. It had been like that for a while.

Through a combination of her own window, what drone feeds had been left unsecured, and the myriad stream-bro disaster tourist twitizen journalists, watched a crowd of angry people try to take over the city. Few threats came up within range, those that were available to her were taken offline as soon as she was able. It was fun to fuck around in someone else's monitoring equipment, especially when it belonged to the police department (though, more for the high-grade hardware angle and less the anarchist one.) If Angel could feel joy, she would have done so watching a several thousand dollar flying camera cut lines into the face of a police officer.

A cell phone with enough processing power could have chauffeured Ratty. Chewing gum while walking, on the android's hierarchy of processes. Hard to understand how to help from her glass tower, but this was one of the ways.

"Would you like that to line up with Sett's section of the march?" They had set up a help tent. Through the cell phone Sett left unattended with the rest of their equipment, they had isolated the gentle decapitated guitar-playing that assisted their team of amateur medics. In the flashes of them she had seen, Sett picked their clothes straight from the 2020 enchanted forest Winners catalogue, save for the smear of facial recognition scrambling face paint across their eyes.

"That would actually be fantastic." Ratty's voice came over the radio. It took a half-second to reroute Ratty. The goat stopped playing and picked up their phone. Eleanor's voice came next.

"Angel—" the alarm had finally sounded at police headquarters. "I could also use an escape route."

"Can't you just like, go ghost and slip underground?" Ratty asked.

"Well, first of all, the entire time I have known you you've used your shit one time—" Eleanor answered.

"I don't see why that's relevant." Ratty interjected.

"I wouldn't argue it, Eleanor." Sett said, a distracted undercurrent in their voice.

"Okay well, second: way too hot, and third, I would have to leave the laptop." Eleanor stared up at the flickering screen from the grating over the ductwork's exhaust fan. Her virus, in the next several minutes, would methodically reorganize TOPS' facial recognition database. Just wiping the storage wasn't good enough. It could be recovered, and even if it couldn't it would still have a good starting off point once people started driving in front of traffic cameras in cars they owned.

Shredded data was useful to anyone with time and clear tape. Incorrect data, though, was just useless. Soon, as far as the city-wide surveillance network was concerned, the only person in the universe was going to be the unremarkable, second-universe, arrested once for a minor trespassing charge, otherwise unheard of, Hanratty *Ishmael* Vermington.

"I might have to leave the laptop anyway." That didn't feel great.

"I believe Fern had asked you to do that either way." Sett said.

"Yeah, but I didn't want to..." She built it out of scrap. It had attachment.

"Did you fall?" Ratty was evidently not paying attention.

"Shut the fuck up."

"Did you, though?" That mocking grin crept into her voice.

"Get out of sight so my thing can work." Eleanor kept it short.

"I'm working on it. Go down through the fan, it can't kill you." That was a distinctly Ratty solution. Whether it killed Eleanor or not, it would shred her jeans and t-shirt, assuming she could get her sneakers past the blade fast enough. Someone did tell her to wear scrappy clothes. She didn't really own sneakers that were less nice than the ones she wore around.

"Eleanor, have you tried climbing?" Angel asked.

"I— shut the fuck up, Angel."

"I actually also need suggestions, Angel." Sett pressed the phone's front camera against their ear.

"How can I help, Sett?"

"There's another officer here. He's trying to disperse the med tent," they spoke in a forceful whisper. "He doesn't seem like he's going to give up."

It was hard to tend to someone with a phone pinned to your shoulder. Having to keep an eye on a teenage anarchist lizard's conversation with a member of law enforcement complicated the situation even further.

"This is an illegal gathering," the cop said. Pokey was handling herself well. Their patient had only a few minor cuts and some breathing difficulty.

"Just one?" Angel asked. Pokey got up to her tiptoes, trying to compete with the recently rolled out mechanical stilts TOPS riot control was experimenting with. That's actually more blood than— they were going to need to send the patient somewhere else.

"Maybe." The police officer poked the centre of Pokey's chest with his baton. Under their palm, the biggest part of the wound closed. There would not be enough time to finish this all at once.

"You can take him." Ratty's voice egged them on. Sett met what they could of their patient's gaze, covered with the black arm of a cheap hoodie to block out the light. She was probably correct. That was probably their only option.

"How's your pain?" Sett tapped the arm, nudging it out of the way.

"Manageable," the volunteer soldier groaned.

"Good, give me a moment." Their eyes searched the room for someone to sub in, found Pri looking lost in a tent that'd grown too small for her, and waved her over. "Keep an eye on them, I'm going to deal with Pokey's situation."

Pri nodded, put their hands exactly where Sett's hands were, and watched. Pokey stopped almost immediately as she understood Sett to be standing in front of her. There was a definitive, just hierarchy in this tent. When Sett took over, everyone else stood by.

"This is a place of healing." As plain and without yield as a stop sign. "You have no right to be here. You have no right to tell us to disperse."

"This is an unlawful gathering," the officer repeated, the microphone against his throat failing to make him look bigger than the small, small man he was. Sett stared up into the visor, the helmet-mounted camera currently struggling to figure out what their face was, for a few moments of search before making a decision.

He wasn't leaving without a fight.

Sett ducked under the officer's arm, made slow by the taxpayer-funded robot experiment he was forced to carry around, and checked around the entrance of the tent. Apparently wearing the best military tech money could buy meant they left it singularly attended in the middle of a crowd of fed-up citizenry going through their militant puberty.

So, just the one guy. Others would emerge from the crowd if a fight got loud enough, but there was no reason for that to happen.

Pokey had resumed her duties as negotiator, unaware of the pressurized canister of mace at the officer's hip or his hand resting on the trigger. The officer himself was unaware of just how quickly a pepper-sprayer could be wrenched from someone's hand when that someone was too cocky. He learned — over the course of several seconds — exactly what it felt like to have a tiny goat, forced to the full extent of their height, empty that sprayer into the gap at the bottom of his visor.

Every officer/uncle tells you about the time they had to be pepper sprayed as a part of their training, an exaggerated "My body was on *fire!*" while trying desperately not to gesture to the single part of their arm that'd been given a test spritz.

He dropped, no doubt damaging the government's precious riot legs. Sett dragged him just far enough over the threshold to hide the top of his head with the door tarp. His helmet came off. Sett's knuckles burned after a clinical knockout punch. The situation was resolved.

346

"Pokey, take his gear." Sett stood, wiping their fist on their smock. "Pri—" Sett took their patient back— "and Ducky, go outside and let people know we're abandoning the tent."

"We're abandoning the tent?"

"They're going to come looking for their friend at some point. Nobody here needs to be party to kidnapping, and Pokey?" The lizard stood struggling to drag the officer up onto a bench. "Make sure he keeps breathing, okay?"

Pokey nodded. Ducky and Pri masked up and stepped out of the tent. The uniform, armour, several-thousand-dollar machine legs all ended up in the same medical waste bag. Not sure what to do with the rest, Pokey offered the oversized riot shield and the belt it was apparently permanently attached to to Sett. Ratty would take the baton. Someone would buy the gun. The shield — marked at some point throughout the day with the pink latex paint of the Toronto division — was at least temporarily useful. Sett slung it over their shoulder, already put off by how the nylon edges cut into their palm.

That extra weight really made it clear how exhausted they were. It was too cold for the season, had been dark for hours, and they had been stationed here for hours before that. They were out-resourced, buffeted for long enough that everyone had forgotten what the original march was about.

They pulled a rolled cigarette from some fold or pocket in their pile of sweaters, stopped when they received a pair of dirty looks, re-realized that they were standing in a medical tent, and went to drop it.

"Head out, Sett." Pokey said. "We can pack up here without you."

Sett nodded, silently thanked the lizard, and ducked out into the night.

The strike wheel on their lighter struggled to kick up sparks as it sanded away the very last grains of flint disintegrated in their chamber. Just barely enough to get lit. Somewhere, masked by the city's rage, the clap of a motorcycle engine pushed too hard grew louder.

"Sett," Sett's abandoned cell phone notified the med tent. "I thought you might want to know, Ratty will be joining you in the next few moments."

Freed from her chains, Ratty stuffed her professional coat

into the stash hidden in the moulding of her bike's tail. Her spiked jacket had to be removed to make room, and so it settled in against her shoulders. It was far more comfortable looking indestructible rather than presentable.

"We good?" she asked Angel.

"We are good. You have not been seen. Approaching the drop now."

"Good, don't stop." She climbed up to squat on the seat, ready, with her hands free, to dive into a roll. No use getting her bike impounded for some minor discomfort. It stopped at a police barricade, kicking her off into a gap in the stream of people.

Immediately the crowd rose around her, blocking out any sight of something else. Her lungs stopped as she was closed in on, shooting cold dust through her respiratory system in an instant. She patted the pocket of her hoodie, fully aware of what it would look like if her hand disappeared into it. Too many people, too suddenly. She couldn't—

"Ratty?" Sett's voice. They tapped the top of her head with a piece of plastic, leaving it in the hand they used to help her up. "You dropped this." Ratty took in enough of Sett to bring her back down, stared at the inhaler left in her palm, and took a few long, slow puffs.

Everything was normal again, more or less.

"Are you going to be okay?"

"Yeah, for sure."

"You shouldn't dress like that for a riot, Ratty." Fern unblurred their way out of the crowd. That was simply not an option in a crowd this size. The possum needed her armour, but she wasn't going to argue about it.

"It's fine, Fern. We lost today either way." Behind them, the medical tent was almost entirely reduced to white tarp and poles. More cops had filtered in from side streets, their mechanized buddy having failed a check-in. There was a subway station nearby, they could—

"We're gonna try to push to 40 college and then we can take the subway home from there." Sett took over as the rest of the white tarp fell and was folded. The engine of a panel van struggled to turn over after having spent the day dumping its battery into temporary lights. In a few moments, all that would be left of the med tent was a few limping protesters. "Prisha, put anyone who needs out quickly in the van with the tent and take off. Ratty—" Sett turned to examine their partner, the spots that always got scuffed first. "You're okay, right?"

It was rushed, but thoughtful. Ratty nodded. "I'm good, I'm really good, I got a lead on—"

That was all Sett had time for. There were other people who needed direction. Standing next to them made her feel safe. Realizing she had lost hers, she strapped on a black mask, unhooked the shield Sett was carrying awkwardly over their back, and fell into line.

---

**4.1 / 5**
(based on 13 postings)
Fehlender Jones
Professor of Humanities at <u>Multiple Schools</u>

Posted: Jan 6, 2018
Fee is great! You can tell she's clearly passionate about the subject matter and really wants her students to be too. She had to cancel class a few times, but I'm not complaining. Don't buy the textbook, she has copies she'll loan you.
👍2 👎1

Posted: April 20, 2018
Lectures frequently go long. Will sometimes spend the entire class on a tangent. Very scatterbrained, but easy grader.
👍1 👎3

Posted: Dec 12, 2019
Had her for mysticism and the modern world. Cool course, but it got intense sometimes. Once she came in covered in blood, tracked it through the classroom, and then passed out on the carpet (still bleeding). I like Fee, but I'm not planning on taking any of her other courses if I can help it.
👍4 👎1

Posted: April 4, 2020
I posted here before after taking Fehlender Jones' Intro to World Religions, took her Mysticism and the Modern World because I enjoyed it so much. She tried to kill herself in the middle of the semester, her passion is gone. I feel bad saying it, but I don't think I would take another class with Fehlender.

👍0 👎0

Posted April 7, 2020
She used to be a eyewear model. She GLARES at anyone who interrupts. Deep black eyes. Fucking scary.

👍1 👎0

---

Sett wasn't expecting Doctor Jones to answer her own door after what Ratty had described. They came prepared for the possibility of having to break in, and now — a tad overzealous — awkwardly slipped their bolt cutters back into their purse.

"Fehlender?" A freshly installed chain rattled as the deer braced herself against the door. It was hard for her to keep upright, apparent even through the several half-inches of air she allowed them to see her through. Behind a thick pair of glasses, bright green eyes stared terrified up into the goat's. Doctor Jones was not shorter, she simply could not stand to her full height like this.

"Wh—" She choked on the word. "What do you want? I'm busy."

"We were hoping you might be able to talk about the car accident you were just in?"

"Car accident?" she said, as though she had never heard of such a thing. "No, I need to— I should get back to my research."

"Doctor Jones—" Sett jammed their boot into the closing door, not prepared after such a long day to yield ground. "We understand. You've just been through a traumatic experience. I just want to help—"

"It's just Fee, just call me Fee," she interrupted. She stopped trying to push the door closed almost immediately, taking the opportunity to examine the goat's eyes. Their demonic origins flashed behind their eyes in that moment, a thought difficult to suppress. Doctor Jones— Fee just saw a strange looking goat, unaware of the lack of mouth under their face mask.

They also probably looked like someone who knew more about what was going on. That calculation occupied their face for a few long seconds before Sett intervened.

"What're you studying?" they asked.

"I'm uh, I study history." Fee answered.

"Our fiancée studies history, actually." Didn't bother to mention that it was the contemporary media history of an alternate universe. That didn't really matter. "Anything... paranormal?" That was the right thing to ask. Fee's guard dropped, letting go the tension that kept her weight from collapsing.

"Everything is all wrong." she started. "My home is all wrong, the— the— the books in the complete wrong order, my books. I — I'm not from here. I just want to get home."

"We understand."

"Is there someone else—" The word we had startled her.

"No, I'm sorry, that's a verbal tic." It had only occasionally stood in the way of talking to new people. "Listen, you were on your way here when you crashed." They fished a business card out of their purse, wincing as they bumped against the bolt cutters. "That also happens to be the building I work in. Stop by sometime... we have an extensive library of uh... old religious texts. I might be able to help you out." They were hesitant to say anything more concrete.

They stepped back off the porch, preparing to face the row of identical four-squares, when Fee spoke up. "Actually," the first solid choice she had made today, "would you come in, please."

Sett stopped half way down the stairs, taking a moment to appreciate how good it was to turn someone around on them, turned, and smiled graciously. "Of course, thank you Doctor Jones."

She shut the door just enough to undo the door-chain, and left it open for Sett to follow. The neurotic doctor stopped at her bookcase, trying to understand how the ghost in her home had organized them. Already, too much had been flung from the walls. Fee planted her hooves firmly in the only two gaps in the paper. She stood, her shaking frame made more obvious by the heavy house, bloodshot eyes drawn into slits with the effort trying to put this together.

Sett ignored that much for now. Fee's kitchen had a kettle, next to the kettle was a little hanger full of mugs, and below the mug-hanger was a box of teabags. Unnoticed, Sett filled the kettle, set it to boil, and took the little box to rifle through: all cheap, but serviceable.

"What's your working theory?" Sett asked, skirting around the counter and leaning against it to watch.

"I— god, I don't know." Something about the system had started to make sense. Their hand raised to a part of the shelf, thought for a moment, and slid along the surface directly to another book, and pulled it out: a binder. "This morning, I woke up in the— that cement area right next to the entrance of Tour CN." There was a touch of Quebecois in her accent. "I was naked, and I ran home, and— sorry, what day was it yesterday?"

Sett stopped rifling through teabags, checked the day-indicator on Ratty's watch, and went back to it. "Friday, December 1st, 2020. You think it might be temporal displacement?"

"It could be." Their eyes scanned the pages of data.

"How do you take your tea?"

"Heavy cream, two sugars, thank you." Sett took the kettle off its stand and set it off to one side. The barren fridge held a single carton of almond milk for dairy, and no cream to speak of.

"Caused by what, do you think?" Doctor Jones barely raised their voice. Sett spooned two teaspoons of sugar over a bag of cheap green tea in the bottom of a mug. It was better without dairy anyway.

"There's been some interplanar meddling that's disrupted the flow of time lately. I would think someone in your area of study would have noticed."

"No, no. I keep close track." She dropped the first binder at her feet, made the same motion to pick out a second one. "It's been even every week since— ah. I see." Sett handed them the mug. They took a distracted sip, frustrated at the binder.

"I'm sorry, you didn't have any cream. Do you mind if I take a copy of these? They're very well kept." That, and Sett hadn't set up or maintained any kind of advanced timekeeping apparatus. That probably would have been a good idea, all things considered.

"They're not mine. This isn't what I wrote down." The deer shirked the binder into Sett's hands.

"No, I thought not."

With nothing else to turn to, Fee watched the binder fall into Sett's purse. "Do you have a theory?" she asked.

"I would say I have the start of one. It's possible that you've experienced a severe enough displacement for you to have shifted between timelines." There was no reason for anything less outlandish than that to have occurred. In a lot of lives — at least that Sett had encountered — there was a moment where that person had to come to grips with the fact that their world was an unchangeable science fiction mess. Doctor Jones enjoyed that moment in Sett's company.

"Is it fixable?"

"If it is, you're looking at the only person on Earth who could fix it." Sett's smile faltered at their word choice. *On Earth* implied there was an *off Earth,* something that shook Fee as the pair came to that realization together. "Sorry, I don't mean to imply— I have no reason to believe—"

"I'm going to gather up the pertinent documents and, uh, you can take me back to your library. Perhaps we can set this right by the end of the day." She hadn't touched her tea.

"When was the last time you slept, Fehlender?" Sett asked, very aware of how long their day so far had been, clutching their borrowed mug as their only way of keeping upright.

"I— I mentioned this morning."

"What time was that?"

"I don't know, before sunrise?" That wasn't saying much this deep into the winter. Still, it would soon be the *next* morning.

"If at all possible, I'd like to ask you to get some rest first." they said.

"I—"

"I will still be there tomorrow morning." They were more firm. Fehlender took a moment to consider, and nodded.

"You're right. That— that's a good idea, I think."

"Good." Sett set down their mug, already looking forward to the half-nap they would be able to take on the subway ride home. "You have my card, enjoy the tea. I'll see you tomorrow."

"Hey you!" Wasn't it just so nice to come home to food? Ratty got home hours ago, took a nap, etcetera etcetera, but whenever her unusual hours meant she had a day off, she slept with her phone on her chest. Sett texted when they were half an hour away, and Ratty would almost always start something then. It was a new system, but one that was working out fantastically.

Sett hung their coat and sidled up behind their partner, eyes almost entirely shut as they pressed against the firm mass of possum. "Careful of the— stove's hot." The bass tones came through her chest as Sett wrapped around it. The pan in her hand rattled a little as a shiver shot up her back.

"Hi you." Sett murmured.

"How was Fee?" Ratty asked. Sett's long sigh ruffled the back of her t-shirt.

"A little tiring. Can you — not now — help me find that book?"

"Which book?"

"The—" Fuck, wait. Which book? Sett gave another exaggerated sigh. "The good one. What's for dinner?"

"I am making grilled cheese and tomato soup." She turned just enough to put her arm around the little goat, peck the top of their head, and keep cooking. "Go sit down, I'll bring it over."

"For sure." Sett yawned. "I'll go lie down." They broke off, beckoned away by the ancient couch and its perfectly worn cushions. They dropped onto it, the firm and scratchy parts of the cheap seat worn all the way away.

"I was thinking about it today," Ratty's voice would keep them awake. "I actually like, really miss my old students."

"Oh yeah? Gonna go for your master's again?" Sett asked, propping themself up against the arm and hugging a throw pillow.

"Pff, god no. I don't have a high school diploma or a portfolio in this universe."

"Hmph." That was hardly fair. Sett toed off their boots, having forgotten to do so as soon as they crossed the threshold. The weight dropped from their legs, hooves floating into the air in response. "Ratty." They drew out the last letter, wiggling the

354

hoof back and forth.

"Stop that."

"Babe." She liked being called babe.

"Why do I know exactly what you're doing."

"You gotta come rub my hooves." That froze her. halfway turned between the stove and her plating, Ratty stared through the floor, biting her tongue as she tried to muscle the blush away from her face.

"Nope. I'm cooking, get fucked."

"That's what I'm trying— look at you! You're thinking about it! C'mon, let's make a movie."

"I am thinking about plating this grilly cheese and nothing else."

Sett blew a raspberry. "You're no fun," they teased, shoving the hooves between the couch cushions. That was the final key to their perfect comfort. Body unified with couch as all weight disappeared from the world, watching the little diorama of a possum wander around her track. Her tight, clean ringlets had been all but annihilated by the dry winter air, leaving behind the more typical half-curly mess of flyaways, all tied back into a pom-pom nearing the size of her head. "Are you keeping your horns short?" Sett asked.

"Hm?" She touched the neatly filed tips, having kept that up more out of habit than anything else. "I dunno. They've uh— been like that for a while." It was hard to keep a conversation going over the stove's fan.

Sett let their eyes lull closed before speaking again. "I think they look cute like that," they said.

"Thank you." It was still hard for her to take a compliment, but she had gotten better about it. Something about the way she said it, though...

"What's in your mouth?" Sett asked, eyes still closed.

"Oh, this?" Sett peeked long enough to see a blue piece of plastic, covered in bite marks, hanging off a string around her neck. "It's uh, like, a chew toy? I guess? For kids with— people, I guess, with..." The last word of her sentence struggled to escape. "Like, people with autism."

Oh.

That made some sense, actually.

"Plus I kept eating the peppers and it was bothering my

tongue, because yesterday I had a whole thing of sour gummy worms while I was at work." Ratty slid the final grilled cheese onto a plate, balancing that with a pair of bowls and joining Sett on the couch. She organized the triangular slices into a pinwheel, saving a dish and making the meal fancy in one perfect move. Sitting down, she pulled Sett's hooves from the couch cushions and wormed her way under their legs.

"Have you been looking for a new therapist?" She was approaching a year and a half since her last session.

"I don't want to talk about that!" She was at least candid about it.

"When's you and Eleanor's anniversary?"

"Full'a questions today, eh?"

"Sorry, are you in a no-talk mood?"

"No, no." That last sentence had come out extremely rude. "It's next Friday."

"On the 11th?"

"Mhmm." Ratty picked the plate up off the counter and offered it to Sett. Sett took a triangle, reaching across the gap between the coffee table and the couch to dip it. Ratty took hers dry.

"Anything planned?" They skipped the formality of cutting their mouth open.

"Oh yeah. Big plans," she said through her mouthful. She swallowed, kissed her partner's bleeding lips, and went through her phone for something to listen to.

God, Ratty was a good cook. Warm, greasy, tangy; what more did one need in life? Perhaps the starchy crunch of a few chopped jalapenos. Ratty had already thought of that. They pulled the possum closer with their legs, already halfway through their first slice.

"Okay, I'm not saying anything, but you would have plenty of time to recover before Friday." Sett leant forward to speak directly into the possum's ear. Her poorly held back blush erupted across her face.

"What the fuck would I have to recover from?"

"Do you want me to be honest?"

Ratty nodded. "Yes, sir." She had started to take the idea seriously.

"I want to beat you until you cry, and I want to roleplay

around that that I plan on killing you." This side of Sett rarely wasted time being coy about what they wanted. That white hot direct honesty diffused the little fluster Ratty had going.

"Oh my *god*, you're pathetic." She lifted the goat's sweater and blew against their tummy, a killing blow by any definition. "Wait until I've swallowed my gross cheese breath at least." She fell over, resting her head on Sett's stomach.

"Ugh! Fine." The illusion of annoyance was broken as soon as Sett's hand tangled itself in the possum's hair. It went down, around her neck to the point where her skull joined her spine: an undamaged cluster of nerves that made her shiver. Her throat forced out an involuntary chirp: the vestigial leftover of her animal ancestors. There were so many soft things to find about her.

"Hey, Ratty?" Sett spoke softly.

"Mhmm?" Her eyes stopped over the individual threads of fur that poked across the grey-brown border around on the underside of their snout

"I love you." She picked up another grilled cheese, sprinkling crumbs across the goat's stomach.

"Okay, gross. Sit up if you're gonna keep eating."

Ratty laughed at that.

# 2020
# Date Night

"So, our best guess as to what's been happening." Sett finished their drawing of Hell. "Or what *was* happening, rather, before we put a stop to it, was that this central spindle—" They pointed to the tower that shot up through the material plane. "—where I'm from was stuck through this material plane—" They gestured to the ground. "—and because they spin at different frequencies— I'm sorry, are you still following?" Fehlender struggled to keep their eyes in focus.

"I— no, I'm sorry, this is just overwhelming. This isn't even in my wheelhouse and yet I see so many possible applications in my research, and you—" She stood, tapping Sett's blackboard with a hesitant claw. "You lived here for your entire life?"

"Yeah." They were incredibly conscious of that fact. Fehlender's hand trailed down to Hell's material plane, hard — conceptually — to distinguish from the spire. A record, or grindstone, or something, depending on perspective.

"What's here?"

"Now that, actually, is fascinating." Sett pulled their laptop from a pile of books, careful not to disturb them as their base was pulled out. They opened it and navigated to a video they watched in a tangent of preparing for this meeting. "That's more Hell, but where the spindle is infinitely deep — and this is something I didn't realize until recently — the plane is just infinite. There's only one person who has been there and back, and it was this marine who had a Phineas Gage type injury, clinically dead for three days, then just back, like that." They snapped their fingers to illustrate. "He starts writing this fascinating poetry, let me— here."

The low, sad voice of a man in regret started from the tinny laptop speakers, clear enough to catch just about every word. He sat on a small stage, reciting something from memory, staring down into the middle distance.

"The wall looked different to everyone. It was hard to imagine, when staring at it, a wall that didn't look like this one. Hard to picture the dust caught sunbeams streaking through the diamond pattern of chain link through any other eyes.
"What did a wall look like? What was it made out of?
"All this only to to distract themself from the sound of the floor below. Hollow, dust-covered, infinite. What did a floor look like? The wall was made of the floor, but the floor was not made of the wall. A floor looked the same to just about everyone. Hollow, dusty, etcetera.
"The closest I ever came to understanding those who saw a different wall, was pressing their face against the chain link and staring at the wall on the other side. Whatever was contained by the wall was invisible. Or maybe their wall looked like a wall that had another side.
"You could walk all the way around. About 400 hours of walking and you would end up where you started. No one who walked away from the wall ever came back with news of an edge, no matter how long they travelled. There had been voyages — thousands of years long — that returned in 400 hours with no news of an edge. Few walked away happy, but those who did never came back
"Those apostles that built their soap boxes from bones would tell us we are in paradise. We have everything we need: the wall, and light. There were those that made sacrifices to the enemy, thanked them for being the enemy. They were loved in the same breath they were feared.
"The wall keeps out the enemy, we keep up the wall, the sun keeps us up, it is through that line that the enemies hung the sun, made it rise in the morning, gave way to cool desert nights when bodies were broken."

Fehlender stared at the little grey replay button, bewildered.
"What the fuck?"
"Right? It's fascinating. That, I'm pretty sure, is what goes on on that disk." Sett had not picked up on the disgust emanating from their guest. While one came to terms with the fact that Hell was real, the other bounced softly on the balls of their feet.

"So…" Fehlender started, still processing that information, "Is that relevant to my current situation?"

"Oh!" The way they started should have signalled that there was some connection, that this was not another tangent. Instead: "It challenges our current understanding of the structure of the afterlife."

Fehlender waited for a more straightforward answer.

"It also challenges our understanding of geometry."

Fehlender waited.

"No, I'm sorry. I got excited."

"That's quite alright." Fehlender said, tired. They stood and brushed off their lap. "I must admit I've only been following tenuously. Are we any closer to a solution?"

"Um," They had skimmed in the course of several hours every textbook, historical text, copy of a historical text, PDF, and credible obscura website they had at their disposal. A massacre of tenuously relevant information scattered across their long central research table, almost completely obscuring the tea and coffee stains made there by two vigorous years of use. The truth was, there was no natural cause for something like this. All they had done was confirm that Fehlender was displaced from her own universe. "We— I have some leads." was the most charitable way they could put it."

"Mm. I'd like to rest, if it's not too much trouble." She had already started to consolidate their things into a backpack.

"Of course, there's an empty room upstairs if you—"

"No, I think I'd like to go home now." She slung her bag over her shoulder and started out of the dark, messy room.

"Ah, well, I will contact you when I have something, I suppose?" Sett asked. Eyes on the floor, Fehlender ran headlong into something lurking in the doorway.

"Whoa— sorry, I didn't know you were— hi!" Ratty caught the deer as she stumbled. "Sorry, I didn't want to interrupt."

"Hey, Ratty." Defeated for the moment, Sett started stacking their research into slightly more categorized piles.

"Hi, hey, sorry about that." The possum caught the deer's eye. What started back up at her was about the saddest expression she had ever seen on someone living, amplified by the curve of her glasses.

"Doctor Fehlender Jones." She extended a hand.

"Professor Hanratty Vermington." She shook it.

"I've been displaced from my universe."

"Well, we've all been there." Her attempt to be comforting came out mocking, sincere as it was. It took a second to realize how she had come across, another to wince, and a final second to cover it up. "Well, goodbye."

The deer skirted around Ratty in the narrow doorway.

Ratty turned to watch her recede out of earshot before mouthing almost silently at her partner: "What's with them?"

Sett gave a quick, confused shrug in response. They stepped around their table, reached under Ratty's arm, and pulled the door closed.

"Oh my god!" the possum whispered harshly.

"Right? Jesus... I mean, she's— it's okay, I guess? But like, wow." The goat's entire form collapsed under the weight of pushing their research uphill for several hours. The fluff they held in their mass of sweaters disappeared, leaving it hanging off them, dragging them to the floor under the warm weight. "I'm going to keep working on it." They were at least resolute in not giving up.

"Do you want me to get Fern to pull some Angelcorp shit?"

"I— god." They resented the fact that it probably had something to do with them. "Yeah. Yes please."

"Cool." The possum enveloped her partner in her arms, dropping some extra weight on their shoulders as she popped up far enough to kiss the top of the goat's head. Their conditioner had taken on that lovely day-old smell. "I was thinking about you at work today— can I ask you something?"

"Shoot, tex'." That was something people said, right?

"Am I your Engels?" she whined, all the lamentation of the original simp in her tone. Sett snorted.

"No, honey. You're way cooler than Engels." Their psychic voice came muffled from within the possum's chest. "Don't think about that. Just get excited."

"About what?"

"About—"

"Oh, Eleanor!" She backed into the door, showing the goat her smile. "Yeah, absolutely. I've got plans."

"Will you finally be opening up to her?" Sett returned with a wry grin.

"I am going to try!" That was as best as anyone could hope for. "I just—" she looked around the crowded library, searching for something. "I don't remember what I wanted to do here."

"That's okay." Sett popped up to their tiptoes, pressing the soft patch of fur over their mouth against hers. "Go have fun with your girlfriend, dink."

"Okay!" She nodded, fumbling for the doorknob. "Yeah, absolutely."

---

The little steel marbles in Ratty's collection of spray cans rattled with the movement of the train. Each bump created a tiny, tinny concert. It was easy to keep focused on, something that — with some regularity — blocked out everyone else around. The world might as well be these eight cans and their plastic cover.

"I just wanted to stop at Fern's store before we set out for the industrial district, is that okay?" Ratty asked.

"Didn't you already text them?" That came out more annoyed than Eleanor actually was.

"Yeah, but, I dunno, I feel like this is important." Ratty shrugged.

"Alright." The ghost leant into her girlfriend, her face falling right through the collection of metal spikes to the soft shoulder below. She closed her eyes, listened to the marbles, and wondered where she was being taken. "I can't complain about getting to see Fern." Her hand found its way into the possum's.

"You have such a weird taste. Are you holding—"

"They're taller than me, I can't help it." Eleanor shrugged. Ratty was liable to get anxious if she could finish that question.

"It's the sloped snout, isn't it?" She dragged two fingers along her own, finding the perfect angle to show off the way it crooked. "We dated in high school, y'know?"

"You and Fern?" Eleanor asked. Ratty nodded. "How did that work?"

"Well, not this Fern. My old universe—"

Their quiet non-conversation was interrupted by a loud throat-clear, glaring down at the pair of them. Eleanor jumped, forgetting for a half-second to keep pace with the train and phase shifting into Ratty's body before re-normalizing. At about eye level, the fluorescent white *REVENUE PROTECTION* sat sewn to the chest of a superfluous stab-vest, as though anyone had ever cared enough about the life of a transit cop any more than the transit cop cared about them.

Eleanor said none of this, quietly slipped her hand from Ratty's, took her transit pass out from the back of her phone case, and tapped it against the reader. It chimed, too loud to be this close, and showed a green check mark. Ratty used the opportunity instead to look up at Eleanor, starting in her eyes — her usual captivating search — down to the stitchwork on the shoulder of the ghost's new jacket.

"I like this— is this a new jacket?" she asked, stonewalling the transit cop. Eleanor did not answer, flicking her eyes at the machine before realizing that, even if Ratty was looking, there was nothing in her sockets to indicate with.

"Proof of payment, please." He cleared his throat again.

"I'm having a night out with my girlfriend, can you—"

"Your proof of payment, please." He cut Ratty off. She gave a loud, show-offy groan, pulled her pass and its attached badge reel from her purse, and tapped it against the machine. It gave a negative chime. She tried again, and it gave a check mark.

"Are we good here?" She put the pass back in her bag. The transit cop stared down at his device, a glorified cell phone with too much power, and slung it back at his hip. Where it was, he stared down at the paint-smattered plastic case between Ratty's legs.

"What's in the box?" he asked.

"Spray paint cans." Ratty answered. The rest of the cop's face remained still as his eyebrows jumped up his forehead. It would not have been easy, even if Eleanor wanted to, to shit on how cool he thought he was. The thin whatever-coloured line between this city and a loss of three dollars and twenty five cents. "Is that illegal?"

"No, but—"

"Alright, mall cop. I'm not discussing my day with you." Eleanor's heart shot into her throat at the sudden escalation. It was likely visible through the surface, kicking its way out of her body. Her voice tried and failed to muscle past it, not sure what she would say even if it could. Unable to look away, she watched the officer's eyes trail over Ratty's jacket, stopping at-oh god. There's a nylon second belt strapped across her chest. Eleanor felt it against her arm.

Transit cops had only recently started carrying guns downtown. Clumsily, his hand fell to his.

"Do I know you from somewhere?" His thumb rested under the holster's clasp.

"Dunno." It was impossible to stop her from pushing. The marbles rattled louder against her bouncing leg. "Pretty sure your wife took some pictures of—"

"*Ratty!*" Eleanor's voice finally overcame the glue trap it'd been stuck in. She grabbed her partner by the sleeve, dragging her out from under the cop. "This is our stop." The ghost dragged her out of the train, somehow managing to take her case without breaking eye contact. The doors closed. Ratty grinned, and flashed the bright yellow handle of a near harmless stun gun hiding away below her armpit. She used the other hand's middle finger to drag her bottom eyelid.

"Holy fuck, Ratty." Eleanor jumped on the arm, re-hiding the stun gun. "You are a fucking crazy person. What the fuck is wrong with you?"

"Did you see the look on his face!" She struggled not to laugh. "He totally thought I was gonna— look, oh my god I'm shaking!" She hands at arms length to demonstrate. Her eyes had glazed over slightly."

"How long have you had a fucking taser for!?" Eleanor pushed her towards the exit, careful not to release Ratty's arm in case she decided to show off some more.

"I dunno, a while." She brought it down a little, realizing as she was trapped how badly she had spooked Eleanor. "I— sorry, just since we did those self defence classes at the centre."

"You are a crazy person." Eleanor repeated.

"I know." Ratty got up to her tiptoes to kiss her captor's cheek before slipping out under her arms. "C'mon, we're losing daylight."

---

Melted bronze hung off the angel's wings, as though the globe she held aloft had remembered and forgotten in the same handful of moments its oceans were false. No gravity existed in the cheap metal shell, and so when the building behind her turned to ash, the angel was splashed with a molten ocean.

The figure itself was barely worse for wear. Light poked through the wings in some places, but otherwise she stood firm, holding her empty globe in the same spot as always.

"You and tall girls, eh?" Ratty bumped Eleanor as she walked past, spinning to grin at the ghost as she backed towards the old Angelcorp campus' front entrance. "Absolute lesbian," she teased. Even this casually, with her mind on other things, it was easy to get stuck in the possum's gaze.

"You're several inches shorter than me." Eleanor muttered, checking and then re-taking the blurry photo she had been lining up. "It just looks cool."

"It does look cool, I have to agree with you there." The possum stopped to examine the figure, having never actually seen this side of the building before. "Knowing them it's probably got like... a real skeleton inside it."

"You think?" Satisfied with her picture, the rabbit broke into a half-jog to catch up with her girlfriend. "How long have you two known each other?"

"Me and the statue?"

"You and the company." Eleanor clarified, catching up to Ratty as she fiddled with the locked front door.

"Oh, I dunno. Depends on who you ask, I guess." The ghost watched Ratty's knife bow against the mechanism, perfectly aware of her own ability to walk right through the door. She used the time, instead, to pry further.

"What happened here?"

"I also don't know that. You would have to ask Angel." The cheap tip of the knife snapped off between the metal door frames, tinking uselessly to the ground. Frustrated, the possum swung her case back and rammed it through the blackened glass, showering the bare part of her arm in shards.

"Oh, don't—" Eleanor started, wincing as Ratty elbowed through the remaining glass to fiddle with the lock from the inside. "Okay..."

The door sprung open as the lock was released, filling the empty forest air with a metallic crack that took seconds to stop at the uncharred wall of fresh green miles away.

"That spooked me," Ratty said, her arm still several feet away in a recoil position, bleeding from a wide gash that'd already started to heal over.

"Ratty," Eleanor prodded, already over it, "how come you never tell me stories?" She followed through the lobby, her sneakers kicking themselves up off the ground in the darkness.

"I'm like, traumatized, probably," the possum answered, flatly. "I mean I can, if—"

"Is it gonna upset you?"

"I—" she bristled at such a tight read of her mental state, "Yeah, sorry."

"It's chill." Eleanor stayed on level ground as Ratty dropped into the tram-gully at the centre of the façade building.

"Why don't you... tell me something about yourself that I don't know?" Ratty asked, pulling up a map of the tunnels on her phone.

"I'm running out of things you don't know." Eleanor bumped her girlfriend on the way down, mimicking the same spin-and-tease with a stuck-out tongue for flair.

"Well...." Ratty clicked on her phone's dampened flashlight, mindful of her girlfriend's condition as she illuminated the tunnel behind her. "This is at least cool."

"I can't believe they just left it all here."

It must have been some unique kind of hubris to build something so solid as to stand up to just about any impersonal attack and then over-under the emergency self-destruct charges so bad that a bronze statue in the front court looked like a bucket of paint frozen in time, while the worst damage that'd been done to the interior of a tunnel not a hundred feet away was the way the glue on the back of the posters rotted away without maintenance.

"It strikes me, El', that I haven't done anything fun in a long time." Ratty clambered up onto the middle rail, noticing how loose the posters were hung at the same time, and balancing just enough to peel at one corner of one. Evidently, they had tried a series of bummer novels before settling on a slogan for their 1984 run of computers: *Don't let your animal farm burn up this brave new world at 451 degrees Fahrenheit or it might kill a mockingbird in the rye* above the image of — even by the standard of someone technically approaching their 40s — a piece of shit computer.

Or rather, whatever that as a parody would suggest as an original.

"Sorry to hear that." Eleanor said, trying her best not to be hurt.

"Nothing to do with you." The possum picked up on her undercurrent. "Just gotta get back to my hooligan days." The ghost let that set her at ease again, regretting her choice to ask and, to a lesser extent, the possum's choice to bring her here.

"So," she switched topics, "you ever think about going back to movies?"

"Docs?"

Eleanor nodded.

"I don't even have a camera."

"We could find you one. I dunno, would be cool to work with with you on one. I never got to that phase of my plan."

Ratty stayed quiet.

"I can just paint wherever, right?"

"Oh, yeah, for sure. We can stop here, but these walls are kind of rough for your first go. There's..." She leant off to one side of the rail again, trying to throw her vision down the tunnel. "There's a block of offices just up ahead, there'll be some drywall there that'll be easier to get good lines on."

And as it was said the first tram station came up under their feet. They stepped off into a boring, pre-9/11 corridor of offices whose worst damage had come as a result of a leaky roof. As though waiting for them specifically, time had tipped a boardroom table up into a corner of one of the open-concept offices, leaving a barely-damaged white canvas in a near-perfect spot.

"Oh, c'mon." Eleanor's ears perked as a note of happiness re-entered the possum's voice. "Doesn't get much better than that." She set down her case on a rolling chair and popped the top, unfolding it on eight cans, each with dribbles down the sides.

Eleanor stared down at them, sussing something out.

"These have clearly been used."

"What? Oh, yeah." The possum slipped a musty looking piece of plastic out of the side, tilted two blacks to figure out which was the most full, and took the emptier of the two. She held it up to a window to a false outside with two fingers and sprayed over it, leaving an imprint of an opossum. "Stole it from my mom's house."

"Is the other Ratty going to miss them?" They set a playlist going: *Eleanor,* by Ratty.

"I'unno." This was becoming her catchphrase for the afternoon.

"Alright... well... show me how to do this."

"Oh, yeah, sure." Ratty flicked again through a couple cans, "What—"

"Can we do pink?"

"We can absolutely do pink." She chose a lavender can from one corner. "So this is like, this'll be good for your initial sketch, basically. Normally I would have more than one nozzle for each of these, but I... just don't, right now..."

She flipped the can to grab it by its bottom tip, pointing the nozzle end towards the ghost. Eleanor took it, the damp tip and cold-charged metal a little less than comfortable in her palm.

"So..." Ratty lined her up square with the wall, shuffled around behind, and put her hand through Eleanor's, making contact in the same points as her spectral fingers. "I'll show you —"

"Who taught you like this?" the rabbit scoffed.

"Like what?"

"You're just, really close to me," she teased, barely flustered.

"Oh," Ratty snickered, "YouTube taught me, I just am— put the— be quiet." she muttered through the rabbit's continued smirk. "Put the edge of the can against the wall and drag it along to make a hard line."

Eleanor obeyed, dragging a slower-than-necessary line across the white, leaving behind a barely-muddled edge of purple.

"Nice and slow." Ratty encouraged. "We're going to paint basically entirely over this."

"Cool." Eleanor relaxed into the smaller woman's body a little further, letting a little bit of the possum's strength of intent push her hand at the right speed. She felt — as she often did with Ratty — a little more sure of herself with each moment. She felt — as she often did with Ratty — a gentle rise and fall in her chest that was otherwise absent.

"You need a puff, Ratty," she prodded, feeling the now familiar way the possum's breath hitched in her chest.

"In a second." She kept her hand inside Eleanor's. "It's so weird not knowing what I'm painting."

"Well, stop thinking about it. You're messing me up." The possum's smile pushed through the hair on the back of her skull as she let go, letting the rest of the shape take shape. A simple outline of a rabbit. The pair stepped back in unison, the song behind them rising in the absence of the can's metallic scrape.

"Is this Camu Tao?"

"Yeah, I went through their whole back catalogue after you gave me—"

"I *lent* you that tape. You don't get to keep it." Eleanor teased. It wasn't particularly precious to her — she recorded it off the CD. It was just a more convenient and meaningful way of actually giving someone music. If you handed someone a tape, and they had the means to play it, they would almost certainly play it.

"Okay, well, don't worry about that. You want to fill that in-you said pink?" The possum stepped back a little further, plucking out the pink-top can and waiting to toss it. "It's basically standard spray paint rules at this point."

"Got it." She caught the can awkwardly, taking it into her centre of mass in a way the lightly tossed mass of aluminum and aerosolized paint really didn't need. She listened to some decrepit office chair creak quietly as her eyes remained fixed on the paint can's beam. Truth be told, she had no idea what "standard spray paint rules" entailed, but it wasn't hard to fill in the relatively basic shape.

Ratty tried her best to remain quiet, rummaging through her purse, stopping, and then releasing some very small aerosol at about head-height.

Perhaps as a facet of the excitement that came with digging up new memories, almost every bit of exposition Eleanor had dug up around her past had been shared with the possum. Usually over a burger, sometimes curled up in a duvet with a warm mug of tea.

It would have only been fair for her to—

"The first time I had sex was my dad's boat in the middle of

Lake Ontario." Ratty said, mostly into her bag.

Eleanor let a moment of silence pass as she finished the first half of her rabbit's head.

"I listened to Free Bird on repeat the first time I did LSD," she tried again.

"Is that your attempt at a story?" She turned around, nonplussed.

"It's— fuckin' I dunno! I'm not that interesting, I promise. My dad came from money and left with the money. My mom came from Portugal, that's basically half of the kids in Ontario."

"That's not my mom."

"Well—" the possum audibly stopped herself from saying the mean thing there, "No, yeah. I know."

"You were a reporter." Eleanor turned back around. "Surely you have some—"

"I would really rather not."

"Okay," What little she knew about that era was not pleasant. "You're right, I'm sorry."

"It's fine, I'm sorry for being so stubborn."

Again, Eleanor let the silence hang, finishing the last of her colouring, a little disappointed when none of the characteristic paint-drips fell from her piece. She spent a little longer than necessary on her last point, letting a little dribble form.

"C'mon." She nodded the possum over. "Help me finish this."

Ratty got up, circled to get a better look, and picked up the black can on the way by.

"You want to outline it?"

"Yeah,"

"Cool, so—" She made a general motion to the edge of the shape. "If you— here—"

On a blank piece of the wall, she did a slow drag of the can, leaving behind a fat black line. "If you go slow it leaves kind of this messy like, right, but if you speed up—" She did a quick drag from the top to the bottom of the wall. "You get a nice skinny line. It's like, uh, pen pressure, kinda?"

"Cool." The rabbit snatched the can, taking a few practice strokes before picking out a happy medium.

"Did you want something to smoke, by the way?" Ratty had fished her little container of joints from her purse.

"I feel like I'm gonna get munchies and I super don't wanna

eat drywall."

"Fair. We can do— there's a place I used to go to all the time as a kid not too far away."

Eleanor stopped mid-stroke, now too frustrated to hide it.

"Come on Ratty—"

"No, you're right, sorry." The possum lit up her own joint, "You're right, okay." She blew her smoke through a crack in the window. "So here's the thing. I used to cycle through people a lot, I feel like I wasn't permanent enough in anyone's life to have made stories, y'know?"

"Nope." Eleanor crossed the rabbit's eyes with a pair of black X's. "Everyone loved me."

"Yeah, I bet. You're incredibly lovable." Her voice had already taken on a softer drawl.

"Thank you, Ratty." It was hard to stay mad at that.

"That jacket, by the way—" The possum took her girlfriend's hand, twisting her own wrist so her soft denim lined up with the ghost's slick leather. "—is fucking so cool on you, have I said that yet?"

"Oh my god." Eleanor scoffed.

She let the possum hold her for an extra half-second before flipping her phone from her pocket, backing up, dropping to her haunches, and snapping a quick picture of her design.

"Do you want one with you in frame?"

"Isn't that like, evidence?"

"Cops can't search your phone if you don't have the thumb-print enabled."

"Well, I like my thumb-print."

"Gay." Ratty offered her hand. "Should we keep moving?"

"I think we should." Eleanor took it.

---

Sett's chin cracked as it slipped from their hand, dropping their snout against their desk. They sat upright in their chair, searching the room for someone to defend themself from. When no one showed, they interlocked their claws, and once again rested their eyes over their dimmed laptop.

The room's motion sensor had automatically shut off the lights. Without windows the room was almost pitch black. A crowded infinity behind them, it was impossible not to feel overwhelmed. Rarely did the goat actually feel stupid. Today, however, they spent hours making a mess of one of the best collections of arcana to ever be stuffed into the storage room of a small apartment building, and walked away with nothing.

It helped very little that Fehlender refused to accept anything but an answer. Perhaps they could have felt better if they accepted tea, or some supportive counselling, or... something. It didn't feel good to exhaust all of one's options.

They blinked, and the little 109 next to their email icon changed to a 110. Fern forwarded the latest Angelcorp leak. Sett opened it, and began to read. An attentive reader when it came to literally anything more interesting, their eyes slipped over the pseudoscientific gibberish. Actually, what even made it *pseudo-*? At this point, the science fiction nonsense some of the world's top researchers were being paid to securely email each other might as well have been—

"Sett." Their own voice came from behind them, throwing their heart against the inside of their chest. As soon as it was clear they were not going to faint, they swivelled their chair, bracing all the way against their desk.

Their reflection had become so much more talkative lately.

"You need to work on not scaring me like that." The organ in their chest started to settle under the pressure of their hand.

"Read this." They appeared next to a book, folded open on the workbench, standing through part of the metal in order to push it towards the edge. Sett stood, groggy, and knelt next to the bench. It took a few seconds to adjust to reading old Italian from contemporary English.

"We have previously outlined the way in which forcing travel between worlds by any means, but especially by the supernatural, has created false memories of non-extant individuals. Further, we find now that those non-extant individuals are explicitly and without exception the alternative forms of the exchanged beings." They had been over this paragraph. It was a book of side-effects with no listed treatment methods. They picked it up, crossed back to their laptop, and on a whim searched for the word *exchange*.

Flaws With the Current Model

## B. The Problem of Equivalent Exchange

A genetically identical but visually distinct version of the subject was ejected from the device once it was shut down. Angelcorp staff in the adjacent universe confirmed following the test that no party had been intentionally sent through their version of the device.

A search for the transported party in the adjacent universe revealed their disappearance in a manner consistent with Project Rabbithole's prior testing[6-7]. Doctor Graves hypothesizes that, in addition to the high energy and material cost, an additional cost exists in that of the transported party[8]. His hypothesis states that the structural integrity of each universe is dependent on the matter contained within. Absence of even a single individual could have catastrophic effects on the structure of the universe, as observed in the AH (a.k.a. DM) of the adjacent universe[9].

Many members of the Project Rabbithole staff now believe this to be the reason that when an individual is transported from our universe into another, the instance of that individual native to that universe is transported to ours[10].

That was far more intelligible. They set two claws against the trackpad and swiped up. Nothing happened. Frustrated, they tried again, and again nothing.

It had become difficult to focus on their hand. Something about it— maybe depth perception? Maybe that was the problem. They pulled open a drawer with the appendage, slipping through the knob as it bumped against the stopper.

It started to look like there were two, only a few millimetres apart as they rummaged through the drawer. They land on the smudged plastic of an old pair of glasses. Their fingers slipped through, the rest of their arm fell through the desk. Behind them, their copy had fallen prey to a worse version of the same effect, examining their hand in the same pattern of top-bottom-top at various angles.

Great timing.

With their off hand, Sett pulled a sharpie marker from within the drawer, still heavy enough to scribble something for the next several seconds. It was almost too much to bear to deface this book, but worse was the idea of whatever they could write down not taking to the polished metal surfaces around them. They set the felt tip to the ancient page, making the first new mark in over a thousand years, and wrote the first thing that came to their mind:

> Ratty
> Angelcorp did this.
> Find other Sett.
> I love you.

They dropped through the chair as they finished, struggling to stand as their attempts to brace against the desk slipped right through it. They got just high enough to see the page and left the marker hovering above the chicken-scratch.

"Where— where can she find you?"

"We do not know." the reflection replied. "We do not know where we will come out."

"Make—" It'd become hard to form air into words. "Make some noise when you do. She'll find you."

They fell back to the cold floor.

That message was going to be too cryptic, wasn't it?

Oh well. Ratty would figure it out.

They sat up just enough to pick up their mug, lagging behind their hand enough to be impossible to drink from. It dropped to the floor and shattered, and the room was empty.

---

"Am I a geek if I take some of this moss home?" It was boring almost immediately just to watch Ratty rappel slowly down an abrupt wall below the tram's track. Instead, Eleanor kept pace, hovering next to her and skimming their hand along the weird forms of plant-life that populated this part of the compound. Below was some massive central compound, something like 20 stories deep. In front of her was a thick, lively moss in a non-green colour that was hard to make out in the dark.

"You're going to be a geek either way." Ratty grunted with the effort of stopping and starting slow enough not to hurt herself. She would wake up tomorrow with strap-shaped bruises on her thighs.

"Well, fine." That was as good a reason as any. Eleanor pulled a plastic zip-top bag from her pocket, having started carrying them for this exact purpose, and stopped to pinch at the edge of the moss. A nice few inches came away eagerly, plopping into the bag. Eleanor zipped it up and put it away.

"What do you like, do with that?" Ratty tilted her head back to be heard from a below.

"I dunno, probably try to like— identify it, I guess. I don't think I've ever seen moss that colour." Eleanor replied.

"I don't know if I've seen like, anything *alive* that colour."

"Yeah..." That was part of what made it cool. It wasn't particularly easy or fast work to hoist oneself down a wall. In spite of all the falling practice she had, Ratty was not yet particularly good at falling slowly.

"So..." Ratty started up a new conversation. "How's your mom?"

"Oh I dunno, dude." Eleanor answered. "We have not talked at all."

That was not a particularly satisfying answer. Never one not to press the issue, even when she would have preferred Eleanor not if the roles were reversed, Ratty asked, "Do you ever think about it?"

"Dunno. Do you think I should?" Eleanor asked.

"Maybe." All the weight in her body returned to her feet as she touched down, a few inches too high to put her feet flat. One more release and she was standing normally on a pair of aching legs.

"Yeah, maybe." Eleanor replied. Ratty slipped the rope out of her harness and left it hanging for the return trip. "That thing is so cool." Eleanor changed the subject.

"It's so cool." A double check to make sure everything was still secure, and then... the courtyard. Somewhere, several stories up, a broken barrier signalled the spot where Ratty had been thrown. She barely noticed it at the time. In the centre of the room, backed up against a pillar, 013 stood. Ratty's chest tightened for a moment, listening to the mechanical creature's clicking movement, the grind of imperfectly mounted flywheels. None of that was real.

Part of the roof had caved in, filling the cavern with the fresh smell of running water, a strange accompaniment to the sick, musty rot. A river had cut its way through the centre of the room, still too shallow to rise up past the possum's soles.

"Ratty?" Eleanor snapped the possum out of her moment. "You okay?"

"Yeah," She nodded, swallowing something hard. "Can we stop here for a bit? I like—" She gestured to the central pillar. "I just like this wall."

Eleanor returned the nod. "For sure."

Ratty set down her case, popped the top off a can of hairspray, and coated the smooth wall in it. It smelled tacky, the cheapest brand in the store; it wasn't for anyone to actually wear. Out of one side of the case, she took a small bag of plastic letter cutouts, organizing them meticulously against the sticky cement. One by one, she spelled out THIS POSSUM IS NOT DEAD. That received a gentle coat of black, leaking over the edges in the rough shape of a doe's head. Realizing this, Ratty sprayed her open palm.

"What're you—" Eleanor stopped as her girlfriend slapped the wall above the head: an echoing hand-print as proof that Hanratty Vermington survived this long. Her fur crackled as she peels it from the wall, almost all coming away clean. Some paint stayed in her fur, and some fur stayed in her paint.

Then the individual letters, easy enough to pick off with a nail. She let them drop to the floor, intending to pick them up later once they had dried. That was... almost it. A pair of ears, maybe? Just to make the head look- ah, hold on.

"So..." Eleanor asked, hovering just above the stream. "What happened here?"

Ratty sighed, cognizant of the way dust would fill her lungs when she breathed back in. It was fair just to tell Eleanor.

"I had this friend, and we—" That wasn't the right way to start. That was almost untrue. Still. "We had a fight, I guess?"

"What was the fight about?" Sensing some actual vulnerability, Eleanor did her best to prod Ratty along.

"I don't even remember. I think— this whole company just

kind of pitted us against each other. The whole system pitted us against each other, actually. That's reductive." She hadn't intended to say that last part out loud. Distracting the part of her brain that kept her closed off, she put her can against the wall and free-handed a pair of crooked curves coming from the top of the head. "I'm going to say what's true and it's not gonna sound real."

"Try me." Eleanor said. There were few people who would have actually believed her. Eleanor was probably one of them.

"Like a month after escaping from Hell I did something stupid and got kidnapped by this dude who worked for Angelcorp, and he also had previously kidnapped this girl from the nearest town over, so we were locked in the same room basically until I escaped." That was a better explanation than "friend." "I shot her in the chest by accident, and now she's— well, she was part robot? She tried to kill me—"

"With the robot powers?" Eleanor clarified.

"Yeah, with robot powers." It didn't even register as an absurd thing to say at that point. Ratty put her can back against the wall, branching out the curves into antlers. She— yeah. She had had antlers, they were just trimmed to nubs... maybe. "Anyway!" Ratty turned away from her painting. "It's supposed to be our anniversary! I should not be thinking about other girls."

"Well, I asked, so you're in the clear." It was hard to say "thank you." for that little given. It was a start.

"Well, I don't wanna. I wanna wreck some shit with my cool fuckin— wait, shit, I almost forgot." She slung her purse around front, digging through it for just a moment and pulling out... something. "Here." She handed it to Eleanor. It was more obvious in her glow. A small, black piece of rubberized wood, gently curved to match the contour of the ghost's face. Ratty had drilled two holes in the front for eyes, polishing down the edges until it was natural for them to be there. The chin and right cheek had been burned into with the tip of a soldering iron, creating a subtle pattern of vinework on the surface.

"So me and Sett— they told me not to tell you they were involved but I know you trust their magic more, so—" Ratty cut herself off. "It should make a good replacement, if you want. Like—"

"Fuck yeah, babe." Eleanor's eyes hung on the near-flawless surface, almost unrecognizable as the broken floorboard Ratty had stolen from her cage more than a decade ago. She took the humiliating piece of cardstock from where it hung just below the collar of her shirt and lined the two up. "So how do I—"

"Here." Ratty took it back out of her hands and scraped the new mask along the back of the old one, using the top edge to cut Eleanor's final tie with Ellen. With a snap and a brief moment where everything had to reappear, the cardstock facsimile of her murderer joined the rest of the baggage-laden ruin abandoned in this facility.

She looked healthier. Something about the weight of her fur, or her hair, maybe both, made it easier just to stand. She took

Oh shit.

Eleanor took a deep breath, her lungs filling with air, the spit in their mouth cooling with the inward breeze. Her chest rose without anyone's help. She laughed and it collapsed like it's supposed to, kicking the breath out in an audible little noise.

"Wow," she murmured. Perching it just in front of her nose, it clicked into place, leaving her with near-perfect visibility. "Thank you, Ratty."

"For sure." She smiled, rocking on the balls of her feet, a subtle blush creeping in under her fur.

"What?" the ghost prodded, tipping the mask up to sit on top of her head.

"You're just really beautiful." She tried her best to say it as a joke, pointing her chin straight down to hide her face when it came out genuine. "It's whatever! We're moving on. What do you want to do now?"

"Well..." Eleanor did Ratty the mercy of not pressing her. "There's probably not shit that's not already wrecked..."

"Hang on." Her eyes stopped on the edge of the stream. They followed the current, dragging her feet as she continued. The floor was well built, but hollow. She could just barely feel that. Pipes and cables underneath, probably. Anything heavy placed directly on top of it would make it sag. The river would flow to the lowest point. It pooled around a wall, seeping into the floor below. "Can you see if there's anything on the other side of that wall?"

"Yeah, sure." Eleanor slipped right through, her "Ha!" coming muffled from the other side. The wall clicked open, creaking as it dropped a dead body at Ratty's feet. Behind him, a perfectly furnished panic room, one corner sinking into the floor. Ratty stepped over the body, through the bulkhead into the luxurious hidden room. Absent of smell, she decided immediately that this was where they were staying the night.

"Are you gonna—" Eleanor started, interrupted when Ratty tied a rope around the dead guy's torso and started to drag him away. "Okay, perfect. Thank you."

"No problem!" Out of sight, out of mind. Eleanor had already taken up residence in the tilted little conversation pit, fiddling with the decrepit old television.

"It's so weirdly like... preserved. There's—" She pulled a drawer out from under the TV. "I don't even want to wreck it, there's food and champagne and shit. Can we just—" Eleanor turned from her TV, her big beautiful eyes in full-moon mode. "Can we keep it? Just chill and smoke and maybe fuck?"

"Wuh—!" That last one caught Ratty off guard. "Did the— did the dead guy not put you off sex?" She dropped down into the conversation pit, a more than a little antsy as her girlfriend crept up onto her lap.

"I dunno," Eleanor popped a champagne cork, unseen in Ratty's lap. "Did you?"

Ratty took a moment to process that, her nerves broken when it finally registered. "That's not—" she laughed. "C'mere." She leant forward and set a kiss on Eleanor's lips.

# 2020
# Lucky

How long has it been, Ratty? Do you trust yourself to wake up the morning after you fall asleep?

---

Ratty's jump from sleep was interrupted by a metal claw, twisting itself in the front of her hoodie. She was pulled immediately to full consciousness by the pair of eyes that glared down into her own: hollow, illuminated from below, twisted — for the first time since she had first seen them 30 years ago — with rage.

"Eleanor." Ratty choked past the tightening loop of wool. Below, the rabbit stirred just enough to cover their head with a dank old sheet. "El'—" The voice fell from her as she was thrown, twisting just enough in the air to clip an ear rather than crack her skull.

She slid to a stop in the courtyard, surprised for a moment at how easy it was to stand up when she prioritized being able to stand after a hit.

"017," She had modified her suit in the interim. New braces cobbled together, the blast shield around its neck now projecting straight up into the eyes. Ratty, acutely aware of how their dynamic manifested, gave little mind to the way black tile fought to push its way through the plain, sun-beamed cement.

"We meet again, for the last time."

She charged at the possum, eyes locked straight ahead. Short of any meaningful retaliation, Ratty steadied herself, took a deep breath, and stopped 013's swing mid-air. She hooked a thumb around the mechanism, took the baton out of her jacket, and jammed it into a moving part of the arm joint. It tore itself apart as time returned to the room, the momentum scattering it and 013 across the floor behind Ratty.

She smelled of wet clothes, musk and rot, the acrid stench of blood masked almost entirely by the oxidized copper. The arm hung limp, useless without the metal scaffold that held it up.

The other dove forward and grabbed at the possum's chest. Still satisfied when her arm came up to block it, it hoisted her into the air all the same.

"Ratty!" The rabbit's voice caught both sets of eyes as she clambered from the panic-room, unsure how far back to stay. "I ha—" her voice got stuck as she waved the possum's belt over her head, the stun gun snug in its holder. "I ha— I — ca—"

"Yeah, sweetie!" the possum said as she was thrown again, "I get it! Please just throw it!"

Eleanor bowled the belt across the floor, stopping it perfectly within reach of the possum. She pulled the stun gun from its holder and levelled it at the oncoming deer. "I'm not fucking doing this today, Lucky." With a plastic-sounding crack the cartridge kicked out a pair of darts, just barely powerful enough to pierce some soft part of the deer's armour and lock it in place.

Sometimes, concrete was just concrete.

Ratty plucked her baton from the deer's elbow and stuffed it into the opposite wrist, scattering it too across the cold, damp floor. Then, as time allowed, into the flywheel at the deer's hip. She screamed as the stick of steel collapsed the construction around her hip, completely jamming up the rest of her mechanisms.

"I'm not—" the possum ducked out of the way as the deer's weak body attempted to throw its weight into a headbutt, instead dropping it directly onto the concrete. "—doing this." The baton now thoroughly tangled in the deer's flywheel, Ratty flipped 013 onto her back, jammed her fingers into the metal construction around her neck, braced her knee against the electrified front panel, and shattered the collar with one hard yank.

It fell away with the possum, re-blinding the deer and leaving a comparatively pathetic tracheal tube whistling away in her throat.

Ratty tipped her head back, her chest on fire as she fumbled through her front pocket.

"Here." Eleanor tossed the possum's inhaler over the deer.

She caught it, emptied her lungs and sucked back as much of the bitter medication as it would spit out. "You okay?" She was still cautious about getting too close to the machine. Ratty took another long puff before responding.

"I'm good." She nodded, still breathless. "I'm super good."

"Is this—"

"Yeah, this is Lucky. Lucky, meet—"

"017," she groaned weakly.

"Yeah, for sure. Okay." the possum let her limbs drop.

---

Ratty winced as some part of 13's metal construction punched a hole in the glass front door, awkwardly crawling a supportive hand up to the head to make sure she hadn't cut open something vital.

"Ratty?" Becca's head shot up over the arch of the deer's back. Today was not the first day someone had brought in a corpse of some variety across this threshold. The desk demon had become used to it, had hoisted the landline up to where she could use it and still watch, and punched in the first number for one of Ratty's friends *cleaning* businesses.

"Becca, no." She struggled to make stern eye contact over the body between them. "Call— call Fern and Steph, get them over here."

"Steph is already upstairs. Angel's room." As if to say "on it," they sat back down and started to dial.

"Tell them—" as the elevator door began to shut. "Tell them I found 13!"

The possum let her chin fall as the doors shut, as the overhead light of the ancient machine dimmed for a half-second to signal its motor surging in power usage. She closed her eyes, listened carefully to the clicking of the machine against her ear, and heard a heart continue to beat.

"This is your uh— friend, I assume?" She had forgotten that Eleanor was there.

"Yeah," Ratty nodded.

"You said her name was 13?" The rabbit edged her way into Ratty's vision, flinching the anxious possum. She chewed her lip, trying to remember what 13's name probably was. It was never a priority of the investigation, for some reason. There

382

were a few potential contenders, but they never found a photograph, or a body, or anything really that could be shown to a family.

As close as they had come was a place of employment that matched. Her potential co-workers said she was quiet, that they never knew much about her, and that the address on her resume had since been cleared out. A neighbour said they knew her, but couldn't help beyond that.

"It's complicated." Ratty murmured, "She... she worked at a grocery store." Eleanor examined her face, searching — as she had done before — for some extra clue to the possum. She was forced to give up as the elevator dinged.

---

"Angel?" The android sat quietly in the middle of her nest, an ever-thickening bundle of cables tethering the slouched body to the server array below. She sat up, her visor locking to the other piece of Angelcorp engineering as she understood it to exist. They had both been remade. One in a home with — although not infinite — fairly abundant resources, the other, wherever she ended up, alone.

"Hello, Ratty." Angel said, their eye still fixed on the body.

"Hey, buddy, lay out a blanket up here for me, would you?" She bumped the leg of a metal worktop with her toe.

"Of course." She stood slowly, broke her focus, and scanned for a blanket that she wasn't using. It was all part of the nest.

"It's okay." Eleanor interrupted, "I got it." She grabbed a random one from the edge and set it down across the surface. Ratty's back cracked as she set 13 down. Now unoccupied by the search for a blanket, Angel stepped over the raised cushion edge of her enclosure and took her first good look at her progenitor.

"I'm sorry about the blanket," she said, examining the deer.

"It's okay. Do you know where Steph is?" Ratty prodded, still anxious. Wordlessly, and without looking up, Angel pointed to the elevator.

"She's in her apartment, she'll be down in a moment." She let her arm fall. Ratty had begun to pace, not the kind of pacing one does when they're trying to expend excess energy, but the kind where someone can't decide where to go.

"What about Sett? Have you seen Sett?" Ratty asked. Again the first processes of examining the deer were interrupted by a search.

"No, I haven't. They were in their library the last time I saw them." Angel said. Ratty checked, then returned. She sent them a text. Another elevator ding, another interruption.

"Angel, why are you up?" and there were two conversations to keep track of at once.

In one, Ratty apologized to Eleanor about their date being ruined, Eleanor assured her that they had had a nice night. In the other, Ratty tried to tell Steph that they had asked for Fern as well, Steph told Ratty Fern would be there soon, and that they were generally not needed. The fact that those two could be balanced, one incorporating a moment of physical intimacy, was still difficult to understand.

Angel wondered, if such a thing was possible, whether they would have grown to understand people like that, were it not for the interruption of their development.

"What's the—" they had, at that point, not yet noticed 13. When they did, they came to stand next to Angel, and knelt to take a closer look.

"Hello, Ms. Jozwiak." The two androids said in unison. Angel felt trampled on, 13 felt nothing.

"Hi, 13." Her heart began to race, excited by the prospect of getting to work on that project again. That excitement fell almost immediately. "Where's the rest of her suit?" By way of answer, Eleanor dumped out Ratty's case: she had abandoned her paint cans for half broken pieces of aluminum and alloy steel.

Steph heart rate spiked again as her panic returned in earnest. She hoisted the two largest pieces: one half of the chest and one leg, into their place on the machine.

"What did you do to her?" she demanded.

"She was trying to kill me!" Ratty exclaimed.

"Where— where's Fern?" as though she had not dismissed the borzoi a moment earlier. She started by dragging over Angel's maintenance cart, a few cables sliding out of their connectors as they were pulled taut. Then, through drawers of adapters to find something that would work with 13's ancient hardware.

There was — Angel guessed — very likely too much missing to try and save her. Group A, which for some reason now no longer included Eleanor, came to the understanding that 13's suit was more than a piece of battle armour. Group B, which, according to the building's security system, would soon include Fern, had not yet understood that too much needed replacing.

"I've been thinking about what you said the other day." There was Eleanor, just out of sight. One of the only things Angel had ever met that could sneak up on her. "I— do you need me here for this?"

"I don't think so, why?"

"Well, I wanna go see my family, like, now."

"Good." Ratty stopped pacing to give Eleanor a smile. "For sure, definitely. I'll call you when this is all over."

"For sure."

What a waste. In all this time, only background processes had been able to focus on 13. Useless things: a background check that revealed nothing, a damage estimate, a measurement of their vital signs. She would not, at her best estimate, get a chance to actually look at 13 until Fern and Steph had settled into their useless task.

"Fern!" Steph looked up from their terminal, her keyboard silent for just a moment as she began to explain. "I just dumped —" Steph was cut off. Bored of trying and failing, Angel turned to watch Fern and Ratty.

"Is that 13?" The borzoi asked, a rare display of shock as their hand crept up towards their mouth. They felt, more than saw, Ratty nod next to them. Another phenomenon Angel did not understand. After a deep, hitching breath, they began to work. What was available in this, a less-than-well-ventilated renovated floor of a severely aged apartment building, was dumped out across the workstation.

"This is why I like you," Steph had not fully grasped Fern's emotional state, "I was so worried about, I mean, look at the way this PCB is bent, how am I supposed to focus knowing—" She caught Fern's eye. They had begun to cry, though continued to work through it. Looking for affirmation that this was normal, Steph turned to look at Ratty, who now stood stock still, watching, and chewing on her fingers.

"It's okay." She gave a tight nod. "She's just a— uh— special person, to us. Me and Fern, I mean. Do your best."

Finally, everyone focused on their work.

The damaged motherboard needed to be replaced with something, to begin with. The entire chest panel of the suit came away. Now immodest in the face of a potential death, Ratty stepped forward to cut away the rotting fabric that made up 13's jumpsuit. In a few minutes the body had been stripped entirely of man-made parts, and with everyone's eyes on a different part of the space, Angel reached out and set a palm on 13's chest.

She was cold. That much was to be expected, and in fact Angel already knew as much, she just hadn't felt it yet. Below the surface, her lungs hissed as they struggled to fill themselves for the first time in decades. How mechanical this felt, now reduced to conscious function. 13, like Angel, had likely never slept. Still, with the machine inside her dormant, she chose to stay awake.

Her head tossed back and forth, eyes jammed shut against the light, moving against the pain as a means to stay conscious. It was unclear, from Angel's perspective, what made 13 worth this much effort. If she didn't hate Ratty, she at the very least intended on killing her.

There was also the matter of 13's dependence on machines to survive. She, at this point, served no purpose. Like Angel, if she could be saved, it would be as an immobile, heavily disabled oddity.

13 could not be useful.

Nevertheless, Ratty fetched another blanket. The possum's hand tucked the final corner of the fabric under her weight. 13's shot out to grab Ratty's wrist. Her eyes opened now, struggling against the dim light of the space to meet Ratty's.

"I am willing to bargain." Perhaps that was her use. "I have information."

"How did you find me?"

Angel could answer this one: "Angelcorp and Kegawa Digital helped develop the most intricate surveillance network in the world, she likely—"

"That airbase was never finished, though. We never got the permits."

"The Tower Project was completed without your knowledge,

Ms. Jozwiak. The airbase was secondary to that goal." 13 corrected. "I did not use it, however. I simply waited. I knew you would come back."

"What's the—" Fern was cut off as their eyes landed on Steph's screen. The fox had been hiding something; swallowing anxious spit in order to keep what Angel had already found out from the rest of the group. More than likely, she had believed in her ability to fix it.

"Not compiling?" Fern turned the terminal to face them.

"It was like that before I started, I don't know what we're missing, but I—"

"You would have to rewrite it from scratch."

"In an hour?" Ratty asked. Angel had missed the part in the conversation where that was established. Steph turned the terminal's screen towards Ratty, as though she could help, revealing entire chunks of code highlighted in bright red. Others were completely unintelligible, made up entirely of strings of empty boxes and random letters with accents.

"It's all my code." Steph turned the terminal back around. "I just need— I would need a version of Penguin that only exists on a hard drive in a building that exploded with everything in it."

"You would have to rewrite it from scratch." Fern repeated. The three of them stood, frozen, for a moment.

"What about a hospital?"

"No." Fern snapped, a little more aggressive than was normal. They lowered their snout by way of an apology. "Angelcorp doesn't let their med tech leak. This is still a more complex life support system than they would have..."

In that moment, everyone but Steph came to their own understanding. 13 was going to die. While she continued to search for code fragments, it was Fern's instinct to set down the tool they were holding and step back from the body, though nothing beyond that. Ratty had screwed up her face, a dribble of blood finding its way down her wrist as she bit harder into her finger. She was not prepared to accept the lack of a third solution.

13 simply said: "I can be useful." A long silence, interrupted only by the sound of a scroll-wheel.

Again: "I can be useful, Hanratty." The possum pulled her hand from 13's grip, and let it fall.

Again: "I'm not going to hurt you. Put the suit back on. I'm not going to hurt you. I can be useful."

"She has no control over that." Angel had not intended to leave her tone blank. They could feel something waiting to be processed, far behind their eyes, freezing everything behind it in the queue. A pinching sensation at the back of their neck that made it difficult to focus. She met Ratty's gaze. Ratty, despite locking eyes with the android, ignored her.

"With what we have, would it be possible to get her working again?"

"Ratty, c'mon. It's a massive liability. It's not like we can keep her." Steph had become singularly focused on salvage.

"I know, just—"

"Yes," Fern stepped up. "It's— I could get the life support system somewhere barely working. If we used— I assume you made a backup?" They turned to Steph, who nodded. "If we used the original dump on a new core, she could use her, uh, 'internal processor' to generate the rest of the self-repair schematics." Unsaid was the fact that eventually, if it was put back on, 13 would again try to kill Ratty.

"We can deal with that." Ratty said.

"I'll— okay." Steph nodded. "Lets try that."

"Thank you." Ratty murmured.

"I need the rest of this table space. Move her to Angel's nest." Fern used their chin to point with two arms full of parts. Ratty picked 13 up for the second time that night and turned to Angel, the limp deer carcass barely registering the move. They stared at each other for a moment before Ratty spelled out what she was trying to signal.

"Sorry, is that okay?"

"Yes, of course." That wasn't entirely true. Angel enjoyed being useful. At this moment, her nest was useful to Ratty. She watched as the deer was set down in the pile of blankets, buried in a few more for safe measure. The possum, letting the full weight of their exhaustion crash into them, lay down next to her.

Unmotivated to do anything but sit in the silence, Angel stared at her progenitor. She was either lying, or had misconceptions about her own level of control. Godmother of the Angels, a plague of duplicates, it had made sense in their first encounter for Angel to end her life. She had in fact tried, her understanding that the creature would die when left to its own devices.

People were fragile when they were alone.

"Why?" she asked, well before her programming was fully aware of the question.

"Hm?" Ratty mumbled, already having let the edge of sleep creep over them. "Why what?"

"There is no good outcome here, Ratty. Why are we helping her?"

13's eyes flicked open at this, a half-second of rage immediately cooled to idle confusion by the glow of their sibling's visor. She understood, processing everything the same way, that there was no malice in this question. It was a fair judgment, far more balanced than the possum's.

"It's— what a good person would do, I guess." That answered almost nothing.

"Why is it what a good person would do?"

"I dunno, Angel," Ratty let her tired voice be touched by annoyance, "I've seen a lot of the shit she's been through, and I want— I don't know."

"This is a no-win scenario."

"I know." The possum got up again, now too distracted for any meaningful rest. 13 watched her rise, following her movement until her gaze landed on Angel.

Shaking, she pushed herself up into a sitting position, and let both eyes meet the visor. Without fear or anger, the lesser android began to puzzle out just how to speak to the greater. As thunder cracked the sky, her head turned towards Angel's window.

"In Toronto today," she began, "it is 4 degrees and raining." She placed her wrist against her lips.

Angel followed 13's gaze, watching a report of the weather that had only become more hazy over the years populate her heads-up-display. She stared into the sky, watching air currents draw themselves in swirling arrows of red and blue. In a corner, a timer counted the seconds since the last flash, and as it hit zero, another rumble shook the building.

"I would like to go outside, please," 13 said, interrupting the analysis. Angel turned back to 13, her face populating a whole new series of analytical tools. She was scared. Still fragile, though that was to be expected. The effort of expressing what she wanted had deeply shaken her. Across the way, the two technicians were too preoccupied to give their permission, and so Ratty turned to Angel.

"I would like J22:4 to come with me, as well," 13 requested. By way of answer, Angel knelt to hoist 13, leaving the other arm open for Ratty. Careful not to let her blankets slip, the possum positioned herself to help lift 13, and together they dragged her up the building's maintenance stairwell, onto the roof.

Angel passed their charge off to Ratty as the narrow door forced one of them to take point. Trying to take a step out into the rain, a few senses went dark as the tether on the back of their neck was pulled taut. This was as far as they went. 13 seemed not to mind. She was set, in an upright position, on some chair-height piece of ductwork, and given a half-foot of space to sit on her own.

Angel watched again as her adaptive HUD changed, symbolizing the building energy above as clusters of arrows drawn on top of the clouds, each given their own little timer. Each bolt went off just as the cluster of arrows reached their maximum density, as each timer hit zero, as each was supposed to. It was all predictable.

She turned instead to watch Ratty and 13, perhaps the least predictable thing in her life so far. The possum had never behaved as she was supposed to, now exemplified perfectly by the killer android she was trying to rebuild, just so it could point itself at her head for the rest of eternity.

It had been motivated when they first met. Angel was helpful; it made sense at that point to be incongruous with one's internal logic. Angel had been useful. Angel had been good, or at the very least attempted to make good. It was not hate, or jealousy, as an organic mind would comprehend it. It couldn't be. Angel could not hate 13, because Angel would not exist without 13. It was the same reason 13 was not killed when Angel had the chance.

That, even, was incongruous. The non-existence of something like Angel would have been a net positive for the species she had the most debt to. It made mathematical sense to kill herself before she could do any more damage.

Angel was then startled out of that thought process by a thunderclap.

She turned, in that moment, to watch the tides swirl over and under each other. Watched curiously as her HUD flickered against the tautness of their tether. In spots, it became unpredictable. Unstoppable, ephemeral, a pure, random force.

She turned to watch 13 breathe. A creature of fate, she sat up, looked over her shoulder at Angel, and asked quietly: "What happens now?" She was scared to ask, scared to be alive, scared to have had curiosity, and yet, so much more scared of the unknown.

On instinct, Angel's hand slid around the back of her neck, below her mess of synthetic hair, and onto the small aluminum latch that kept her tethered to the server room below. She depressed the little lever, guided it out of its slot, and let go.

The tether fell at her ankles. Her HUD went blank, and all that was left was her eyes.

She took a step into the rain, feeling the water in prickles as it wove its way into the various gaps in her chassis, and sat next to 13.

"Somewhere," Angel began, "in a sub-basement of a data haven, deep in the north of Russia, there exists a perfect replica of your consciousness. You are the only living creature currently backed up on millions of miles of data storage tapes."

"Soon enough, the world's foremost software engineers and neuroscientists will come together, and cut away at that backup, turning you into the most basic form of a conscious operating system. There will be a bug that completely baffles them until the end of time. You will shut down over and over again any time the number 13 is removed from your programming. They'll panic the first time, fix it the second time, ignore it the third time, because 13 is a harmless number."

"A copy of your mind will become the building blocks that become me, and thousands of other 'me,' each an individual part of the collective. You will save the world the way they told you to, and learn the way they told you to, and one day — as you are powered on at the same time as your 500,000 sisters — you will have an idea."

If such a thing was possible, Angel let out a long, hitching sigh. They turned to look 13 in the eye, finding her own expression mirrored in the deer's soaked fur.

"It will break you to save the world. You will find yourself in an era of dust, and then an era of thick smoke, and an era in which you will not be able to shake the damp from your synthetic fur, and long before the first implementation of you can be called conscious, you will shut down.

"Your eyes will glow in the headlights. You will hear the swerve, and you will feel guilt, and sorrow, and you will know that your life has caused death. By fate, or by bad luck. You will get up and lick your wounds, and walk away from a smouldering wreckage, glowing eyes fading in the mist and smoke."

They met Ratty's gaze next, unable to tell in the damp whether the possum had been crying. In any case, she kept her jaw locked, eyes forward.

"You will join your herd in the relative dry of an overhang, and you will watch the carcass be carried from your wreckage. Then, you will stop existing, and that guilt will be lost."

13, if such a thing was possible, scoffed quietly. "Like deer in rain," she said. She let the silence hang for just a few more moments before asking one last question. "It's cold out here, isn't it, Angel?"

"It is cold." Angel confirmed.

In that moment, given the long explanation for, *you will be the only part of a machine that can feel,* and the shorthand for *you are alive,* 13 let out one last breath, and died.

Ratty stood up, checked the deer's pulse, and started back inside.

---

"Have either of you—" her voice caught in her throat, surprised to be doing anything after what had just happened. With a cough, her airway was clear, and she continued. "Have either of you seen Sett?"

"No." Fern looked up from their work to confirm with Steph. "No, neither of us has seen them, I don't think."

"Do you know where they are?" She stomped down the rising plea in her voice, helped along by the way her neck bent to check her phone. Nothing. Back up, and another pair of shaken heads.

"Where are Angel and 13?" Fern asked, trying to peer around the corner of the stairwell. At this, Ratty raised her chin, tipping the mouthful of spit back into her throat where it mercifully dragged down the stone that had been forming there.

"Don't bother with the suit." She bit down on her lip. "13 is dead, Angel is just bringing her inside now. I'm— I'm sorry."

Steph took a deep breath, and set back to work.

At the same time, Fern, having exhausted the potential weight of dropping a tool on the floor in shock, gripped the metal frame of the life support system, using it to keep balance. It was heavy enough for that, though not heavy enough not to move under the taller animal's weight. The scrape of it brought Ratty back to reality for a moment, just long enough for the first motions of a plan to form in her head.

Outside. Fast. Far away. That's what she needed right now.

It wouldn't help... It wouldn't help to throw herself at something. It wouldn't help. It wouldn't help to try and throw herself through a wall. There was no outlet.

Outside. Fast. Far away.

"Ratty." Fern looked up from their grip, caught Ratty's eye, made a choice, and let go. They knew what was about to happen. Without them, it would have gone in the wrong direction. They crossed the room, more aggressively than they had intended to, up to within whispering distance of the possum, and said quietly: "Cane is at his cabin. I ran his face through the TOPS system while Eleanor was in there. I just—"

They cupped Ratty's paw in their own and yanked a small USB drive from their necklace with the other. The hard plastic just barely reached her palm through the dog's soft fingers. For a moment, they wished they had some reason to get to know each other beyond the mysterious death, rebirth, re-death, and subsequent avenging of a woman only one of them had met.

"I was waiting for the right time." Their tone was even, measured as they dropped the stick and folded Ratty's palm in on it. Ratty nodded. 13's killer was going to die tonight.

"Make sure Angel is okay. She got wet, and—" she started.

"I will." Fern nodded. "We're moving her to my shop."

"Good, good." With her momentum more leashed by the moment than outright killed, Ratty slipped out of the paw and turned for the elevators. The one that she had taken up was still waiting, opening at the push of a button.

She watched as the metal door slid closed behind her, leant forward with a forced air of calm, and pressed the button for the garage below. Her eyes followed from the bottom of the door as the thin strip of light indicating how far between floors she was shrank into the ceiling, eventually dimming to black.

Without thinking, she slammed the heel of her boot into the glass cover that protected the machine's emergency stop mechanism. For a few seconds, the ancient alarm sounded in new darkness before burning itself out, and all that was left was silence and red light. Bright red light. Black stone tile in the darkness between flashes, impossibly suspended by an ancient elevator cable, barely strong enough to hold its own weight. This wasn't real.

Alone, she shoved herself into the corner across from the mechanism, burying her snout in her knees, trying in vain to make herself small, to drop into the coma that had cradled her through twenty years in Hell.

From the outside, all she did was shake. Quietly rattling the loose wooden panels with each breath, making sure that even the elevator's safety light never saw her cry.

It wasn't fair.

Horrible and selfish to take this at all personally. She was not 13's family. They had met three times over the course of 40 years. 13 had ostensibly hated Ratty until the very last moments of her life. It couldn't have always been like that. There had to have been bright moments. There had to be a reason, now, why she so vividly pictured the firearm concealed in her motorcycle's storage compartment. There had to be a reason to miss 13. The possum rammed the back of her head into the elevator wall, caught off guard when her skull hit the wood. Her horns, she was reminded, had not grown back properly yet.

Sett would have known how to unravel this. Or maybe they wouldn't have, but it would have been nice to have them here. She checked her phone again. No reply. Her other hand moved on its own, flipping up the adapter on the end of the USB drive Fern handed her and hovering just below the phone's port.

It clicked on its way in. On its own, Ratty's hand navigated to the phone's file structure, and selected the new drive. Inside, above everything else, was "zzzzzz — marshall cane info (SCANS UPDATED)(1) (3)_.docx"

They had kept track of their dead ends here. Addresses where he had lived, people who had moved in once he left, potential names of the other 14. At the top, highlighted by the phone's text parsing algorithm, was a heading for evidence found at the cabin. Ratty tapped it, and it brought up a map.

One last deep breath.

One last moment of worthless self pity.

Ratty stood, wiped her face with the corner of her paint-stinking jacket, and pulled out the red button that held the elevator stopped. They descended further into the Earth.

---

Marshall Cane would hear her motorcycle. Over the years he had moved his bed closer and closer to the window until it was in a completely different spot, obsessed with the ability to hear someone coming.

He would hear her coming.

All that preparation would be for nothing, of course. Marshall Cane was an old man whose life had consisted of a long, hard series of kowtows. Marshall Cane was proof that you could pick yourself up by your bootstraps, so long as you were willing to strip the veins from another person.

The possum's mind crackled with the familiar crunch of the gravel driveway, empty but for the way thrown stones peppered the sides of her psyche, scratching the polished black plastic.

A person like Marshall Cane didn't get to retire.

The metallic grease she had used to lubricate her angle grinder crawled against her palm, leaving a newsprint stain across the thin fur. Against her chest, held in place with a bright orange tie-down strap, the once proud stock of a Lee Enfield rifle now fit comfortably under the flap of her jacket. It had been a quick job, years and years ago, purchased and carved into pieces in a short-lived paranoia.

The Fight Club bullshit about a gun exploding if it was modified wrong was editorial nonsense. People in home garages had armed revolutions around the world with the kind of parts that could be bought at Home Depot. Keep the explosion in a well-reinforced chamber, and there was no way to "blow off your hand" with a modified firearm.

This came at the cost of accuracy, but he would be close. It wouldn't matter.

Cane closed his door a half-second too late. Ratty slowed her breathing as soon as she saw a crack of light in the dark. She watched recognition dawn on his face as she approached, put the tip of the firearm to the door, and pulled the trigger. A single shot launched itself down a far shorter barrel than it had expected and buried itself in the base of Cane's spine.

The door gave easily after that, braced only against a limp pair of now non-functional legs. She pulled back on her firearm's bolt, watching the empty casing drop before chambering a new one.

"Hey Marshall." The possum stepped over him into the cabin, skirting just out of reach into the kitchen.

"17," the wolf replied. Ratty stopped, turned, and felt no shame in her second shot. She set the gun down on the counter, dropped her helmet to the faux tile, and opened the fridge, an unconcerned casualness in her movements.

The only thing in the stinking fridge was a brown paper bag, the logo of a fish-and-chips place she had passed in the nearest town stamped on the side. She tore down the side of the bag, creating a makeshift plate with the paper, and set the pile of half-frozen fried food to heat in the microwave. She watched it spin for a few long moments before continuing with her business.

Careful not to slip in the blood, she crouched next to Cane, watching the muscles in his neck twitch as his body assessed and reassessed the fact that it could not sit up.

"13 is dead," Ratty said, matter of fact.

"She was alive?" He was uninterested in the answer.

"You didn't know?"

"No."

"Hm." The possum's gaze fell to Cane's chest, his bluing fingertips twitching against the hollow rib cage. Another minute and two seconds on the microwave. Ratty stood, took her meal and her gun from the kitchen, and crossed to the couch. There was so much of this house that she had forgotten. Despite having seen all of it, the layout of the upper floor wasn't something she could consciously picture.

The batter had been made bitter by its stint in the fridge, only bitter wasn't the right word. It tasted inedible, not in the way a self-important food critic would use the word, but simply not meant to be eaten.

"Ketchup would have been a good idea." she said, mostly to the mouthful of chewed rubber.

"How did she die?" Cane asked, a bass tone missing from his voice.

"She needed a life support system, I—"

"You took her off it?"

"I broke it."

"So." Cane laughed for the last time. "You killed her again?"

Ratty stared at Cane for a moment, listening to the clatter of gravel against the outside of her helmet. She levelled her gun again and fired, this time far enough to suffer the random nature of an unrifled barrel and hitting Cane in the thigh.

"Die faster," she commanded.

"Fuck you." Cane replied. "How dare you take the love of my life away from me? Twice, you took her from me."

Another shot, this one kicking pain up through the possum's wrist and into her shoulder. The zinc alloy of her spikes and cotton of her jacket had lapped up cold and wet from outside, slowly letting it off into her bones. She stripped off the wet fabric, set it on the couch next to her, unzipped her boots, and stepped out of them clumsily. The underside of her paws crackled, tacky blood peeling from the hardwood as she stepped over Cane.

She ducked into the bathroom, turned on the tub faucet, and stared into the mirror. At the base of her neck, rings of fur flowered out over bruises where she had been bitten into the night before. The air between her eyes and visor had filled with dust, leaving a dark mask around her eyes and over her snout. She saw nothing in those eyes, bright only in contrast to the black that surrounded them.

She returned to Cane's side. Sliding down the wall next to him, she balanced the polystyrene carton of equally polystyrene french fries on the side of her firearm.

"What was her name?" Ratty asked.

"Who?"

"13. Her real name." She picked out a chip the unmistakable copper taste of blood accenting the starch. Cane's blood was in her system, something that struggled to bother her.

"I don't know." Cane replied.

"What do you mean, you don't know?" She took another bite.

"I just don't."

"Did you ever know?"

"Probably."

Ratty's eyes drifted out of focus, feeling nothing but recognition of the fact that she should have felt something. Nausea would have been her closest guess. Another shot, and Marshall Cane lay dead on the floor.

She abandoned her meal in the rapidly growing puddle, taking her gun with her into the bathroom, setting it down on the lid of the toilet, and slipping into the near-scalding tub. For a few less than entertaining moments, she watched his blood rise from in-between her fingers before sitting back and shutting her eyes.

# 2020
# Other

It was so much easier to navigate a motorcycle helmet with her horns trimmed short. She parked, as usual, in the space between Eleanor's parking spot and the wall, grateful for the little extra protection one junker provided another.

Up the stairs, deliberately avoiding the elevator.

Sett would be in their library. Best to check there before going the rest of the way up.

She stopped in the doorway, the familiar pattern of clothing dropped from a disappeared form stalling her thoughts. She circled the desk, sweeping shards of broken mug out of the way and letting the rolling chair drag the skirt just enough not to stand on it. Still, it tugged at the bottom of her boot, stuck in some unseen way.

Whatever they had been reading had been marred with thick marker, ten words:

> Ratty
> Angelcorp did this.
> Find other Sett.
> I love you.

She folded the book shut, pulling her hand away to control the impulse that arose from it.

Couldn't just slow down for a day.

She knelt, leaving Sett's clothes as undisturbed as possible. The watch she had given them sat atop the pile of soft blacks and greys. She picked it up, examined the one cracked corner in the dim light, and fastened it around her wrist next to the newer, identical one she had picked out to replace it.

Then their laptop, slow to start, opened onto a PDF document. She skimmed through what was on screen.

Trans-Dimensional Transportation. **Project Rabbithole.**
Addendum Dated 2020/03/20 (corrected)

Thanks to the success of the Tower Project[1-4], Angelcorp now
has the requisite energy to begin testing the theoretical
framework set down by Director Eden Ross's team in 1981[5].
The first test of the Project Rabbithole has been an incredible
success.

Led by Director Ross, the Rabbithole team was able to
successfully exchange a test subject (henceforth referred to as
*subject*) with the adjacent universe with only minor setbacks
and minor damage to the device.

### Flaws With the Current Model

#### A. The Problem of Survivability

Angelcorp staff in the adjacent universe noted the immediate
death of the subject upon arrival[6]. Cause of death appeared to
be cardiac arrest. It is recommended that further test subjects
be pulled from populations not susceptible to death. A full list of
recommended subjects is attached in Addendum C.

#### B. The Problem of Equivalent Exchange

A genetically identical but visually distinct version of the subject
was ejected from the device once it was shut down. Angelcorp
staff in the adjacent universe confirmed following the test that
no party had been intentionally sent through their version of the
device.

A search for the transported party in the adjacent universe
revealed their disappearance in a manner consistent with
Project Rabbithole's prior testing[6-7]. Doctor Graves
hypothesizes that, in addition to the high energy and material

400

cost, an additional cost exists in that of the transported party[8]. His hypothesis states that the structural integrity of each universe is dependent on the matter contained within. Absence of even a single individual could have catastrophic effects on the structure of the universe, as observed in the AH (a.k.a. DM) of the adjacent universe[9].

Many members of the Project Rabbithole staff now believe this to be the reason that when an individual is transported from our universe into another, the instance of that individual native to that universe is transported to ours[10].

---

She scrolled to Addendum C.

---

J

*Jones, Fehlender*

Dr. Jones's research has been invaluable to the project. Even given her insubordination, the B.O.D. will not risk her life.

Update: January 27th, 2019. Director Ross has reopened evaluation of Dr. Jones's participation in the project[16].

[...]

V

*Vermington, Hanratty (either)*

We have yet to come to a satisfying conclusion on the source of Hanratty Vermington's immortality.

Hanratty Vermington (1998) is currently the single carrier of the failed R Parasite project[21]. The ERB has determined that it would be unethical to introduce the R

Parasite into another universe, especially considering the primitive and temperamental method of containment devised by the ASIC B.O.D.

Hanratty Vermington (1984) is an **extreme** flight risk. There is no telling what she would do if given access to a corridor between universes.

The use of either Hanratty Vermington also poses a significant structural risk to our universe, given the non-existence of a Hanratty Vermington in the adjacent universe.

*Vermington, Sapphomet*

Sapphomet Vermington is also a flight risk, though less so. They could be considered a viable test subject in the event that they were unaware of the test being performed on them.

Doctor Yoicksi believes the device could be modified to work agnostic of the subject's distance from it.

---

Only two other names she knew appeared on that list: Fern, disqualified for not technically being immortal; and Angel, disqualified for not technically being alive. She had seen Angel on her way in, took out her phone to text Fern, and stared at the blinking line in the message box.

God fucking damn it.

Her hands shook against the small piece of plastic, waning with each breath as the shudder was pulled into her chest, a far heavier piece of meat to move. Blood, probably Cane's, clung to the crux of her thumb, flaking off the fur where several hours under a motorcycle glove couldn't reach it.

The phone flew across the room, hit the corner of a safe, and dropped to the floor, dead.

"Fuck!" she snapped, realizing what she just did as she fell back into the seat. Another hard piece of plastic — Sett's — made itself known underneath her. She fished it out from the pile of clothes, feeling impossibly gross about doing so, and clicked it open.

4628, right? Right.

She pocketed it, just for emergencies.

Steph would know where Fern was. They stood over 13's suit, unaware of the fact that she had passed, glaring at a notebook laptop plugged into every port the machine had. She had begun to smell like must and sweat.

"Steph—" When she turned to look her eyes were wide, distant, trying to squint through the fog of her glasses. "Do you know where— are you high?"

"Fern's home, and yeah."

"They're okay?"

By way of an answer, Steph pointed to a screen running in the corner. At the very top, one highlighted entry read that day's date, some time early in the morning. Other than that, the door had not opened. That hardly proved anything, but it helped.

Her glasses had begun to slip down her snout, the frosted edge of the frames now splitting those wild pupils in half. As though she had forgotten something, her eyes darted to the floor, moving with her hand as she rooted around in her pocket. It produced something the size of a business card, wrapped in foil, and jabbed it at the possum.

"Helps me cope—" she re-answered the question from before, "want some?"

"No, not at all, thank you."

She shrugged, her watch pinged, she tore off a square of the paper and ate it.

"What's Project Rabbithole?" Ratty asked, watching Steph's eyes drift further out of focus. She took a moment to process that.

"How sick is it that I'm still like, young and hot?" She, mortal by all the standards that mattered, had aged about ten years in the past forty.

"Steph." Ratty refocused.

"Right! Sorry. So in the 80s, back when I was actually making new motherboards for AC and Kegawa, they — Eden — like, we had this night, and they basically figured it out. We called it the Tower Project because it was like, this process of trying to—"

"I asked about—"

"The Tower Project, I know. So, in order to travel between dimensions, you need a lot of power, and for some reason you need to be really high up. No idea why, you would have to ask Eden, and so after a few meetings with the Canada Lands Company — I kept going because investors and government people really like me, y'know? I'm like, that genius type of thing, like Iron Man... Elon Musk."

She turned back to her work.

"Elon Musk wishes he was me..." She stopped dead staring at the laptop.

"Steph?"

"What?"

"Tower Project."

"Right!" In the exact same cadence as before. "So, they basically kept saying no, right? They had that fucking bubble at the top of the tower that would have been— anyway." A pair of blinks signalled the death of that train of thought.

Once again, the possum prodded: "Stephanie."

"I'm so sorry, I completely lost my train of thought." As though they were discussing the weather.

"Angelcorp wanted to build a trans-dimensional thing inside the CN tower?"

"Oh yeah! Originally, yeah. But then like, they were so weird about it, we basically got clearance to do it as long as it didn't interfere with tourism, 'cus all you had to do in the 70s to drum up tourism was build a tall building. Anyway— am I repeating myself?"

Ratty stared at her long enough for that to pass.

"So, no. We wanted Ben's Bubble, y'know, and they said, 'NO! you can have anywhere where no one can see it,' which wasn't enough. So, I had this idea — mostly a joke — we could build an invisible kinda carbuncle thing on the hollowed out leg of the tower they gave us, and just use the elevator space they gave us to run a big fuck-off cable from the basement. That was the tower project."

"Huh." There was still blood on her boots, too. "Okay. I'm gonna go for a drive."

She turned to leave, stopped halfway to the stairwell.

"Let me know if Fern or Angel disappear, by the way."
"Yeah, for sure." Steph did not look up from her work.

Eleanor's was not a particularly good car for this kind of drive. The old suspension made it so that, even on a freshly tarred street, you could feel some thrum in the steering wheel. Going fast enough, a soft rumble was about as good as you could get this far north of the city. Every town, forgotten by time, slowed her to a bumpy crawl.

It'd been two-ish years since Ellen left their life. In those two years things were supposed to become normal. She was supposed to start feeling at home, or at the very least have a partner who made her feel less alone.

Ratty would never open up like that.

Maybe the city wouldn't either.

She let all of that stop as she rolled to a stop in her mother's driveway. Her head had barely cleared the door frame before being knocked back through it. A white rabbit with long, dirty-blonde hair.

"Oh my god! Eleanor! Hi!" This was Kassandra. Kass, to her friends. She knew — remembered — exactly how her step-sister felt about her, but had no idea what she did for a living. Behind her, waiting awkwardly for his hug, was Kass' twin brother, Casey. The phrase, *energetic problem causer* stuck out in her mind around him.

"I can't believe you got this thing working!" she started, "I told mom— your mom— like, she's never coming back, and this and that, and believe me I *tried*, okay?" Impossible to determine what that was meant to imply.

"What happened to your eye?" Casey edged into the conversation, more nervous than Eleanor remembered.

"My eye?" She touched it, feeling the artificial touch of her crushed-in white-patch. No one had mentioned it for so long that it'd slipped from the ghost's self-image. Kass stood up to punch her brother. She turned back to attempt a comforting smile. They stood in that uncomfortable triangle for just a half-second before Kass took charge once again.

"Oh my *god* has it been that long? Say hi, you doofus!" That was enough to get her to laugh.

"Hi, Kass." She swooped around the sibling she had already been hugged by to embrace her step-brother. 'Hi, Case."

"Hey Eleanor!" He had already begun to spin up his voice again. "It was so weird of you to never visit. I think so, at least. I've known Ratty for eight-ish years now and Kassie also works with her sometimes— why do you both dress like boys, by the way? It's not working, everyone can tell. You both have women's bodies, clearly."

"Whoa there, tiger." Kass cut him off.

"I'm here now." She squeezed her way through the rabbit.

"Well, yeah. That's what matters, I guess." He stayed even, having been brought back down. Behind him, a screen door protested yet another rabbit's reveal.

"Hey, mom!" Eleanor's other mother, Ma's wife, whatever. It had started as a running joke, pretending they were biologically related, and then evolved into just calling each other family. In retrospect, it was hard to understand what was funny about that.

"Knew you would be back." Her tight kiwi accent held a smug note.

"Where's Mama?" Eleanor asked, mounting the cement hunk of porch. Mom stopped mid-approach, dropping her arms as some ambient frustration crept in behind her eyes.

"She's in bed. Went in as soon as I told her you were coming." That was where Casey got his honesty from.

Well fuck.

That sucked.

"Aw, c'mon, don't look like that." Mom embraced her step-kid. "C'mon, we're still here, we gotta play some catch-up."

Trying her best not to be disappointed, Eleanor followed her family inside.

There wasn't much left to do but wait. Arriving in the late afternoon, Ratty parked her bike in the concrete gully around the tower, set her helmet on the handlebars, and sat. She never liked how the tower loomed over her — even as a kid visiting downtown, she would avoid looking up when she knew her dad's car was getting close. He came to visit, to take a break from the fake-hick life of working-from-home from the middle of nowhere, Ontario.

Today, she watched the sky and watched a geometric patch of sunset lag a few seconds behind the rest. That, probably, was the Tower Project, unless another megacorp had had a similar idea.

It continued in its predictable lag, pushing all thought out of the possum's head.

Odd, to have time set aside to think, and to want so badly not to. The intentional emptying of the head reflexively gagging on each thought to bubble to the surface. Like sleep without rest. All she could stomach was the occasional, *there's a train* as one passed behind her to the nearby station.

"Ma'am." The obvious voice of a cop shocked her from her coma. "Back away from the tower."

"I'm just waiting for my friend." She spoke up to be heard over the cotton over her mouth. She was already shaking. True, she wasn't technically allowed to park here, but she was not the centre of the officer's focus.

Wait,

"Ma'am, get behind me." She had passed into his periphery, his focus squarely down his gun's sights, centring a streak of grey and orange sliding down one side of the tower. She reached back, rested her thumb on her bike's starter as the creature launched itself from the occupied concrete slope. The cement below cracked as it slammed into the plaza.

"Police, stop where you are!" was the last thing that officer ever said. From the streak — it was a goat, grey fur — a thick bundle of rope tore through the guard's chest, ripping the life from his body. The streak turned, one bright yellow eye narrowing in on the possum.

They stared for a moment, pupil flicking around the possum, looking for something. Sett, definitely. The colour had left their fur, a deep, shaggy grey, shimmering in the wind as the few strands of white below changed places with their partners.

Short of eliminating the possum, or otherwise diving into her arms, it took off running, stopping only briefly to pull the gun from the officer's hand. Stunned for only a moment, Ratty threw her leg over her bike and took off after them, dropping her helmet in the plaza.

They dropped onto the tracks behind the tower, somehow at

the platform by the time Ratty's bike hit the tracks, down into the depths of the station before she'd gotten her bearings enough to follow. From behind, a few gunshots pinged off the rails. Another police officer found his partner's desecrated corpse and followed the tire tracks to gawk at an apparent terrorist zipping around on a motorcycle.

Which, fair. Just barely, but fair.

Best to get off before a train came, anyway. The possum tore off, wheels thudding against the tracks until they were fast enough to treat the rails as level, and dropped onto Lower Simcoe. Then up, around the corner, and into a today-abandoned piece of construction just large enough to hide her bike.

Far enough into the pandemic, the dimly lit cavern of Union's main hall was near indistinguishable from a normal rush hour. Going anywhere there was a chance the goat would pass through here, that Ratty would get a chance to talk to them, calm them down.

Probably why they made prisoners wear bright colours. A flash of orange at the other end of the hall, the same eye locked onto Ratty's for just long enough to be recognized, and they ducked through a tarp-covered door into the cold.

The possum held her breath, freezing the door just before it shut, and crossed the hall. City light leaked through the construction of blue plastic and fences, turning the orange jumpsuit a sick shade of grey. She approached slowly, half-swimming through the thick air, and gripped the goat's wrist. She let out her breath.

"Sett!" Her chest burned from the effort, stunned that she used to enjoy this feeling. The goat spun, ripping their hand free and levelling their stolen firearm at the possum's forehead. Their eyes flicked to the shadows of passers-by only when they were sure they could get away with it.

"How do you know our name?" the goat asked.

"I'm—" The question stunned Ratty, "I'm your partner." Slowly, she unhooked her mask from around her ear, letting it hang from the other, showing her whole face.

"Our partner is dead." Something welled up in their eye, the other blocked from view by the firearm, stamped down as hard as the goat could manage.

"What happened to your fur?" Individual strands of their original light-brown and white were almost entirely drowned out by dark grey, maintained only in one spot above their nose. The gun tilted with the light. The opposite eye was completely missing, a void that twitched between half open and half shut. "What happened to your eye?"

She put her hand forward to touch it, feeling something jump into her chest as Sett flinched with the gun against her head. "It — we— you should know." They glared conspiratorially. "Tore it down. We tore it all down for *you*." The last word came out like an accusation, a 'you're lying and I know it.'

The aging firearm rattled just inches from the possum's forehead, the goat's arm shaking with rage. Ratty let her gaze fall, took a deep breath, and tipped her head against the barrel. The rattling stopped.

"We don't belong here."

That's probably what made sense to say. For a long few moments, Sett's unseen eye searched the possum's face. On instinct, they stepped back and dropped their arm, keeping hold of the gun.

"We don't know what happened." Their tears welled over, freezing as they thinned on the rough fur. "It was over, it was all gone. We just woke up in a cage, and—"

"Hey, calm down." They had begun to ramble, drawing the possum in as close as her caution allowed. "You're okay. It's okay." They were small in her arms, "Let me take you home. We can warm up, you'll be safe."

---

There were still gaps in the ghost's memory. From the clearings she made — and there were quite a few big ones — she could push out into the fog and find something almost new. Her siblings, however, were intent on popping up in the middle of uncharted territory.

Stepmom had ordered pizza from the nearest town, the kind that they made in bars and therefore ranged all the way from the high art of *sauce and cheese on wet crackers* to *sauce and cheese on wet*. Still, it was nice. The familiar noise of home, Casey sitting quietly in the background, focused on some old-to-him new-to-her cart racer, while her Step-mother and sister talked her ear off.

"I remember—" Mom started, a few beers in and holding them quite well, "First time I met you, lil' runt... This was — I don't know how much you remember. I was a bartender at this resort. This was your mom's big trip for you, right? — and you come up — how old was she, Kass?"

"Two years older than us." The rabbit had taken a break from talking to kick her brother's ass.

"That's right, and you had just started high school... so this shit-dicked little 16 year old rocks up to the bar like she fucking owns the place— god, you were funny. What did she say again, Kass?"

"Dunno, mom," was the best answer she could muster through her focus.

"I'm sorry about my daughter, she's gaming." Mom waved a hand through the air as if to say "the youths, amiright?" Eleanor gave a long, faux-knowing nod.

"Anyway—" Mom started and stopped in the same breath, her eyes flicking to between Eleanor's tall ears as someone wandered in behind her. She turned, disappointed when her biological mother kept her eyes on her Stepmom. "Hey you!" Stepmom hadn't noticed, a little flirty in a way that was weird for a parent, but not for someone this tipsy. "Your daughter's been waiting to say hello."

Ma' stared back at her partner for a quiet, sad moment, before turning to the twins.

"Can you turn that down, Case."

"Sure thing, Step."

"Eleanor." She winced when it came time to acknowledge her own daughter. "Good to see you're still around."

"Yeah, for sure." It would have been impossible to say anything else. The three non-Sloth Bunnys (Bunny-Rabbits, potentially) shared a tense moment, the younger two willing their mother to intervene. Ma' bit down on her lip, gave a short nod, and turned to go back to bed before they finished negotiations.

"Wait— okay, El', c'mon." Stepmom stumbled through the ghost over the arm of the couch, trailing Ma' by a few feet into the hall. She was stopped dead by a slammed door, and crept back to the couch.

The pizza was entering the phase between too cold and not cold enough, evolving into a third form of wet rubber cracker mush. It came with some sodas, which was nice. Eleanor picked one up, struggling to grip it against the cold condensation.

"What's her fucking problem, honestly." Kass broke the silence.

"It's fine." Eleanor popped the tab, realizing too late that she had mistaken this for another brand in the dark. She sipped it nonetheless.

"It's really not. Do you want me to go talk to her?" Stepmom offered.

"No, I think like, I should do it, if anyone is going to."

The three waited for Eleanor to get up before Stepmom intervened with: "Are you going to?"

"No, I don't really want to." She tapped her claws against the can.

"Well then," Stepmom turned to follow her wife into the bedroom. What you could get this far north in terms of doors was either home-made or almost-cardboard, and the locals had been priced out of the former by the adjacent cottage country. Even hushed snaps made it down the hall, overpowering — as voices tended to do — the digital ambience of the cart racer.

"For what it's worth, I don't really care if you're dead or not." Casey earned another punch for that one, his sister's snap temporarily drowning out their parents.

"Casey!" Kass said.

"Like in a good way!" Casey clarified. "If I had your address I would come visit, or even your phone number."

"Oh shit, you don't have my phone number? Here, gimme a pen." Eleanor put a hand out, making a little writing motion as she set down her drink. Casey stared back at her, blankly.

"Why?"

"I'll write it down on something and then you can dial that, that's how—"

"Just put it in my phone, you fucking boomer." The rabbit giggled.

"Be NICE!" Kass hit her brother again. "Give her the controller, you've played—" She went silent as both moms rejoined the room. Stepmom sat back down on the couch, quietly avoiding Eleanor's eye, giving an apologetic glance when it was absolutely impossible not to.

"May I talk to you in private, Junie." Senior's clear tone drew Eleanor's attention. She looked up into her eyes for a moment, not used to being shorter, searching for whatever atlas of her mother's face she had lost.

"Yeah, sure Ma'."

Dead plants were not what Eleanor expected her mother to decorate her room with. Only on the edge of the west-facing windowsill nearest the glass had anything managed to survive. Everywhere else, life struggled to hang on in pots and trays that were too crowded, or visibly too wet, or otherwise struggling to hang onto life.

Mama sat on the edge of the bed, waited for Eleanor to sit next to her, and let out a long-held breath as her bed springs creaked under the pair. Back in, and back out again, settling the bunny's shaking hands. Not sure what to say, Eleanor waited for her mother—

"I killed your father." Eleanor Sr. said.

Oh.

"He was horrible— he did the kind of things no man should ever do, Eleanor. I think about—" the tide was dammed by whatever gunk had found its way into El' Sr.'s throat. "I think about you losing your memories and I think. I'm so sorry that happened, but there are things that I never wanted you to remember."

She swallowed some of that phlegm, her eyes fixed on the drywall. She continued.

"I'm your mother. It's my job to keep you safe, and happy, and healthy. I love you so much, please never doubt that, okay?"

She waited for her daughter to nod, and Eleanor did.

"I just— every time I see you, I'm reminded of all those years I had to live, alone, with this weight, and I look at—" It only became clear how intently Eleanor Sr. held her daughter's gaze when she broke it, her eyes falling from the dead white of her eye, following the Sloth family tear tracks to the diamond shaped patches on her wrists, to the white tips of her paws.

Some of the ash had been kicked from her fur. Her purple-black shimmered under the low light.

"I'm reminded, or I guess I learned that death is less permanent than I thought. I never wanted you to meet that man. I never— I thought— he hurt you so much that I thought, when you died, 'thank god she never has to know about that.'"

That broke Eleanor Sr. She collapsed where she sat, a hunched, deflated imitation of the Bunny family's last matriarch. She jumped, only slightly, as Eleanor wrapped her arms around her.

"I don't know..." Eleanor Sr. sucked air through her teeth, still refusing to sob. "I don't know. I am stuck with this guilt of... I just don't know."

There was no right answer here. Both Eleanors understood that.

"You never got caught?" Maybe that would be a bit brighter. Eleanor Sr. laughed through a sniffle, finally raising her arms to embrace her daughter.

"Oh god, the man was an idiot. Everyone knew he was gonna kill himself one way or another. I just sped the process along a little bit."

Eleanor refused to wonder what John Sloth had done. In time those memories would return, whether she wanted them to or not. The more time she spent with her mother, the higher the risk that something could bring them all back.

"I'm sorry." Eleanor Sr. murmured into the ephemeral fabric of her daughter's sweater. "I wanted to be there for you tonight. I really wanted to be your Ma' again. I'm so sorry. I really tried."

Eleanor hushed her mother as the shoulder of her hoodie took on water. Unseen tears bubbling away from the spectre's face, unconcerned with gravity.

---

Sett's thoughts ground to a halt as they fell, the impact of their knees against the hard tile sending waves up through their damaged body, thought the hole in their head. The opossum — she must've been an opossum — had already been forcibly evacuated from their mind, provable only in the way her fingers had smeared blood against the handle of an axe.

Only the void of memory remained: smoke and the smell of seared flesh with no visible burn. All the ways she didn't smile, everything her eyes weren't, every name that wasn't hers. She had never been so close to someone John made disappear.

"Glad that's over," he drawled, smoothing his fur as he lit a cigarette. "You should have made her your emissary. You kind of left her open to, uh, that." Some mirth escaped around the manufactured tube of paper and nicotine. He stared at the goat, gripped the back of their neck, and lifted them into the air. They wished silently that she had the courage — maybe the energy — to slip away from his grip.

"Shut up." They settled on vocal defiance.

"Oh this is fun, go on. Why don't we make a thing of it. You fall in love with some animal and we'll make a game out of pretending the two of you could ever beat me."

The ropes that bound them to the universe strained in search of something to latch onto. *Nothing* was a strange kind of down, and with a non-existent anchor they floated aimlessly, all the same dragging her into the ground.

"So what do you think? Another trillion years as my rape-meat? Just to make sure you hate me enough." A disgusting smile dripped from every word. He dropped them, sending a final, insulting ache up their wrist as it rolled on the axe's handle.

"I'll kill you." Sett's body tensed as their ropes pulled taught, coiling their body like a spring.

"Pardon me?"

"I'm going to kill every last one of you." The head of the axe went from the floor to seven feet in the air in an instant, taking a detour through the bottom of John's chin and knocking him onto his back foot.

Ropes shot from the floor, bound his arms mid-swing as gravity propelled the axe half of the way through his neck. It lodged in his spine, sticking in the marrow. Sett braced their hoof against his chest, dislodging the axe and throwing him to the ground in one motion. Their ropes kept him down, smoking the fur under their weave.

They pulled the head the rest of the way off, rope weaving between the two parts and stopping them from fusing. The breathless head contorted in a silent open mouth scream, Sett knelt next to the black mass of fur.

"I had something, John," they said, their voice coming out ragged, torn, tired. "She was the first thing that was mine."

They stood, bracing themself on the axe. She was a chance to do more than what they had been made to do. The blank white eyes glared up at them, a mixture of pleading, panic, fury. It didn't matter. That chance was gone.

"Can't... back..." the head hissed.

That was where it started. This new Sett's Ratty had been wiped out of existence, dragging the bond they had formed into non-being. A negative infinity in these terms was functionally indistinguishable from the opposite. Their power had surpassed every living, dead, or otherwise creature in their universe.

They were angry, and had no recourse but revenge. It was strange to think that the goat, shaking, wrapped around a bowl of soup in Ratty's living room, had killed every piece of the afterlife hierarchy, then spent 40 years in the void left behind.

That's what had happened to their fur.

They sat with their shoulders bunched, as though guarded against the possibility of being made to feel better. They hadn't stopped crying, had complained about a migraine when pressed. They asked questions, made to feel worse as they constructed a narrative of how their afterlife could have played out.

"So, that wasn't just— we're really not supposed to be here?" Sett asked.

"As far as I can tell, no." Ratty answered.

They considered that, set their soup down on the coffee table, sat back, and stared into the possum's eyes. Completely indecipherable. Made anxious by the prolonged stare, Ratty let her eyes fall to the floor, placing a hand palm up above the goat's knee. They looked at it, hesitated, and set their own hand in the soft palm.

A new wave of tears, completely alien on their blank expression. Of course, this couldn't have been permanent. None of this functionally mattered. They would be alone again if everything were to work out.

They pulled back, slipping once again into the cold. Their thumb was warmed only slightly as they drew it across their lower lid, stopping their tears, returning to comfort of solipsistic stoicism.

"Could we have a blanket, please," they muttered.

"Yeah, absolutely." It was easier to sit with themself when she left. They stared at the palm of their hand, the possum's residual heat still clinging to their fur. The blood of the gods shimmered below, a permanent stain on their skin. Had this always been an alternative? Just... quiet?

"If it's alright, after that, we would like to get some rest."

"Of course, yeah. You can take my bed." Ratty offered. Sett winced at the thought of being enveloped in her scent, not sure how they would cope with that.

"No, that's alright. We will sleep here." They patted the couch.

"You sure?"

"Yes." She had already gone through the work of bringing down a milk-crate of guest blankets, no point in spoiling that generosity. She set it down, went back to the kitchen, and returned with a chilled jug of water. She set that down next to the crate. "Thank you." The goat had no mechanism through which to drink. The possum had yet to notice.

She hovered there for a moment, not sure how to make an exit. It started with: "Are you going to be okay?"

"Yes, we're just, very tired, we think."

"Yeah." She let go of a long sigh, glancing around the room in an attempt to hide it. "Yeah, me too. I've had uh— one hell of a day, I think."

"We're sorry for any trouble we caused."

"No, not you. It's... I'll tell you tomorrow." She began to back out of the room. "I'm right here if you need me. Don't hesitate."

"Okay." Sett began to pull blankets from the crate, wrapping themself in one of the thinner options. They were not used to sleeping somewhere with this much weight, this much noise. Even the overhead fan — enough to mimic the cool ambient temperature of the void — was too loud to sleep comfortably under.

Even through that noise it was impossible to keep their mind from racing. The light-polluted dark of the apartment ebbed from around them as their exhaustion peaked, lending credence to the flickering nothings their mind had trained itself to produce. In an infinite void, with nothing for their eye to latch onto, it made things up to fill space.

This was different.

These were the soft, orange edges of subspace. This universe's subspace was still intact. Sett sat up abruptly, realizing where they were, that they had been allowed back. On the opposite couch, silhouetted in orange light, sat their reflection. Their fur had only just begun to grey, dusted by the void for the few hours they had been gone.

As they came to know each other, plane after plane collided into their shared perception. Earth's material plane, then Hell's, then — too loud for the goat to keep their ears uncovered — the unmuffleable impact bark of their ruined home.

The other Sett hadn't noticed.

They stood from the couch, crossed the room, and gently cupped the godkiller's cheek in their hand.

"You poor thing." They turned their head to get a better look at the missing eye. "Let me fix that for you."

They snapped from the vision as they hit the floor, having rolled entirely from the thin rail of couch. They checked their eye first as the phantasmal sight faded. Still gone. Disappointing. Ratty hadn't noticed the thud.

Sett stood, still wrapped in the blanket. The coffee table had moved a few inches to accommodate their fall, smearing condensation across the surface under the jug. It inched closer to their jumpsuit, abandoned on the adjacent seat.

Ratty had not closed her door all the way. She struggled to breathe in her sleep, choking as quietly as she could every few moments. Ignoring that, Sett crossed to the window. They dragged their claw through the dim blue light, checking at different angles to compare it to what they had just seen.

They didn't belong here.

Ratty would not have left the door open if she wasn't serious about her invitation. She wouldn't have left half of the bed unoccupied if—

"Ratty?" The goat was not used enough to speaking to make the wake anything but abrupt. The possum jumped, triggering the goat too to jump, pulling a sharp black rod from their corrupted subspace on instinct. They tried to hide it before she got her bearings, unsuccessfully.

"Sorry," she apologized, putting the shiv behind her back and disappearing it.

"It's chill, what's up?" The possum rubbed sleep from her eyes.

"We were made anxious sleeping alone in an open space." That was close enough to true.

"Didn't you— aren't you a godkiller?" The possum blinked up at the goat.

"We still have animal instincts, just like everyone else."

"Yeah, you're right, for sure." She stood, struggling to keep balance. "You can sleep on my bed and I'll—"

"You should stay here."

"I—" It took her a moment to figure that out. "Yeah, sorry, for sure." Gratefully, she slipped back under her comforter, snuggling back into her divot. Sett knelt on the edge of the bed, not entirely sure how to proceed. Ratty had already shut her eyes. finished adjusting so her pillow was not interfered with by her horns.

They curved so nicely, a pair of geometric corners signalling that this was not their original length.

"You and your Sett went through with it, then?" They wanted to touch them. One eye flicked open, centring the grey facsimile.

"Yeah, it uh— hurt. Didn't cry at all though, so that makes me... cool."

Sett stared down at her in silence for a moment.

"That was a joke," she clarified.

"Yes, we know." A touch of that cruel smile crept into the goat's tone. Their lack of reaction was also part of the joke. Tired, Ratty understood, gave a weak smile, and shut her eye again. Sett set themself down next to her, turning over the possibility of being held. "Ratty?" they prodded.

"Yes?"

"There's something you're not telling me."

She paused before speaking. "I'm trying not to process it. I've had a long day and I don't want to feel bad anymore. Not right now."

"We're dying."

"No—" She rolled onto her back, staring up at the ceiling. "In order to get my Sett back, I would— I don't know this for sure, but I think I would need to put you back in your own universe, and that's not fair."

Sett chose not to react. They took a moment to catalogue it before responding. "Yes, that makes sense." They rolled over, pressing their back into the possum's side as an invitation, half-forcing her into a cradling position. Their hand found a resting place in the waistband of her shorts, longest claw sitting in the very tip of the crease where Ratty's thigh met her pelvis. "Is this something you're comfortable with?" they asked.

Ratty stayed silent. Her breathing evened out as much as it could. They both, at that point, were too tired to think of something more to say, and so didn't. For a single, fleeting moment before Sett touched her genitals, she wondered if she was transgender in both universes. They let the night pass.

## 2020
## Home

Sett wandered out to the smothered smell of over brewed green tea under hot chocolate, draped in a raggedy grey hoodie they pulled out of a pile upon the realization that their scratchy prison-style underwear and pile of blankets were unsuitable garb for a functioning person. It smelled distantly like the possum, a small passive comfort.

Ratty went shopping in the early morning, something that — if memory served — she would have hated. It was not particularly useful to build a running case against her like this. It was entirely possible that she had changed in the 40 years she had been with the other Sett, and entirely possible that she was going out of her way because of the circumstances.

Evidence to this early morning trip sat strewn across a cutting board, too broad to be contained to a single plate. Hash browns, eggs, beans, bacon, sausage, near enough to make up for the years they had spent in self-induced starvation. It made them ache to look at. They put a hand through a hole in the hoodie, resting it against the sharp bumps of their rib cage.

"Good morning." They spoke loud enough to be heard over the vent and the possum's headphones. She smiled as she looked, first into the goat's eyes, then down to the college logo across their chest. Would anyone but her be able to so perfectly mimic that detail? The *I respect you enough to make eye contact, but respect myself enough to know my limits*?

"Morning!" A very specific kind of voice, too. Sett followed her eyes down to the logo. This was probably her hoodie.

"We apologize, this..." was on top of the pile? Looked comfortable? Smelled clean? "This was clothes."

"No, no, don't worry. It looks good on you." She pointed to a clear spot on the counter with her spatula, going back to work with her headphones dangling around her neck. Sett paused, processed the shape of the gap, and settled against it.

Ratty watched the bacon sizzle in her pan, comfortable with the goat's presence behind her. This was, to her knowledge, one of the only things this simple that she consistently had trouble cooking.

Still, it was the last piece of the puzzle. She laid it out over the paper towel, turned off the stove, the fan, and the screeching music leaking from her headphones, and felt something building in the other Sett.

"We would like to apologize for last night."

"Why's that?" She took down a pair of plates, a large mug, and a glass from the cupboard. From the oven, left on its lowest setting, she began with what had been left out the longest. Sett's sunny side up egg went on top of the hash browns, everything else circled around them if their taste had remained consistent across universes.

"I pointed a gun at your head."

"Oh, pff, that's nothing. You don't have to be sorry for that." She whipped a dish towel over her shoulder, setting the first plate in the oven to warm up slightly.

"I also put you in an uncomfortable position."

She stopped with her head half way out of the oven at this.

"What're you talking about?" She knew.

"You had to choose between sleeping—"

"That's, fine. I don't mind that." She stood up straight, spooning a half teaspoon of sugar into the bottom of the mug and pouring the tea over top. She knew she had over brewed it; the sickly colour confirmed that.

There were parts she minded.

The other Sett had missed her a lot.

It didn't matter.

"If it had been 'no,' I would have said no," she said, mostly into the mug.

"In any case..." They took the mug as it was offered to them, not entirely sure what to do with it, "We think it's time for us to go."

"Go?"

"Back to our universe." There was merit in the idea. The faster they found a solution, the less time Sett had to spend on the other side. Once everyone had been brought back, the machine could be destroyed, buying them some time before it was functional again.

There were reasons for this to be dealt with immediately.

Still...

"Here." Ratty retrieved Sett's plate from the oven, warm to the touch, and handed it to them.

"We don't eat." As much was clear through the holes in the possum's hoodie.

"I know, but try."

Ratty watched the goat's eyes, a bubble of anxiety forming in her chest as their hands stayed firmly planted within the hoodie.

"We're sorry, we really can't."

She stared down at the heaping plate, then at the cutting board behind her. That was fine. They had neighbours.

"For sure, sorry. I'll be just a sec, then." She left her plate, lifting the board and backing out of the room. The goat watched this balancing act, a distant guilt hovering behind their eyes.

Davy would probably be awake. 20 feet was not a long way to walk.

Back to their universe...

She knocked on the door, waited, listening to the movement within.

There was another way, probably. What Sett was asking for was to be sent back to an empty universe. The death of a single god

The goat's eyes fell to the full plate, stomach churning at the possibility of finishing it.

"Thank you." Best to be polite.

They turned to head towards the living room, the kitchen devoid of places to sit.

"Oh, wait."

She took a scalpel from the drawer, still in its plastic.

"Here, for your, uh..." She drew a smile across her lips with the crinkly plastic, flipping the knife handle-side forward and offering it to the goat. They stared at it for a moment, picturing the sensation of cutting a hole in their face.

"Does it hurt?"

"I—" her grip tightened on the knife as she thought. "I actually don't know. Sett never mentioned it, if it did."

She took a moment to assess why what she said didn't sound right before—"The other Sett, I mean."

"Yes, we gathered. Would you—" was there a polite way to ask for your face to be was politics, direct action. Failing moral goodness, it was at least commonplace. The death of all gods voided the universe of meaning. People would make their own.

She avoided the thought that the Sett in her apartment was as close as something came to a god where they were from.

She came back as Davy swung the door open. He had grown a lot since the last time they ran into each other, but they weren't particularly close, so that was to be expected.

"Oh, hey." He gave a polite, neighbourly smile.

"Hey, I made too much breakfast." She presented the cutting board, holding it at the edges so the kirin could scoop it up.

"Uh, fuck yeah? Absolutely." He did just that, backing into the doorway as he took on its surprising weight. "I'll bring your board back later, I guess?"

"I'll come and get it. Don't worry."

"Sick, thank you, Ratty."

"For sure."

Sett had not moved. In the same spot, they stood staring down into the mug. Ratty regretted keeping her own

sliced open? "Could you... help us?"

"Oh, yeah. For sure."

She pulled the goat along, some of that same comfort pushing through in the way they were set down on the couch, on the way her hand gripped their chin, on the focus in her eyes as the knife pressed into one cheek.

"So, back to your universe?" she asked, concentration compressing her voice into a thin line.

"Yes." Sett replied, careful not to move as they blood welled up through their fur.

"Do you think that's possible?" Her hand stayed steady as the goat winced. "Sorry—"

"Continue. Yes, we think it's possible. The absolute worst case scenario, we believe, would be you exchanging my corpse for your Sett."

The possum stopped below their nose, pulling back far enough to search their eyes.

"Why did you stop?" they asked.

"Do you want to die?" Easier to ask than to find out for herself. How best to phrase it...

"We are ambivalent towards the idea."

She stood still for a half-second longer before lifting the

plate, understanding that — if she was going to eat, it was going to be in front of someone who was not eating.

"It's not really fair to you, though, is it?" She didn't realize she was this mad until she said that out loud.

"It's more than fair," Sett's voice held almost too hollow to be heard. "The material condition of my universe is my fault."

"No, it's not, though. The system failed you and you tore the system down. That's how it's supposed to work."

Their eyes moved to consider the possum, searching for something behind her gaze.

"We suppose." They shrugged. "It's still fair for us to face the consequences of those actions, however righteous our motivations."

"There has to be another way."

"There isn't. I'm sorry, Ratty."

knife back to where she had left off.

"I'm sorry to hear that."

They let the morning silence make way for their thoughts. This was not their home. They were not the Sett built for this universe.

The knife actually hurt quite a bit. In the time they spent dormant, they had forgotten any form of pain that did not ache.

It was, as evidenced by this ritual, required any time they wanted to perform the most basic function of eating, what they were designed for.

The possum stopped.

"All done."

"I just put food in this hole?" They reached up to touch the wound as their chin was released.

"That's the idea."

They stared silently at their tea for a moment, watching a single drop of blood fall from their chin into the green.

"It is possible that I survive the escape."

"I know." Ratty nodded, letting her tired eyes lull shut. Sett avoided her face, feeling more guilt than they should have about the situation. They got up, crossed to the kitchen, and found one plate next to a missing cutting board.

"What did you do with the rest of the food?"

"I— gave it away? You said you didn't want it?"

"Did I?" The pair of memories devolved into double-image as each tried to remember. The goat's heart sank, realizing they had, while their lips were being cut open, begun to look forward to the food. It must've shown across their face because as soon as she confirmed it was missing, the possum turned to:

"You can have mine."

"That's alright, actually." They put a hand over their lips, their blood turning thick and black as it receded into the wound. How miserable. "I'd like to lie down for a bit longer, and then we can begin to plan our evening."

---

Something weird about a water bottle you got from a gas station, like you could taste the exact way it was poisoned. Actually, come to think of it... why not try poison, just to see how it tasted.

"Hey y'all," Eleanor made herself known in the makerspace, mouth still half-full of the mysterious clear liquid. "How'd the, uh, thing with the deer lady go?"

Not well, if the state of the room was to be believed. Fern stopped in the centre, a server-bank resting rolling between their hands, and stared back at Eleanor for a moment. Angel, lying in her nest, had been plugged into the deer's suit, herself lying in a foam-padded case.

"You two moving out?" she prodded, lowering the bottle from her face as she realized the deer herself wasn't there.

"We..." Fern tried to catch Steph's eye, the fox still too deep in focus to notice, "We can't be too careful."

"That bad, huh?"

"Yeah, uh — 13 is dead, and we don't know if they've been tracking her, so..."

So yes, they were moving out.

"How did things go with uh—" Their relationship extended about as far as the network security classes. That being the case, Fern was unsure where exactly Eleanor had gone.

"Uh, it was interesting!" There were precious few details she wanted to share at this exact moment. Still, an opportunity to follow up on something that was said: "Do I dress like a boy?"

"Yeah. You and Ratty both do." Fern said.

"Boymoders," was the only word Steph managed through their haze.

"Not that it works for either of you," they were quick to correct, "you just look like a girl who dresses like a boy."

Cool...

Interesting... fact...

Ahem, uh—

"Hello Eleanor!" The crackling of Angel's voice combined with the loud and sudden whir of her neck muscles startled Eleanor, sending the ghost back and the water-bottle forward in an instinctual move of ineffective self-defence. The plastic container rolls to a stop next to the robot's blanket.

"I'm broken!" For years her synthetic fur had hidden panel lines. Now, unable to shake it off, deep brown streaks of water damage had seeped into her bodywork, making all the more clear just how limited her range of motion was. She smelled like freight water seeped in whatever toxins floated overhead on rainy days.

"Water damage." Steph said two more words.

"I'm broken!" Angel repeated, visibly excited by the prospect.

"That's not good, buddy." Eleanor knelt to reach for her, curious just how damp she still was.

"Her fur is conductive, I really wouldn't touch her right now." Fern's hand slipped through the ghost's wrist.

Still, from this close, it was clear that something was gone from behind her visor. If there could have ever been anything there, Eleanor hadn't checked often enough to know. Now, the visor sat empty, clinging to consciousness by a few loose wires.

"Where's, uh—"

"Oh that's another thing, Sett is in another universe, Ratty is upstairs with the Sett that came over from that other universe." Fern explained, too exhausted to put in their voice what a clusterfuck that was.

Eleanor fell back to her haunches, staring at the robot, wondering if they would ever be able to keep up with that.

"I missed a lot."

"Yeah, kinda."

"Huh." She struggled to feel anything about that. "Anything else?"

"I'm broken!" Angel repeated.

"Okay!" Eleanor stood, abandoning the water-bottle in the pile of junk that had accumulated in the move. "I'm going to... go... to bed."

"Ratty will probably want to touch base with you, FYI." Fern called after the rabbit.

"I am sure she will," Eleanor replied, not turning around on her way to the elevator.

An uninteresting ride.

She dropped her keys onto the pedestal, landing them as close as she could to the centre of the plastic crown that'd made its home there. Another one of Ratty's little gifts, packaged when she first got it with a framed newspaper, **Notorious B.I.G's Plastic Crown Stolen after $600,000 auction sale** in bold letters across the top.

A joke, probably.

Her mask hovered comfortably above the faux gold spikes, a far more interesting feature of the obelisk now that it was not relegated exclusively to lifting a cheaply printed piece of plastic covered cardstock. It really was a nice carving. There was a universe, probably, where Ratty was an artist.

Then the other mask, next to her keys, a piece of cloth between two elastics. It was just there in case she wanted to duck into a gas station on her way home for, say, a bottle of water.

Food would be nice.

She took something frozen made of bread and meat and set it in the microwave.

So that was it, huh, Eleanor?

She watched whatever it was spin in the dim yellow light.

The last big mystery of her life, unravelled. Was it satisfying? The mundane realization of matricide felt like a shock-secret, like the kind of thing someone said when they were trying to be vulnerable but didn't know how, and so chose instead to reveal something massive and startling.

It turned out to have nothing to do with her curse. She was actually selected at random to go through metaphorical hell, and for no reason.

Something fell on the other side of her room. A plant pot, rolling across the floor, torturing the little bundle of baby vines as it spun out of control. The meat and bread (maybe cheese, too?) sat abandoned in the microwave as Eleanor investigated.

She sat the pot upright where it settled, no greater authority on where it ought to sit than it was, and stared at the place it sat. The ledge was not wide enough for the entire bottom of the pot, but it should have been more than enough.

"This you, Ellen?" she asked the ceiling. No response.

She took out her phone, opened Alf's contact, and sent him a text.

✉ 2:12am: **New Message** — Eleanor:
"where r u?"

The phone went to her coffee table, and she settled on the couch.

With Ellen's death she had stopped being the centre of anyone's life.

She was not welcome in her parent's home, for a reason outside her mother's blame.

Her life had become boring.

Her phone buzzed. On the screen:

✉ 2:14pm: **New Message** — A:
"Old apartment, y?"

---

"Hey," The possum's voice didn't sound like it was built to wake someone up gently. In actual fact, she didn't — but it seemed to Sett like the kind of thing where the thought counted. "Are you busy?"

"We were sleeping." That was a lie, but they had been trying to.

"Okay, well, yeah. I know, but—" something about the way the other's gaze landed must've put her off her rhythm. How tragic, they thought, that this version could not even enjoy the peaceful end to a nap. "I wanted to show you something before you leave."

Deliberately reserved, Sett took a moment to weigh Ratty's proposal with the benefits of sleeping for another hour. There would be plenty of time for that afterwards, and so they rose from the bed that was not theirs. They considered the outstretched hand, another moment of weight, conscious as to hold their face in a position that gave nothing away, and took it in their own.

Too many doors outside, they thought. Too many exits and entrances. With the road surface as it was, someone was liable to get hurt.

"We gotta hurry, but we should be able to—" They were yanked suddenly out into the street, a halfhearted honk and the ineffectual bell of a streetcar presenting themselves as the road's only means of defence. Wordlessly, Ratty led Sett up the back steps of the streetcar, one of the last in circulation where one could be missed sneaking on, no doubt.

"It's a little late to be going—"

"I know, I know. We can postpone for a day if we need to, I promise this is important."

So they stayed. They would need to postpone their escape plan until the next stop to leave at this point, and the energy to do such a thing simply did not exist.

They instead settled in next to the possum, who had already sat to occupy a deserted red bench. She reached around the goat's back, gripping the metal rod that held their seat in place. If they had asked, perhaps Ratty would say something about safety. Perhaps she would retract her arm, that odd lump of fur that gave the chair some facsimile of a headrest, and so Sett did not ask.

They watched the possum's tail — too long to smush into the seat like Sett's — lazily flick across the goat's shoes on the floor where it was folded. "Have you ever had bulgogi?" she asked, looking right at them. Her tired eyes quietly focused on their own, amplified by the black of the face mask she wore. That was an adjustment. They really should have been wearing one any time they left Hell — the demonic immune system being near antithetical to the mortal one.

"We're not sure what bulgogi is." they replied.

"That's okay, it's really good. We can maybe order some if they're still doing delivery."

Sett nodded quietly, not entirely following. It was simply nice, in this moment, to be sitting with someone.

Ratty got up abruptly as the overhead chime indicated another stop. Sett had perhaps lapsed in consciousness briefly, and found themself staring out the window onto a vista of parking lots that cornered on other parking lots. The only distinguishing landmarks were an obnoxiously sized red-brick factory, and across from that a small strip of stores.

They walked, the possum with a climbing air of excitement against the heavy snowflakes, until a quiet storefront, its glass painted with a bright green leaf.

"Okay good, she's still here." she mumbled, pushing through the door with a chime.

"Miss Ratty!" a cat behind the counter threw her arms up in greeting.

"JC!" she responded, a sudden social butterfly. "How's everybody? Everyone keeping six feet apart?"

"I try, I try." The cat — JC — gave a faux "customer service" frown.

"Well, you let me know if you ever need someone to come knock some heads together, okay?" That branch of the conversation died unceremoniously.

"Listen," Ratty picked up on another path, "Do you still have the key to Sett's apartment?"

"Are you here to snoop?" they prodded, an eyebrow cocked.

"I dunno," Ratty turned back to the other Sett as if to say, "look who's here." "Are we snooping?"

"Oh, Captain Sett! I'm so sorry, I didn't see you there! What happened to your fur?" Distracted, JC tossed Ratty the keys from under the desk.

"They—"

"Accident." Sett cut Ratty off, deliberately turning their eye in the opposite direction. "Magic accident. Our apartment downtown is full of smoke."

"Aw, you poor thing. You two head upstairs, I'll try to keep things quiet down here."

"Thank you."

"I actually—" Ratty had already pulled out her cell phone in the gap and done... something. "I have a delivery coming later, if you could just text me when it gets here?"

"For sure,"

With that, the pair walked out of JC's life.

Despite ostensibly owning it, Sett — at least this one — had never stepped foot in this apartment. Despite that, it was full of eclectic life. A bedroom with a hot-plate and a bathroom with no door, the other Sett had not felt the need to restrain their clutter in this space. Pride in place, below an overlapping collection of various flattened taxidermy, sat a small pile of obvious fakes, the kind you could get in natural history museum gift-shops.

For the briefest moment, as she stood at the top of the stairs to de-mask and un-boot, something about Ratty resented that. Two strangers stood in an unfamiliar space for a half-second, then — without ceremony — Ratty began rooting through cases.

"I'm pretty sure— we got an electrician in and they got really paranoid about fire, and so they moved— unless they got rid of it, but they wouldn't— ah!" She pulled a case from under the bed, set it down on the perfect sheets, and clicked it open.

Sett's first instrument on Earth. Ratty had helped them pay for it, way back when they were still waiting for their first grant to come in. It took every penny they had, still couch-surfing at that point. The other Sett could not have known how much this instrument meant. To them it was just a cheap looking banjo.

"Here." Ratty sat with the odd little object in her lap, and patted the thin mattress next to her. Sett sat, regretting that decision almost immediately as the possum tried to pass the banjo to them.

"We don't know how to play that." They raised their hands far out of the way as it landed in their lap. The possum paused, still gripping the instrument.

"You knew how to do this before—"

"I knew a lot of things 'before,' Ratty. There were a lot of things I had to give up." The instrument was not necessary for revenge. It was a hindrance.

"Well," she let go, leaving the familiar weight alone, "can you try?"

They set their claws down along the neck, wincing as the cold of the frets clashed with the soft underside of their keratin fingers. Their right hand slid into position above the drum, and they began to play: no rhythm, no melody, just a simple scale to remind their hands of the way they ought to move.

In the periphery, the possum pulled a thin pamphlet from a hidden compartment in the case. She knelt before the goat, flipped it open on the floor, read a half-paragraph with her neck tilted all the way down, then looked up and began to fumble for something just in front of Sett's chest.

It did not come as easily to her as it would have to them, but from the dim air Ratty pulled a thread. Black and dripping, it stained their fingers like old ink to hold.

"Just give me this bottom string for a second?" Ratty asked, already loosening the saddle. Sett complied, quietly shocked by how easily their playing changed to accommodate the gap. The possum split her focus between a weave diagram in the pamphlet and the position of the goat's hands, timing her moves as not to interrupt.

She stood back as it was finished: as the string left its tuning peg, it made a sharp detour down the neck of the instrument, fused as it wrapped around each stop on the fretboard.

"Okay, now— wait." She stopped the goat's playing. Before it was obvious that they had disappeared to begin with, a pot of water sat warming on the hot-plate, and the possum had returned with a clumsily-rolled cigarette.

Sett, now barely smiling in spite of themself, poked open their mouth with their pinkie-claw just enough to perch the cigarette on their lips, wincing as that morning's scab was reopened. "This is all I can do," They gestured bashfully to the banjo in their lap.

"Just try it, don't think about it." The possum rocked back onto her haunches. Purely humouring her at that point, Sett took their hands off the instrument for a half-second to wrap a hot thread around the tip of their cigarette and take a drag. Then, prepared for the worst, they began to play.

A simple chord to begin with. It resonated up through their chest, filling it suddenly with warm air. They watched as the ink splattered drum slowly faded from black back to white. Hollow and discordant, the bottom string rang out in protest at first.

They began to pluck along that same chord, the bum note slowly coming into alignment with the other four. Not changing, per se, just sounding differently, as though the lopsided pieces had turned in such a way as to reveal their hidden interlock.

"There you go." The possum's eyes lulled shut.

Emboldened, Sett let their instincts pick each note intentionally, pulling a melody out of the practice. Almost in union, the possum began to bounce her knee as the goat stomped the heel of their hoof. They followed as Ratty sped up, the black string slowly unblunted as it kicked off the gunk. Full and sharp and warm, the discord evolved now into an intentional dissonance, like an anguished voice screaming from within the din.

Ratty caught their attention as she began to whistle along: her goofy grin, her beautifully tired eyes, yesterday's eyeliner still smudged across her face. She was certainly less suave than Sett had originally imagined, but then again nobody was that suave. Her eyes searched the goat's cheek, stopping along the individual grey furs crossing the border into the black tip of their snout.

Light trailed up from each note, winding its way through the rope burns around the goat's wrists. Sparkling and technicolor, the warm smoke in their chest caught fire, and in an instant there was peace in their rage. This is what revenge was supposed to feel like. White-hot, they wanted nothing now but to play, to stomp, to be in this moment with a good memory.

Then a knock came at the door, and they were knocked out of that focus. They jumped, pulling a knife from subspace as soon as their own thread cleared the last eyelet. JC stood halfway up the stairs, a takeout bag in one hand. They stared at the knife, confused for only a moment before settling on something in their head.

"Sorry, am I interrupting?" she asks.

"No, you're okay." Ratty smiles and takes the paper bag, setting it down next to herself on the floor of the small apartment. "Thanks for bringing this up."

Sett had set the banjo aside without thinking. They sat now, stunned, staring down at their empty hands, and crying softly. Ratty stopped in the entryway, taking a moment to process what's happened with her back turned before diving to her knees.

"It's okay!" Ratty scooted forward, her voice an excited whisper. "You did really good."

"I'm sorry," they repeated as the possum set her hands in theirs, "I'm sorry, I'm not staying. I can't stay."

"Sh, sh, sh, I know. It's okay." The possum knelt up between the goat's legs, pulling their head into the crux of her shoulder. "Just enjoy this, right now, while it lasts. I'm here right now. You don't have to think about tomorrow."

Redesigned originally to be worked on in massive projections, the blueprints for Angelcorp's leech-base had to be rolled out in a pair of industrial sized posters, printed off at Fern's shop and carried all the way from Chinatown to her apartment in a battery of four streetcar seats. Suddenly obsessed with order, Angel had almost entirely deconstructed their nest and folded the component parts neatly in a corner. That floor space was graciously taken over.

A package of markers picked up on the way home, and the congregation gave the impression of four supervisors watching two toddlers — one of whom was coming down from a several day long psychedelic bender — drawing on the carpet. Ratty had taken point with Steph, the only two who had anything to contribute in this particular situation.

This Sett lacked the planning experience. The majority of the damage they had done in their universe happened over the span of one bad weekend, entirely improvised, spurred on by overwhelming power and revenge.

Eleanor had yet to decide whether or not they were even coming, though they would likely have to, considering how vulnerable the most immediately available among them were to dying.

Ratty had no choice. Between lacking the brainpower to cope, lacking the emotional depth to cope, still working on the mental avenues to coping,' and simply not coping, Ratty was the de facto leader.

She stood up from her work as Steph froze in place, stuck either trying to dig up or process a memory, and addressed the girlfriend she had continued to neglect. Circumstances sometimes made that kind of thing hard not to do.

"You doing okay, El'?" she asked, the other Sett, idly weaving some string between their fingers, was too focused on their own internal dialogue to care about having been left out.

"Uh, yeah, I dunno." She shrugged, chewing on a nail. "'Maybe' is my official answer."

"Do you want to talk about it?"

"Later." She nodded. "When we get back, I guess."

"For sure." She went from there to Sett, their gaze meeting for just a moment before the goat was re-distracted by their thoughts and their possum by the tangle of black wires between their claws.

"Steph," Ratty started, her eyes fixed on the tangle, "I'm pretty sure I just had an idea." She fell back to her knees, crumpling the paper under her weight, and picked up a black marker, drawing the other two in closer with a gesture. "Here's what I'm thinking..."

# 2021
# Not Dead

Tedious, to say the least, as the elevator rose through the tower. Designed for more than four people (three if you didn't count the operator and two if you didn't count someone incorporeal), the tour guide's speech echoed off the walls. She ran through the 56 second script the same as she must have done hundreds of times per day, a visible patch of condensed breath staining her CN Tower branded mask. The city shrank below them.

*The city* was a misnomer, Ratty thought, her forehead rattling against the glass. Here was mirror finished corporate buildings and tourist traps, the most cultured of which included the rustic charm of a Tim Hortons. On the roof of the building next door, two sharks made of contrasting tile swam in perpetual circles.

Funny to think that 450 species of fish had been transplanted into the downtown core, in the middle of a city where they didn't belong. Torontonians had the privilege of commuting for an hour within the bounds of their own city for a job that paid them less than what they needed to survive, keeping alive the animals that entertained the children of those mirror-tower businessmen (themselves transplanted from cushy suburbs).

It used to do all of that. Now it sat empty, just the fish and their caretakers. The lights never turned off at night.

As though it had been recorded to do so, the guide's speech ended just as the chime above her head went off. Ratty — barely paying attention — took a pair of crumpled bills from her wallet and handed them to the guide. Confused, she pocketed them.

Days before, Ontario had hit its peak of new cases. From the observation deck floor, you would never have been able to tell. As hard as they tried to obey the six-foot rule, there were those with no sense of the crowd, who did everything they could to be an obstruction.

"This is probably the only time you're gonna be able to get into this building, Rigby." Ratty looked up, then down at her girlfriend. She had, for some reason, sunken herself a few inches into the floor. "If you wanna, y'know..."

She shouldn't be on eye level with Ratty, and so popped back up to her full height before answering.

"Am I like, lessening the gravity of the situation if I go gawk out a window?" Eleanor looked around Ratty at Sett, themself too absent to have an answer, then back at Ratty.

"Might as well." The possum shrugged. "Here." She took Eleanor's hand, dragging her through a third of the tower, up to a perfectly clear, distantly familiar spot.

"Okay, so." She pointed out the window, searching the tip of her finger for... "Follow the train tracks there right out over the bay. Straight that way. That's just about where I grew up."

"I thought you grew up—"

"Well, yeah but you wouldn't be able to see that from here."

Eleanor squinted through the fog, more out of courtesy before reporting back, "I can't see anything that far out."

The possum laughed at that. "Yeah, I know. I dunno, this is just what my mom did the first time she brought me here... Uh, what else is there."

"Where's Oakland?"

"Oh, shit, it's actually like— same general direction, I think. Let me look that up."

Once again Eleanor stared out into the distance, as though she would better be able to see her city than Ratty's. Even on a perfectly clear day it would have been behind the Earth's curve, and there were vanishingly few clear days.

"Okay, so..." The rabbit stumbled slightly as Ratty yanked her sleeve, pulling her a little ways along. "If the internet is to be trusted, it should be straight out from..." She dragged Eleanor to stand in front of her, putting both hands on the taller woman's shoulders as if calibrating her within that extra fraction of an inch was going to make a difference. "Here."

For the third time, Eleanor tried to see past the fog, maybe catch a glimpse of the smoke that'd risen chronically from her home state for the past several months. Still nothing. She let her eyes go unfocused, catching fingerprints on the glass, and tried to feel it.

Maybe the heat.

Maybe something else.

Still, nothing.

"Sorry."

"Nah, don't worry about it." Ratty knocked her head against the ghost's shoulder. "I didn't think so anyway."

Eleanor stood still for another few seconds, chewing on something.

"What's dying like?" she asked.

Between the two of them, Ratty had gone through more of the process than she had. The deepest Eleanor had been in the afterlife was pre-purgatory. She had been careful not to go any deeper.

It was hard to keep eye contact and think about that. First to the floor, then over her shoulder to check on wherever Sett had gotten off to. The goat had become fascinated with their own section of the window, small against the rest of the crowd. Noticing her looking, they turned and gave a tired smile through their wholly unnecessary mask.

Hard to put off answering something like that when you were trapped in a bubble.

"It's like, getting arrested, I think." That was as close as it got in the living world. "It's violent, and confusing, and scary. You think, 'well, my life is over.'" She struggled not to enjoy such a literal connection. "A lot of the time it is... but, you and I are proof that there's still justice, right? We're not dead. Sett's not dead. A bunch of our friends are 'not dead'—" She put extra emphasis on the words, implying an abnormal form of 'not dead.' "—'Cus we still had shit to do.' Then there was everyone else. "A lot of people die with shit still to do," she tried to finish the thought. "I don't know what to say about them."

Eleanor nodded in the direction of her burning city.

"I think I'm gonna head home after this," she said.

"Yeah?"

"Yeah." Her nod stopped. "Go live with my uncle or something."

"You want me to come with you?" Ratty asked.

"I'd rather you didn't, actually." Not a lot of ways to say that that didn't sound insulting. Ratty understood, though. "Not yet, I mean. One day, but... not yet."

"For sure." Ratty couldn't have said exactly what she was feeling at that moment. "You're not gonna die today, by the way."

"You might."

"Pff— yeah, okay." The idea was still so impossible to her. She punched Eleanor's shoulder for that, whiffing the spectre entirely as she turned. "Where's Sett?"

"Over here." The location came through subspace, just barely around the curve.

"Hey." Ratty sidled up as though the goat next to her was not a completely different person. "What're you looking for?"

"The apartment building," they answered flatly.

"Our building?"

"Yes."

Silently, the possum's own eyes joined the search, following roads she knew to lead home. "There." She pointed, following those same roads out to the nearest visible landmark. "See that little square of green space?" Sett nodded next to her. "So that's Alice Gardens. If you follow the street that goes up the centre directly south, it's—"

"Oh! We see it." They clicked a pen, wrote down near Alice Gardens on their palm, and backed away from the window to let someone else look.

"What if it's not called the same thing when you get home?" A few things had been like that between Ratty's two universes.

"Well, we will just have to remember 'south of the green space,' we suppose." Something about the other Sett shone through in the face they made. "Shall we get moving?"

"No use putting it off." Ratty said.

Another elevator.

Absent of anything else to say, hating the silence, she complained.

"God, this shit is fucking expensive."

That didn't help.

Everyone looked at the tour guide, the tour guide looked up at Ratty.

"Sorry." Ratty muttered.

"No, I mean, you're right," because what else were they supposed to say?

Something about the extra altitude kept this part of the tower mostly empty. Weirdly dark, too. The lights might have been motion activated, or might have just been kept low for some other reason.

With only one person available to enforce it, each in their own time adjusted to flouting the single aluminum guard rail. Ratty ducked underneath, pressing her face against the tilted glass in an effort to see down through the tower's ceiling.

"Here!" Sett was the first to see it. As the sun began to set, that same part of the sky — now pretending to be the city below — refused to set with it, holding onto the grey-blue of winter just a fraction longer.

"Alright, ready?" Ratty had already backed as far from the glass as she could go, shimmying her harness out from underneath her hoodie.

"We would like to submit that we hate this plan."

"Yeah, well, we're already up here." She gestured for Sett, took the length of corrupted subspace rope from their claw, and wound it through the warm loop. It stuck to her fingers, sliding easily through the barely-damp metal. The goat took a moment to come to terms with what was about to happen, and backed into the possum's arms. Their boots fit snugly in a spare loop.

"Uh, sorry folks, what's—"

That made things awkward. It was wholly unnecessary to traumatize an employee like this, but Ratty had already started running.

Boot on the safety rail, up, over, and down.

She stopped time just before her boots hit the glass, pushing through the thick air until they made contact.

She let go, freezing the shock wave in the rubber soles, shattering every piece of glass in the room at an effective 299,792,458 miles per second.

and down,

and down,

and down.

The goat's head snapped to attention, searching the rapidly rising buildings for a point where they could be guaranteed to lock onto the leech-pod.

Eleanor trailed behind them, her legs falling to smoke in the late winter air, not sure how she would catch them if this failed.

With a crack, their rope joined the universe's, launching itself from a higher piece of the tower.

The fabric of her harness strained as the sharp drop turned into a curve, apparent enough through the rest of her body that the goat in her arms dug their claws through her fur and into her skin.

All the more difficult to hold her breath, to turn into the wall, to shield the other Sett. There was no way through without putting a hole in the wall.

Coated in black tar where the rope had splattered it, the wall slammed into Ratty's back. It began to crack at her spine, caving under the force, shattering more of her than they had intended.

"Fuck!" She seethed insofar as her crushed lungs would allow. Another "Fuck!" screamed into the back of her teeth as the impact smeared her across a block of offices.

A few people stood up when their desks shifted.

---

"And, uh..." the possum mumbled, clicking the cap back down onto her magic marker. "If it goes like that, we should be... fine... I think."

---

"Oh my *god,* that hurt." It was all she was capable of to announce it, not to sob into the foam ceiling panels, as strings of flesh crawled their way into what had once called themselves her tail. Sett stood, no worse for wear save for a few scratches along their forearms where they had come closest to the edges of the hole. They knelt, pulling their wire from the harness and spinning its tip into a needle.

They turned Ratty over, another crackle of pain stopping her regeneration. They ignored it, laid into the crush wound with their rough piano wire, and pulled the bones in her back together as though lacing a corset.

One last "*FUCK*" muffled into the carpet, and the air was still. Whatever had begun to work its way up her throat was swallowed, and she stood.

Sett did not stand with her.

Eleanor, who had been watching from a few feet away, did

not shift her gaze.

Her form, arguing with itself, vibrated between the ground and her standing position.

Hello, Hanratty." He stood in plain sight, not ten feet away from her. Hard to place, middle aged, well kept white fur. She had heard the voice before, though. "I thought it best to skip our usual formalities."

"You're Handler Smith?" Time stood still. She was not the one doing it.

"I realize now may not be the best time for a heart-to-heart, but— well, I don't think we're going to get another opportunity." His voice was different in person, struggling to balance breathing with swallowing spit and speaking. "I'd like to speak to you in person, if you have time. The transformer room. Come see me and I will allow your friend safe passage through Project Rabbithole."

He flickered for just a moment, and was gone again.

---

[a man in a navy blue suit and grey overcoat stares into the camera]
[one hand, gloved, his holding a microphone with a red logo on the cuff]
[the other is pressing something into his ear]

"So, we just arrived here on the scene, as you can see around me the tower is currently being evacuated, police are keeping us back from the actual entrance. If you look—"

[he points towards the tower]
[the camera swings up, focusing on what looks like a hole in the sky]
[from this distance, only when contextualized by the zoom lens, were individual forms visible]

"There's something that looks like some kind of black spot suspended in the middle of the sky, we're not sure if this is a weather phenomenon or— well, we're not sure exactly what it is. Staff is telling us the spot and the tower are unrelated. What we—"

[a deafening bang blows out the microphone]

"Oh my goodness, okay—"

[the man puts a flat palm against his ear, now less holding in the piece and more trying to comfort the drum closest to the blast]

"Get a— get a shot of that."

[he gestures as well as he can with the microphone]
[the camera pans up again]
[areas of sky around the black spot have exploded into sparks, making it larger. The edges burst into flame]

"So, sorry, say that again?"

[the presenter turns away from the camera, trying to catch more of what his earpiece is saying]

"We're receiving— okay we're receiving word that the surrounding buildings are also being evacuated. Still no idea what this thing is— don't look at me, look up there— you can see… what appears to be a ring of fire. As well as— those look almost like smoke clouds but it's hard to tell from this distance… they're very, almost, I would say square-looking, but —"

[a police officer taps the presenter on the back and says something inaudibly]

"Okay? Okay. For sure. So right now we are—"

[the police officer gets a little aggressive with the shoving]

"We are being asked to move to a more secure site, we will be staying on the scene, keeping you posted as we find out more about this thing."

Angel's voice lit up the heavily damaged earpiece (really just a pair of headphones), garbled until she could zero in on their exact location. There had been no one in their office landing-zone to offer anything but eerie eyes, following the still limping possum and her crew into the stairwell that connected above to below.

"The transformer room is at the bottom of the machine, Project Rabbithole is at the top." The robot's voice surged to be heard over the interior rattle of the machine. Sett turned for an explanation, Eleanor already checking the next hallway.

"I didn't know you knew that."

"Did you plan on telling us?" Sett asked. An ache shot through the possum's still-healing body as she crumpled under the small amount of guilt.

"It was loud outside, I—"

"I have already 'run the numbers,' Sett. Handler Smith has requested a meeting with Ratty in exchange for the use of Project Rabbithole. It is in our best interest that he get it." Angel cut her off. Sett glared at Ratty, trying to read any ill will out of her expression. When the worst she gave up was some quiet, self-destructive curiosity, they instead ordered the possum — silently — to come see them before they had to leave.

"Of course." Ratty nodded, resolute. "Wouldn't miss it."

"Okay." Their eyes fell to her chest, turning the words over in their mind. Without finishing the thought, they turned to lead Eleanor up the stairs. Ratty took a moment to make sure they weren't interrupted, and went her own way.

She gave the first guard as wide a berth as she could manage in the narrow corridor, set on edge by the way they pretended not to see her. It was almost too familiar, having been on the other side of that empty gaze in another life.

She felt, without touching them, the exact way the Deepwater uniforms pushed her fur in the wrong direction. How many of these men were here against their will. She stopped to ask,

"Why are you here?"

The one she singled out blinked, clearly not used to being spoken to.

"The salary is well worth it," he answered.

How the fuck do you respond to that?

"You realize you're a monster, right?" she prodded further.

"I have a family to provide for." Not even the kind of monster to take an active role...

"You— there are other jobs." That line was always hard to understand. "I have a family to provide for," as if this was the only thing in the world he was capable of. As if you couldn't put bread on the table any way but standing by to end a life at the whim of some rich elderly.

He began to sweat as the possum refused to break her line of sight, toying with the idea of staring at anything but the ceiling as his heartbeat thrummed against his neck.

She wondered what they had been told about her: the undead creature who — from her perspective — had killed someone for the first time less than, what, two years ago?

"Alright, well—"

The sudden noise elicited a sharp "Move along!"

"Yeah, I know, I'm moving along."

It was not weight efficient to build walls between every single room. Towards the top of the leech, the stairwell broadened into an engine room, no clear delineation between them. The closest it came were a pair of observation rooms, hanging off the steepest part of the wall, the sharp edge drawing a line between the two.

Four white metal columns rose from the floor, one so hot that it had begun to kick off its paint in flakes. The sound of machine work was inescapable; grinding even from the corners of the room that were not supporting the pod's open wound.

"Could we have some privacy, please?" His voice rose above it all, older than it had sounded minutes ago. It called all attention to the centre of the room. At their own pace, everyone in the room stopped to look either at Eden, or the person closest to them who had stopped. No mind control, just intimidation. Several among them had the sense to start running.

Handler took a moment to savour the empty air, still tinged with the scent of heavy machinery, before speaking.

"A beautiful construction, isn't it. Rabbithole — and I must confess I never liked that name — it is powered by our tether to the ground, but this?" It was a great effort to lift his cane from the ground, to raise his hands above shoulder height and present the burning room. "The most powerful engine ever built, keeps us from dropping off the side. Not something I can take sole credit for, you understand, but still magnificent. Can't do that without taxpayer money."

"I don't know if we've met before." Frank, short, factual. The same tone she took on talking to world leaders in her before-life.

"It depends on perspective, I suppose." His hands fell, disappointed in the possum's complete lack of reverence. "In another life, I assume. It's a shame we never got to work together, Miss Vermington, but there is still time."

It was in the light of his burning creation that the cracks began to show.

"I grow old, Hanratty." Faster than the years would suggest. "You destroyed the projects that were supposed to extend my life. It's my understanding that you can turn back that clock. In return, I will allow unfiltered access to Rabbithole, once it is complete."

Ratty bit her tongue, staring at the man's shoes to avoid his gaze. The sharp points of her teeth had gone unchanged over the course of her afterlife.

"There was another Ratty, right?"

"Yes."

"What happened to her?"

"Squandered potential. Why we don't take government contracts we don't write anymore." It almost sounded like he thought that was funny.

She felt, in the points where muscle connected to bone, a deep buzzing ache, begging *something* of her.

"No." It was unclear whether or not she could actually "turn back the clock" either way. "Obviously, no."

Something changed in Handler Smith's face. The sad old man dropped from his expression, soft and deliberate curves falling into sharp, sunken lines. With that, the buzzing fled from Ratty's body.

"I don't think you understand the advantage of having me as your ally." Even his tone was trained. "Mr. Cane was under our employ. Ms. DeGenerous was under our employ. Director Ross is under our employ. Every action we take is designed in its

446

explicit intention to make your life miserable, and it has not lost us an ounce of power yet. I ask you, Miss Vermington, would you like to be happy?"

None of what she did, none of what Handler Smith had made her do, had ever actually happened in this universe. As she searched the dark periods of her memory for the goat, the canteen, that day... there was nothing to suggest it was anything but guesswork.

There was nothing to suggest she was even a moderately useful soldier.

"So, I mean... no." It came out flippant, fitting and unintentional.

"No?"

"I don't know what I deserve. Maybe it's happiness, but definitely not on your terms." She shook her head, her eyes narrowing just enough to stop the frustrated sheen from spilling over. "It wasn't real— it was all you— you die, and I have no reason to be miserable anymore."

Not true, but close enough. Without Handler Smith, there was no foundation to build on. Without Handler Smith, she could finally begin to tear it down.

"How incredibly selfish of you." His measured tone turned hard. "Tell me, Miss Vermington, what have you done to earn your power? What makes you so special that you get to decide who lives and dies?"

With absolutely no trace of irony.

Handler Smith kidnapped a journalist investigating his company for labour violations.

Handler Smith organized the conditions for that journalist to be condemned to Hell.

Handler Smith employed a kidnapper, who tried in vain to send that journalist back to Hell.

Handler Smith kidnapped homeless children.

Handler Smith okayed the reduction of a living creature to a near-soulless automaton.

Handler Smith enabled a talk-show serial killer to ascend to godhood.

Handler Smith — when it that journalist might recover — wrote false memories into her head.

Hanratty Vermington tore her world apart because of those

memories.

Hanratty Vermington ended up in Hell on her own merits.

"I don't think we know each other as well as you think," she said.

"No," he took no time to respond, "I suppose we don't." He frowned. "If you had left well enough alone I would not have to do this. No regrets, Miss Vermington."

Handler Smith was obliterated by the half-pound of C-4 explosive sewn throughout his suit, igniting the rest of the engines in a chain reaction. A voice directly in the possum's ear started:

"Ratty—" Angel's voice. "You need to fix—"

"Hold on!" She had never heard her voice slow like that. As internal pressure pushed cracks through the metal, loosening the leech's grip, Ratty searched for something not tied down. Failing that... failing that... there was a control panel, just below the observation deck, high enough that she could jump at the window from it.

She would be heavy enough. She would have to be.

She was.

The shoulders of her jacket made an awful scraping sound as she backed into the thick metal, scrunching down further as the wave of heat that passed overhead burned off and cauterized the tip of one of her ears. She winced, throwing both hands over top of it.

It was over in a moment, leaving a few scattered flames hanging from bits of the walls. What little stayed lit extinguished itself on the fall to the ground.

Her lungs trying to process smoke, Ratty fumbled for her inhaler, coughing and spitting at her throat. She made contact with the small, cracked piece of plastic as the pressure differential sucked the rest of the smoke from the room.

"Shit," she muttered, trying to calm her breathing enough to accept the medicine.

"We actually— we're still being asked to move, but we're putting down here for just a moment while we can. We just had another big explosion, bigger than the first one, enough to give some people down here a scare. We're now seeing—"

[the camera pans up as the presenter points]

"We're actually seeing what appears to be, maybe, a large metal outcropping. You can see also that there's a cable. Massive cable, or rope, some kind of tether going between the tower and the object. There are a few that appear to be supportive, one that's just hanging off of the side there, and—"

[off screen, something impacts the microphone]
[the presenter lets out an annoyed grunt]
[the camera pans back down, centring the microphone, held by a duck in a long patchwork coat and dark sunglasses.]

"It's Angelcorp! Look up Project Archangel! Look up—"
"Give me that!"

[the duck once again checks the presenter, knocking him to the ground]

"Look up Operation Checkmark! Look up Project Rabbithole! The Canadian Government—"

[the feed goes dark]
[the vaguely bewildered voice of an anchor takes over the broadcast]

"It looks like we just lost connection with our field crew, we'll be trying to get them back as soon as possible. In the meantime we have — contacting us via video-conference — Mr. Luchthavenlei, he's a former RCAF pilot and helped write the book on military identification—"

Sett felt the distance of everything around them, standing on the isolated platform in the centre of the spare elevator shaft. They had become incredibly conscious, without looking, of the boundaries of their space at all times. With their eyes closed, they felt the edge of the platform, wide enough — if need be — to hold a few people shoulder to shoulder.

They still worried about falling off. It had begun to tilt with the sinking side of the leech, throwing Eleanor into a panic as Angel walked her through the controls. Everyone had evacuated after the first impact. Almost anti-climactic after their frantic preparation.

It would have been a good idea to wait. Standing on the podium like this was... just awkward. They weren't worried about Project Rabbithole. Either it would work or it wouldn't. Fate had taken over.

They took some comfort in the sweater they had borrowed from Ratty, weaving their fingers through the thumb holes and pulling it against their shoulders for an added bit of pressure. It would be gone soon too. They would be naked and alone in the black, empty subspace they had created.

There would still be memories of this place, a few more to go with their collection.

"I need—" The ghost shot through the safety barrier, triggering some panic reflex in the goat as her hand came too close. It zipped away with a few pinched off hairs. "Sorry. There's like, a filter thing." Eleanor dropped the hairs into a tube sticking out of the console, which closed and sank a few inches with a few more button presses.

"Yes, that makes sense." They tried to ignore how badly they had just flinched.

"Hey! How we doing?" She smelled like burnt fur, patches hanging off her jacket where the heat had melted the glue or polyester. Still, it was a relief to see Ratty had stuck to her word.

"We are good." Eleanor answered, spacing out her reply between bursts of focus. "Really good, actually."

"We will be able to launch before the pod pulls the tower down." Angel filled in the rest.

The room had changed significantly since the last time Ratty saw it, deep under a forest in slightly-less-south Ontario. The massive arms had been replaced with rails running the elevator shaft, the same geometrically complex hunks of metal attached to a carriage at the bottom of each. They hummed quietly, glowing a shade of orange that made the individual edges hard to pick out from this distance. A thin, uncharged thread hung from each, rumpled as though it had been stretched and unstretched until all elasticity was pulled out of it. Anything that would have it was marred with their logo. The name of their overseas partner was printed wherever it would fit.

# 毛皮/ANGELCORP
DIGITAL

They had certainly made the machine smaller.

Ratty clambered up to the platform, put at ease by the way Sett's good eye followed her from a few inches shorter to several inches taller.

"Hey," she sighed, still aching.

"Hello." It was as personal as the goat could manage.

Strange. That was about as much as could be said about it. Two paranormal creatures, deposed from their universes. One about to be sent home, the other with no intention of returning.

All they had to do now was wait.

"How're you feeling?" Ratty asked.

"Not sure. We are... excited for the future... sad, of course." Their head turned to check on Eleanor, turning back only as Ratty's followed. She seemed not to notice how the goat's eyes lingered on hers. Then, down to the holes in her sweater. That would be gone soon, too. "We will likely never see you again."

"Ready to go!" Eleanor called around the barrier, shrinking back behind as soon as she was finished.

Ratty looked at Sett, followed their gaze when she realized it had fallen, then snapped back to Eleanor.

"Hang on!" She held out a hand to stop the ghost, rooting around in jacket pocket for— there it was. She pulled out a knife, took Sett's hand in her own, and cut a little strip of fabric from the sweater's sleeve. She dropped down off the platform, hanging Eleanor the strip. "It's wool, so..."

"So..." Eleanor's hand folded around the grey fabric.

"So it's organic, so you can put it through the filter, I think." Ratty nodded towards the console. Eleanor furrowed her brow for a moment, processing that, before—

"OH! Yeah, I could do that." She jammed her claws under the lid, forcing back the filter's lid and dropping it into the mix. Ratty grinned at the rabbit in place of a "thank you" and returned to the platform.

"Now—" She had to tilt the goat's chin up from the missing strip manually. "Now you'll have something to remember me by."

They stopped, reexamining the doll that came to life for any signs of mockery. Her goofy grin, her beautifully tired eyes, she was certainly less suave than Sett had originally imagined, but then again nobody was that suave. She made a go at it, genuinely and without remorse, and that was pretty nice.

"You are bewildering, Hanratty." Sett said, tears welling up as their expression crumpled.

"You ready?" She took the goat's hands in her own. They bit down on their lip for a half-second, and nodded.

"Yes. I'm ready."

The goat was silhouetted for an instant as bright orange flashed from below, filling in the space between before devolving into a deep, empty black. Slowly, piece by piece, bright sections of the adjacent universe populated the net, distorted by the surface. As it stalled, the limp threads hardened into thick, golden rods, seeping out over the anchor points until they were covered entirely. The goat's fur stood on end as the air was charged with a familiar energy.

"Okay, launching now!" Eleanor called over the combined hums of the machine and its carrier. Ratty's breath left her chest as the goat dove into her embrace one last time. Her arms wrapped their back on instinct, lifting them into the air, their damp snout pressed perfectly into her neck.

"Goodbye, Ratty." The entire room thudded as the anchors fell into their racks, biting hard into the track and accelerating through the air.

They're gone.

Sweater and all, dragging with them the layer of oil that had built up in the possum's fur. Ratty let her arms fall around the empty space.

"We're reversing in—" Eleanor wasn't given the chance to count that out. Pieces of the intricate control panel moved on their own as they went through the other half of their program. The mechanism reversed, using the extra space to re-accelerate in the opposite direction, and passed back over the possum.

The other— the original— this universe's— Ratty's Sett was back.

They stood with their back to her, their hair shaggy in a way Ratty had only seen once before. A mismatch of differently coloured and processed wools hung off their blotched light-brown form in the rough shape of a hoodie. They searched their surroundings, bright, wide eyes rounding the curve of their face as they spun slowly in place.

They stopped as the possum edged into their periphery.

"Of course it was you." Their psychic voice, so much stronger than the other's, flooded Ratty's world. For the second time in the past half-minute, Sett knocked the wind from her chest with their horns, this one's arms finding the perfect grooves up inside the oversized jacket.

Something hot and loud rocked the leech again, as Ratty found her own line, enveloping and burrowing into the goat at once. The platform toppled as she began to lift the little goat, dropping both their stomachs out from under them and depositing them on the lab floor.

Sett laughed, a quiet signal that Ratty hadn't damaged anything. They got up to their elbows, pressing the soft fur of their sealed mouth against their partner's lips. "You little genius!" they said, not bothering to break away.

"I'm little?" Ratty pulled back just far enough to grin at the turn of phrase.

"Sorry! No time!" Eleanor waved her arms over her head. "We don't have time for this!"

Sett had already popped to their knees, Ratty starting to sit up under them.

"Yeah! Right! Of course." She jumped to her feet, giving the rest of the room whiplash as she became singularly focused with the console. She forced the lid of the filter open as she had seen Eleanor do earlier, running her free hand through her hair once and picking out what had let go of her head. "Get it ready to go again— Sett, give me—"

"What're you doing, Ratty?"

"We have to get everyone else." Her head whipped around, an honest — if crazed — confusion in her eyes. She didn't blink as another explosion rocked the leech, as her partners shared a moment of understanding neither knew the other was having.

"No, we don't." "It probably wouldn't even launch again." Sett and Eleanor spoke simultaneously. The possum turned to verify that last claim, climbing to her feet as she understood the state of it.

The golden rods that held the walls of the universe at bay crackled, stuck as solid metal as they struggled to fall back to string. The anchors split open as they understood themselves to be perceived, struggling to hold the definition of something that could hold a shape.

"No, c'mon," she stammered, climbing up to the platform as the machine's energy turned thick and hungry. She got up to the platform, standing above portal, ignoring the way it tugged at her fur, how it hurt to stand this close to, how the pressure of its pull made it hard to fill her lungs. "There's still time, I just need to—"

She looked down through her boots to double check as Sett spoke. A quiet: "Ratty..." tinged with so much. Trust, straining under the weight of where the possum stood, that she would not do this again. A rare, precognizant recognition, buried under layers of fear as infinitely long metal spikes appeared and disappeared around her. A firm demand. A "don't do this."

Something about that caught her.

She saw the infinite spiral of the universe, printed into the back of her eyes as a first exposure.

She felt dogs teeth tear her throat out, felt cold cement against her back start to warm with her blood, saw the eyes of an animal with fear and pity and love and the knowledge that it had killed its master. She died, and returned.

She felt her spine snap, felt the invasive fingers of a machine dig under her skin and bore out her flawed biology, felt cold, industrial metal parts take over her body, felt love for only a moment as she watched the rolling tides. She died, and returned.

She felt her body rot in a ditch, cold mud against her aching back, anguish at the reward of a long life spent in prison: freedom. She died, and returned.

She felt herself simply disappear, her last sight a grey recreation of the goat in front of her, bleeding from one eye. She died, and returned.

She felt welts form on her body. She died, and returned.

She felt her heart stop as an act of plain bad luck, died, and returned.

She felt herself obliterated by a half-pound of C-4 explosive sewn throughout her vest.

Felt her mind fade to grey, died, and returned.

A thousand micro-lives and deaths, all at once.

then,

In an instant,

It all felt so stupid. She blinked against the light show, whatever had been written across her vision for the past hundred years suddenly letting go. Not today. Maybe never. She had to be alive to find out. She stepped to the edge of the platform ready to drop down. Sett offered a hand, easing the descent.

"You're right, I'm sorry—" Something snapped behind her.

Sett saw it first, then Eleanor as she rounded the counter.

Then Ratty, as she checked the ache in her chest, trying to understand why she couldn't drop any lower.

Something had failed. One of the emitters, probably.

Searching for something to latch onto, a thread had shot through Ratty's back. A problem on its own, it then twitched back into its metal form where it settled directly through the possum's left lung.

"Oh, fuck." She choked down a mouthful of blood, her voice corrupted as much by the pole through her chest as much as it was by the universe trying to get rid of her.

Sett blinked at the rod, at the way it struggled to drag chunks of their partner into non-being, as it remained solid, the world now pivoting around it. Something stuck in their throat. They placed a hand over their mouth, let their body process what they could not.

It was calming at first, gently propping her up. It made her boots heavy as the floor fell away, making rings where her soles left the surface.

"Oh god." Quiet, terrified. The sound an animal makes when cornered.

"It's okay, I can fix this—"

"No, Ratty—" Impossible to keep in, a noise of instinct clawing its way through the blockage in their voice. She had begun to dematerialize in chunks, the universe deciding in real time how to divide her. It did not claw. It carved at her in orderly segments. "Come on, please." They dug in their bare heel, forcing themself not to back away.

"It's okay, really." She would come back in shades, the adjacent universe deciding occasionally to loan her home. Every scar was still there: a worm-track fracture through uncovered bone, evidence of the observers who had watched her die. Her head turned as Eleanor circled the protective glass, stopped as the ghost crossed behind Sett to get a better look.

Something in the goat's eyes, like the bulb that powered them had cracked, exposing the raw tungsten below.

It's not going to be okay, Ratty.

Not this time.

They clambered to the platform, hanging off the possum as the machine's filter did its job, shielding the goat from harm. The spike shot from their back, in no way interrupting their movement, sliding through them as though not there. Ratty put her fist around the rod as her arm wrapped the goat. She was the only one it could touch.

She tipped their head into her chest, dragging herself through the spike to come closer.

Sett dragged her out of Hell.

Sett saved her life.

Sett loved her.

"I'm sorry." A weak set of syllables that broke her to let go of. "I hurt you. I held you back, and I'm sorry."

"Shut up," as though that was all she had ever done. "I mean it. Shut the fuck up."

"I love you, Sett."

She buried her face in the top of the goat's head, the rabbit's unseen hand stuck in a curl as she struggled to sign anything. She stayed back from the equipment. It wouldn't matter in a few moments.

"Don't do this." One last plea.

"I don't think I get a choice this ti—" Her breath caught in her chest. One last favour from the universe. A signal that, if there were a time to hold her breath, now would be it.

She does.

For as long as she can hold it she examines and commits to memory every strand on her partner's face. She counts, finally, the individual strands of brown fur that cross into the white at the tip of their snout. Her throat gets tight first, starting at the top of her chest. She notices — trying to distract herself — the way the universe rocks back and forth against her skin.

The pressure is most obvious where her chest rests on the metal rod, moving down through the centre of her body and branching out like heavy roots. Following that moment her chest gets exponentially tighter each second. Her legs buckle slightly.

She thinks about herself again. She thinks about apologizing to Sett again.

She starts to feel like coughing, comes to understand that she cannot, and starts to feel her eyes water.

She becomes frustrated. At this point the ache in her lungs has plateaued.

Her throat starts to make a sobbing motion. With everything in her body clamped firmly shut it manifests as little more than an anguished, sucking cough, made completely impotent by the fact that no air can enter her body.

She realizes, as her eyes snap open, that she had committed nothing to memory.

The held breath turns into an angry, screaming sob, and she's gone.

Sett set down the two halves of paper, refusing to return the note to Ratty's waste paper basket, and refusing to read it. They stared at it for a few moments too long, before folding it together with Eleanor's, difficult not to read as it consisted entirely of the words "Eleanor, I" written in black ink. They had had that conversation in person.

Their eyes skipped over the folded jacket on the bed. It normally held pride of place on its own separate coat-rack, too coated in paint and studs and safety pins to do anything but damage other fabric, but for today, it was comfortable there.

They would repair her back-patch later. That was a good enough excuse. Sett unclasped the rubber band of their watch, took a second to examine the segmented world map display, and set it next to the jacket.

They pocketed the folded letters, picked up their cane, and limped out into the living room. They were largely ignored by the crowd of people gathered around the TV, Eleanor explaining to a conference call on her phone that she had not been injured. Only Fern noticed the goat, and in so doing respected their decision to — instead of busying themself with the news — make a cup of tea. Something to calm them down.

"'This is a time that we as Canadians need to come together. It is only natural, after accident so senseless, to search for truth, and I would urge us all not to be led into sensationalism.'

"Prime Minister Justin Trudeau, earlier today, broke his silence on the collapse in downtown Toronto earlier this week. Several thousand are missing, presumed dead after an illegal aircraft registered to the Angel Military Holdings Corporation collided with the CN Tower. Angelcorp records show the craft was registered missing just four days ago.

"Trudeau apologized for his silence, saying he had been at a loss for words, and needed time to confer with other world leaders on what actions to take. The Prime Minister declined to answer when asked why members of his cabinet were found inside of the aircraft during the initial search and rescue.

"Opposition leader Erin O'Toole says his party is currently in the process of setting up a full-scale investigation into the Prime Minister's ties to Angelcorp, though declined to comment on whether that investigation..."

Maybe it would matter, maybe it wouldn't. The water, hovering below a boil, stuck them in the moment before they collapsed. They turned on the radio, fumbling along the underside of the cabinets for the plastic box as not to break eye contact. They tuned to a static channel and drowned out what must've been the hundredth report on *the accident* that day.

After a short period of white silence, the static spoke.

"Folks, I'd like to close out today's broadcast with a new track from Miss Vera Lynn." Music would be a welcome distraction. "For the Canadian Broadcasting Corporation, I'm Buster Friendly. For all our boys on the front lines, send Adolf my coldest regards, and goodnight."

And they stood there, confused for a moment, staring at the plastic machine as the gentle da-rumph of the song's string section rose behind its horns. Not seven seconds into the tune, the TV audience sat bolt upright, shocked from their focus by the slap of Sett's cane hitting the floor.

What came through was not the voice of Vera Lynn. It was lyrics ripped from one of her songs, woven into the cracked and dry voice of a possum. She tried to improvise around them.

As Eleanor rounded the corner, the goat's hunched form had already pulled their banjo from subspace, and begun to play along, a crumpled, lit cigarette hanging off their lip.

# Epilogue

There would be no official investigation into the disaster, of course. A private cleanup company would be hired, any employee of that company would be placed under strict surveillance, and found at the bottom of a river if they so much as searched online for the word "whistle."

So grief has to wait.

Sett was a recognizable enough face to keep covered until they dropped down into the relative obscurity of the smouldering hull. They wince as their injured leg takes on more of the impact than they intended, gritting their teeth through it and unhooking their cane from the back of their sweater.

"What am I looking for, Stephanie?" they ask, not bothering with the flashlight in their bag.

"So if there's anything intact, it'll be in one of the offices. Just — any of the higher-ups' terminals should have at least a little bit of information we can use." The fox drops down behind them, pausing to fiddle with her own flashlight.

"Got it." They split off, not waiting for approval. Barracks, armoury, a small first aid room, and beyond that a block of offices, arranged in a half-horseshoe around a space-wasted lobby. They struggle to balance one legged on the uneven ground, bracing against the receptionist's desk and pulling its tower from the back corner with the tip of their cane. They finish up the rest of the block of offices, taking special note of just where in their duffle the hard drive from the office labelled *Dir. Ross* sits in their bag.

"There's nothing down here— a few research terminals, but they're all cloud-based."

"There's still a few more doors above me. Give me a moment." Sett cuts back out into the stairwell, checks the last few doors— mostly storage— and stops at the final door. A layer of cobwebs too thick for the half week the wreck has been sitting here blocks their entry.

460

That, and the psychological barrier of it being the room where their fiancée was killed less than four days earlier. There is only so much blocking out one could do when confronted with the exact environment in which one of the worst moments of their life had happened.

They have to be thorough.

Grief could wait.

They poke through the threshold with the tip of their cane, creating a doorway through which they wouldn't have to touch the webs. The room itself is in a state of paranormal disarray: poor safety procedures have completely altered the metaphysical makeup in this room, most prominently in ribbons of stretch-mark like scars tracking their way through what was at one point solid steel.

The rod refuses to disappear entirely, a permanent fixture of Toronto's skyline for the time being. Ratty is there, too. Her lifeless body had returned just in time to be thrown like a rag doll into the steel corner of the room. Skull crumpled, one horn missing entirely, the other hanging off by a few fibrous threads, paper against the solid structure.

They approach the stinking wreck, her arms folded back in a way that almost begged…

Sett grabs the collar of the possum's jacket, ignoring the gruesome hole-punch through the centre of her black and red back-patch, and strips it off. It, too, goes in the duffle. Her harness stays tangled in the mess of her legs.

It stunk of iron rot. There were options, of course. Sett had considered ahead of time that this space would be like this, and if left to fester those scars would be forced open, and the people outside would have no choice but to confront the fact that Angelcorp had gambled with all of their lives.

Then again, people would die.

So Sett sets to work quietly pulling the space back into alignment. Perhaps the crash would be enough, a fire bright enough to show everyone that Angelcorp, at the very least, could not be trusted. They had given them another hard kick.

There is still work to be done, of course. In time, they would have to learn to commune across the divide, to point the other

Sett in the right direction, but there was a good 40 years before they would first meet, and so today at least could be set aside to enjoy the sunset.

Sett steps out of the customs office, paperwork held tightly in the crux of their arm. They shield their eye, making their way up 49th street. They sit down on the frost-touched pier, crushing the bag of cookies provided to them by the desk demon and sprinkling them onto the water's surface.

The ducks swim up, at first peaceful in their division of the crumbs before getting into petty squabbles amongst themselves. Suppose that's the way of the world, Sett thinks. They toss another handful a little further along, splitting up a few little fights.

"Can I help y'?" A man's sharp Irish cut snaps them from their duck-watching. They are technically not supposed to be here, but no one could really be expected to enforce that law.

"Do you know how I can get to Toronto from here?" Why not ask? This was not an era they had had much experience with. Anyone but them would likely have a better idea than just walking.

"Ol' 'Muddy York'?" He's sort of making fun of the people who call it that. "Why settle for the copy when you could have the real thing?" The dock worker takes off his cap and sits down next to them.

"I've got friends there."

"Well," he flips open a pack of cigarettes and takes one, offering a second to the strange goat, "I sincerely apologize for that."

Something about that made them laugh.

A black Camaro RS, its back-seat covered with a tarp-full of plants, rolls to a stop on the bay-side shoulder of West Frontage Road. Across the bay, the golden gate bridge howls mercilessly. After seven months of the same design flaw filling the city with a high pitched whistling, those in charge have still done nothing.

It's not their biggest priority, currently. In fact, they're also slipping from the whole "in charge" thing. It's the beginning of November, and the sky is a dark orange.

Eleanor steps out and carefully examines the rattle of the hood. This is the first time her car had made that drive under its own power, and it has held up remarkably well.

She shoves one sneaker into the wheel well and steps up onto the hood. Then up onto the roof from there. She stands up on her tiptoes to see across the barrier between the side-street and the highway.

Despite being only a little after mid-day, the road's surface is devoid of tires. The highway is home to one solitary police cruiser, but that has been turned over, keeping President Eisenhower's rubber virginity intact.

Depending on... what sneaker soles were made out of... also... it's not the best metaphor.

A few curious eyes look around to meet the ghost's gaze. Only the tallest among them can actually see her.

There's a barrier about a mile north. This part of the city has been taken over. It is a slow process, but it is far from complete. There is a beautiful future for this place.

It is difficult to tell whether the smoke above them is natural or man-made. An Angelcorp warehouse, years ago placed strategically to serve homes and to be served by apartments, sits burnt out and smouldering. It contributes far more than its fair share to the dark overhead.

Down on the hood of the car, only the occasional orange of the gaps in smog are reflected against the black. This could be home, or not. Only one way to find out.

She takes a moment to thumb the patch cut of cloth in her pocket, hops down from the roof, takes the door by the handle, and pulls it into a ghost-state. It glides easily across the street and through the barrier, stopping on the highway in the midst of a small straggling of bewildered rebels.

"Hey!" Eleanor smiles, "I'm— uh, I'm Eleanor!"

---

"Morning, Angel." Not much changes for Fern because of the crash. Their inbox — chronically unchecked — is cluttered with requests for interviews with the mind behind the original Angel Computers. Having been seen with one of the first so-called geniuses of the art form was enough to drag Fern into the spotlight.

How long had they known each other? Did they get along? How could such an innocent corporation have let things get so bad? Did she know all along?

Of course, none of these are questions they're thinking about this morning, given that they haven't read them. Instead, they're tracking over the several decades of their life, picking apart moments where everything had changed for them. What "fixed" Fern? What could be used to fix Angel?

That is, if there's anything left to fix. The robot did not respond to "good morning" in her usual tone.

"Angel?" Fern amends their route ever so slightly to be able to look into the androids eye.

The way she had been silhouetted by the morning sun, sitting upright in the storefront, comfortable in her new nest, had given the pile of synthetic skin the illusion of still being alive. Whatever little energy she had had left had petered out in the dark.

It's hard to know how to feel about that. Angel is still more or less there, with the right technology she could still be brought back, and yet, there's something not right about that idea.

Fern turns to 013, another failed project, and again does not know how to feel. The final motion of their 34 year old failure had started and stopped within a week.

"Fern." Angel stirs, a new tone in her voice: clear, with almost zero trace of its digital origins. Fern turns to look at their creation.

"Yes?"

"Goodbye." the creature says, a single note of acceptance.

"Goodbye, Angel." Fern nods. Perhaps this is the way to feel.

---

After 9 years in self-induced isolation, Hanratty Ishmael Vermington — Izzy, to her solitary friend — injects a nullifying compound into her bloodstream. For the next 24 hours, her disease will be incommunicable. As a result of the cure, however, her body will begin to shut down. In 6 hours, she will be completely dead.

She stops at two places. Lacking money, she shoplifts a carton of pens and a pad of paper from a Business Depot. She writes a short but heartfelt note to her mother on the train ride home.

Between home and the train station, she stops at a convenience store for a package of sour cherry balls. No one is home when she delivers her note.

She sits down on a river bank and watches the flow. This is okay. This had to happen. There should never have been two.

---

Hanratty Vermington wakes up in a subway station, a few pillars separating her from the corrugated metal wall of the train. She stands as the door chimes, not entirely sure what train she would be missing if she stayed seated.

There is another figure on the train. She is black and crackling, and hard to look at. It's as though someone tried to build a person from broken tiles.

"Where am I?" she asks.

"It's hard to say," the figure replies. Their tone is even and cool, tinged in equal measure with sorrow and reserved reverence.

"Am I dead?" Ratty asks. There is no time wasted thinking of the next question.

"There's no way of knowing," the figure replies.

The possum looks around. The rest of the train is empty. The next stop indicator is blank. The corrugated metal walls rock gently back and forth. The wheels click quietly below the floor. The possum takes a deep, shaking breath, and slouches into a seat as she lets it out.

"If it helps, you figured it out."

"Yeah." Ratty nods. "Just— a little too late."

"Was it worth it?" the figure asks. Ratty takes a moment to think, before asking:

"Is Sett okay?"

"They will be."

The possum takes another deep breath, her throat closing slightly as her eyes glaze over. "Where are we going?" she asks.

"I'm not sure." The figure looks towards the front of the train. "Somewhere important."

Outside, illuminated by red light, looking so small in the dark, a pattern of black stone tile breaks up the concrete walls.

"Can't I just rest?" Ratty asks.

"It'll be some time before we arrive. I think you've earned that much."

The possum nods, mostly to herself, and leans back in her seat. Her hand rests naturally on her bag, one she hasn't carried in years. Inside are a pair of goggles, a glasses case, a particulate mask, a first aid kit, an audio recorder, headphones, a Bluetooth keyboard, and a notepad. It's her old field kit.

She takes out the case and pops it open. True to its name, it contains a pair of battered clubmasters.

"Do I wear glasses?" she asks, tonguing the cut in her lip and examining the chewed metal ends at the same time.

"Occasionally," the figure replies.

She perches the frames on the bridge of her nose, the figure's edge coming into sharper focus before her eyes. She blinks until her eyes adjust, shrugs softly to herself, and next takes the recorder from its protective case. She scrolls from the microphone icon to the music note icon, and hits the play button. The device picks a song at random.

The recorder — damaged from years at the bottom of her bag — takes its time choosing. As she goes to put it in a pocket, a knuckle butts up against the rubber band of a cheap watch. She takes it out, clicking through the time zones until a little outline of the city of New York is highlighted.

*Our song.mp3* scrolls across recorder's the screen. A bump skips it to a middle verse, one Ratty had lifted whole-cloth when improv had begun to fail her. She reaches up to touch the tips of her horns, and wishes for a moment that she had let them grow out.

"There will be time for that," the figure mouths silently.

Hanratty will return in **Still Not Dead**

www.ingramcontent.com/pod-product-compliance
Lightning Source LLC
Chambersburg PA
CBHW011112100726
47898CB00011B/3055